THE 4TH PRISONER

ALSO BY BRANDON HUGHES

The Hero Rule

Barclay Griffith Book 1

THE 4TH PRISONER

WHEN EVIL ESCAPES

BARCLAY GRIFFITH
BOOK 2

BRANDON HUGHES

TENSION
BOOKS

For my children
Paxton, Piper, and Brock

"Break the rules, and you go to prison; break the prison rules, and you go to Alcatraz."

ANONYMOUS, ALCATRAZ ISLAND

"What the detective story is about is not murder but the restoration of order."

P.D. JAMES

THE 4TH PRISONER

ONE

Alcatraz
June 11, 1962

Tonight was the night. Months of planning, scraping, digging, reconnoitering, and close calls with the guards all came down to tonight. Come morning time, when the sun rose, Eddie Howard would no longer be a resident of the most notorious prison in the world. He would succeed, or he would die—no in between.

The guards had standing orders to shoot on sight any prisoner attempting to escape. Assuming he got past the rifle-toting guards, he would have to deal with the water, perhaps the prison's most significant obstacle to an escape. The odds of success were long, and Eddie knew it; after all, there had been nearly forty escape attempts from this place, and all had failed. He knew with an almost cool certainty that death was the most likely outcome of what he was about to embark on, but death would be a welcome alternative to life in this most inhospitable place.

Alcatraz had the reputation as the most secure prison in the world for good reason. The prison stood silent sentry on a remote island in the perpetually freezing, shark-infested waters of the San Francisco Bay. The first structure on the small island was built by the United States Army to stand guard over San Francisco before becoming a military prison in 1868. In 1909, most of the existing structure was demolished, and the current prison was constructed —largely by the prisoners themselves. The bone-white edifice became a monolith to the modern maximum-security penitentiary and housed the nation's most violent and notorious criminals— the worst of the worst. Prisoners often found themselves at Alcatraz because they were too dangerous to be housed elsewhere; every other prison they had been confined to could no longer handle them or hold them. As the old adage went: Break the rules, you go to prison. Break the prison rules, and you go to Alcatraz.

You did not make friends inside Alcatraz as much as you tried not to make enemies.

There were a number of security measures in place to dissuade any notion of an escape attempt. Aside from the natural barrier of the water that was virtually impassable without a motorized watercraft, cold showers were rendered an impossibility to keep the prisoners from acclimating to the frigid conditions that made up the Bay. In addition, there were twelve prisoner counts per day and two dozen armed guards who were a constant presence both inside the prison and outside, regularly roaming the perimeter. The guards also moved prisoners around on a semi-regular basis in an effort to keep plans or even notions of escape from being formed between cell neighbors. It was actually the rumor of one such impending prisoner movement that necessitated putting the plan into effect tonight.

Eddie was not the only prisoner readying to make his move. He would be joining four others in his exodus, and therein lay his first hurdle because the other four men—Frank Lee Morris, John and Clarence Anglin, and Allen West—were unaware they would be joined by a fifth. Eddie didn't care whether he was invited or not, as he was never much for social graces, but he was well aware that this would be his first opportunity to die.

———

IN THE MONTHS leading up to the escape attempt, it was perhaps the prison's worst-kept secret. Practically every prisoner knew what was being planned, but miraculously, the warden and the guards had no such knowledge and would be caught unawares. At least, that is what Eddie believed. If he were wrong, this would be the shortest escape attempt in the history of the penal system. When he caught wind of what was happening, he approached Allen West, who occupied the cell directly beside him. He approached West as delicately as he knew how, which is to say not delicately at all, and got the barest framework of the plan: break out of the cell, get to the shore, and swim to freedom.

Alcatraz was falling apart around them. The place had a distinct malodorous lacquer—the pleasantness of the ocean breeze was besmirched by an undertone of dead fish and rust with the piquant finish of mold. Saltwater was used for showering, washing dishes, and toilets. Over time, the briny liquid corroded the pipes carrying the water throughout the prison resulting in leaks that weakened and softened the cement walls. When Eddie learned that the inmates planned to dig through a ventilation grate in their cell, gaining them access to the interior structure, he began his own dig. He was able to exfiltrate a metal spoon from the cafeteria and use it to work a hole in the wall wide enough to slip through. Though the walls were softened and crumbling, they were still concrete, so the digging took time and multiple spoons as each one wore down. Details of the plan were never fully known, so he wasn't sure what to do beyond getting through the wall in his cell. *His* plan was simple: go when West went and follow him—by invitation, threat, or force (he didn't care which and was prepared for either)—and join the others at some point along the way.

Lights out was at 9:30 PM, and along with lights out came another of the dozen daily counts. Once that count was made, the next count wasn't until midnight, which gave them a timetable to work with. *Lights out* didn't mean total darkness, so the prisoners had to wait until the guards made their rounds before attempting their escape. The warden ran a stern operation, so there was no conversation, no activity whatsoever from the inmates after 9:30. The only discernible sound was that of the slow, rhythmic footsteps of the guards' hard sole shoes on smooth concrete down one cellblock and up the next.

Eddie lay in bed in his tomb-like five-by-nine-foot cell. His eyes were closed not to deceive an inquisitive passing guard but to focus his hearing, listening for any sign of movement in the neighboring cell. After what seemed like hours but was only a few minutes, he heard his neighbor in cell B-140 begin to stir. Allen West was commencing his escape.

———

EDDIE EASED out of his bed and stuffed clothes under the threadbare sheet and blanket to give some semblance of his presence in the event a curious guard decided to pay him a little extra attention. Then, as quietly as he knew, he slid the false grate away from his rear cell wall, revealing a hole not more than eighteen inches wide. Eddie was not a large man, standing approximately five feet ten inches and weighing a hundred and fifty-five pounds, so he did not require much of an opening to squeeze through.

He lay on his back, head toward the wall, then, shimmying along the floor, he stuck his head through the hole—the musty odor of mildew and freedom overcame him. He allowed the moment to take him, but only for a second, and then he began to shimmy and slide through the narrow opening. The edges weren't smooth, and he got hung up momentarily on a jagged piece of concrete. The concrete edge dug into his shoulder, causing a brief panic that he had made the hole too small; however, he grit his teeth, twisted this way and that, and got his shoulders through, the rest of his body following easily.

Standing upright inside the walls now, he immediately looked for Allen West. It was much darker here, so he really had to concentrate on what he was looking at. He closed his eyes for a few seconds, trying to acclimate to the dark, and when he opened them, he spotted West's head poking into the interior wall space.

He ran up to the space in three quick strides, kneeled, and said, "Come on, man. Hurry."

A thrashing Allen West was startled by the voice, turned his head toward the sound, stopped squirming, squinted, and said, "Eddie? What the...what are you doing?"

"Escaping," he said as if the answer were obvious.

West decided conversation was unimportant at that point and went back to moving about, grunting, trying to squeeze through the hole. The opening was illuminated with dim light leaking around West's body, and Eddie could see that the opening wasn't wide enough. *Gotta move*, he thought. He looked up from West and looked around, listening. Then, not seeing or hearing anything, he whispered, "What's the plan? Where are you supposed to go?"

West stopped and turned his face toward Eddie, slick with sweat. He was breathing heavily and said, "What?"

"Where are you supposed to go?" West stared at him as if not understanding, and Eddie shook his head and said, "You're not getting through there. Tell me where I need to go to meet up with the others."

West ignored him and began thrashing about earnestly, his

foot kicking something in his cell, probably his bed, and made a noise.

"Jesus, Al. Just stop. You're going to alert the guards." West continued for another beat before stopping, his breath nearly hyperventilating.

West dropped his head to the floor, got his breathing under control, and licked the sweat off his upper lip. He closed his eyes. When he opened them, he appeared to have made a decision. "Ok, look, you see those pipes?" West croaked in a hoarse whisper, Eddie leaning in to hear. They both looked up at the maze of pipework extending three stories to the ceiling. Looking back at Eddie, he said, "Climb those pipes. There's a landing up there where Morris and the Anglins are supposed to be waiting. If they aren't there, you have to get to the roof. Just find a way up and go." West closed his eyes again, frustration evident. Seconds passed when West opened his eyes and said, "You gotta go now. Go."

From a knee, Eddie looked up at the task before him and nodded. "Ok. Ok."

He stood up and was studying the layout of the pipes, plotting his next move, when West spoke. "You'd better fuckin' make it, you hear me."

Eddie was still looking at the wall of pipework, nodded, and said, "Yeah."

"I mean it," said West louder than intended. He brought his voice down a notch and said, "I mean it, Eddie. Do this." Eddie looked down and nodded before setting off. Before he could take more than a few steps, West made a noise to get Eddie's attention. Eddie looked back, and West said, "Send me a postcard." They shared a quick, quiet laugh, and Eddie was gone.

———

EDDIE JUMPED and grabbed a water pipe. He pulled himself up and found purchase with his right foot, then his left. He was peering up, eyeing his next move—really beginning to sweat now. He reached up, grabbed a pipe, and his hand slipped. He wiped his hands on his prison-issue denim pants and reached up again, making sure of his grip before pulling himself up. He could feel time and opportunity slipping away, so he hastened his pace. Eyes burning from sweat, he ignored the discomfort as he found his rhythm and reached the third-floor landing. No one was there. *Had he missed them? Had he beaten them here?* He darted to his left and then his right, looking for access to the roof. There was none that he could see. He bent over, hands on knees, trying to catch his breath—sweat rolling off his head and face splashing onto the catwalk. Then a noise. A loud noise. A noise that sounded to him like a dump truck being dropped off a building. Eddie ran toward the source, not caring at this point if the guards had been alerted. He couldn't turn back now; had to keep pressing forward.

He ran down the catwalk, hand on the rail as he looked toward the ceiling, trying to find something, anything indicating a way out. It was stupid to think he could go ahead without a plan. Without having even the slightest idea what he was going to do once he left his cell. "Fucking West," he said between breaths. *It was his fault. All of this. Stupid sonofabitch made his hole too small.* Then he heard another noise, quieter this time. He moved, slowly at first, then quickened his pace. *There*! He saw the night sky through a hole in the ceiling, a ladder underneath it. He ran and jumped, landing halfway up the ladder, both feet and his left hand slipping off. He regained his balance and moved quickly up to and through the vent without regard for what awaited him on the roof.

———

ON THE ROOF, his gaze immediately fell on the lights of San
Francisco some mile and a half across the Bay. Standing there in
the fifty-degree weather, bracing against the twenty-mile-per-hour
wind, he shuddered as his sweat-slicked skin cooled instantly.
Every now and again, when the wind was just right, the sounds of
life in San Francisco—music, parties, laughter—would drift across
the Bay and into certain parts of the prison. That was one of the
unknown tortures of being captive on this rock. No discernible
sound was emanating from the City by the Bay on this occasion,
but he had never yearned for freedom as much as he had at this
very moment. Eddie breathed in the salt air, which had come to
signify so much of what was bad about Alcatraz but took on a
decidedly different meaning up here on the roof with freedom
within his grasp.

A gust of wind knocked him slightly off balance and brought
his attention back to where he was. He looked around, spinning a
full three hundred sixty degrees before seeing the source of the
noise that brought him to this point: a large metal air vent lay on
its side. The waning crescent moon didn't give off much light, but
enough for him to see the three men in prison blues crouched and
moving at a quick but methodical pace. He tore off after them.

Eddie must have made a noise because all three men stopped
and turned to look at him in unison. Then, one by one, they stood
up tall. Eddie noticed they were carrying something of some bulk.
Finally, the one in the middle said, "Who the fuck are you?"

"It's me. Eddie Howard." No one was whispering now.

The one in the middle, the one who had just spoken, Frank
Morris, dropped what he was carrying with a muted, heavy thud
and practically ran at Eddie, causing him to take a step back and
into a defensive stance. Eddie reached into his back pocket and
pulled something out; the object glinted in the moonlight. This
brought Frank up short. His eyes went from Eddie to the thing
and back.

"Where's West?"

"He ain't coming." Then, seeing the look on Morris' face, he clarified, "His hole was too small. Couldn't get out." Eddie shifted his attention to the other two men who had dropped what they were holding and were now approaching him and Frank.

Eddie could see now that the two men were the Anglin brothers. He never did know who was who—although they were related, they didn't look terribly alike save for the perpetual look on their faces as if someone had just asked them for the temperature of the sun's surface in Kelvin—so he wasn't sure of the one who spoke first. That person said, "What the hell is going on here, Frank? Where's Allen?"

Frank Morris: "Eddie here says he couldn't get out of his cell."

The second Anglin brother chimed in, "We got no room for you." Then to Frank and his brother: "Let's get out of here."

"Oh, I'm coming," said Eddie.

The second brother responded: "The fuck you are. You deaf, boy? We got no room."

Eddie: "You were planning on West coming along, weren't you? Well, now he ain't coming. I am." That seemed to confuse the Anglins.

Frank: "Sorry, Eddie. Nothing personal, but you ain't in this."

"I'm coming, Frank. Now, we best get moving before the guards find us missing."

The first Anglin brother edged up closer and spoke in a voice dripping with menace, "You take one step to follow, and the guards will sure as shit find you...right where you stand. Get what I'm saying?"

Eddie flashed the object in his hand—a sharpened piece of metal with a thick dirty white wrap on the handle. He said, "They may find me here, but I won't go quietly. I will get at least one of you—maybe all three—but whatever happens, it's going to raise a hell of a ruckus, and no one makes it off this god-forsaken island then. You willing to take that chance?" He looked from one man to the next. He knew Frank well enough to know he was intelligent and pragmatic, but he didn't know the Anglins by anything other than their reputation: unpredictable and not terribly bright. He didn't dare let his guard down.

The first Anglin made a move. *This is it*, thought Eddie in a flash, and he moved his right foot slightly back and raised both hands: his left palm facing out and his right holding the shank, the blade extending from the bottom of his fist—all of it taking less than a second. The Anglin brother didn't even check up, but his momentum was stopped as he shot past Frank, who had him by the shirt.

He turned his head and said, "Let me go, Frank."

Frank struggled to contain the much larger Anglin and said, "Calm down, Clarence, calm down." Clarence Anglin slowed for a beat before trying to buck and twist his way out of Morris' grip. "Clarence," Frank said in a near yell. "Stop!" Then, quieter, "Be smart about this."

Clarence finally stopped moving, but Frank didn't dare ease up on his grip. Frank said, "Eddie's right. If you get at him, there is gonna be all kinda noise, and then what? I ain't goin' back there, Clarence. Hell, we're all here because we done tried to bust out of Atlanta. We get caught here, ain't nowhere else to send us but to the hole—probably forever." He paused to let that sink in before saying, "You want that?"

Eddie remained tensed, ready for a fight, his eyes flitting between the Anglins; the second brother hadn't moved.

The second Anglin spoke up. "He's right, Clarence. And we need to move like right, fuckin' now."

Frank: "Now I'm about to turn you aloose. Can I trust you not to go at him?" After about five seconds, Clarence Anglin gave a single sharp nod. Then, "Ok, I'm letting go." And Frank released his grip. Clarence stood there, his breathing slowing down and staring daggers at Eddie. Frank spoke again, a smile in his voice, "Now let's get the fuck off this rock."

Frank turned and went back to where he had dropped his cargo. Clarence and Eddie stood in a stalemate, Eddie waiting for Clarence to make the first move, which he did. After Clarence turned, so did his brother. Then Eddie followed.

Frank and the Anglins gathered their supplies and made their way to the roof's edge when Eddie spoke. He said, "So, what's the plan, boys?"

"Goddamn it," said Clarence.

"Easy, now," said Frank. Then, "We got to get down to the shore. Just follow us, and we'll be out of here in no time."

Eddie did as he was told. At the edge of the roof, a pipe secured to the side of the building would be their way down the more than fifty feet to the ground. The inmates dropped their cargo off the roof and shimmied down the pipe one by one, with Frank going first and Eddie going last. On the ground now, they regathered their cargo and headed to the north side of the small island. The deflated raft weighed in at more than a hundred pounds in the ungainly, hard-to-handle weight of more than four dozen rubber raincoats. Frank hefted it over a shoulder and led the way to shore. Whether by sheer strength or the adrenaline of the moment, the diminutive Frank Morris wasn't going to be bogged down with his payload.

They ran toward the elevated water tower, passed underneath it, and then made their way down and around the powerhouse to the shore. The waves crashed against the rocky shoreline, the cold, sobering spray hitting the inmates as they reached the water's edge. They dropped their payload on the rocks, took a moment to catch their breath, and went to work.

Frank said, "Alright, me and Clarence are going to work on inflating this raft. John, you and Eddie blow up the life vests." He was having to almost yell to be heard over the surf.

Eddie shook his head and said, "Life vests?"

"Yeah, you fall overboard in this chop, and you're a dead man without one."

Clarence laughed and said, "I guess you didn't know about that. Too bad, asshole."

"Fuck you. Any one of us falls into that water, and we're dead, life vest or not."

"Cut the shit and get to work," yelled Frank.

And that's what they did.

———

ABOUT HALFWAY THROUGH the inflation process, Eddie spoke in ragged breaths—blowing up the patchwork vests by mouth was taxing, and his jaws burned. He said, "Any idea what time it is? Another count is coming soon."

John Anglin spoke up. "We should have until first count after the morning whistle. We put dummy heads in our beds. They won't pass a close inspection, but to a guard making his rounds, they'll look real enough."

This caused Frank to stop blowing up the raft. He turned to Eddie and said, "Wait, you didn't make a mask." This caused Clarence also to stop and look up.

Eddie said, "I stuffed some clothes under the sheets."

Clarence: "For fuck's sake."

Frank: "Forget about it; we're here now. Let's just keep moving, and we'll be in the water before next count. As long as the guards don't look too close, we'll have the time we need."

Vests and raft inflated, the inmates edged the raft into the water. Frank jumped in first, and Clarence Anglin turned to Eddie and told him to climb in. Eddie shook his head and said, "And turn my back on you? I don't think so. I'll get in last and"—he flashed his shank—"should you get any ideas, I will gash this fucking raft and send us all to hell."

Frank yelled back, "Just get in the goddamn boat! Let's go!"

The four inmates climbed in—Morris and the Anglins wearing life vests and Eddie wearing only his prison issues—and they immediately felt the frigid cold of the Bay through the thin rubber bottom of the makeshift raft. Frank produced four cobbled-together wooden paddles and passed them around. Their original plan was to shove off from the island's northwest corner, go around the western tip, make the one-and-a-half-mile journey south to San Francisco, and get lost in the dense urban crowd. What they didn't count on, however, was the assertive current of the San Francisco Bay. As they made their way to the western tip of Alcatraz Island, the current swept them steadily west, and they were expending great energy trying to move the raft toward San Francisco.

The going was rough from the get-go in the small rubber raft, up one swell and down the next, cold water spilling over the sides with each drop. Paddling south was futile against the fast-moving current, so Frank made the executive decision to change course and head for Horseshoe Bay, which lay due west of the prison. Although more than twice as far as San Francisco, Horseshoe Bay was quickly becoming their only alternative for land if they wanted to avoid being swept out past the Golden Gate Bridge and into the Pacific Ocean.

Somewhere around thirty-five minutes into the water, the four inmates' backs and shoulders burned with lactic acid. John Anglin was the first to quit rowing, and it was his brother that urged him on. Clarence screamed: "Brother or not, you take that oar out of the water again, and this boat will be one man lighter." John looked skyward, his face a twisted, painful grimace, then went back to rowing.

Horseshoe Bay *was* getting closer, but so was the Golden Gate

Bridge. The bridge appeared to be getting closer faster, which was an enormous problem. The raft was adequate serving as a floatation device, but was proving to be a bit less so as a mode of transportation; they were being tossed about in a most violent manner.

Over an hour into their escape and they seemed to have made no progress at all. In fact, they seemed to be going backward, and frustration began to set in. John Anglin vomited in the boat—either from fatigue or seasickness—and in doing so, he lost his oar to the rolling black water. True to his word, Clarence dropped his oar in the boat and began to force John over the side. Frank was oblivious as he sat at the bow, churning his oar through the sea as if his life depended upon it, which it did. With all the action happening in front of him, Eddie shrank back to the stern of the flimsy tub in an attempt to avoid the brotherly fracas.

Clarence had John by the shirtfront, John's back arched over the pontoon, causing a rush of water to invade the raft. The cold water rushing in grabbed Frank's attention, pulling his gaze to the rear. He lunged at Clarence and pulled him off John, but in the commotion and amid a swell, John flipped backward, over the side, and into the water.

This caused Frank and Clarence to stop struggling. Clarence, seeing what happened, started screaming, "John! John!" He leaned over the side and dug into the turbulent water as if he could pull the water aside and see beneath it.

Frank said, "He's gone." Getting no reaction from Clarence, he said again, "He's gone! Now get your ass back to work before we all die!" *Pragmatic*, thought Eddie.

Clarence did not get back to work. Not for about twenty seconds when Eddie, a newfound pragmatist himself, said loudly but in a calming voice, "Clarence, he's gone. If we die, then it was all in vain. We've got to go, man."

Clarence cut him a look, and Eddie met his stare, but not in a challenging way. Clarence groped for his oar floating in the shallow pool inside the raft and began to row—slowly at first, then with a strength and determination that shocked Eddie. Then he, too, went back to rowing.

The waters seemed to calm just a bit as if the human sacrifice of John Anglin had appeased some unknown Water God, and it was enough to start realizing some headway to Horseshoe Bay.

Their destination was pitch black, and the moon's phase wasn't providing much additional light; however, the hulking steel behemoth that was the bridge could be felt through the fog. Frank was urging them on. Eddie couldn't hear what he was saying, but it had the desired effect, and the pain the three desperados found themselves in was forced to the back of their minds.

Eddie: "Guys, we're sinking." No reaction. "Guys!" he yelled, "We're sinking!" That got the attention of the other two.

Frank's wild eyes took in the dire state of their escape plan and said, "Start bailing." At that, the three started using their oars to flip the six-inch deep water from the boat. Unfortunately, at that exact moment, the seas kicked back up, and with no one rowing, they began to drift further toward the bridge, and it seemed to Eddie they were being swept to the point of no return.

The water level inside the raft was improving, but Eddie recognized their conundrum: continue to bail water, and they would miss their mark and wash out to sea. Or, stop bailing and row, and they could sink before making landfall. In that instant, he made a decision.

———

THE THREE OF them were soaked to the bone and shivering but continued to work, Eddie waiting for his moment. Eddie quit bailing and removed the prison shank unbeknownst to the other two, who were in survival mode and oblivious to anything else around them. It occurred to Eddie at that moment that even in

the best-laid plans, the mind's survival instinct would take over—
every single time.

Eddie's right arm shot out, and he embedded his shank in
Clarence's kidney, causing the man to spin around, grabbing at
the source of his sudden pain and, in doing so, ripping the shank
from Eddie's hand—the crude dagger remaining embedded in
Clarence. He was groping for the object, fingers grazing the
handle, but unable to secure a solid grip on the slippery, blood-
soaked handle; the blood, his blood, warming him ever so slightly.
That was his last thought as he was pushed out of the boat and
into the water. The frigid water galvanized his resolve, and
Clarence wrestled with the now-deflating pontoon. Eddie dared
not take his eyes off the desperate, drowning man trying to gain
purchase. He felt for his oar, grabbed it, raised it over his head, and
smashed Clarence in the face and about the head until he let go of
the boat to cover his head. *Survival instinct.* Eddie watched as
Clarence drifted farther from the crude boat until he disappeared
into the blackness.

He looked to Frank, who was staring at him in a stunned rage.
Eddie spoke in a dispassionate voice and said, "We were sinking,
and we weren't getting rid of the water fast enough. Now we've
got one less body weighing us down and a chance to survive this
thing."

Frank looked out at the last spot he'd seen Clarence Anglin
before turning his back to Eddie, putting his oar in the water, and
began to row. Eddie had ceded control at that moment and was
shouting instruction and encouragement. Water still weighed
down the raft, but they could not concern themselves with that.
He had no idea how long they had been off the island, but he felt
it had to be at least a couple of hours.

Exhaustion threatened to set in for both men; their adrenalin
stores seemingly depleted. But they kept rowing. Their stroke rate
had waned, but they were putting everything they had into each

pull of the oar. Land was approaching, but so was the bridge, the presence of which was felt more than seen in the fog-shrouded night. The current was aiding their movement in the growing turbulence of the water, but was it carrying them to safety and freedom? Or was it dragging them cruelly out into the Pacific Ocean, where there would be no hope for survival?

They were moving rapidly now. Jettisoning more than three hundred pounds of men allowed the rubber raft to ride higher on the water and, at times, on the crest of the growing swells. They were gaining speed on the way down but getting knocked back on the subsequent rise. Fatigue and despair were fighting for space in the minds of the escapees and were slowly, successfully elbowing past the will and resolve that had gotten them this far.

Tears began to fall down the face of Frank Lee Morris, tears of grit and determination—more than a year of planning the perfect escape. The hundreds of days when making an inch of progress was deemed a successful day. Being on edge and living in fear and worry every single moment that they would be discovered, their plans brought to light, and thrown in the hole for God knows how long. He didn't expect it to be easy, but no one could have anticipated this.

Back, shoulders, forearms, burning, shaking with fatigue in both men, but they doggedly rowed on the verge of collapse and surrender, each knowing how good it would feel to simply put down their paddles and cave to what their minds were telling them to do. Curl up in the bottom of the water-laden boat and pass out; consequences be damned.

Right then, as if on cue, a wave picked up the boat and lofted it high for an instant, high enough that both men dropped their paddles and reached and grabbed in vain, unable to gain purchase. Then the wave dumped them, hard, upside down onto a surface that felt not like water but a brick wall.

———

EDDIE CAME TO, and his first sensation was that of how quiet it suddenly was. He lay face down on a hard, dry surface and realized he did not feel the motion of the sea. He was wet and cold and began to shiver almost uncontrollably. He was scared to move and did not want to open his eyes for fear of what he would see. He finally allowed his eyelids to flutter open, and his first sight was of the barest light in the eastern sky, the lighthouse on Alcatraz Island silhouetted in the foreground.

He'd made it.

He slowly got to his knees and winced at the pain in his shoulders and back. He had a raging headache and groped for the source of the pain; he found a cut and a knot on the back of his head. He then felt the ground around him and allowed his eyes to rove over where he now sat on his knees—a large concrete slab. He slowly tried to stand, pushing himself up off the ground on wobbly legs. He held his arms out and slowly moved about like a blind man walking through an unfamiliar room. With his left hand, he touched something sturdy, immovable, thick, and steel, then pulled back—a stinging pain. He then saw that his hands were scraped, cut, and bleeding. He wiped his hands gingerly on his pants and approached the steel girder. It was too big to put his arms around.

The sky and the area around him steadily brightened, and the object came into focus—it was rust-red and had huge bolts affixed to it. Recognition dawning, he looked skyward and knew instantly where he was.

He then remembered the wave that tossed them here and...*Frank*! He started looking around for Frank Morris. *Where was Frank*? Keeping a hand on the giant steel girder, he made his way around the concrete pad, and there, on the opposite side, lay a figure cast in shadow. He knelt down, keeping a grip on the immovable object, and gave the figure a shake. "Frank?"

He took his hand off the structure and, using both hands, rolled the body over. It was Frank, and he had a large gash on his forehead at the hairline. The skin was wrenched apart, revealing bone and bone fragments. He shook the body twice more and felt for a pulse at his throat.

Frank Morris was dead.

Mind still foggy, Eddie tried to concentrate. *What to do?* A minute passed, then two. Finally, the only conclusion he came to was that he had to move. He removed the now deflated life vest from Frank and tossed it aside. Crouching now, he apologized to the dead man and rolled him into the water. He made his way back around the pylon, looking for a way out, when he saw that the concrete pad connected to land. He gathered himself and was about to step out from under the Golden Gate Bridge onto dry land when he heard a noise that stopped him. He looked back over his shoulder at the source of the sharp sound.

Sirens began to wail. He was now a fugitive. He had escaped from Alcatraz.

TWO

Towne, Alabama
November 23, 1963
2:52 AM

Fall is just now making its presence known in east central Alabama as the leaves are beginning to change, and the mercury is sitting consistently in the low fifties during the day and dipping into the forties when the sun goes down. It's rained steadily the previous two days, and though the damp air chills the solitary man sitting in the woods to the bone, he doesn't feel it—or at least he doesn't acknowledge it.

He is wearing cuffed jeans, a flannel shirt, and a dark blue canvas painter's jacket as he sits, perched frog-like, on the low-slung stone ledge of a well in the dense woods, staring at the house some fifty yards or so in the distance—the house almost escaping the reach of the nearest sodium streetlight. The near-full moon, however, makes up for the light's failings.

The smell of damp leaves, dirt, and sweet tobacco fills the immediate moon-dappled surroundings.

At his workboot-clad feet sits a twelve-gauge shotgun, a sheathed machete, and a red nylon duffle bag with dirty white straps. He is sitting perfectly still save for his right arm working as he chain smokes hand-rolled cigarettes, lighting one off the other and disposing the butts behind him into the abyss of the well. His mind is busy yet thinking of nothing at all—a buzz. The house shows no signs of life as far as he can tell, but he understands the limitations of his current vantage point. He has waited for this time of night, the time when even night owls find themselves in the deep, restful sleep of the comfortable, of the fearless...of the clueless.

He reaches into his shirt pocket for one final cigarette, lights it, and takes a long pull on the shag-filled rollie before setting it on the ledge next to him. He stands up and stretches, having sat for almost two hours. He is not a tall man but is of a solid build; his dark, glossy hair is combed back and to the left, with a few disobedient locks falling across his forehead. He is a good-looking guy with delicate features and a natural squint as if from years of tobacco smoke floating up into his vision. He grabs the twelve-gauge pump, machete, duffle bag, and, lastly, the burning rollie. He stomps off toward the house with a weapon in each hand, the bag slung over his right shoulder, and the cigarette between his lips. The ground is all damp, dead leaves which quiet his deliberate steps.

The man does not so much as check-up as he emerges from the tree line into the open backyard. He reaches the concrete slab serving as a patio littered with a round black wrought iron table and four chairs, a rusted shovel and rake leaning against the house, and a black kettle grill. The porch detritus is joined by a half-burned cigarette that he spikes to the ground after taking one last drag. He pauses at the glass sliding door, surveying the inside of the house, and sees a man asleep on the couch in the glow of the television set. He slides the door open with two fingers on his left hand, cutting one of his fingers on a metal burr on the underside of the handle. He pulls the hand back and sucks the small bubble of blood off the pad of his middle finger.

When he steps onto the orange-brown shag carpet, he is greeted by a faint white noise from the television mixing with the low snores of the slumbering man on the couch; the faint smell of breakfast for dinner hangs in the air. He sets the shotgun against the wood-paneled wall just inside and to the left of the entrance, then slides the homemade cardboard sheath off the machete and drops it. The intruder covers the ground to the couch in four strides, silently raises the machete, and brings it down with a whistling force. There is a dull, wet thud when blade meets flesh, a spray of black blood in its aftermath. The buried blade does not immediately come free when he tries to remove it, so he leaves it.

He retrieves the shotgun and then moves past the couch toward the stairs, looking down at the still figure on the sofa, looking as he did when he entered, save for the eighteen-inch blade wedged between his neck and shoulder. He assaults the staircase two steps at a time when a tall, somewhat wide silhouette appears at the top. Without breaking stride, he holds the pump shotgun off his right hip and lets loose a deafening roar as fire spits from the barrel. The shape is blown back, almost comically so, the man thinks, and as he crests the top of the stairs, he observes the blood spatter glistening in the moonlight on the wall behind the now downed figure.

He racks the pump as he does a hairpin turn at the newel post and steps into the first open door to the left, which contains two single beds separated by a nightstand. Standing in the doorway, he is greeted by two small figures, each seated upright in their own bed. He methodically dispatches the first bed's owner with another fiery explosion, then turns the barrel on the second bed, pumps, and pulls the trigger.

He moves to the next open door on the left and, seeing it's a bathroom, keeps moving. His attention is drawn to a door on the right side of the hallway when it opens. He racks the shotgun, points, and fires; the once-filled doorway is now empty.

He hears clattering in the last room on the second floor and, for the first time, quickens his pace. He gets to the door and tries the doorknob. Locked.

The faint sound of a siren pierces his concentration, which he quickly blocks out with a shake of his head. He racks the shotgun again and fires, blowing a gaping hole in the door at the knob and swinging the door open, which then drifts back partially closed. He pulls a fistful of shells from his jacket pocket, losing one to the floor, loads four shells into the chamber, racks the slide, and pushes the door open with the tip of the barrel. The siren growing louder now, he scans the bedroom, sees a figure crouching in the corner, and pulls the trigger. The blast is deafening in the small space, and the room is lit for an instant by the muzzle flash. He sees he has hit not a person but a giant stuffed teddy bear. He curses under his breath.

He steps fully into the room and scans left to right; his attention is drawn to the sheer curtains billowing in the wind invited in from the open window. He moves to the opening, sticks his head out, and surveys the ground, seeing nothing except the pulsing glow of a red flashing light. *Police.*

He moves from the window and out of the room. He retraces his steps down the hall and then down the stairs, not quite running. At the bottom of the stairs, he looks behind him to the front of the house and sees the cop car through a large picture window.

He doesn't panic as he moves to the prone figure on the couch, grabs the machete handle, and begins to rock it back and forth, trying to dislodge it. When that takes too long, he opts to leave it behind. He turns to go but stops. He raises the shotgun, racks it, and fires. He then calmly walks out through the open sliding glass door and into the wood line, not looking back.

Eight minutes after evil entered the Chatham home, it was gone.

———

KATHRYN CHATHAM HAD SPENT her Friday night cutting dress patterns and practicing sewing on her mother's new Singer. With no school the next day, she stayed up past midnight, hoping to become good enough to make her graduation dress. Fatigue eventually got the best of her, and when she messed up the stitching one too many times, she knew it was time to go to bed. Lying in bed with the lights out, she dutifully says her prayers, and as she waits to drift off, she can only think of the nice man she has come to know these past two months.

He is a police officer who works nights and, whether on shift or not, always has dinner at Gilly's Drive-In, where she works as a car hop. He always orders the same thing: a cheeseburger, fries, Dr. Pepper, and a chocolate shake. She tells him she would get fat if she ate like that every day, and he tells her the caffeine and the sugar keeps him awake for his all-night shift. She likes it when he comes in even though she usually gets in trouble with Mr. Gillespie—the owner—for spending too much time talking to him. She doesn't know how old he is exactly but knows her parents would disapprove of her going on a date with him even though she is a senior in high school and will be eighteen in three months. He asks her out whenever he sees her, and she always tells him her parents wouldn't like it.

At first, he was playful, and she thought he was only kidding, but he recently told her he was serious, and he got a little mad whenever she told him about her parents. He got very angry with her about that earlier this week, and the next night he came in for dinner, he drove off without eating at the restaurant—he'd never done that before.

Why can't boys my own age ask me out? she thinks. This is the second "older" guy to ask her out in the last couple of months. After the first one asked her out, she mentioned it to her father, who said, "Absolutely not."

That guy didn't take it any better than the policeman, though she likes the policeman much better, and she even told the other guy that, which she thinks now may have been a mistake. Of course, she didn't say it exactly like that, but that's how he took it, and, quite frankly, that's how she meant it. She had never had anyone get so mad at her. She thought he was going to hit her.

She merely posited how cool it was to be a police officer and "Who wouldn't want to take a ride in a police car?"

She didn't work tonight because the restaurant is closed until after Thanksgiving. But all she can think about lying in bed is this nice police officer, and she hopes he isn't mad at her. She is sad that it will be over a week until she is back at work and able to see him again...that is, if he comes back.

———

KATHRYN FEELS herself being pulled from a dream-filled sleep like she would imagine it feels to be lifted skyward on a cloud. Her eyes flutter open as she tries to determine if the noise she heard was from a dream or if it was real. She lay there blinking, unmoving, until she hears it again, louder this time, then again. The sound is real, and it's close. She has been bird hunting with her father since she was old enough to heft a gun, so she registers the source of the explosion. Confused and not fully awake, she tosses back her covers and pads toward the closed bedroom door in bare feet when she hears it again, the noise—louder and more violent now—stopping her as if she walked head-on into a wall. She leans her head

toward her door, rising on her tiptoes, listening, straining to hear...
anything. Then, finally, she hears a sound that is unmistakable. A
sound that once heard can never be forgotten. There is only one
such sound: the racking of a shotgun.

She spins on her toes and runs.

———

THE CACOPHONY of the shotgun blast tells Kathryn the
madman is in her room. She is hugging her knees to her chest so
hard that her entire body is beginning to ache; tears are streaming
down her face. She is stifling sobs, conscious that she dare not
make a sound. She registers a siren, but it isn't close enough to feel
safe. She doesn't know if it is the police or an ambulance, but she
hopes it is her friend from Gilly's. *He will save us*, she thinks.

Just as she allows herself to relax ever so slightly, she feels the
blood flowing back into her fingers. She begins to unfurl her legs
when she sees a figure, a head, pop out of her bedroom window.
Her eyes go wide as she gasps and slams a hand to her mouth
before it gives her location away. It's far too dark to make out
anything more than a shape, but it is definitely a man. He looks
left then right, head angled toward the ground; he ducks his head
back inside. Fear grips her, realizing how close she was to this
person as she perched on the roof next to her dormer window. She
begins to shake. A warm liquid runs down her leg; she cries harder
now, silently.

———

OFFICER MIKE GARRETT is cruising his beat in his black and
white 1962 Ford Galaxie with a red bubble gum light on the roof.
The night has been unusually quiet even by sleepy Towne standards, his only call being a non-violent domestic dispute between

the Boones, a husband and wife who aren't strangers to the TPD night shift. One of only two officers working the overnight, he was shaking door handles on businesses in his sector, making sure they were locked up tight. He was checking on Cherry's Corner Store when he heard the squawk of his car radio. Finding the store secure, he went to his car and, half in and half out of the patrol unit, he keyed the radio mic to check in.

He heard dispatch say, "Gunshots," and that was all it took.

In his haste to clip the mic to the side of the receiver, he missed, the handheld clanging to the metal floorboard. At the same time, he folded his long left leg in, slammed the heavy door, ripped the car into drive, and put his foot to the floor. The heavy automobile leaped to attention, spinning its wheels on the wet pavement before gaining purchase and rocketing off, the red bubble gum roof light and siren piercing the black serenity.

———

LESS THAN TWO minutes after receiving the call, Officer Garrett guided the lumbering Galaxie into the driveway of 619 Woods Way, its springs protesting the aggressive maneuvering the entire way. He killed the siren but left the red light on to announce his presence. The gangly patrolman ducked out of the vehicle, ran to the person standing in the neighboring yard, and asked, "What's going on here? I heard there were gunshots?" As he said, "gunshots," he noticed the rifle in the man's hands and took a step back, hand going to his duty weapon when they both reacted to a muffled shotgun blast from the house next door.

"Something bad's going on next door, Officer. I was up taking a leak when I heard the shooting; I called the police and grabbed my gun." He lifted the 30.06 and lowered it back to waist height.

Mike Garrett unsnapped his leather holster and removed the Smith and Wesson Model 28 revolver with the six-inch blue steel barrel. He held it up beside his head in a two-handed grip and moved on the house in a semi-crouch.

He tried the front door and found it locked; tried looking inside through the side panels and saw nothing of the dark interior, and then...a flash and a boom, much louder than the first, and in the briefest instant, he saw the silhouette of a person behind the tongue of fire. He stood, frozen for a couple of beats, before running back to the neighbor who now had a child with him, a boy, perhaps eight or nine years old, and said, "How many people are inside that house?"

The man shrugged and said, "It's a family of five."

The officer nodded, said, "You watch the front; I'm going around back." And he was gone.

Garrett bladed up the side of the brick structure and paused for a five count, trying to control his breathing before peering around the corner. As he watched, he estimated half a minute had passed, and when he neither saw nor heard anything, he turned the corner and edged up to the rear entrance, left palm flat against the cool, rough brick, gun up by his ear.

He stepped through the opening and was slapped in the face by the sulfuric odor of spent gunpowder and the sweet, metallic smell of blood. He was sweating now, causing his peaked cap to slide down his forehead a little, so he took it off and tossed it to the ground. He could barely make out the figure on the couch, so he approached with caution, and when he stepped in to check on the person, his foot squished into the carpet, and he instinctively knew what it was: blood.

He swore to himself for not having brought a flashlight, but he also knew a flashlight would make him a target if the shooter were still in the house. He backed up a few steps from the couch and scanned the room, thinking...and listening. Nothing. Not so much as a creak. To his left, he noticed a doorway and a slight shine to the floor, so he assumed that was the kitchen. He crept sideways toward the room while keeping an eye back to his right. It was unlikely someone would be in the kitchen that time of the night—morning—so he didn't expect to find any victims or survivors, but he couldn't discount the shooter was posted up in there, maybe even lying in wait. Neutralizing the shooter had to be his first priority; there were possibly four other people in the house, and he had no clue as to their status.

The ambient light was low, but his eyes were now well enough adjusted that, as he moved through the kitchen and into the connected dining room, he knew no one was there. Completing the circle back to the room with the body, he had cleared the first floor and turned his attention to the stairs. He was about to take the first step when he heard a familiar sound in the distance. Backup was arriving.

He shook his head to re-focus and put his back against the wall, carefully placing a foot on the first stair, slowly applying weight, listening for any noise the steps may make. The shag carpet muffled any potential sound, so he proceeded, one step at a time, crossing one foot over the next, back connected to the wall, eyes up and moving. He reached the top and recognized the same smells from downstairs. He crested the final step, eyes still up and looking back to the right when he tripped and fell. He lay there for a moment in case the sound brought the shooter out. Hearing nothing, he began to get up and realized he had fallen over a person; he registered that it appeared to be an older female. He wanted to scramble up and run; instead, he marshaled control and gathered himself to rise as quietly as possible. He slipped once when he placed his hand in a patch of blood.

On his feet now, he walked down the hall, and the smell grew stronger as he approached the first room on his left. He stopped at the edge of the doorframe and leaned in, his attention going immediately to the gore on the wall above each bed in the room. He saw each bed contained a lump, thought *bodies,* and moved on, taking a quick peek in the next doorway—the bathroom—before seeing the first room on the right with a large portion of the door-frame missing. He crossed the hall, gun pointed down in a two-handed grip. He saw a supine figure surrounded by dark, wet carpet. He glanced up, taking a cursory view of the room before moving down the hallway to the final doorway on the right, where he saw a hollow wood door with a ragged half-moon chunk blown out of its left side where the knob should have been. He stepped in and stood, listening; the pervasive odor of burned gunpowder throughout the home beginning to burn his nose. He heard nothing but registered the billowing curtains and shuffled toward them a couple of steps. He could just make out the ruined stuffed animal in the corner, which puzzled him before he shook off the errant thought and cleared the room.

———

OFFICER MORRIS ARRIVED on the scene in much the same fashion as Officer Garrett, except when he exited his patrol car, he immediately drew his gun on the armed neighbor. "Drop it! Drop the gun!"

"Whoa, whoa, whoa," said the neighbor, hands going up—left hand holding the rifle by the forestock, right hand empty and open. "The other officer, he asked me to watch the front yard, and he went around back."

The compact Morris moved around the front of his Galaxie—undeterred, focused, gun aimed—and walked down the suspicious individual who dared not move a muscle.

"Look, I'm the one who called the police." Then, seeing the officer's determined movement, he said, "Please, sir, my son." He motioned left with his head. Morris saw the boy for the first time, which stopped his advance without affecting his concentration.

"Jeff!" Officer Morris heard his name and recognized the voice but did not take his attention off the man lined up in his sight. He responded, "Yeah, Mike, whatcha got?"

Officers Morris and Garrett were both rookies nearing one year on the force. They met as roommates at the police academy. Neither grew up in Towne, which was rare for this particular department, so they became fast friends looking out for one another and earning the moniker Mutt and Jeff due to their incongruent sizes and inseparability both on shift and off. It was probably also brought about because Jeff Morris was indeed the shorter of the two, much like the comic strip characters. They tolerated the lazy designation because it was just easier that way.

Garrett sidled up to Morris and, slightly out of breath, said, "This guy's good. I was standing with him when I heard a shot from inside." Morris holstered his sidearm, and the neighbor slowly lowered his hands after a beat.

Morris could hear the buzz in his partner's voice and said, "What did you see in there?"

Garrett put his hands on his hips and shook his head as he turned to look back at the house he just exited. "It's bad."

———

THE TOWNE POLICE DEPARTMENT descended on the murder house en masse; everyone from the police chief to the rookie officers was present and assigned a task, whether it was manning the crime scene log and controlling access, evidence collection, photographing the scene, searching the nearby woods, you name it.

Detective Lieutenant Joe Wilson was the first on the scene: "Which one of you went inside?" Lt. Wilson had an easy way about him both in manner and speech, but he was intimidating—especially to younger officers. He wore his blonde hair in a flattop and smelled of Bay Rum aftershave. Even now, at just after 4:00 in the morning, Lt. Wilson was wearing a white shirt, skinny black necktie, and gray tweed sport coat. It was rumored that he shaved before bedtime and slept in a suit. He had never married and wore his large, round, gold college ring on his left ring finger—he was right-hand dominant and didn't want anything to interfere with firing his duty weapon.

The lieutenant believed there was only one way to do police work: the right way. *There were no shortcuts to finding the truth.* He had little patience for screw-ups on mundane cases, but a crime of this magnitude? Perfection was the only option, and nothing less would be tolerated. He took crime personally, and even the youngest officer in the department would have known that this case would cleave him to his core.

Garrett stepped up and said, "I did, sir," in answer to the lieutenant's question. His steady, matter-of-fact cadence belied the buzzards in his stomach.

"Come with me." Garrett fell in behind the lieutenant as he made for the Chatham's house.

When they reached the steps to the front porch, Wilson said, "I want you to walk me, step-by-step, through everything you heard, saw, smelled, touched, okay?" He fixed him with his blue-eyed gaze and said, "Everything."

Garrett said, "Yes, sir," and, beginning with his arrival, his contact with Dr. Jackson (as he now knew the man to be), and hearing the gunshot from inside the home, he recounted the entirety of what he had done and observed.

Garrett produced the flashlight he'd retrieved from his vehicle and began to lead the lieutenant around the side of the house and into the home, taking the same path as he had some forty minutes earlier.

"Turn that light off, son. I want to see things as you saw them. At least from the outside."

Garrett extinguished the light and led him to and through the rear door. Upon breaking the plane of the open entryway, the atmosphere grabbed hold—the odor of burned gunpowder a hazy memory, the smell of blood taking center stage.

Morris: "Turn on the light."

Garrett: "Sir?"

"You cleared the house, right?"

"Yes, sir."

"Then turn on the light. We need to see what we're looking at."

Turn off this light; turn on that one. He groped for a light switch, found it, and lit the back patio. Seeing that, he flipped the neighboring switch, illuminating the television room. "Dear God," muttered Lt. Joe Wilson at the nightmare revealed by the light cast from the wagon wheel chandelier.

Garrett's back was to the room. When he turned and saw what drew the senior man's attention, he quickly turned back to the wall and said, "Goddamn." He quickly turned to the devoutly religious Joe Wilson, who, not taking his eyes off the scene before him, replied, "Relax, Officer Garrett, your reaction is understood." A pause, then, "But maybe try for a different word next time." The officer nodded, but the lieutenant still did not look at him. Instead, Wilson said, "Tell me about it."

They gazed upon the body on the couch and then took in the gore that painted the cushions and the wall behind it. The figure had a bloody, meaty mass of flesh, brain, and bone where his head had once been, and Garrett mentioned the shotgun blast he observed through the window at the front door. By this point, the neighbor had given them a rundown of the Chatham family, and they made a preliminary identification of the dead person on the couch as Frank Chatham, the family's patriarch.

As they moved on through the home, Garrett narrated, the horror growing worse room after room, light after light.

The route through the kitchen and dining room was uneventful, but they began to piece together what happened as they ascended the stairs.

They saw a spent shotgun shell on a step about a third of the way up the staircase. At the top of the stairs lay a woman whose nightgown was soaked in blood; the wall behind her riddled with buckshot and blood. This had to be Marjorie Chatham—the mother, noted Garrett. Carefully stepping around her, Garrett led the way to each room off the hallway.

The overhead light in the first room revealed a dead boy in each bed. In the first bed to the left, a boy's head lolled off the side of the bed near the headboard, his entire torso showing evidence of violence. The boy in the second bed was blown into the corner and lay on the bed in a heap. He, too, covered in blood.

Garrett consulted his notepad and said, "The Chatham's had one son, Brian. One of these boys must be him, but who's the other?" This was stated as a rhetorical question. They noted two spent shells—one just inside the room and one just outside—and moved on.

There was nothing remarkable in the bathroom, but the first bedroom on the right told a different story. They saw the spent shell in the middle of the hall, which correlated to the damage to the doorframe. Then, just across the threshold, they found a dead girl lying on the floor, nearly cut in half, with the upper portion of her torso lying about thirty degrees off center. The two lawmen surmised she got up after hearing the gunshots, opened her door, and was gunned down where she stood.

Garrett scanned his notes again. "I'm guessing this is Chelsea, but then again, it could be Kathryn." He could only shake his head as they moved on.

They eyed another spent shell further up the hallway and an unspent shell on the floor next to it. Lt. Wilson mentally counted up the shells he had seen. "He had to reload here. Probably fumbled a shell in the dark."

They pushed through a door and turned on the light. No blood—not what they expected. They surveyed the room, eyes falling on the obliterated carnival prize in the corner. Lt. Wilson took the lead further into the room and did a three-sixty. Thinking. After a minute, his eyes fell on the dancing curtains. He walked to the open window, moving the curtains out of his way. He leaned out and stared past the roof's edge toward the ground. Thinking. He brought his head back into the room and looked around before noticing an overturned chair at his feet. He righted the wood kitchen chair, stood on it, and hung out the window up to his waist. He reached a hand back through the open window and said, "Flashlight."

He aimed the beam onto the ground, scanning right then left. Then he focused the beam on the tree line, straining at the limits of the bulb's capability. He clicked it off but kept staring.

A noise. A scrape. Flashlight back on, aimed immediately left.

"Ma'am? I'm Lieutenant Joe Wilson, Towne police department. You're safe now."

THREE

Towne, Alabama
November 18, 2023

Towne County District Attorney Maggie Gamble entered the crowded media room in courtroom four, Judge Malcolm Arnett's courtroom. The media room spanned the width of the courtroom and was positioned at the rear so its occupants could observe the proceedings. The audio was piped in via speakers utilizing microphones in the front of the courtroom where the action occurred. The room also made any television cameras less intrusive; the last thing anyone wanted was for the jury to be influenced by the media coverage of a case.

The narrow room was crowded with reporters from three local television stations, a pool camera to record audio and video, a reporter from the *Towne Tribune*, and a smattering of DA office staff and other courthouse personnel on hand to watch the closing arguments of the most high-profile trial of the year.

The case that had brought them all here was a rape case involving the college-aged son of one of Towne's wealthiest citizens. The defendant was accused of raping a girl he had known his entire life. The pair had graduated high school together, gone to the same college, and were hanging out with friends while home for Christmas break two years ago when the sexual assault had occurred. The trial had been a week and a half of legal warfare, and this was its climax.

When Maggie arrived, her star pupil, her chief ADA, was in the middle of his final remarks.

The dark, cramped space was standing room only and warm from the cameras and computers being used. When Maggie entered, a young intern offered up his seat, which she took without acknowledgment by look or word. She set her Tervis Tumbler of sweet tea on the countertop in front of her and asked the room, "How's he doing?"

Wendy Wade, the most veteran TV reporter in the room, said, "How do you think?" This drew a knowing smile from Maggie while not taking her eyes off the event unfolding in the courtroom.

Through the speakers, she heard Barclay Griffith telling the jury, "...which is right out of the rape defense playbook. *Blame the victim. She was asking for it. She knew what was going to happen when she went to his place after midnight. What else could have been on her mind?* The defense wants you to focus entirely on Ms. Thompson's behavior that night.

"Conversely, they *need* you to ignore not only the defendant's behavior the night of the rape but *also* his behavior the next day when he was interviewed by the police and lied to them for over four hours." He paused for effect before repeating, "FOUR HOURS!" Then: "Why? Why lie to the police at all in this situation? Why didn't he just say, as he wants you to believe now, 'Yeah, we had sex. She came over, I drank some beers, she was drinking vodka, we watched a movie, and then we had sex.'"

His rangy frame relaxed, open as he stared at the jury, making eye contact with each one before continuing. "He lied because he knew what he did. He raped Lucy Thompson and thought he could get away with it. He figured he would give the police a story, and they would believe him because of who his family is and because Ms. Thompson...well, who would believe...how did he describe her to the police?" Barclay picked up his legal pad as if he needed to review his notes when what he was actually doing was building up the moment. Everyone in the courtroom knew how the defendant described the victim; it was repeated ad nauseam in opening statements and throughout the course of the trial.

He flipped pages on his legal pad, ratcheting up the tension. Appearing to find what he was looking for, he said, "He called her a 'clout chasing WHORE!'" He slammed his legal pad on his table, allowing the words to echo around the jury box. In a quieter tone, he said, "Admittedly, I didn't know what a clout chaser was, so I asked Detective Beck Lawson what it meant, and she told you that a clout chaser is someone who tries to feed off another person's popularity or use someone for their benefit." He gave the jury another ocular once-over. "He figured there was no way they would believe some whore over him.

"Folks, she grew up in this community just like him," he pointed at the defendant. "She graduated from Towne High School just like him." Point. "And she is attending the same college he is attending." Point and a pause. "She's studying to be a nurse. Only her plans have now hit a snag. You heard her say how this has affected her life. How after undergoing the humiliation of an invasive SANE examination and rape kit, she can't stomach so much as walking into a hospital or doctor's office." He stood before the defendant and stared at him for a beat before saying, "That's going to make it a little tough to live out her childhood dream of becoming a nurse."

Barclay removed his typewritten notes from the small lectern in the middle of the room and placed them on his table. Maggie had watched him enough to know he was about to close the deal. Speaking in a conversational tone, he told the jury, "What the defendant did not count on was his DNA being where it shouldn't be: inside Ms. Thompson's vagina and in her mouth exactly where *she* told the police he ejaculated—against her will and despite her vehement protestations—and exactly where *he* told the police nothing would be because *he* told the police that NOTHING HAPPENED! AT ALL!" Barclay was all emotion when giving his final appeal to a jury to convict.

He approached the spindly oak rail separating himself from the jury and spoke just above a whisper. He knew that if he got the jury to lean in to hear him at any point, he had them.

He said, "I want to leave you with this: Defense attorneys always make these cases about the victim. Well, now *you* get to make this case about the defendant. When you go back to deliberate and one of you starts in about her going to his place after midnight, which one of you is going to stand up for her and say, 'This isn't about her.' Your only question is, 'Did the defendant rape Lucy Thompson?' That's it. And if you come back with a not guilty verdict, you are effectively saying that if a girl goes over to a guy's apartment after a certain time, then he is free to do to her whatever he wishes." He paused and looked as if he were deep in thought. "My wife recently gave birth to our first child, a little girl, and it terrifies me to think of the message a not guilty verdict will send about sexual assault. We are a community of laws, standards, and values, and I know your verdict will reflect exactly that. When you reach your verdict, you are going to come back out here, and with your verdict, you are going to say, 'Lucy Thompson, we believe you.'" Barclay made eye contact with each juror one last time before sitting down.

Each of them had moved forward in their seats and tilted their head upward in his direction. He knew he had them. But was it enough?

Maggie didn't say a word as she picked up her tea and left the media room, the entire room watching her go. She was a force of a person.

Judge Arnett spent the next half-hour charging the jury before sending them to deliberate. Then, with the jury gone, the lawyers stood and gathered their things. Barclay looked at Stacy Steen, his co-counsel, and said, "Win or lose, we tried a hell of a case."

She was organizing papers, sliding them into her briefcase, and said, "You killed it in your closing." Then she stopped and said, "You think they're going to cut him loose?"

Barclay shrugged. "The defendant looks twelve, and any juror with a son is going to see their son sitting in his place. Not to mention, *rape* is a big word. Really big. It's much easier to convince twelve random people that someone is a murderer than it is that someone is a rapist."

Barclay felt a buzz in his jacket pocket and retrieved his phone. It was a text from Maggie asking him to come to her office.

————

BARCLAY ENTERED the anteroom outside Maggie's office, saying to Sandy Maxwell, "Maggie wants to see me." The veteran gatekeeper gave him an appraising look. Barclay took it to mean she was unaware he had been asked to come to her office.

Barclay knew the informal protocol. He waited for a humorless and on-the-verge-of-retirement Sandy Maxwell to give the slightest nod toward her boss' closed office door. Barclay knocked as he opened the door and entered.

Maggie looked up at the sound of the door opening, grabbed a remote from her desk, muted the wall-mounted television, and motioned for him to sit in one of the chairs in front of her desk.

He said, "I guess you saw it?"

"I did. Well, the last few minutes, anyway. One of the

Morrisons caught me in the hallway as I was heading to the courtroom and cornered me, trying to persuade me to allow his client to get probation. We've been prosecuting him since I was an ADA here. I'm pretty sure I sent him to prison at least twice myself." She leaned back in her chair and said, "Dealing with dumbass lawyers is one thing I will *not* miss in retirement. How either of the Morrison brothers ever passed the bar...I swear."

Barclay laughed, "There's still time to change your mind, you know."

It was Maggie's turn to laugh. "Yeah, right. It's my last week in this office, the governor is set to appoint you as my replacement on Monday, and you say I can still change my mind."

"You could serve out the remainder of your term."

"Nonsense," she said. "When you and I spoke about this last year, I told you then that I was ready to go, but..." They both knew the *but*. After a moment, she continued, "It's been over a year since that awful mess and since the governor owed me a favor." Seeing the look on Barclay's face, she said, "Don't even ask." They exchanged smiles. "So, you going to get that prick?"

It took Barclay a second. "The rape case? Pruitt?" She gave a look that said *who else,* and he said, "Who knows. You know how difficult sex cases are. Girl shows up at a guy's house after midnight, she brings booze with her...and he doesn't *look* like a rapist." He lolled his head back and blew out a breath. "He doesn't even look like ninety-eight percent of the folks we prosecute."

"Can I offer you some advice? About your closing today."

"You mean criticism?"

"No, I mean advice, but frankly, I don't care how you take it." Barclay knew that was Maggie being Maggie, and he respected her for it. "Be careful preying on the jury."

"How do you mean?"

"You have a way of making it personal for them. Putting everything on their shoulders."

"It is all on them; that's their role. They render the ultimate decision."

"That's all true, but you don't always have to be so...on the nose with it."

He leaned forward in his seat and said, "I've lost too many of these damn rape cases with the defense attorney dancing all over my victim, and I've had enough. I was going to say what needs to be said, and if we still lose, then so be it."

"I understand. Just something to think about." Maggie got up and walked to her closet. She opened the double doors and accessed a locked file cabinet inside. She slid open a drawer, withdrew an accordion-style folder, and laid the file flat on her desk. Not removing her hand from the folder, she said, "Are you familiar with the Chatham murders?"

The abrupt change in topic took Barclay aback. He'd been so focused on his current case for the last few weeks that it took him a moment for his brain to switch gears. He finally said, "Maybe," but without much conviction.

"In November of 1963, five people were murdered over on the west side of the city. An entire family was wiped out except for the oldest Chatham daughter, who somehow managed to escape the fate that befell everyone else. It was awful." Maggie grabbed her Tervis of sweet iced tea and consumed half of it as if trying to drown the memory. She set the cup down and said, "I was five years old and still have memories of when it happened. My father was a corporal in patrol at the time, and he was away from home a lot after that. They had the entire force working twenty-four hours a day for weeks, but they never caught the person who did it." Again, she seemed to get lost in the memory. "He became Towne's Boogeyman to a generation of us."

"Why are you telling me this?"

She gave him a look like she couldn't understand that he didn't understand. Then, she said, "I want you to solve it."

He took in that statement and said, "Gee, no pressure there."

She dismissed that statement with a wave. "Maybe you solve it, maybe not, but I want...make that I need you to promise me you'll look into this." Barclay opened his mouth to speak, and she spoke over him. "I'm serious, Barclay. Do this for me." She fixed him with her prosecutor's gaze. "Do it for everyone that lived through it sixty years ago. Towne changed after that night, Barclay. People started locking their doors and sleeping with guns under the bed. They made their children come home before dark. Spend the night with a friend? Forget about it."

She drank from her tea glass before continuing. "Sure, everyone's fears eventually waned, but the wound is still there—consciously for some, subconsciously for many. Others live with the effects and don't even know it because it changed how their parents raised them. Even those who never heard of the murders live in a community forever changed that night." She bore into him with her green-eyed stare that dared you to disagree. "Towne needs this."

"Sure. Of course. Absolutely." A pause, a look out the office window; it was a beautiful fall afternoon. Then a question: "Maggie, I have to ask, why this office?"

"How do you mean?"

"Investigations are the job of the police." He nodded at the brown accordion folder worn along the edges and said, "Why are we...you handling this one? I didn't know we were in the cold case business."

"We're not, really. Chief Joe Wilson gave this case to me last year, shortly before he died. He was the lieutenant over the detective division when the Chatham murders happened, and that case ruined him. He eventually made police chief and did a damn fine job, but that case was an abscess on his soul."

"Why did he give you the case?"

"Joe mentored my father as a young police officer, and he became like a grandfather to me. When he retired, he didn't believe the incoming chief—some hotshot assistant chief from Atlanta PD—would concern himself with the sins of Towne's past, and he didn't want the case to sit on a shelf and rot, so he took the file with him when he left. By that point in his life, he was tired, beaten down about it, and never did much with it. Then, shortly before the cancer finally took him last year, he gave me the file. He trusted me to finish what he started back in sixty-three."

"What have you been able to do with the case?"

"Unfortunately, not much. To be honest, I didn't know *what* to do with it...where to even begin. It wasn't until I attended a conference last summer where the DA and some of the investigators involved in solving the Golden State Killer case spoke. They discussed genealogy DNA and how that led to the killer's identity and arrest. That got me thinking about the viability of solving the Chatham case."

"Where does the case stand now?"

"I knew a retired SBI investigator, guy named AJ Murphy, so I reached out to him about helping us. He's only getting started, but a cursory review of the case file indicated a possible source of DNA in evidence."

"What is it?"

"A cigarette butt."

"And it's never been tested?" he asked, excitement edging into his voice.

"The first thing we did was test the cigarette and had the profile uploaded to CODIS but got nothing. Of course, it is entirely possible it belonged to someone other than the killer. Maybe it was the TV repairman, or the plumber, or any number of other people who had nothing to do with this case."

"So you have a DNA profile; you just need a person to test it against."

"That's correct; however, that brings me to genealogy DNA and why I asked for AJ Murphy specifically. He solved a near-twenty-year-old cold case in Lauderdale County utilizing genealogy DNA. As far as I know, that was the first and only Alabama case solved using it."

Barclay was taking everything in when his cell phone buzzed. It was a one-word text from Stacy Steen: *Verdict*.

Barclay cleared his throat and said, "We have a verdict, so I need to, ah..."

"Of course. Go on. I'm right behind you."

Barclay stood, "Talk about this more later?"

"Nope, I'm done. It's yours now."

"But..."

She waved him off. "You'll know better than this old woman what to do with this case with all this new technology." Barclay knew that wasn't true, and he knew that Maggie didn't believe it either. "My only suggestion is to meet with AJ yourself; sit down with him and talk through it. Where things go from here is entirely up to you...Mr. DA."

Barclay forced a smile, seemingly caught between staying and going.

Finally, she said, "Don't you have a verdict?"

———

EVERYONE STOOD in the packed courtroom as the jury filed back in. They had deliberated a little over an hour, which Barclay took to be bad. He figured they wouldn't convict this kid of rape without giving it tremendous consideration; he expected them to deliberate into the next day at least.

As they waited for the jury, Barclay leaned over and whispered,

"Remember what I said. We knew from day one this was going to be a tough case, but this was a case we had to try. The evidence demanded it, and our victim demanded it. So if it's not guilty, hold your head up. You can be sick about it tonight, but we have to be strong for Lucy." Stacy nodded without looking at him, her knuckles white from gripping the edge of the table.

This was the worst part of the process for Barclay; he wanted to throw up. He looked back over his shoulder at Lucy Thompson, gave her a slight smile and a nod. She looked back, impassive with her tear-streaked face. Barclay faced forward, closed his eyes, and said a silent prayer.

The jurors filed in one by one, the courtroom quiet as a graveyard. When the last juror was seated, the judge ordered everyone else to do the same.

Judge Arnett broke the silence, saying, "Has the jury reached a verdict?"

"We have, Your Honor," said juror 147, a bookkeeper for a local heating and air company. She was not who Barclay had expected to be the foreperson.

"Please hand the verdict form to the bailiff." The foreperson did so, and the bailiff walked the folded piece of paper to the bench and handed it to the judge.

Judge Arnett unfolded the paper and read, "We, the jury, find the defendant, Alfred Alan Pruitt, guilty of rape in the first degree as charged in the indictment."

The judge had warned everyone in the courtroom against any outbursts, and, save for a giant sob from Lucy, there was no audible emotion displayed. Under the table, the two prosecutors bumped fists.

The judge polled the jury, and after determining the verdict was unanimous, he said, "Mr. Pruitt, the jury having found you guilty, I now adjudicate you guilty and remand you to the custody of the sheriff pending sentencing."

This drew an outburst first from his attorney, lobbying against custody until sentencing. Then, before he'd gotten a half-dozen words out of his mouth, Pruitt's mother burst into tears, yelling, "My baby, my baby, not my baby!"

The judge rapped his gavel, demanded order, and told the defense attorney that he'd need to file a motion if he wanted bail pending sentencing. The judge then adjourned court.

———

MORE THAN AN HOUR after the jury's verdict and maybe ten minutes after Barclay and Stacy had met with Lucy Thompson in the adjoining witness room, Barclay was back in the courtroom alone. He looked around the empty room and reflected on the day's verdict. He thought about the months of work that went into this case. He considered the effusive gratitude from Ms. Thompson and her parents. He never took for granted how fortunate he was to have this job.

Then, in the solitude of the empty courtroom, he allowed his pent-up emotions to come forth.

FOUR

Barclay sat in his office, the only light diffusing the room coming from a lamp on his credenza, the streetlights, and the neon-glow of storefronts in the square below his second-floor window. He usually found himself mentally and physically drained after a trial, particularly one as lengthy and emotional as the case he had just prosecuted.

Post-trial, he preferred to bathe in the semi-darkness and think about...nothing. Simply sit and get lost in the music. Tonight, it was his Melody Gardot station on Pandora. He allowed the music to wash over him until he could finally will himself to go home.

He was into hour number two of sitting, listening, and decompressing when a rap on his open door brought him out of his reverie, and he swung his chair around to face the distraction.

"Hey, Boss."

A smile creased Barclay's lips at the sound of the familiar baritone emanating from the silhouette filling the door frame. He rocked forward and out of his chair and met the welcomed interloper on the other side of his desk, sharing a handshake and a brief but firm embrace.

"Congratulations," said DA investigator Winston Fitzsimmons, moving into the room. The starched white shirt and neat-as-a-pin appearance contrasted Barclay's: rumpled dress shirt, sleeves rolled up, shoes and tie removed.

"Thanks, Fitz. That was a big one for sure." Barclay returned to his desk chair, and Fitz took a visitor's chair, the gun on his hip beneath his jacket making for a tight squeeze.

"Hate I missed it. Heard you had a hell of a closing."

Barclay shrugged and said, "You'll have more opportunities...I hope. Why are you here so late?"

"Just got in from running down a couple of witnesses for Gary's attempted murder trial. A witness and the damn victim didn't show, so I've been working with the PD to round them up."

"You find 'em?" Fitz gave Barclay a look that said, *Did you really just ask that*? Barclay smiled and said, "I'm only asking, brother." Despite the company, he was melting back into his chair. He needed to get up and go home now, or he'd never leave.

"Rosie texted me the verdict a couple of hours ago, so maybe I should be the one asking you why *you're* here so late." It was Barclay's turn to give the *Did you really just ask that*? look. Fitz smiled and said, "It's so damned peaceful here at night." He got up, walked to the window, looked down at the square and people moving about, and said, "Savor this one, Boss."

"This was my last trial as an ADA." He shook his head as he stared at nothing in particular, then said, "It didn't fully hit me until after the verdict this afternoon, but...that was it."

Gardot's "Worrisome Heart" began to ooze through the Marshall speaker on the scarred bookshelf tucked in the corner of the room, and Barclay leaned back and closed his eyes. There was a long silence between the two. So long, in fact, that Fitz thought the prosecutor had fallen asleep. He made a move to leave when Barclay said, "You want to be my chief investigator?"

"How's that?"

"You heard me."

"Well, shit yeah."

"Good, you're hired."

Fitz was waiting for more when he finally said, "You serious, Boss?"

Eyes still closed, he said, "Rosie is retiring with Maggie, and I'm betting Stubbs won't be too far behind." Barclay opened his eyes, rocked forward in his chair, and said, "Regardless, I was going to ask you."

"Sure you were." There was a smile in his voice.

Barclay slid open the front door of his credenza and retrieved a bottle of Blanton's and a glass. He filled the glass with more than usual and slid it across to Fitz. He refilled the glass on his desk with a similar amount, then set the squat bottle on the desk and capped it. "Cheers," he said, raising his glass to Fitz before taking a big sip.

After a few beats of silence, Barclay spoke. "I've got us a project to work on."

"Which is?"

"It's actually Maggie's." He gave a brief overview of the Chatham murders: the facts as he knew them (which were extremely limited), why Maggie had the case, what it meant to her, and why they would give it everything they had to solve the sixty-year-old homicide.

Fitz nodded, then said, "You'd better be getting on home, or Brittany's going to have your tail."

"She's at dinner with friends. I knew the jury would get the case at some point today and expected a late night."

"Who's watching the baby?"

Barclay smiled and said, "My parents."

Fitz laughed a big laugh. "Oh, man, what I wouldn't do to see the great Grover Griffith *the third* changing a diaper."

They drank a little more and talked a little less.

It was nearing 8:00 when Barclay said, "We'd better go ahead and leave, or neither one of us will be able to drive home."

FIVE

November 21

Barclay and Fitz sat in the conference room inside the district attorney's office. The two were dressed casually: jeans and a hoodie for Barclay, tan 5.11 tactical pants, and a navy performance golf shirt for Fitz. The shirt fit the investigator in a way that made Barclay a little jealous. Barclay was just over six feet tall and in excellent shape; however, despite the investigator's playing days being far behind him, the six-four former collegiate tight end looked like he could still run a slant route or seal off the edge if he needed to. The coming week promised to be hectic, and they were both eager to dig into the Chatham murder file. Few places were as quiet as a DA's office on the weekend.

The conference room was well-appointed and rivaled that of any private law firm. Prosecutors met with victims in this room, the DA gave press conferences from this room, and serious plea discussions were held at this very conference table. Maggie Gamble made it a point to ensure this room gave the best impression to anyone invited in.

The dark gray walls were trimmed in rich mahogany, which went along with the thick mahogany conference table polished to a mirror-like finish. The conference table had an ornately carved edge matching the carvings on the thick table legs. A crystal water service was set on a matching sideboard against the wall at one end of the big table. Above the sideboard was a large framed sepia-toned photograph of the town square from more than one hundred years ago. One wall was floor-to-ceiling windows, while the opposite side was built-in bookcases housing the office's legal library. The room perpetually smelled of citrus furniture polish.

A box of dark roast coffee from The Knockbox sat on the polished conference table, and they were enjoying a cup when two men entered the room in the middle of a war story.

Chief DA Investigator Gary (Rosie) Roosevelt strolled in, his paunch straining at a too-tight golf shirt, his mustache working over a hidden mouth. A man of similar age followed him into the room laughing; Barclay assumed this to be AJ Murphy. He got the impression the two had not seen each other in a while.

"Barclay, Fitz," said Rosie, "I want you to meet AJ Murphy." Murphy was straight out of central casting. He was broad-shouldered, wore his white hair shorn close, and had a white fu manchu mustache. He was wearing a short-sleeved mint green fishing shirt, revealing meaty forearms, and blue jeans with cowboy boots that were obviously his everyday wear, and he was overweight the way large men grew heavy with age. Oakley blades rested on his head, and reading glasses hung around his neck.

Introductions were made, and shaking hands with AJ Murphy was like shaking hands with an oak tree. The first thing Barclay noticed was his blue eyes, which danced with scrutiny. His lined face spoke of experience, and his voice had Barclay wondering if he'd swallowed a bullhorn after gargling gravel.

"Coffee?" offered Barclay as everyone found a seat at the table.

Coffee was poured—Rosie drinking his black while Murphy tipped a splash of cream into his.

Rosie said, "AJ here retired from SBI, what, three years ago?" AJ nodded, and Rosie continued, "They brought him back to start a cold case unit to look into unsolved homicide cases across the state." He looked at Barclay and said, "This is the man Maggie trusts with the Chatham case."

"Thank you for taking the time on a Saturday to help us out," said Barclay.

AJ waved a hand and said, "I love this stuff. I just need to know you're committed to this case because without buy-in from the DA, these cold case investigations won't work."

"I wouldn't waste your time if I wasn't serious about this case. Maggie Gamble was my mentor, and I aim to do whatever I can to see this case solved and this killer brought to justice. Tell me where we begin?"

"The first thing you need to do is let the PD know you will be taking a hard look at the case. Let this be your first lesson in politics, you hear me? You don't need their permission, but you will need their help, so try and avoid pissing them off from the jump. They may see you solving this as making them look bad. I don't know the chief over there." To Rosie, he said, "You think he'll be ok with this?"

Rosie began nodding and said, "He will...if we do it right. I'll handle that."

"Good," said Murphy. "I would ask the chief for a liaison for this case—a detective or even someone on the command staff to communicate with about the case. Whoever they assign to you, make sure they know that you will not do anything on the case without them knowing about it—and then make sure you do it. You don't need to blunder into this case right off the bat, you hear me?"

Rosie eyed Barclay and said, "I'll square it away with the PD.

In fact, if you want a particular detective assigned to the case, tell me, and I'll make it happen."

Barclay nodded, already with a name in mind. He said, "How should we begin investigating this thing?"

"Right," said AJ, "well...who's going to be the lead investigator for this office?" He bounced his gaze between Fitz and Rosie.

Rosie spoke up, "This is all Fitzie's. I put my papers in, so this will be all him."

"Fitz," said AJ, "Don't talk to anyone about the case. Don't ask anyone who they believe did it or even who the suspects are. You need to go at this fresh without *any* preconceptions, you hear me?"

"I can see that," said Fitz.

"Get into the case file. Read the witness statements and detective supplements." Murphy leaned forward, moved the paper coffee cup toward the middle of the table, and said, "Learn this case. The better you know it, the more likely it is you'll know when you see something significant. You'll also be better prepared to know when someone is lying to you or lied to the police back then." AJ stood and refilled his cup, skipping the cream this time. He remained standing as he sipped and said, "The age of this case presents its own challenges." To Rosie, "Any idea how many of these folks are even still around?"

"I'll have to give that some thought." Rosie also poured himself a second cup of coffee as he pondered the question.

Fitz said, "Any other advice?"

"Yeah, get a look at the evidence; all of it and right up front. The last thing you need is to get off into this case only to discover later that evidence is missing or was never collected. I've made that mistake myself, and it can completely upend an investigation."

Fitz was taking notes on his iPad. "Anything else?" he asked, eyes still on the tablet, Apple Pencil working.

"Once you start, don't stop. Not until you run down every

lead, exhaust every resource, you hear me?" He paused, then said, "You picked one whale of a cold case to start with. Most of the folks involved are probably dead, moved off, or their memories will have faded." He surveyed the triumvirate before speaking. "And Barclay, if you're going to need DNA before you feel comfortable prosecuting this case, think long and hard about even stepping off into this."

"How do you mean?" asked Barclay.

"Most DAs, all they want to know in these old cases is: 'Do we have DNA?' In those instances, I know right then who I am dealing with. You have to make that decision now because while DNA in a cold case is possible, you don't need to go in expecting it; way too many variables in a case this old. Chain of custody alone could make any DNA evidence you *do* have inadmissible." Barclay felt the intense scrutiny of AJ Murphy's blue eyes. Barclay knew he wanted this for Maggie, but he was beginning to add AJ's approval to the list of reasons to solve this case. "You tell me today that you're committed to seeing this case through, and I will commit to assisting you in any way you need." He paused, then said, "I'm serious. Whatever you need."

As for DNA, Barclay knew they had a profile but no idea if it even belonged to their killer. Even if it did, he thought, it was worthless without a name, and that didn't even factor in the chain of custody issue, which he hadn't considered until Murphy mentioned it. So, no, Barclay didn't need time to think about it. He'd already made up his mind about the case before walking into the conference room that morning, but now, now he was ready to get after it.

———

A POST-COFFEE BATHROOM break was called, and Barclay, Fitz, and Murphy were back in the conference room, settling in around the table. Rosie left to go fishing, for which he was suitably shamed.

They each got a fresh cup of coffee, and Barclay said, "I've got to say, AJ, when Maggie told me about this genealogy stuff, I was intrigued. How did you come to use it in a case?"

"I saw a television show about a cold case murder that was solved using genealogy DNA, and a case I was working on immediately came to mind. I reached out to the lab from the show, a place called Genome 23, and spoke to a lady named Katrina Anderton. Probably the smartest person I have ever talked to, let me tell you.

"It took her about three months, but she came back to us with a last name. It wasn't a very common name, and it just so happened the current police chief knew of a guy with that last name who was about the right age. So we got his DNA, which matched semen on the victim's shirt, and just like that, an eighteen-year-old rape-murder of a high school student was solved." He shrugged as if it were all in a day's work, then sipped his coffee.

"How did she do it? This Katrina Anderton." Barclay said.

He shook his head as he took another sip of coffee. "She explained it, but I'm not even going to try. I will tell you that the first thing you have to do is forget what you know about DNA as we use it, you hear me? The DNA profile we get from DFS uses only about twenty genetic markers whereas genotyping—which is what the private labs do—uses hundreds of thousands of markers."

"Damn," said Fitz.

AJ nodded at him and continued: "The reason is that the Department of Forensic Sciences is only interested in who matches the profile exactly, whereas the purpose of genealogy DNA is to cast the widest net possible to get as many people as possible who share some of the DNA of our suspect."

Barclay nodded.

"In your case, DFS used up all the genetic material to create the DNA profile from the cigarette butt I submitted, so we had to find more source material. A cardboard machete sheath was recovered from the scene, and there appeared to be a smear of blood on it. A nylon duffel bag was also found with what looked like blood on one of the straps. The sheath was found in the house, whereas the bag was found out in the yard, so we opted to use the sheath for testing based on its proximity to the crime scene. We're still waiting for the lab to get back to us on that.

"Anyway, the lab, they do their own extraction, and I'm going to skip a lot of the science stuff that I don't fully understand, but they get the job done."

"Huh," said Barclay.

AJ tapped a finger to the side of his head and said, "Smart." He followed that with a look to Barclay like that was the only explanation needed.

Seeing Barclay about to speak, he said, "I don't know how she does it other than by any means necessary." He tapped the side of his head with his finger again, and Barclay replied with, "Smart."

"Yep. Hopefully, when it's all said and done, she has it down to a specific person. But, of course, that doesn't always happen. Like I said, in my first case, the closest she could get was a family's last name. She told me about a case where she got it down to the parents, and the cops just had to figure out which of their children was the killer."

"This is crazy stuff."

"It's definitely a game changer for cold case investigation." The retired investigator appeared to weigh something in his mind when he said, "Just conduct your investigation as you would if this weren't available to you. As I said before, don't expect genealogical DNA to drop a name in your lap. It could certainly happen, but don't sit back and expect it—definitely don't wait on it. You'll need to lay the groundwork so any results you do get from the lab will actually mean something to you. Otherwise, you could get a lead without any idea how or even *if* it fits, you hear me? Shoe leather is going to solve this case, so I suggest getting out and getting to work."

SIX

November 28

Fitz was standing outside his house when the blacked-out Tahoe arrived, not bothering to pull into the driveway. He walked around the front of the SUV, opened the door to a Modest Mouse song, climbed into the front passenger seat, and passed Barclay a coffee.

Barclay took a sip and said, "One day, you're going to have to tell me your secret." He put the coffee in the cupholder and pulled away from the curve.

Fitz smiled with the cup at his lips and said, "It's all about the beans." He took a sip. "And the vanilla-kissed cream I put in it."

Having read the Chatham case file, they agreed they wanted to go to the house where everything occurred and see it firsthand, maybe conduct a walkthrough if the current owners would allow it. Pictures were one thing, but they wanted to get a spacial feel for the scene both inside the house and out.

As they made their way to 619 Woods Way, Barclay said,

"Rosie spoke to Chief Greenhaw and told him we are looking into the case."

"Who did the PD assign to be our contact?"

"Lawson."

This drew a reaction from Fitz.

Barclay said, "I specifically asked for her."

"You know I trust you, Boss, but are you sure about that choice?"

"Very sure," was all Barclay said, and he sipped his coffee.

Fitz shrugged, unconvinced, but he didn't belabor the point. He said, "Did you mention we were going to the house today?"

"I did, and I even invited her to join us." He caught Fitz's look in his periphery and said, "I figured she would decline. I didn't expect she would burn a Saturday—particularly the Saturday after Thanksgiving—simply to take a cursory look at a sixty-year-old crime scene. She's been at this too long to get too excited." Barclay glanced at Fitz and said, "At least they won't be able to say we haven't included them in this."

Fitz nodded, seemingly placated for the time being.

After several minutes of riding with early 2000s alternative music serving as the soundtrack for the drive, Fitz turned the radio down. He said, "All I'm saying, Boss, is that Lawson... she's...well..."

"A bitch?"

"Your word, not mine," said Fitz, holding his hands up, his left holding his coffee.

"She's a strong female." Barclay shrugged, eyes staying on the road. "She doesn't take any shit from anyone and doesn't apologize for it. A lot of guys don't like that—especially old guard police."

"Come on, Boss, you know I don't play it like that."

"I know you don't, Fitz. And I agree she can be a little rough around the edges, but I expect she's had to fight tooth and nail for every inch she's gained on the force, and I imagine below the sand-paper exterior is some insecurity."

"So you think she's weak," said Fitz in a tone that said Barclay had just made his point for him.

Barclay laughed. "Detective Beck Lawson is not weak. She has busted her tail to get where she is, and it would probably take a heck of a lot less work to lose all that she's gained, so yeah, I believe there is a little bit of insecurity there. I bet you and I would have the same thing in her shoes." More silence, then, "Look, I agree she can be a bit..." Barclay searched for the word "...disagreeable, but that is precisely why I asked for her. She's a damn good detective—maybe their best when it gets right down to it—and she won't be intimidated by the case. I don't need a half-committed yes-man along for the ride simply to check a box with the PD."

"I agree with all of that, but do you really think she is just going to jump in with two feet on this case? It's sixty years old, Boss. She's got her own caseload to deal with. Recent cases. She may even resent you for bringing her in on this. She won't simply grin and nod because you're the district attorney."

"And that right there, Fitz. That's why she's perfect for this case."

"Because she's going to hate you for this?"

"She won't hate me for bringing her in on this; her pride won't let her. She'll know she was handpicked, and she's going to accept the challenge. She may not accept at first, but I know her well enough to know that everything about this case, the sense of injustice on what was done to that family with no one ever being held responsible, the opportunity...no, she won't hate me for bringing her in on the case. She'll get dug in. She'll like it...a lot. And *that's* what she'll hate me for if we don't solve it."

———

THE HOUSE WAS LOCATED in Towne's west end, which, over the preceding half-decade, had suffered the penalty of growth. As Towne grew, the population matriculated east, sending much of the west side to seed. In recent years, however, gentrification was taking hold, investments were being made, and the depreciated neighborhood that sprang up in the post-World War Two era was seeing renewal grab hold.

Almost twenty minutes after picking up Fitz, Barclay steered the Tahoe into the neighborhood of Forest Hollow. Woods Way was the main road of the subdivision and traversed more than a mile from the entrance to the rear of the neighborhood where the Chatham house was located.

"The odd numbers are on my side," said Fitz. Barclay got to the mid-five hundreds and slowed. He crept to the six hundreds, and they scanned the curb, the mailboxes, and the houses, looking for the street numbers. Fitz was announcing the numbers he was seeing: "Six-eleven, six-thirteen, six-seventeen, six-twenty-one."

Barclay stopped in the roadway as he approached a dead end that was the terminus of Woods Way. He leaned up on the steering wheel and looked right, then left, then behind him. He then rolled the front driver and passenger windows down and continued to look around. He put the Tahoe in park, and he and Fitz got out of the SUV.

Barclay walked around the front of the vehicle to the passenger side, stopping at the corner of the hood. He looked to where the house should be and then produced an aged photograph about four inches square taken by police the morning after the murder. The picture was printed on thick stock and was only slightly faded by age. It reminded Barclay of pictures he'd seen in photo albums at his grandparents' home. The photograph was a wide shot of the home and showed the police tape around the perimeter, as well as a police car in the foreground and a police officer standing in the front yard.

He edged toward Fitz and held the picture out in front of them. Fitz pointed to the left side of the photograph and said, "Well, there's that house." His eyes flitted to the house to the left of the property, and the portion of the house visible in the photograph matched the house that currently stood in that spot. The roofline and the curve of the driveway were the same as depicted in the photo.

"That's definitely the same house," said Barclay. "Now, where is the Chatham house?"

"Ain't here, Boss."

In the space where the house should have been, the house to the right now encroached on a large portion of the property.

Barclay reached in through the front passenger window and dropped the photo on the seat. He said, "Let's knock on some doors and see what we can find out."

They chose the home to the right because it looked more modern than the rest, giving a feeling of a recent renovation and likely habitation. Fitz rang the doorbell and knocked on the door. They could hear music playing inside, and he was about to knock again when the door opened.

"Can I help y—Barclay?"

Barclay said, "Mr. Jackson?"

"Well, now that we've established who we are, what can I do for you?"

"Mr. Jackson, this is my chief investigator, Winston Fitzsimmons. Do you mind if we step inside for a minute?"

"Not at all. Come on in."

As they stepped inside, they were met with the scent of fresh paint and sanded wood floors. Barclay said to Fitz, "This is Walter Jackson, president of Towne Bank and Trust, and his son is Luke Jackson—local lawyer." Then: "Moving in?"

Walter Jackson followed Barclay's gaze around the empty space and said, "Oh, no. Luke and I recently finished a pretty extensive renovation, and he is trying to decide if he wants to move in or put it on the market."

"How long ago did you buy this place?" Barclay said as he stepped further into the living area, looking around.

"Oh, we didn't buy it. No, this is the home I grew up in." At that moment, things clicked into place for both DA and investigator—the *Dr. Jackson* from the case file. Barclay and Fitz exchanged a look which prompted Mr. Jackson to say, "What's this about?"

"We're taking a look into local unsolved homicide cases, and—"

"Ah," Mr. Jackson interrupted, nodding. "You're here about the Chatham murders."

"We are. But, Mr. Jackson, I would ask you not to mention this to anyone...for a lot of reasons."

"Of course. In my business, discretion is paramount, so rest assured no one will hear a thing from me." Mr. Jackson gestured at the cavernous but empty space. "I would offer you a place to sit, but as you can see..."

"We understand, and we won't be long. If I remember correctly, it was your father who called the police that night?"

Walter Jackson stilled himself as he remembered that night. "Yes, that's correct." All joviality gone, his countenance darkening. "I was supposed to be in the house that night." This was news to Barclay and Fitz. "That's right, I was supposed to spend the night with Brian and Steven, but I had gotten into a little trouble at school earlier in the week. Set off a stink bomb at the teacher's desk." He smiled wanly and continued, "The whole class had to leave the room. Anyway, as punishment, my father wouldn't let me sleep over at the Chatham's. It'd been planned for a week, and I was devastated."

The realization that Walter Jackson likely averted certain death cast a pall over the room.

"Wow, that's...I had no idea." Not sure what else to say to that, Barclay pressed on. "I didn't see a statement in the file. Did the police talk to you that night? About what happened?"

"No. They talked to my father, but that was it."

Fitz cleared his throat and said, "Do you remember anything from that night? Or maybe the days leading up to that night? Anything that may shed some light on what happened?"

Walter put a hand to his chin and looked to the ceiling. He slowly shook his head as if discounting thoughts or memories that popped up. "I remember waking up to my father yelling at my mother—something about a shooting. I ran downstairs and out the door behind him. I remember he held a hunting rifle while wearing his pajamas. That stood out, I guess. That and all the police. They were running around, some shouting." He paused before adding, "I also remember seeing them bringing the bodies out on the stretchers."

This wasn't helping. Fitz repeated his earlier question: "Anything leading up to that night?"

Walter was slowly shaking his head when he stopped. He said, "Seems like I remember Kathryn Chatham talking about someone calling their house and hanging up."

"She told you about this?" asked Fitz.

"She didn't tell me, no. I have a sister her age. Sylvia. Sylvia Burrows. Burrows is her married name. She and Kathryn were best friends at the time and told each other everything. They also didn't think about little nine-year-old ears hanging around."

Barclay said, "That name sounds familiar."

"She's a semi-retired Realtor. You've probably seen her signs. She's who I would suggest speaking with. Like I said, best friends back then. Of course, the murders changed things between them. My mother and father did not want my sister hanging around Kathryn after that. As if murder could rub off on another person."

Fitz: "She still live in Towne?"

"She does."

"Anything else you can think of?" asked Barclay. "Anything at all?"

Walter shrugged. "I was nine."

He gave Barclay and Fitz his sister's contact information, and as they were walking down the steps of the front porch, Barclay turned and asked, "What happened to the house?"

Walter leaned on the doorframe and said, "It sat empty for a number of years. No one wanted to live there, so my dad eventually bought the place. I don't know that Kathryn ever knew he bought it. It sat empty for so long, serving only as a haven for morbid curiosity seekers and a childhood rite of passage destination. It was deteriorating to the point that it was becoming dangerous. I eventually had it demolished and hauled away, and the lot sat vacant for many years. When the area began to come back, Luke had the idea to remodel this house, and we expanded onto the property."

"You mind if we take a look around?"

"Not at all."

"How far back does the property go?" asked Fitz.

Walter moved down the steps and off the porch. He walked to the corner of the house and looked back into the woods. He pointed and said, "There is a barbed wire fence at the rear of the property. Be careful walking back there because the fence is in pretty bad shape and may be down in some places. I don't want you inadvertently walking into it."

"Who owns the property behind the fence?" asked Barclay.

"That I don't know."

They continued their conversation for another minute or so before Fitz and Barclay embarked into the densely wooded terrain, where the first hints of autumn were just beginning to reveal themselves. The wilderness remained untouched, making their initial progress slow as they high-stepped their way through the dense underbrush—Barclay soon regretted wearing loafers.

They came to the barbed wire fence, or at least what remained of it. They split apart here to cover more ground, and each found a low spot in the dilapidated fence to step over.

Beyond the fence, the trees thinned out. As the area opened up, a surreal sight came into view—nothing short of an automobile graveyard. As far as the eye could see, there were old vehicles in various states of decay. Due to proximity, they had to speak up to be heard across the expanse of ground that separated them.

"I've got an old Mustang Mach One laying under a fallen tree over here, Boss."

"I've got an old truck over here with a tree growing up through a rusted hole in the bed. The trunk must be six or eight inches around," said Barclay. After walking further into the woods, he said, "This collection is incredible."

They wandered farther apart the further they walked in, eventually losing sight of one another between the trees and the abandoned vehicles. Finally, after about twenty minutes, they had retraced their steps and emerged from the tree line onto the well-manicured lawn of the Jackson house—Fitz first, then, maybe two minutes later, Barclay walked out.

"Anything?" asked Barclay.

"There's an old well back in there—"

"A well?"

"Yeah. Past the property line, maybe thirty yards or so."

Barclay didn't say anything for a minute, scanning the property. Then he said, "Can you pull up this property on your phone?"

"Sure." Fitz opened the maps app on his iPhone, found the property, and switched to satellite view. He held it out to Barclay, who grabbed the phone and held it where they could both see the screen. He used his fingers to zoom out and move around the property.

"There," said Barclay. "There's a road, what, a quarter mile or so from where the tree line begins?"

He looked up at Fitz, who nodded and said, "Looks like an old logging road. You could park a car there, come in through the woods, do what you needed to, and get out without anyone ever seeing you."

"Where's the well on here?"

Fitz took the phone and moved around the property with his finger. He zoomed in and said, "Somewhere in here." The satellite image was taken when the leaves were still on the trees, so the leafy canopy hid anything on the ground.

Barclay reached over and pinched the screen for a wider view. He said, "The most direct route from the rear of the house to the road would take you right past the well or very close to it."

"What are you thinking?"

"I don't really know. I'm curious if anyone saw the well that night."

"Even if they did," said Fitz, "They didn't have any reason to look in it."

"True, but I'd like to see if we can get a look inside it now."

"Seems like not enough sugar for a dime, Boss. Getting down into a well like that. I mean, even if there is something, it's been down there since 1963, just sitting in water. No way it can be of any value." Barclay didn't respond; he was staring into the woods. Fitz continued, "We don't even know if that logging road existed back in sixty-three or that the killer was ever in the woods at all."

"Remember the first officer on the scene saying he heard at least one gunshot?" Fitz nodded. "And Dr. Jackson heard two, maybe three shots." Another nod. "And by the time the police made entry and cleared the home, no shooter." Understanding played across Fitz's face. "We have to look at what makes the most sense. All other exterior doors were locked, so it stands to reason he came and went through the back door."

"And escaped into the woods."

"Exactly."

"And potentially right past the well."

Barclay said, "I know it's a long shot, but we need to take some chances. If we're going to solve this case, we are going to have to get lucky, catch a break. And we catch breaks by doing work."

The two men began walking back to the Tahoe, and as they walked, Barclay said, "Remember the Roger Loman case? Ol' doper found in the drainpipe of that pond on the Hawthorne property?"

"Stabbed a couple dozen times, shot in the head?"

"That's right."

"Yeah. I remember. What about it?"

"Sheriff got a tip the body was down there, and rather than send a man in, they brought in that search and rescue team from Georgia to search the pipe with a fiber optic camera and found the body."

"Ok." Fitz's tone indicated he didn't grasp the relevance.

"Well, after that, Sheriff Gillespie went out and bought one of those cameras."

"Ah, so you want to send a camera down into the well," said Fitz.

"You got it."

They began making their way back to the truck, and Fitz said, "Can't hurt, I guess. Want me to get on that today?"

"Not yet. Add it to the to-do list. We need to get organized first."

They got to the truck, and Barclay executed a three-point turn. They rode in silence and were almost to the subdivision's entrance when Fitz said, "Where to now?"

"Time to go see a realtor about a murder."

SEVEN

November 30

The district attorney's office was buzzing on Monday morning; the din of activity that was week two of a trial term. Phones were ringing, witnesses walked in with subpoenas asking where they needed to be—unwilling or unable to bother reading the piece of paper they'd been served with—and prosecutors were on the move preparing to do legal battle.

Barclay had been the first one into the office by a couple of hours and was working through the Chatham case file and making notes in preparation for a meeting later in the day. Quiet jazz emanated from the Marshall Bluetooth speaker on the floor in the corner; a candle was burning on a bookshelf, filling the room with the spicy scent of bergamot.

A phone rang, and it took Barclay four rings to locate his cell under the phalanx of paper.

"Detective Lawson, you calling to cancel on me?"

"Cancel on the DA? Shit, no." Their professional relationship went back a few years, so any pretense of formality was absent. "I was actually calling about moving the meeting up to this morning. Fitz just delivered a subpoena, and I have to be in court this afternoon."

"Why were you given such late notice?" Barclay was annoyed by this. It's not how he wanted his office to run.

"An out-of-town witness can't get here until tomorrow, so they're moving me up. No big deal."

"Ok. When were you thinking? I can be there whenever."

"Be here in half an hour?"

"I can do that," said Barclay. "Grab Fitz if he's still in the building. Tell him to stay there, and I'll head on that way."

The call ended, and Barclay grabbed his suit coat from the valet in the corner behind his desk, told Peggy, his assistant, where he was going, took the stairs to the first floor, and exited the building.

———

THE TOWNE POLICE station was housed in the Arnold Gillespie Municipal Complex—a sixties-era four-story brick building with a flat roof and wide marble steps leading from the sidewalk to the front entrance. The building occupied an entire city block and housed municipal government offices, the police department, and the municipal court. To many, the building was old, but it was decidedly new when considering the age of the structures around it. The interior walls were blue-gray, and the floor was gray linoleum. A new stand-alone police station and municipal court building had been rumored for over a decade but appeared to be nothing more than idle chatter by city politicians. The place always smelled of disinfectant tinged with body odor.

Barclay entered through the glass front door and was buzzed through to the back with a show of his badge to the officer manning the front desk and the pronouncement that he was there to see Detective Lawson. He made a mental note to request a key fob granting him access through the employee entrance.

Once through the electronic security door, Barclay turned left, walked to the end of the hallway, and entered a stairwell, which took him to the second floor and the detective division. TPD detectives were divided into four divisions: robbery/homicide, crimes against persons, property crimes, and the narcotics unit. All of the detectives were housed in a single large room with the recent exception of robbery/homicide—they had each been assigned their own office, which caused slight malcontent among the other detectives despite the offices being small, stuffy, and windowless.

Barclay heard Fitz's voice coming from the detective's office when he rounded the corner. He appeared in the doorway and saw the detective typing on the computer. Then, seeing Barclay, she leaned back in her primitive desk chair, which groaned in protest.

Lawson's office was cramped, so Barclay suggested meeting in an interview room. The detective nodded, rocked a squeak, stood, and led them down the hallway.

———

After getting an overview of the Chatham case, Lawson said, "I really do wish you would stick to regular cases. You know, we make arrests, you convict them."

"That's all I'm trying to do here," said Barclay.

Lawson gave a look and said, "This case is like sixty years old."

Barclay spread his hands and said in a slow, semi-condescending way, "Come on now, anyone can solve a *fresh* murder. It takes someone truly special to solve something this old, no?"

"Nothing can be easy with you, can it?" Barclay detected a slight...something. Something that said the detective was giving him a hard time the same way a big sister razzes her younger sibling. But he wasn't sure.

"Look, if you're referring to last year and the Clements case, we solved that one." Lawson made a noise.

Detective Beck Lawson was a Scandinavian-looking woman in her mid-forties—a milkmaid in business casual. Not quite tall enough to be considered tall for a woman, she had a soft, round face and a build that reflected her commitment to the gym when she wore the right clothes. Her white-blonde hair was always worn up in a ponytail that hung past her collar, and she wore minimal makeup because she felt wearing makeup on duty made her look weak. Her blue eyes and light skin tone gave her a look that stood out, and she had been told, "You're hot for a cop," more than twice. She wanted to extend her police-issue ASP whenever she heard it, though, and bring it down right behind the person's ear. She was divorced with no children and had never remarried. "He just couldn't get over the fact that my gun was bigger than his," she told her co-workers in her dry sense of humor when the divorce was announced.

A hard-nosed investigator, she was highly intuitive, and nothing escaped her eye during an investigation. Once she got on a case, she didn't stop until it was solved or she had exhausted every lead.

Barclay expected the veteran detective to be all over this cold case. Like all cold cases, it presented opportunity. An opportunity to accomplish what no other lawman had been able to up to that point, the significance of which would not be lost on her.

"We can get this done, Beck," he said.

"Yeah, yeah, yeah. What do you need from me?" Barclay had her.

Fitz spoke up. "First, just read the case file. There isn't much to it, so getting up to speed won't take long."

"What're your thoughts on the case file itself?" asked Lawson, understanding well the importance of a quality case file, the heart and soul of any criminal investigation.

Fitz shrugged and said, "I don't know enough about everything that happened to know if any information is missing, but what *is* in there is organized and detailed. Honestly, I was expecting worse."

The sound of the neighboring interview room door opening and closing and the scrape of chairs on the concrete floor could be heard; muffled voices began.

The intrusion interrupted Lawson's thoughts before getting back on track. She said, "Any suspects?"

Fitz said, "No suspects yet, which I believe is a good thing right now."

"How so?"

"We need to approach this with an open mind, and focusing too soon could hamper our ability to do that." He saw Lawson chewing on this in her mind. "I don't know if anyone was developed as a suspect back then or not; there wasn't anyone listed in the case file. I also haven't spoken with anyone who worked on the case originally. I wanted to have this meeting first before we stepped off into it."

Lawson nodded and said, "So, what's the plan?" She eyed Barclay and said, "I know you have a plan."

"Not this time," replied Barclay. "I have ideas, but this is new to me, and I don't want to get too far ahead of ourselves. We did speak with someone Saturday and—"

"I thought you were just going to check out the scene."

"We were, but the house was gone."

"Gone?"

"Gone. We made contact with the neighbor to see what we could find out, and it turns out he was a witness that night." Then, seeing Lawson's expression, he said, "Well, witness may be a bit of a stretch. He was just a kid, and it was his father who called the police when the shooting started."

Barclay recounted the rest of their conversation with Walter Jackson. After which, Lawson said, "I guess we need to speak with this Sylvia Burrows."

Fitz nodded and said, "We went by her place after leaving Mr. Jackson. No one was home, so I left a card. If I don't hear back by the end of the week, I'll go back out there."

Barclay jumped in and said, "Back to the topic of the case file, neither of the Jackson children was interviewed by police, so we don't need to look at the file as exhaustive." Barclay could see the veteran detective's mind working. "What are your thoughts at this point?"

Lawson tipped her chair back against the wall and gave a drawn-out, "Hmmmmm." Then: "I think we start by making a list of the witnesses we know about and how they fit into the case. Then we figure out which of them are still alive." She came forward in her chair and said, "What about the cops from back then?"

Fitz: "Haven't gotten that far yet. We've read the file, visited the scene, and had that interview fall in our lap. So that's where we are right now."

Barclay: "We'll want to view the evidence before we get too far in. Know what we're working with."

The detective nodded and said, "Who all knows we're looking into this case?"

"The two of us from my office, you and your chief, and I have a retired SBI agent consulting. He's an experienced cold case investigator who'll help us keep this thing on the rails."

"Best we keep this circle small," said Lawson.

"I agree," said Barclay. "If the person who did this is still out there, there's no reason to advertise we're coming for him."

"It's certainly going to be the biggest challenge of my career, but let's go get him," said Lawson.

"Hell yeah," said Fitz.

Barclay was about to speak when a woman's wails came through the shared wall of the interrogation room next door.

"What is *that*?" asked Fitz.

Lawson laughed, saying, "Ol' girl's been using her roommate's credit cards; outfitted her boyfriend's whole damn apartment with them. We've been trying to get her in for an interview for a week. She agreed to come in today with her lawyer, and I'm guessing the detective just showed her the still shots from the surveillance footage from all the stores where she and her boyfriend have been shopping."

EIGHT

December 1

Barclay and Lawson arrived at the Forest Hollow entrance almost simultaneously despite driving in from opposite directions. Barclay was coming from the courthouse, whereas Lawson had been looking for a witness when she received the phone call—the same call Barclay had received from Fitz: "You need to get out here. Now."

It was mid-afternoon underneath a gray sky, and the cacophony of construction greeted them as they exited their vehicles. "What the fuck?" was all Barclay could think to say as he stood next to the open door of his Tahoe.

Lawson was climbing out of her silver police-issued Dodge Charger with her phone to her ear when she said, "Let me call you back." She closed the car door, looked back at Barclay, and said, "This is not good." More than a dozen marked sheriff's department vehicles lined the narrow street.

Having visited the scene once before, Barclay led the way, anger driving him to the former Chatham home site when he drew up short. "You've got to be shitting me?" he said under his breath.

"Have fun with that," said Lawson.

"Towne County's new district attorney, Barclay Griffith, has just arrived on the scene," said the raven-haired television reporter as she deftly sprinted toward them all legs, hair, and stilettos holding her iPhone out in front of her in landscape mode. Barclay rolled his neck left and stared off into the distance, trying to gather himself.

The reporter said, "What can you tell the viewers on this Facebook Live broadcast about what's going on? We've been told a body has been found."

While Barclay was experiencing a slow burn, Lawson was a beat away from full-on rage. Barclay said, "Hey there, Wendy. You know I can't talk about any of this right now. I haven't even seen for myself what lies beyond the crime scene tape—"

"But you can confirm a body has been discovered."

"Sorry, but no, I can't. It would be irresponsible of me to confirm anything that I have not seen for myself, don't you think? Would you *really* want me to confirm something I don't have firsthand knowledge of? Isn't that journalism one-oh-one? I would hate for you to be getting all of your fine followers up in a tizzy only to be wrong, Wendy." It was her turn to grow flush with anger. "I'm guessing since you are asking me for confirmation that no one else has confirmed this story of a body either. That right?" Lips tight, eyes narrow. That one stung. *Good,* he thought. He knew pissing off the county's primary news source, especially after less than two weeks in office, was a bad move, but at this point, he didn't care.

"Please keep us informed of any developments," she said to his back, the sunshine in her voice belying the storm clouds in her face.

They heard her addressing her loyal followers as they walked across the yard where the Chatham's house once stood.

"That damn Wendy Wade," said Lawson.

"Eh," said Barclay, rolling his sleeves up and loosening his tie as they walked, "she's just doing her job. It's that dipshit coroner or Sheriff Gillespie who tipped her off. That's who you need to get pissed off at."

Fitz was waiting for them at the tree line where the yellow tape marked off the start of the crime scene; he was wearing his own irksome expression.

"Talk to me, Fitz. What in God's name is going on here?" said Barclay.

"Well, I did as we all agreed. I got the S.O. out here to the well with their fiber optic camera. It was me, an investigator for the sheriff's office, and a deputy. Investigator Ramos is the only one trained on this equipment, so she runs it and watches the monitor with Deputy Jarrett assisting."

"What are all these people doing here then? It's not even their jurisdiction," said Lawson.

"I'm getting there. Jarrett's feeding the cable, and I'm watching the monitor with Ramos, not making heads or tails of the video feed. The water down there is dark and murky, all sorts of crap floating in it, making it hard to see. Finally, after about twenty minutes or so of bouncing that camera around down there, Ramos sees something. Or at least thinks she does." A branch cracked, stopping Fitz, and they all looked up to see the county coroner tromping out of the woods—out of shape and out of breath—barely able to duck under the tape. She eyed the three of them as she passed, not speaking.

Lawson cursed under her breath and looked at Barclay, who told Fitz to go on.

"So Ramos is instructing Jarrett where to fish the camera— reel it in, let it out—when she yells at him to stop. She's pointing at the screen, and all I see is a greenish cloud with some dark areas, but when she tells me what she's looking at and traces it with her finger, it's clear. There's a body down there, Boss."

———

INSIDE THE TAPE NOW, Fitz guided them to the well, ducking and sweeping branches out of the way.

"What the heck is all of this?" Lawson asked.

"It's an old car graveyard," said Fitz. They stopped a moment and took in the surroundings. Old, rusted cars and trucks dotted the wooded landscape. "Must be forty or fifty out here. Some really cool vehicles."

"Interesting," said Lawson, not sounding like she meant it, and they began to walk.

As they walked, Barclay asked, "Why is half the sheriff's department here?"

"As soon as Ramos identified the body, she goes to calling her people. I asked her to hold off until you get here and we have a chance to talk it through, but she sputters on about protocol and other bullshit and calls her captain, and here we are. They must've run code out here because it seemed like they were swarming this place before Ramos hung up."

"It's not their jurisdiction," Lawson said again.

"I told her that, and she kept talking about how we were using their equipment."

"Chief Greenhaw is going to have a damn come apart."

As they approached the well, which appeared to be more or less in the center of all the old junkers, a dozen or so uniforms came into view, and Barclay stopped and asked, "Do we know whose property this is?"

"It's owned by a guy named Lockhart," said Fitz. "Name doesn't mean anything to me, but you grew up here." Barclay slowly shook his head as he tried to place the name but couldn't. "I tried to find a phone number, but nothing."

"How'd you write the search warrant?"

"I gave the landowner's name, the latitude and longitude of the well's location, and a descriptor using the street and approximate distance from the roadway. As for probable cause, I kept it vague; said we were looking for evidence in a homicide case."

"Seems a little thin," said Lawson. "A judge signed off on that?"

Fitz: "I went to Arnett; we have some capital with him. He did say that if it were anything more than sending a camera down, he might not have been so generous."

Barclay: "If Arnett signed the warrant on the idea that we only wanted to take some video, we might want to go ahead and get another warrant to enter the well and retrieve the remains. We have time now that the scene is locked down, and I don't want Arnett to think we weren't being upfront with him about our intentions."

Lawson said she would handle the second warrant.

Barclay said, "Alright, let's talk about this for a sec." He eyed Fitz and said, "What do they know?"

"I gave them the story we agreed on. That an outside agency received a tip about evidence from one of their homicide cases potentially being in the well. As a favor to the agency, we offered to check the well to save them a trip out here until we could establish the veracity of the tip."

"So, no idea this is related to the Chatham homicides?"

"No. Not unless they figured it out on their own, and, well..." Fitz didn't like to talk poorly about other law enforcement, so he didn't finish his sentence, but the other two understood what he was saying.

"Ok, let's go see what we've got."

———

WHEN THEY ARRIVED, they saw not a hive of activity but a combination of investigators and uniformed deputies standing around, taking turns looking down into a well that had no bottom.

"For fuck's sake," was Lawson's response to the scene.

Barclay shared her sentiment with a groan. Scanning the area, his gaze finally landed on Towne County Sheriff Arnold Gillespie, III. The sheriff was not hard to locate—he was a stump of a man who looked, Barclay thought, like an insincere television preacher. Adorned with every conceivable piece of tactical gear strapped to his belt, vest, and uniform, Gillespie seemed like a walking armory, rumored even to carry a hand grenade hidden away in one of his cargo pockets. He also touted a beast of a vape pen, and his head was currently lost in a swirling cloud of billowing white smoke.

When the smoke cleared, Barclay made eye contact with the sheriff and walked over to where he was holding court. "Hey, Sheriff."

"DA," said the sheriff in thinly veiled disdain. Barclay knew Sheriff Gillespie did not care for him. The sheriff was close to Richard Kingery, a former ADA believed to be Maggie Gamble's heir apparent. He and Kingery had gone through the police academy together prior to Kingery going to law school and had a grand plan to serve the county as sheriff and district attorney. The Kingery hated Barclay as a political enemy; ergo, Gillespie hated Barclay by proxy. Seeing Barclay get the appointment over his buddy only exacerbated the situation.

In turn, Barclay didn't have much for the high sheriff. He viewed him as lazy and incompetent, only getting elected because of his name. His late grandfather's restaurant, Gilly's Drive-In, was nearing its seventieth anniversary and remained a Towne food landmark. In addition to being a restauranteur, his grandfather served four terms as a state senator. The sheriff's father was Arnold "Gilly" Gillespie, Jr., a politician in his own right, having followed his father's footsteps into the public domain, serving as a state senator for twenty-four years before moving on to serve as a United States Senator for another twenty-four years and who had only recently retired from public service. The Gillespie name carried weight in Towne County.

The sheriff's interest in notoriety trumped his interest in the truth. *Get in, get out, get the headline* was how he viewed his job, and this, Barclay knew, was the reason he was horning in on a case over which he held no authority.

The sheriff's office had a reputation of top-notch police work pre-Gillespie, and the man had managed to erode all of that in three short years. The best investigators either quit or retired, and they were replaced by Gillespie disciples who viewed cases the way their boss did: arrest-oriented versus conviction-oriented. They wanted an arrest to crow about with little regard for whether or not the case they put together could be used to obtain a conviction. Getting them to do any follow-up on a case post-arrest was like pulling teeth. *We made the arrest. We aren't sure how the prosecutor could have screwed it up,* was the prevailing sentiment of investigators under Gillespie's leadership. That was not a sustainable situation, and it would come to a head at some point in Barclay's tenure. He was sure of it.

"We appreciate you letting us use your equipment, Sheriff. We can take it from here."

"Well now, Barclay, no need to be like that. After all, my investigator is the one who discovered the body. She's already in this case—"

"As a witness, Arnold, that's it. She's not investigating this. It's the PD's case, and they will take it from here."

A sardonic, *let me tell you something, boy* look creased his jowly face; Barclay resisted the urge to slap it off of him. "Barclay, son,

I'm here, and I ain't going nowhere, a'ight, so why don't you tell me what this is really about."

"Didn't my investigator already tell you?"

"He told *my* investigator some bullshit story about a tip and a homicide in another county."

"Good, then you've been read in." Barclay turned and walked to where the camera monitor was set up, signaling Lawson and Fitz to join him.

———

AROUND THE SCREEN NOW, Barclay nodded at Ramos and said, "Show us what you found."

Investigator Ramos was a shade over five foot five, not skinny, but not fat either. She was olive-skinned with brown eyes and wore her brown hair in natural loose curls that brushed the tops of her shoulders. She wore a short-sleeved maroon dress shirt and gray slacks with her service weapon in a black leather holster on her left hip. She worked the DVR controls, rewinding to a point in the video and pausing it. She produced a pen from somewhere and, using the tip, outlined the image as she spoke.

"How far down is the body?" Lawson asked.

Ramos consulted the screen and said, "Sixty to seventy feet, give or take." She spoke with a light rasp to her voice.

The four of them edged up to the well and peered down into the chasm. Staring into the black, Fitz said, "How far down does the waterline begin?"

"I'd have to go drop the camera again, but I'd guess maybe forty, fifty feet or so."

They returned to the monitor, silent in thought, when Ramos spoke up. "Hey, Fitz, I'm sorry for how all this went down, but I don't call the sheriff, and it's my ass. I'm trying to hang on 'til retirement, and as disgusted as I am with much of what goes on in that office these days, I need this job."

Fitz said, "It's all good, Sally. We're glad we didn't lose you when everyone else got out." After the mass exodus of investigators after Gillespie took over, Sally Ramos was the most senior and likely the only one of the current lot who could get a job anywhere else. The sheriff hated her, and she knew it. She bore his contempt because she was a woman who was very good at her job. Her complexion, combined with her last name, did not do her any favors with him either. She knew he referred to her as Señorita Ramos behind her back—and sometimes to her face—despite the fact she was from the Florida panhandle.

"What's the next step?" Barclay said, speaking only for the benefit of the small circle.

"I think we treat this as a rescue operation," said Lawson.

"Fire department?" said Investigator Ramos.

The detective nodded. "I'll call and get them out here for retrieval." To Ramos: "Can you hang around? You're the expert with this thing."

She nodded. "As long as you need me." Then, "What's this about...really."

All eyes went to Barclay, who said, "Not here. Let's get clear of all this, and then we'll talk." Nods all around. "Heads up."

"Someone needs to go make a statement," Sheriff Gillespie said louder than necessary as he approached.

"A statement?" asked Barclay.

"Yeah. To Little Miss Prom Queen," said Gillespie with a vague hand gesture toward the road.

Lawson said, "I've spoken to Chief Greenhaw, and he is preparing something for her."

Gillespie stared at Lawson for a beat, then grunted and waddled off, yelling to his folks to clear out. "They don't need us, boys. Let's leave it to the *professionals*." His voice dripped with derision.

"Asshole," said Fitz.

Barclay said, "When did you call your chief?"

"Didn't."

———

THE WOODS BEGAN TO CLEAR, and Barclay said, "I didn't see anyone keeping a scene log."

Ramos said, "I know who was out here. I'll make a list."

"I'll call my folks, let them know what's going on, and get the fire department out here," said Lawson, reaching for her cell.

"The sheriff's right," said Barclay. "Someone needs to give Wendy Wade something, or this thing will spin out of control. I'll go talk to her." Thunder rumbled in the distance. "Perfect," he said, looking skyward.

Barclay had made it about twenty feet when he heard Fitz say, "Ah, shit."

"What now?" Dread in his voice as he turned around.

Fitz stared at his phone and said, "Wendy Wade is getting her statement."

"That fuckin' Gillespie."

"Not him, Boss."

Barclay narrowed his eyes, confused.

"The dipshit coroner."

———

IT HAD TAKEN a couple of hours, but they were now prepared to enter the well and recover the skeletal remains, the Towne Fire Department leading the retrieval effort. A steel tripod straddled the open mouth of the well with a pulley dangling from its apex.

A thick, twisted steel cable ran through the pulley with an anodized aluminum auto-locking D carabiner on the end dangling over the opening. The cable was being threaded from a wench affixed to the front bumper of a fire department pick-up truck.

Three light stands had been erected around the site, and the generators powering them, loud at the initial crank, soon faded into the background as white noise.

Water containing a corpse was bound to contain dangerous contaminants, so, for the last twenty minutes, a firefighter was being outfitted in a DUI CXO Select Hazmat Drysuit in preparation for making entry into the well. The three men helping rescue diver Tracy Cone were going over last-minute safety checks. Their primary concern was ensuring all seams were watertight and oxygen flowed into the helmet. Tracy was the first and, to date, only female certified rescue diver in the county, and her slight stature made her the ideal choice for this confined space.

The site was crawling with TPD detectives and command staff, with uniformed officers manning the crime scene tape, keeping out folks who didn't belong, and logging those who did. Several firefighters, all dressed in navy blue work pants and t-shirts, also stood about, ready to assist as needed. Chief Greenhaw suggested calling out a retired anthropology professor he knew was living nearby to be on site for the retrieval. Everyone agreed it was a good idea.

Barclay heard the distinct click of a shutter prompting him to pivot and discover Towne County Coroner Joan Vance taking photos with a Nikon DSLR camera. He approached the rumpled Vance—stringy brown hair plastered across her sweaty forehead in the autumn cool—looking uncomfortable in a green, black, and yellow flannel shirt and black leggings, both a size or two too small. The garments strained and stretched over the ample contours of her body, creating a series of unflattering and exaggerated bulges; every seam and button seemed ready to surrender, producing an unkind silhouette.

Barclay said, "I'm going to need you to stop with the pictures. This isn't a social function."

The coroner ignored him, peered through the eyepiece, and snapped another photo. Barclay grabbed the lens and pushed the camera down. "Joan, that's enough."

"You obviously don't understand my role here. I conduct an investigation alongside the police, and these pictures help me document the scene."

"Please, Joan, you're the coroner. Your job is to pronounce death, bag the body, and get it to forensics for an autopsy. That's it." Joan Vance was universally disliked by law enforcement. It was well known that she was often Wendy Wade's inside source, and she was notorious for speaking to the media about things she knew nothing about, compromising more than one investigation as a result.

The conversation was gaining interest from the group.

Joan fumbled for a response before saying, "But I'm law enforcement."

"No. You're not."

"But Barclay, I've always done this. Taken photographs."

"Yeah, and it's weird. Why do you need a couple hundred photos of a dead body?" The coroner raised the camera to eye level, and Barclay said, "You take one more photograph, and I will have you removed from this scene. You don't leave the scene, and I will have you arrested for obstruction."

The standoff was on. Vance had the camera up but not lining up a shot. After a few seconds, she lowered the camera and let it dangle around her neck. Barclay said, "Thank you." He leaned in and whispered, "You ever make another statement to the media about a case, and the only death scene you'll be called out to will involve roadkill."

Vance walked off toward the crime scene tape, and Barclay focused his attention on the rescue effort, noticing for the first time everyone was staring at him. He said, "We about ready to go in?"

People started moving again, including Tracy Cone, who was making her way to the well with the aid of a person on each side, her drysuit difficult to maneuver in. At the well's stone edge, one of the firefighters attached the carabiner to a stainless steel ring affixed to the rear of the harness she was wearing and went through safety checks one last time.

With the help of four firefighters, one for each arm and leg, she allowed herself to be lifted and suspended mid-air over the opening. Her assistants tilted her so she entered the cavity face down. As the wench began to let out cable lowering her into the abyss, the rain began to fall, lightly at first, announced by the slapping of raindrops onto foliage, then grew more steady; the operation staying reasonably protected by the remaining canopy not yet decimated by the fall season.

Her helmet was mounted with three cameras relaying live video footage topside—one facing forward and one each facing left and right—and a flashlight that guided her way. The head of the TFD rescue dive team, Captain Dow Graves, remained in constant contact with Tracy via the mic in her helmet.

Barclay and Lawson stood over the opening, watching the bright circle of light get smaller and dimmer as Tracy Cone descended deeper into the chasm; Fitz and Ramos were at the bank of monitors—one for each camera—watching the diver's video feed.

"She's nearing the waterline," announced Graves. Then, the diver disappeared into the blackness, her weight belt dragging her through the water. Barclay and Lawson walked over to the video feed.

"How are you doing, Tracy?" asked Graves.

"Fine," came a strained reply.

"She should be better now that she's in the water," Graves said to the folks at the monitor. "That initial dry drop sent blood to her head, but that should dissipate."

The thirty-six-inch flatscreens showed a remarkably clear picture of the green, murky water. Then, just over two minutes after the descent began, a skeleton came into view.

"Stop the cable," Ramos yelled to be heard over the din of the generators.

Graves spoke into the mic: "Tracy, they've stopped your descent. It's all you from here. You tell me what you need me to do."

"Ten-four." The video showed her twisting and turning, surveying the scene. She was refraining from touching the bones, unsure of their frailty. "Ease me down slowly. I want to get a full view of what's down here."

Receiving the signal from Captain Graves, the wench began letting out steel cable. Eyes were glued to the screen, watching, captivated. The skull, lulling to one side, disappeared at the top of the screen as Cone continued her descent. More skeletal remains could be seen as she flowed downward until she reached the bottom of the well.

Graves noticed the slack in the cable and said, "Tracy, there's slack in the line. You good?"

"I've reached the bottom."

"Roger that. What do you need us to do?"

"Pull me back up. I've found something."

———

THEY ALL WATCHED as the wench reeled her in, water dripping off the cable as it broke the surface, until her feet broke the plane of the low-slung stone edge. When she cleared the opening, they saw she held something in her hand. Tracy's four handlers rushed to her, this time wearing thick rubber gloves, and righted her as they guided her from over the gaping mouth of the well to solid ground. She was gently lowered to the ground, where she was set down on all fours and told to take a moment to gather herself. She handed the object she brought back to one of her aides, who rushed it over to the makeshift command post. One person unhooked the cable from her harness. When she signaled she was ready, two men stood her up, careful not to get any potentially contaminated water on themselves.

She was unsteady on her feet, having been upside down for nearly fifteen minutes; they guided her to a nearby tree for support.

Back at the monitor station, the object was laid on the white plastic folding table on which the monitors sat. It was the stock of a rifle or shotgun. Barclay, Fitz, Lawson, Ramos, Graves, and Greenhaw were at the table when the object was laid down. Fitz and Barclay exchanged a surreptitious glance that Lawson saw.

"A gun stock," Investigator Ramos deadpanned. Then, seeing the exchange of looks, she said, "Wait, is that the evidence you were looking for from the tip? You think this is evidence in a homicide case? Are they looking for a long gun?"

Barclay was deep in thought. How much should he tell, and who should he tell it to? He came to a decision to buy more time. Ignoring Ramos' inquiries, he looked up and said, "Let's get the bones up from down there." He looked to Graves and said, "Is your diver good to go back down?"

Graves keyed his radio and said, "Hey, Cone, you good for another go?"

Tracy Cone remained in full gear because removing any portion required full decontamination, and she knew she'd likely have to go back and retrieve the remains. Her tinny voice came back through the radio, "Yes, sir. We need to discuss how you want me to bring everything back up."

"The PD got an anthropologist on the phone while you were down, and they said the bones should be fine to handle. How much of the skeleton were you able to locate?"

"I'm no doctor, but it looked like a lot of it, sir."

Graves nodded and said, "About the gun stock. Any reason you thought to bring that up with you?"

"There's a gun down there. Either a rifle or shotgun, but that stock goes with it. I was briefed that I was looking for potential evidence in a homicide, so I grabbed it. I will get the rest on the next dive." Again, at the mention of the gun, Barclay and Fitz exchanged eye contact, which, again, did not go unnoticed by Lawson or Ramos.

Barclay felt bad about the false pretext of the search; he never expected it to get this far. However, if that gun turned out to be what he suspected, it would assuage his angst.

After a lengthy discussion regarding the best way to bring the bones up, Tracy Cone was hooked back up to the steel cable and sent down almost eighty feet into the earth.

———

TRACY WAS DOWN eighteen minutes on the second dive as she gathered all the bones she could find. The bones were brought up using a bright yellow water recovery body bag. The bag was made of vinyl-coated polyester scrim mesh and had several clamshell drains, allowing the water to run out while maintaining the integrity of the evidence when it was pulled from the water. The bag was carried to a well-lit area with plastic tables for examining its contents.

Once the bag was handed over, she went down for her third and final dive, which was quick, only six minutes—long enough to grab the gun and what appeared to be blue jeans, a tattered swatch of cloth roughly ten or so inches square, and a single sandal that was almost certainly white before going into the muck. Once back on dry land and upright, she took several minutes to regain her legs before the decontamination process began. First, the suit was scrubbed down with the industrial strength cleaner Blue Gold by her handlers using long-handled stiff-bristle brushes. Then, covered with white suds, the next step was being hosed down with water. Once that was done, it was safe to remove the dive suit, and she did so to a mini celebration from her peers. It was a job few people wanted, and fewer people could do, so every member of the team took great pride in a mission accomplished.

While Cone was being scrubbed down, Lawson, Fitz, Barclay, and Ramos found a spot away from the table where the bones were being laid out by the professor who had just arrived. It was the focus of everyone's attention, so their absence went unnoticed.

Lawson spoke before they had stopped moving. "Alright, what's the deal with the gun?"

Barclay held up his hands and said, "I think the first thing we need to do is tell Ramos what's going on." Hearing herself singled out caught her by surprise. "Now Sally, I'm trusting you with this information, and I do not want you going to your boss with it." Seeing the sheriff's investigator about to protest, he said, "Wait, that's not fair. I understand you have to do what you have to do, but any discretion you can give us would be appreciated. I think it's only fair that you know the truth, and I do *not* want the sheriff to know about it. When I explain it all, you'll know why."

Barclay spent the next few minutes giving Sally Ramos an overview of what they were doing—looking into a cold case—and why they were exploring the well.

"As far as the gun goes," Barclay began after he got Ramos up to speed, "according to the case file, the shooter used a twelve-gauge shotgun. We believe it was a twelve-gauge because of the spent shells at the scene. The police also located a single unspent shell that matched the spent shells. I know the gun found in the well is a rusted mess, but it's definitely a shotgun, and, at first glance, at least, the bore of the barrel appears to be that of a twelve-gauge."

"That could have been tossed in there at any time. Besides, it can't tell us anything in its current condition," said Lawson.

"I agree it likely doesn't have any significant evidentiary value, but if it is, in fact, a twelve-gauge, it has to be the gun. Why else would someone toss a shotgun into a well?" No one could argue with the logic.

"But what good is it then?" Lawson asked.

Fitz said, "Gives us an idea about his route from the house. We know a logging road runs through this property, and the most direct route from the road to the house and back takes you past the well. It's not much, but it's something."

"If nothing else, it's eye candy for the jury, something for them to see and even hold if we ever get this case to a trial," Barclay offered.

Ramos said, "But who is that down in the well? Any chance it's one of his victims?"

"Everyone in the house that night was accounted for," said Fitz, "so, no, it's not related to the murders. It could be someone who fell in for all we know. You saw how low the wall around it is."

"Let's keep an open mind about it, but we probably don't need to focus too much on it right now. We'll let the ME's office deal with it for the time being," said Barclay.

Fitz said, "A cause of death will be next to impossible to determine, let alone an identification."

"Let's have a chat with the anthropologist and see if he has any ideas."

———

Darkness had fallen especially hard in this wooded area; however, the trio of six thousand-watt mobile light towers provided ample illumination. The rain had also ceased but had left a damp chill behind.

Retired anthropology professor Dr. Raymond Bass was a stoop-shouldered man who wore a brown wool sportcoat with too-wide lapels and suede patches on the elbows over a tan sweater with a blue Oxford shirt collar peeking out above the crewneck. The thin white hair on the top of his head was blowing in the breeze like a wisp of smoke as he walked up and down the length of the table, leaning over the bones in concentration. He wore a headlamp for an added light source.

They were awaiting a medical examiner from the Montgomery lab to advise on adequately securing the bones for transport for an autopsy. That was not normal procedure, but Dr. Fred Stanton had an anthropology background and a keen interest in unearthed bones. He had asked the bones be left out until he could make his way to the scene, which wouldn't be until his work in the lab was completed for the day.

In the meantime, the bright eyes and nimble fingers of Dr. Bass were inspecting the bones. He had directed the assembly of the bones, and on the table was a skeletal structure that he estimated was fifty-five to sixty percent complete.

He had identified the skeleton as being that of a white female. He demonstrated as he spoke about how he could determine the person's race by the skull. He held the gray-white skull in his gloved left hand and placed his right index finger vertically from the lower jaw to the nasal cavity. "The fact that no part of my finger loses contact with the bone structure tells me this skull is that of a Caucasian. If it were, say, African-American, my finger would not lay flat on the skull from the front of the jaw to the nose."

As for the sex, he indicated the width of the pelvis and told how a female pelvis lays flatter than a male's pelvis. The design being owed to childbirth, he explained.

"Back to the skull," he said, holding it out with his left hand and, with a gloved right pinky finger, he pointed at a fracture. "We call this a cob-web fracture. As you can see, it is depressed in the middle with micro fractures radiating from the center." Looking at it, Barclay thought it looked as if someone had hit an egg with the back of a spoon.

Dr. Bass continued, "There is clearly blunt force trauma, but I'm afraid that still doesn't get us very far. That could very well be the result of being hit in the head, or it could be the result of an accident such as a person falling into the well and hitting their head on the interior stone wall as they careened toward the bottom."

He assessed those around him and told them that beyond that, he saw nothing remarkable in the collection of bones but conceded the medical examiner in the bright lights of the autopsy suite would be better suited to make that determination. He also recommended collecting and sifting the silt at the bottom of the well to locate any remaining bones which "were almost certainly down there" and "could be helpful to unlocking this mystery."

He continued: "There is an anthropology team with Florida Gulf Coast University that I recommend you reach out to and get them down here. They do a wonderful job recovering bones and other remains. They are thorough and meticulous and will find it if it's there to be found. Also, they will photograph and digitize all of the bones so that when it comes time for trial, you don't have to produce the actual skull. Instead, they will reproduce it exactly with a 3-D printer. It's quite fascinating, really."

Almost as an aside, he remarked the skeleton was in exceptional condition and, in response to a question, said that it could absolutely have been down there for over fifty years due to the cold temperatures of the deep, underground water.

As for the jeans, sandal, and fabric, they would be taken to the police department's drying room before being bagged and submitted for forensic examination.

———

AS THE SCENE was breaking up—bones, gun, and clothing items gone their respective ways—Barclay, Fitz, Lawson, and Ramos reflected on the day's discoveries.

A plan was formed to get a crew back out in the morning for a once-over of the immediate area in the daylight. In the meantime, TPD would send a patrol officer to sit overnight to maintain the integrity of the crime scene and discourage any curiosity seekers who watched Wendy Wade's broadcast.

The significance of the day's findings was not immediately known and may well wind up being of no significance at all, but the fact that their search yielded anything served as a shot in the arm moving forward. Who knew how far it would carry them, but it was something, and although investigating homicides was a zero-sum game, momentum, regardless of its source, was never discounted.

NINE

December 2

The Magnolia Pig was widely considered the city's best barbecue, serving customers ranging from blue-bloods to blue-collar. That's where ADAs Stacy Steen, Sam Willoughby, and DA Barclay Griffith were enjoying lunch and discussing a robbery trial set for jury selection at 1:30 that afternoon. Actually, Sam and Stacy were discussing the trial while Barclay tagged along for the three-block walk, the barbecue, and an impromptu interview...he hoped.

The day before, Fitz took Lawson's advice and completed a spreadsheet listing each person enumerated in the Chatham case file. He approached it as he would any other case by cataloging the name, identifying them as a law enforcement or a lay witness, and summarizing their expected testimony. One name stood out to Barclay because it was the only name he recognized.

The waitress delivered the check, which Barclay grabbed, telling the two prosecutors to head on back and get ready for court —he'd be back at the office shortly.

Barclay hung out at the food- and dish-strewn table for another fifteen minutes, watching and waiting. He finally gave up and made his way to the register by the entrance and handed the check to the young girl behind the counter when Larry Butler came out from the kitchen wearing his trademark blue short-sleeved Dickie coveralls, white v-neck undershirt, red and white International Harvester mesh-back cap, and Tampa Nugget stuck in the corner of his mouth. He was also known to carry a white(ish) terrycloth hand towel, and it was hanging over his shoulder. He was walking around his restaurant, cleaning off tables, and speaking with patrons.

Barclay handed over his Amex without looking at the girl, said, "Be right back," and made his way across the restaurant, meeting the barbecue man at an empty but trash-filled table. He said, "Hey, Larry."

Larry was eighty-one years old and painted with the patina of decades sweating over a smoke pit. He peered over his shoulder as he tossed paper goods, wax sandwich wrappers, and plastic utensils onto a plastic tray and said, "Well, hello there, Barclay. How are you?" He spoke in a phlegmy voice, the mere sound of which made Barclay want to clear his own throat.

"I'm good. Busy as you can imagine but adjusting."

Ignoring the table for a moment, he faced Barclay and said, "Congratulations, by the way. I haven't seen you since taking over for Maggie." He leaned in conspiratorially and said, "You know she used me to cater all of her events, right?"

"I know, Larry. I've been in that office for a while now."

"Of course," he said with a forced laugh. Then, "You here for lunch?"

"Just ate. We're in the middle of a trial term, so we slipped down here for a quick bite...food was great as always." Larry nodded as if he knew his food was good and didn't need anyone telling him so. He went back to cleaning the table when Barclay said, "Do you have a minute? To talk?"

He stopped cleaning, looked at his watch, and said, "It is lunchtime."

"It'll only take a minute."

Larry looked back toward the counter, saw a short line waiting to order, motioned to the booth he was currently clearing, and slid in with Barclay taking the opposite bench.

"I recently learned that you were a police officer at one time. I never knew that."

Larry's eyes went wide, and, cigar bouncing with each syllable, said, "That was a long damn time ago. What's this about?"

"When you worked for the PD, did you have anything to do with the Chatham homicide?"

Butler's eyes narrowed as he removed the chewed, wet stogie from his mouth. "What do you mean 'did I have anything to do with it?'"

"I mean as a police officer. Were you involved in any way?"

Larry leaned back and took in a deep breath. He swiped a hand across his stubble, generating a raspy noise as he seemed to be thinking. "Well, yeah, I stood guard outside Kathryn Chatham's room at the hospital. I remember the chief sending me over there thinking that whoever did that to those people may want to finish the job."

"So you were working that night?"

"No, but when the brass got to the scene and saw what they had, everyone got called in." He studied Barclay and asked, "What's this all about?"

It was Barclay's turn to lean back in thought. He stared at Larry before finally saying, "I was cleaning out some old files and came across this case. I had never heard of it before and did a quick read of the summary, and"—he shrugged—"it sounded interesting. I gave it a cursory read, and when I saw the list of everyone involved, yours was the only name I recognized. I saw you as I was about to leave a few minutes ago and figured I'd bring it up."

A man and woman in their seventies walked by the table and spoke to both Larry and Barclay, who returned smiles and thank yous in response.

Barclay couldn't read the look he was getting across the table and was about to speak when Larry said, "You looking into the case?"

Barclay began shaking his head and said, "Nah. Too old, too few of the major players are still around." Barclay felt self-conscious about saying they were mostly all dead. "It sounds like a horrible case."

"Yeah. Awful." Larry plugged the cigar back into his mouth and stared at Barclay with a hollow affect that unnerved the prosecutor.

Barclay slid out of his seat and said, "Well, I need to get back to the office. Appreciate your time, Larry."

Larry Butler remained seated and didn't say anything. He watched as Barclay slid out of the booth, paid his bill, and left the restaurant.

TEN

December 3

The Tincturist held all the pretense of the prohibition era, but the veneer was real, and the experience was as authentic as it was unique. Outside of the occasional cosmetic update required of a century-old bar, the walnut, brass, and gilt were entirely and painstakingly original, which made this drinkery the envy and the model of resurgent rathskellers cropping up in cities ten times the size of Towne.

The place smelled of a combination of orange and cinnamon and whiskey with a piney undertone. A hint of smoke from times past clung to the tin ceiling, but in a pleasing way reminiscent of a richer time when people had time to talk and enjoy a drink. A time of leisure when time itself didn't matter.

The interior was dim without being dark; the whispers of patrons, the clink of ice in glasses, and occasional muted laughter wafted across the room.

The national cocktail renaissance experienced no rebirth in a city with a place like The Tincurist to call home. After all, there must be death for there to be a rebirth. A Phoenix must die in fiery fashion before rising from its ashes. And Tincs, as it was known colloquially, had never so much as had an irregular heartbeat.

Senator Arnold Gillespie, Jr. sat at the crowded bar, dressed in a charcoal suit—off-the-rack but expensive—and a lavender tie with a green flower pattern. He was sipping on a Vesper Martini, the high-octane cocktail sitting clear in the chilled Nick and Nora glass with the lemon twist draped languidly along the rim. He had white hair in a conservative cut and a thin white mustache—drawing more than one comparison to Hal Holbrook, a comparison he did not care for. He was on drink number two and enjoying the jazz trio providing the evening's soundtrack, allowing his mind to drift to poignant moments of a life spent barside at this most elegant watering hole. Each of his twelve election victories was celebrated here as the favorable returns poured in; he'd mourned his father's death in this hallowed space and drank to his retirement here just over a year ago.

Interspersed with those landmark life moments were deals reached, alliances formed, and enemies vanquished. The senator had commandeered the space for an after-hours Star Chamber on numerous occasions, doling out what he had deemed *political justice*. He shook the wistfulness from his mind, downing the last third of his boozy companion in a single gulp, holding up his empty glass to the bartender.

"Right away, Senator," replied the old salt behind the bar.

"Senator Gillespie," came a voice cutting through the din of the jazz, memories, and libations.

Gillespie did a half turn to his left and said, "Barclay Griffith, there you are." He motioned to the tufted leather barstool beside him. "I've had a devil of a time keeping this seat empty."

"I apologize, Senator," said Barclay as he stepped up into the seat. Despite the long day at work, he was in his suit and maintained his buttoned-up appearance. *If you're wearing a suit in public, the jacket is a must, and your tie should* always *be properly tied with a dimple and never allowed to hang loose from an unbuttoned collar.* He'd worn a suit hundreds of times and still heard his father's advice every time he donned one. "I had a television interview that ran long. Spent twenty minutes filming B-roll if you can believe it."

"Please, call me Gilly. And I understand exactly what you mean." He raised his right hand as if swearing an oath, said, "Forty-eight years as a public servant," and lowered it. "I'm very familiar with the media." He spoke with a twinkle in his eye.

Barclay had to contain the urge to roll his eyes at the *public servant* comment; instead, he nodded and ordered a Sazerac when the bartender set down the senator's Vesper. He also thought how silly it was to call an eight-something-year-old former United States Senator by an adolescent nickname.

"Thank you for agreeing to meet with me. I know the last thing you want to do at the end of a grueling day is meet with a has-been politician, especially when your wonderful family is waiting on you at home."

"Of course, Senator." Gillespie stopped his glass at his lips and gave Barclay a look. "Ah yes, Gilly. Sorry about that." The senator winked before taking a drink. "I'll be honest; I was surprised to get your phone call. I trust everything is ok?"

"Yes, yes, everything's fine. I wanted first to congratulate you on the position." Then, as if on cue, the bartender set Barclay's cocktail on the bar and slid it to him with a "Cheers, sir."

Gillespie raised his glass and said, "Congratulations. I know your father is very proud of you."

"And my mother, brother, sister, wife—."

"Of course. I didn't mean anything by the exclusion. I just know your father well. He was a longtime supporter of my campaigns, you know."

Barclay didn't know—but wasn't surprised—nor did he care. He flashed his most disarming smile and said, "No offense taken," and they clinked glasses and took a drink.

Barclay's ear had wandered to the jazz trio, and he was trying to place the familiar refrain when Gillespie, eyeing his glass, said, "Do you know why we clink glasses when we toast?"

"I've heard it said that it was borne out of trust...or rather lack thereof."

"Trust?" said the Senator, giving Barclay a sideways look.

"It's said that the Romans began the practice of toasting to spill a little of each other's libation into one another's cup to prove one hadn't poisoned the other."

"Interesting." Barclay thought the senator appeared a little embarrassed that Barclay had an answer. "I'd heard it said that the clinking of glasses was to ward off evil spirits, simulating church bells as it were." He thought for a moment and said, "But I like your reasoning the best." And he smiled.

Ever the politician, Barclay thought.

"Eh, who knows," said Barclay. "I think they're all great stories, but they're also probably all wrong." They shared a strained laugh. Barclay took a drink, complimented the bartender as he passed, and said, "What's the other thing you wanted to discuss, Senator...Gilly."

"How's that?" As he passed, the bartender placed a small wooden bowl of cashews between the two men.

"You said you wanted to 'first congratulate me on the position.' Usually, when there's a 'first,' there's a second or third to follow."

"Yes, yes. You'll have to forgive me." He held up his glass, "I got a little head start; I'm afraid these Vespers don't always agree with my memory." His cap-toothed smile stood out against his November suntan.

"Too much of anything is bad, but too much good whiskey is

barely enough," said Barclay. Gillespie fixed him with a look. "Mark Twain."

"Ah, yes. Mark Twain." Barclay couldn't figure this man out? Had he embarrassed him again? Should he be showing more reverence? Barclay was not easily intimidated, and he was sure Senator Gillespie relied on a bit of a bullying factor when trying to get what he wanted.

"I hear you're looking into the Chatham case."

That got Barclay's attention. He said, "Who told you that?"

Gillespie sat up a bit straighter, perhaps sensing an opportunity to seize some control back of the conversation, and winked at Barclay over the rim of his glass—*he likes that move*, thought Barclay—and he downed the remainder.

"That two Vespers for you, Gilly?"

"It's rude to count."

"Yes, it is," said Barclay with genuine laughter, which the senator joined in. "Another round," he told the bartender.

"Sam, have the drinks delivered to the lounge, will you." The bartender nodded. "Let's go somewhere a little more private."

Despite how Barclay felt personally about the senator, he respected the power enough to follow. He thought about Brittany at home with their daughter and felt a little bit sad and a little bit guilty, but the lure of discussing the case was too much to blow off. So he dashed off a quick text to his wife, saying he'd be home later and he'd explain then.

The men entered the members-only 8-9-8 Room at the rear of Tincs. The senator greeted the tuxedo-clad stoic at the host stand and said, "My usual table, Tommy, and my usual cigar." Tommy nodded. Gillespie turned to Barclay and asked, "What cigar can I get for you?"

Barclay looked at the host and said, "My usual cigar, Tommy." A nod in return.

A look of surprise from Gillespie. "I didn't know you were a member."

A shrug. "Why should you?"

The cigar lounge continued the theme of dark wood and oxblood leather masculinity. The rich aroma of fine tobacco enveloped the air in a warm and inviting embrace. The lighting was soft and subdued, with the dulcet sounds of the jazz trio from next door playing over the multitude of speakers that made it sound as if they were still in the bar. Various paintings of dogs dressed as British royalty lined the walls lit by sconces. A nod to the original owner's sense of humor in an otherwise humorless setting.

It was too early for the room to have a crowd of any significance, so the round booth in the back provided plenty of privacy.

Seated now, Barclay asked again, "Who told you we're investigating the Chatham case?"

"So you are?"

"I didn't say that. I'm just curious who is saying such a thing." Barclay guessed it was his son, the sheriff, and wondered how he'd found out.

A mischievous grin creased the senator's face. "Barclay, I may be retired from public life, but this is still my community, my constituency. You don't think I know what goes on here?"

Barclay was beginning to remember why he never cared for the man. "Yeah, well, I'm not sure what your son told you, but we had our reasons for checking that well." He was careful not to tell the senator an outright lie. "Obviously, no one expected to find a body down there."

Their drinks and cigars arrived on silver platters carried by two different servers. Gillespie's cigar was clipped as he liked it, while Barclay's was punched as was his preference. A black Colibri Quasar torch lighter was placed on the table.

Barclay was lighting his Fuente Double Chateau when he noticed the senator's cigar of choice. "A Cuban Cohiba. Nice."

Gillespie shrugged as he lit his stick. After taking a couple of puffs, Barclay said playfully, "Smoking contraband? And you a U.S. Senator."

Another thousand-watt smile. "People don't care about that Cold War bullshit anymore. Besides, it's just a cigar."

"Ah, but as Rudyard Kipling said: A woman is only a woman, but a good cigar is a smoke."

"I'll drink to that," Gillespie said and did. "Now, about your investigation."

"Well, we're in the beginning stages of determining who the girl is."

Gillespie bared his teeth in a smile and said, "Very smooth, Mr. Griffith. You know damn well I'm not speaking of your investigation into some random body found at the bottom of a well. I was referring to the Chatham investigation." Another puff, then his expression changed, "Wait, you said girl. How do you know it's even a female?"

It was Barclay's turn to give a sly grin; he was allowing himself to enjoy this tête-à-tête. As he spoke, he was looking at the fledgling cigar ash, admiring the even burn. "That's right. Your son left before the anthropologist arrived." He took a drink and a puff, dragging out his response. "How we know isn't important, Senator. Just know that we figured it out." He looked at Gillespie and got what he expected: a look of annoyance. *He's yet to correct me about his son being the source.*

"No need to be cute, Mr. DA. I only want to help."

"And how can you help?" Barclay did not try to hide his skepticism.

"I'm willing to offer a reward for information. Say...twenty-thousand?"

"To identify skeletal remains from a well?"

Gillespie gave a look that said *we both know that's not what it's for*, but he said, "Sure. For the girl in the well."

Barclay was beginning to feel a bit silly about keeping this up, but he didn't want to come clean. Not right now, and certainly not to this guy. He said, "As you said, this is your community—has been for a long, long time. For the sake of conversation, what did you know about the Chatham family back then?"

A drink and a long toke on the Maduro Cohiba. Now he was the one drawing out his answer. *Copycat.* "Not much, really. Kathryn Chatham worked for my father at his restaurant."

"So you knew her."

A dismissive shrug. "I knew who she was, but that's about it."

"You two were somewhat close in age, right? Surely, at some point, you were up at the restaurant while she was working."

"I was in college when all this happened, and I believe she was still in high school, right?"

"She was a senior, not exactly a May, December romance."

"No romance at all," snapped the senator.

"Of course not," Barclay deadpanned. "Anything else you can offer? Since you want to assist, of course."

"You'll do well to know who you're talking to at this table; I still carry weight around here. My name is on the police department, for Christ's sake." The current building housing the Towne Police Department was built in 1962 with public funding secured by the late Arnold Gillespie, Sr., when he served as a state senator for this district. So, while the building housing the police department was christened the Arnold Gillespie Municipal Complex, it was named after the senior senator and not the man sitting across from him, which Barclay well knew. He considered explaining the Law of Transitivity but sipped his Sazerac instead, registering that his drink was warming.

"And?" Barclay said after a few moments. He knew he was treading precariously, antagonizing a person of his companion's stature.

Irritation flashed on the senator's face but vanished with equal speed. He said, "I can get things done; resources, manpower, whatever you need. But maybe you're not serious about this—just looking for a headline: *New DA Looks into Gruesome Cold Case.*"

Like his forgotten cigar, Barclay was doing a slow burn, weighing his response. The senator took a drink and peered at the ash on his own cigar, a weightless two-inch gray, black barrel defying Newton's law, and said, "Are you sure you want to pursue this?"

Barclay's eyes clicked to the senator. "As opposed to what? Ignoring it?" After a beat, he said, "Damn, man, you just offered a twenty-thousand dollar reward. Now you don't think we should pursue it? Which is it, Senator?"

The lounge was beginning to crowd, and the hum of the post-work crowd was competing with the jazz music.

"I'm just saying that it happened a long time ago; only the oldest of us have much of a memory of it. Kathryn moved away sometime after being unable to deal with the loss. So why get folks' hopes up for an unsolvable case? It's a pipe dream at best, Barclay—surely you see that. Getting this all stirred up, doomed to fail, will not bode well for you. Surely there is an easier case for you to make your name with."

Barclay pulled a stray tobacco leaf off his tongue and said, "You really think that's what this is about? Me making a name for myself?" The senator opened his mouth to speak, and Barclay cut him off. "Look here, we may both serve in public office, but that is where our similarities end. Until you become a prosecutor, you don't know anything about why I do what I do." He paused, allowing two men he recognized as civil attorneys to walk past before he leaned in and hissed, "A cold case is a victim without justice, a family without answers, and a killer among us." Then, he jabbed at the senator with his cigar clenched between his fingers and said, "That is why I won't ignore this case. Fail or not, it *will* get everything I have, period."

ELEVEN

December 7

The evidence room for the police department was located in the basement of the Arnold Gillespie Municipal Complex, among a musty labyrinth of mechanical closets, HVAC systems, and storage rooms. Throughout the building's lowest level, numerous drop ceiling tiles were missing, affording a view of the building's skeletal frame and flashes of bright blue Cat 5 cable carrying high-speed internet throughout the utilitarian brick edifice.

The interior of the evidence room contradicted the entirety of the antiquated basement where it was housed. Ten flatscreens lined the wall opposite evidence tech Frankie Drake, who manned an old metal desk in a sort of ante-room. Each television monitor was dedicated to a specific camera in the room.

Barclay, Fitz, and Lawson walked in while the tech was on the telephone. Hearing only her side of the conversation, they determined she was speaking to a detective about getting evidence pulled for review.

While she was on the phone, Barclay wandered over to the bulletin board, which had a smattering of mugshots commemorating TPD's brushes with the rich and famous. Barclay's favorite was the skinny, shirtless, boney-shouldered Hank Williams wearing a cowboy hat. Hank Senior was arrested in September 1952 for public drunkenness and disorderly conduct for his behavior at the Dabney Hotel. Pinned next to the photo was the four-by-eight police report, yellowed with age. The report listed the arrestee's personal particulars, the charges, and a handwritten note that his bond was twenty-five dollars. Barclay had heard the story many times about how the then police chief allowed the country singer to sleep it off on his office couch, and the two went out for breakfast the following morning.

Frankie Drake ended her phone call and greeted the men with a smile. No one knew quite how old she was because her brown skin was smooth and practically ageless; however, she had been an evidence tech with the police department for so long that no one could remember a time when she wasn't. As the custodian of every piece of physical evidence seized by the police department, finding a job in the criminal justice system more important than hers would be difficult. She had testified in dozens of cases Barclay had prosecuted, and he knew her to be sharp and excellent at her job and on the witness stand.

She had a personality few got to see. She took her job seriously, and only when she was off duty would she truly let her guard down. The first time he saw the fun side of Frankie Drake was at the retirement party of a TPD lieutenant. It was held at a local bar where she proved to be lethal with a dart in her hand, annihilating all comers to the dart board. Losing over and over to her that night had the competitive prosecutor ordering a dart board from Amazon before he left the bar. He had been practicing at home on the off chance he ever got another shot at her.

The four of them exchanged pleasantries, and she hit Barclay with "When are we throwing darts again, " drawing a pseudo-angry expression and a "Whenever you're ready" retort. She laughed as she turned toward the chain-link enclosure that was the evidence room. The entry to where the evidence was held was guarded by a keypad that scrambled the digits zero through nine when it was activated. That way, when Frankie keyed in her six-digit code, a distant onlooker could not discern the numbers simply by finger placement. She entered her six-digit PIN, which triggered a buzz and a click, then stepped into the evidence cage. Once inside, she made certain the door was closed and locked behind her. Lawson had notified her the previous day that they wanted the evidence from the Chatham homicides made available for review, so she was gone only a few minutes when she reappeared pushing a cart carrying two brown card-board boxes approximately three feet long, two feet wide, and two feet deep. The boxes looked practically brand new, rein-forcing what they already knew—this case had been long forgotten.

As she rolled the cart to Lawson, she said, "There is also a wooden door back there labeled 'Chelsea's Bedroom Door.' It's wrapped in brown paper. You want me to bring that up?"

The three of them looked at one another, trying to decide. Lawson made the executive decision to leave it. They would look at it later. They had enough to do without dragging that out.

Frankie had the detective sign her name on an electronic signa-ture pad acknowledging receipt of the evidence. Then she unlocked the evidence viewing room—the only place the evidence could be moved to until it was taken to the courtroom for trial.

The stark white viewing room contained a large elevated marble table surrounded by ten wooden bar stools with backs. The room also contained a camera posted high in each corner as well as over the doorway to prevent tampering with or removing evidence and, more importantly to the police, a method to document their actions in the event a defense attorney wished to accuse the police of malfeasance with regard to the evidence.

Lawson set the boxes on the white-and-gray-streaked marble slab and slid the cart out of the way; she removed the lid on the first box.

She began pulling out individual paper bags and handing them to Fitz, who placed them on the table. The bags were folded down from the top and taped over the seams; a description of the bag's contents and where that item was located was handwritten on the bags with a black permanent marker. In addition to the item description, the bag had a number written on it. This was the item number of that particular piece of evidence assigned as the evidence was collected. The number consisted of the year the crime occurred, followed by a dash and a number. The investigation began with *One* for the first item of evidence and continued sequentially until all the evidence was collected, bagged, numbered, and accounted for.

They emptied the contents of both boxes, covering most of the large, cold marble surface. Lawson set the empty boxes aside, and she and Fitz began to inventory what they had one bag at a time. Fitz had his iPad propped up and, using an attached keyboard, logged the evidence into a spreadsheet. Lawson would read the item number followed by the description written on the bag, and Fitz would record this information. It took them about forty minutes to catalog everything in the two boxes.

Although forensics has been used in some rudimentary form or another for the better part of three hundred years, the application of forensic sciences as it is known today has exploded exponentially over the last thirty years. When the murder occurred in 1963, anything other than fingerprints and blood typing was well outside the scope of a crime lab's capabilities. As a result, Lawson, Fitz, and Barclay viewed most of the collected evidence much differently than the original investigators had sixty years ago.

First and foremost, their collective minds were on DNA. Barclay thought back to the words of cold case investigator AJ Murphy about DNA and not getting hung up on requiring a hit in order to proceed with an arrest and prosecution. Barclay understood his point and knew he would not need a DNA match to take an otherwise strong case to a grand jury; however, he also knew DNA was low-hanging fruit and, practically speaking, biological evidence was the quickest, easiest way to rule someone in or out of a case. In addition to the cigarette butt, they were all aware that the machete sheath and the duffle bag contained potential biological evidence. With that in mind, they had discussed it before arriving at the evidence room and collectively decided to search first for any additional evidence that could be sent off for forensic testing. In order to make that determination, each bag of evidence needed to be opened and examined.

In addition to observing the evidence, they photographed each item before they opened it to document the condition it was in prior to them handling it. Once opened, they photographed the evidence itself so they could reference it as needed, saving them the time and trouble of having to come back to the evidence room.

The first item they opened was described on the outside of the large bag as *machete sheath* and was listed as being found lying on the floor in the den just inside the sliding glass door. There was a three-inch by two-inch white sticker on the bag that Barclay was unfamiliar with. Upon closer inspection, he determined it must be the label affixed from Genome 23, the genealogical DNA testing lab. This sticker contained the lab's identification number for that piece of evidence and a barcode for tracking purposes within the lab.

"Looks homemade," observed Lawson when she removed the item from its container. The sheath was two pieces of sturdy cardboard stapled down one side, across the bottom, and up the other side, leaving the top open to slide the machete in. She passed the item to Barclay, who, like the other two, wore black latex gloves to avoid contaminating the evidence with his prints or DNA while also protecting themselves against any biological material they may come in contact with, such as blood.

Barclay turned it over in his hands, examined it top to bottom, and pointed to a spot on the cardboard with his right pinky finger. The discoloration had been circled with a black ink pen. Barclay figured that someone at the lab circled the mark so the tech would know what part of the sheath they wanted to try and extract DNA from.

"That's how the dad got it," said Fitz. "Machete right through the clavicle...then a gunshot blast to the face for good measure." No one said anything, lost in thought about those early morning hours and the sheer horror that unfolded. Fitz broke the silence with, "Man, fuck this guy."

"Fuck this guy," responded Barclay, the familiar refrain between the two when dealing with an especially bad actor.

The next item up was a cardboard box approximately twenty-six inches long, two inches tall, and six inches wide. They instinctively knew what was inside: the eighteen-inch bush machete used in the murder.

Lawson used her pocket knife to slice the tape along the edges and opened the box. Inside was a dirty, rusty, blood-stained blade connected to a battered handle wrapped in some kind of cloth. All three of them silently took in the fierce-looking instrument of death before it was photographed, cataloged, and resealed.

A bag containing a heavier object was selected next. Inside was a chrome flashlight approximately sixteen inches in length and had the trade name *Winchester* stamped on the outside edge of the large bulb assembly. Lawson removed it from the bag, and it was covered in black dust.

Barclay reached for it, and Lawson said, "Be careful. That's fingerprint dust, and it's a bitch to get out of clothes." Barclay withdrew his reach and leaned over for a closer look. There was some confusion as to why it was bagged, and they all agreed to ask an investigator about it. The handwriting on the bag said it was located on the floor of the den. This jogged Barclay's memory.

He said, "The case file contains a sketch of the floor plan that denotes where each piece of evidence was located before it was collected." Then, to Fitz: "When we're done here, let's match up everything with that sketch. See if we're missing anything. It also may help establish a narrative." Fitz nodded as he typed.

The next two bags Lawson handled were bedsheets from the boys' bedroom. Inside each of the two bags, the sheets were wrapped in thick brown paper, like a butcher may wrap steaks. She removed the paper-wrapped packages from the first bag and slid her knife along the seams, slicing through the tape. She unwrapped the package carefully, not wanting anything to escape. She pulled back the overlapping flaps, the old paper making a crinkling noise, and revealed a crusty, dark brown mass. In the lighter areas, she could see the sports images that adorned the sheets. "Man, fuck this guy," she said more to herself than the other two.

Lawson gave the other two a look that asked, *You want to see any more of this?* They both shook their heads, and she re-wrapped and re-taped and re-bagged. Like the previous bag, she initialed on the seals where she re-taped. She was now in the chain of custody for this and every piece of evidence they would open and inspect. She was taking her time, being meticulous because that's what she did and how she worked, and why Barclay wanted her involved with the case.

The next bag contained the same bloody sports-themed sheets. The bag and package were opened enough to confirm the accuracy of what was written on the outside and re-sealed and initialed.

The next bag contained the nightgown Mrs. Chatham was wearing that night. Like the sheets, it was dark brown and stiff with blood. As with the sheets and all of the clothing in evidence, there would be a time to open them up and spread them out for a more thorough inspection but now was not it.

Another bag was opened to reveal the father's bloodied clothes in similar condition as the other blood-soaked fabrics they'd seen up to this point.

The next bag contained a twenty-four-inch square cut of blood-soaked carpet from the top of the stairs—where Mrs. Chatham was felled. Again, the bag was opened, contents verified, re-sealed, and initialed.

And so the process went for a similar cutting of carpet from Chelsea Chatham's room and Chelsea's bedclothes.

The following two bags went together. The first bag was labeled *red nylon duffle bag* with the location being at the edge of the woods, and the companion evidence bag was labeled *approximately twelve feet of rope located inside nylon duffel*.

As with all other evidence bags to this point, the contents were cataloged, photographed, and re-sealed. A note was made by Fitz that there was what appeared to be a small smear of blood on one of the straps.

The next bag they opened contained eight small envelopes, seven of which held a single spent shotgun shell, while one envelope held a single unfired shotgun shell. Each envelope was labeled with the location of its recovery.

So far, nothing of what they had seen figured to hold any clues to the killer's identity. The blood was almost exclusively that of the victims, and the spent shells wouldn't have fingerprints due to the heat of the firing process evaporating any water vapor—which is what fingerprints, in essence, were.

Barclay held out slim hope of possible fingerprints from the unspent shell, but the ridged surface made for a particularly challenging place to lift a usable print. The same could be said for the machete sheath, as paper products were notoriously bereft of fingerprint evidence. Their only real hope was that the shooter had touched the brass head of the unspent shell, but even that was unlikely to yield anything useful.

The last item of evidence was the smallest in size. Barclay knew from the external markings on the manila-colored envelope that it was the cigarette butt. The envelope bore the telltale bright yellow sticker affixed by the Alabama Department of Forensic Sciences. When ADFS receives a piece of evidence, a sticker is affixed to the box or envelope that contains the evidence to be tested. The sticker listed the case number as assigned by ADFS and a barcode assigned to that specific item. The barcoded sticker is scanned every time it is moved from one place to the next, establishing an electronic chain of custody. Barclay knew that, in this case, the chain of custody at the lab would not be the problem. If they encountered any chain of custody issues, it would be in the collection and storage of evidence collected sixty years ago.

A cell phone rang in the sterile space; Barclay, Fitz, and Lawson all instinctively reached for their phones. Fitz fished his cell from inside his suit coat and eyed the caller ID, which only showed a number.

He said, "Hello?" Then, "Yes, ma'am, thank you for calling me back." He slid off the stool and walked to a corner of the room.

Barclay and Lawson began putting all the bags back into the boxes. Barclay had taken Fitz's iPad and checked the spreadsheet against each bag as it went back into the box to ensure they had accounted for every piece of evidence in the spreadsheet and also to ensure each piece was going back in for storage.

Barclay said, "We need to establish the chain of custody on this cigarette, or we won't be able to use it. I don't guess the envelope says who found it?"

"Nope, and I have no idea what kind of evidence logs they kept back then. Even if we discover who collected it, we'd better hope they're still alive."

Barclay shook his head. "Just get me a name. That satisfies the law. Now, we don't get a name, and we're busted on this."

Fitz returned to the table and said, "That was Sylvia Burrows. She and her husband have been out of town visiting family. We can go by her house when we leave here."

"You two go," said Barclay. "I've got to get some stuff done in the office."

Barclay opened the door to leave and told Frankie they were ready to return the evidence.

She got up from her desk and moved to the cart to return the evidence boxes.

She said, "You going to tell me why you're interested in a case from 1963?"

"You going to give me a rematch on the dartboard?"

TWELVE

Sylvia Burrows lived two blocks from downtown, which meant she and her husband owned a small but expensive home. Either the Burrows had money, or she had spotted a good opportunity as a real estate agent.

Fitz and Lawson parked on the narrow street because there was no space in the short driveway already holding a large cream-colored Cadillac sedan. Like each of the sixteen homes lining this residential street, the Burrows' home evoked images of New Orleans with balconies and copious amounts of wrought iron. The narrow, two-story gray Victorian-style house had three white columns on the first-story porch and four on the second story. Between each column hung ferns cascading down the sides of their hidden pots.

The two investigators walked up the brick driveway, careful with their steps due to the buckling caused by time and tree roots. They took the off-shoot brick path from the driveway to the front of the house and climbed the brick steps to the black front door with gleaming brass hardware. Fitz rang the doorbell, and they could hear the dull bells resonating inside. The etched glass in the door distorted the figure answering.

They were greeted by a woman much older than the photo on her business website. The thought must have occurred to both investigators at the same time because they exchanged a glance before Fitz spoke: "Mrs. Burrows, my name is Winston Fitzsimmons, and I'm the chief investigator with the district attorney's office." He gestured to Lawson and said, "And this is Detective Beck Lawson with the Towne Police Department."

Sylvia Burrows was a short woman with tall, light purple cotton candy hair, a lot of gold jewelry, and heavy makeup on her crepe-paper face. She wore a black blouse with a loud design, white pants, and sensible shoes. "Please come in," she said with a gesture and a jingle.

They followed her through a jet wash of floral perfume, and Fitz was instantly transported to his grandmother's house. The ornate living room was encrusted with gold, velvet, uncomfortable-looking furniture, and Hummel figurines everywhere: on shelves and in glass-front cabinets, sitting on tables and sideboards.

Fitz and Lawson stepped carefully, afraid a stray breath could break something.

She clapped her hands together and said in the most southern of drawls, "May I get you two officers anything to drink? Eat?"

"No, ma'am," said Fitz, but Lawson said, "Coffee would be great...and cookies if you have some."

"Excellent," she said, clasping her hands in front of her, and was gone; the quickness with which she vanished surprised them both.

Fitz gave Lawson a look. The detective said, "What? Between here and going through the evidence, I didn't get lunch."

Fitz was about to speak when Mrs. Burrows appeared with a silver tray of Danish butter cookies. She placed the tray on the oval glass and gold coffee table and said, "The coffee will be ready shortly. Won't y'all two have a seat?" She gestured to the gold silk brocade sofa that looked as inviting as a log.

"Now, Mr. Fitzsimmons, is it?" Fitz nodded, and she said, "How can I help you?"

He was about to answer when he saw Lawson grab a handful of the blonde cookies, prompting a double take. He gathered himself and said, "I want to talk to you about when you lived on Woods Way."

"Oh my," she said, bringing a hand up to her throat. "That was a long time ago. What could you ever want to know about that?"

They were interrupted by a slightly stooped balding man wearing a gray windbreaker over a plaid button-down, tan slacks, and brown Rockports.

He rounded the corner into the room and said, "Sylvia, where is my—" He pulled up short when he saw the two visitors.

"Tommy," said Sylvia, "These nice folks are policemen." She put a hand to her throat and turned back to Lawson. "Or is it police*woman* now, dear?"

"Detective is fine," Lawson said as she popped a cookie into her mouth.

A nod from Tommy Burrows, then, "What's wrong? Who died? Did somebody die?"

She shooed him with a hand and said, "No one's dead, Tommy. They just want to ask me about the home I grew up in." She turned her attention to the couch and said, "Right?"

"Yes, ma'am. Sort of," said Fitz.

"We need a lawyer?" Tommy asked.

"No, sir," said Lawson. "No lawyers. We just have some questions about an old friend of your wife's."

"I better call a lawyer."

"Oh, sit down, Tommy, for heaven's sake."

"I have to go unpack." And with that, he turned and left.

"Don't mind him. He just needs a nap."

"I don't need a nap," Tommy yelled from the next room.

"I'm sorry, dear; you said you wanted to ask me about an old friend of mine?"

"Yes, ma'am, Kathryn—"

A beep came from the kitchen, and Sylvia Burrows was up and out in a blink. Fitz, who sat on the edge of the couch, flopped back and let out a frustrated sigh.

"The coffee," Lawson said, reaching for more cookies.

Sylvia walked back in with a full coffee service, and Fitz stood and walked toward her, hands out, offering to take the tray. She handed it off to him, and he sat it on the coffee table.

On the etched silver tray sat a tall silver urn, a silver sugar bowl holding a small silver spoon, and a tiny sterling pitcher of cream. All three of them poured a cup and doctored it to their tastes.

Fitz said, "Mrs. Burrows, we have some questions about—"

"Coffee's good," said Lawson, drawing a look from Fitz.

"Why thank you," said the appropriately pleased host. "You know," she began, leaning in as if to share a secret, I dated a police officer for a while." She smiled a broad, toothy grin. "One summer home from college." She raised her eyebrows as if to say *how about that.*

"Does Mr. Burrows know about this?" asked Lawson with a wink, and Sylvia threw her head back and cackled.

"He doesn't, so don't tell him," she said, placing a hand on Fitz's knee and giving him a knowing look.

"Now, as I was saying," Fitz glanced down at his knee then flashed a look at Lawson, who mouthed *What* with a mouthful of cookie, "Kathryn Chatham," Fitz continued, putting his eyes back on Sylvia, "you lived next door to her growing up?"

"Yes, I did." She got a wistful look and said, "I haven't thought about her in years." Fitz let the silence stretch. Sylvia broke it by saying, "Such a terrible, terrible thing that happened to her family."

"Well, that's what we'd like to speak with you about, Mrs. Burrows."

"Really? Me? But why?"

"We just want—"

"Oh, dear."

"Yes, ma'am. We went by her old house—"

"Her house isn't there anymore. My father bought it and tore it down."

"Yes, ma'am, we—"

"Kids. Making it like some sort of carnival sideshow," she said, tsking and shaking her head.

"Yes, ma'am. We spoke to your brother while we were there. He's the one who told us to contact you." Fitz paused, waiting for the interruption. Instead, she stared at him, so he continued. "How well did you know Ms. Chatham?"

"We were best friends. We both moved in about the same time before we even started elementary school. For the longest time, we were the only kids in our part of the neighborhood, so me and my brother and Kathryn and her brother were usually at our house or theirs. She and I were in the same grade and even dated some of the same boys."

"How about after high school? Did you two keep in touch?"

"Oh yes. We both went to college at Auburn, and though we drifted apart a little during that time—I joined a sorority, and she did not—we always tried to make up for it when we were home for the summer."

"I see."

Fitz leaned in as he said, "You mentioned what happened to her family. Can you tell us anything about that night?"

She nodded slowly, sipped her coffee, and said, "I remember waking up to all sorts of voices outside and police lights coming through my window. I walked downstairs and saw my mom staring out the living room window. Then, I saw my father and brother in the front yard; my father had a gun. I remember being scared when I saw that."

"What did you do then?"

"I ran outside. My mother began yelling my name, and I think she grabbed at me, maybe even getting a finger on my nightgown, but I ran up to my father, asking him what was happening. He yelled at me to go back inside with my mother; he said it wasn't safe to be out." She took another drink. "My brother was out there, and my father didn't make him go back inside." She gave a mirthless laugh and said, "You know, that's what always stuck out to me about that night—my brother—my younger brother—was allowed to be out in the middle of everything, and I had to go watch from inside."

Lawson leaned forward and refilled her cup, then held the urn out to the other two, who shook their heads no.

"Do you remember anything odd or maybe something that sticks out in your mind about the days or weeks leading up to that night?"

She contemplated that question for maybe half a minute when she said, "No. Nothing." Fitz detected pain in her voice. A pang of helplessness that caused him to feel bad for her.

"Was she seeing anyone? Dating anybody?"

"Not that I remember. It wasn't because she didn't have boys asking her. She was such a beautiful girl. But, no, she had a job that kept her busy most nights of the week. Just not much time for boys, I'm afraid."

The main reason for this interview was the hang-up phone calls that Walter Jackson mentioned, but Sylvia didn't seem to have any recollection of that. Fitz didn't want to ask her about that directly, not wanting to plant the memory himself. His mind was working, trying to elicit the memory without specifically bringing

it up. The last thing he wanted, or needed, was her telling them
what she thought they needed or wanted to hear.

He finally said, "You mentioned the two of you were close.
Did you confide in one another?"

"Of course."

Fitz nodded. Thought for a moment. Several seconds passed
when Sylvia said, "Do you think this was about her? What
happened to her family?"

"We don't know, Mrs. Burrows. Any reason we *should* think
that?" Lawson asked. The old lady looked between the two investigators, worry in her expression.

"I just don't know. Maybe if I thought about it."

"Take your time," said Lawson.

She considered it for a long minute and began shaking her
head. "I just cannot imagine anyone wanting to hurt her or her
family."

"Unfortunately, Mrs. Burrows, someone did hurt that
family."

Fitz made a decision. "I'll level with you, Mrs. Burrows. The
new DA and the police department are looking into this case—"

She twitched and said, "You're finally going to arrest
somebody?"

He put his palms out and said, "No, ma'am...well, we are
looking into it. But obviously, this is a very old case—"

"It's not that old, Mistuh Fitzsimmons," Sylvia drawled with a
grin.

"Well, in cop years, it is." They all laughed. The levity a
welcome sight. Fitz grabbed a cookie both because he loved
Danish butter cookies and to buy himself a moment to think. "We
know what this case means to this community...what it so clearly
means to you, and we want to give it one last, best look." Sylvia
drank her coffee, and Fitz did the same more out of hospitality
than actually wanting to drink it. "We went by to see the house

and, like I said, saw your brother there. We spoke to him for a few minutes, and he said we should come speak to you."

She looked to Lawson, then Fitz, and said, "That's the second time you said that. What did my brother say? Why did he tell you to talk to me?"

He was doing his best to hold off planting a potentially false memory. "He said you and Kathryn would speak about things... privately." He paused and, getting nothing said, "He mentioned how, you know, little brothers don't always get noticed, and he may have overheard some conversations."

Sylvia Burrows was a very sharp lady. She leaned back in the cloth wingback chair and took on a thoughtful pose.

Fitz and Lawson exchanged a glance. The veteran investigators had conducted hundreds if not thousands of interviews between them. They had been at this point before, many times—a sort of crossroads. The moment where you knew, just knew something was there. You teetered on the precipice of an answer from a witness or suspect, knowing the next words out of their mouth either catapulted the investigation forward or ground it to a screeching halt. They exchanged a slight nod and a look that said *this could be it.*

After what felt like an eternity, Sylvia, still staring off, said, "There was a guy...a police officer, actually."

THIRTEEN

I have to go to the bathroom."

"No shit," said Fitz. "You had four cups of coffee."

"Seriously," said Lawson, "I really have to go."

"Yeah, well, hold it."

Fitz was piloting his black Tahoe like he was navigating the backstretch at Talladega. He had dialed his boss, the district attorney, as he entered the vehicle before the sound of the slamming car doors finished echoing through the cabin of the SUV. Barclay said he was on his way to attend a county commission meeting, to which Fitz said, "Skip it."

Investigations thrived on energy. Like a shark, it had to stay moving. Stagnation starved it of oxygen, choked it out. There was nothing like that moment during an interview when a piece clicked into place. Whether a confession, a statement that corroborated a damning piece of evidence, or something, anything that moved the case forward in any way, when an investigator heard it and understood its value, any frustration or fatigue was eradicated. Replaced, instead, with purpose, drive, and determination.

Sylvia Burrows didn't break the case open by any stretch.

However, for a case that had been hopelessly mired in apathy and indifference brought on by the passage of time and the natural human aversion to failure, the information from Kathryn Chatham's next-door neighbor and best friend may as well have been the name of the killer himself for the jolt it gave Fitz and Lawson as her memory unlocked and kept them at her house for more than an hour.

The last vestiges of daylight were moments from surrendering to the dark when Fitz steered the Tahoe into the empty courthouse parking lot and into the parking spot closest to the employee entrance on the East side of the building. The LED light standards bathed the lot in a soft, blueish glow in contrast to the harsher orange-tinted light above the employee entrance. The area around this side of the courthouse was deserted, the only sound the clanging of the flagpole's counterweight against the aluminum pole as a stiff breeze kicked up, the cold wind eliciting a curse from Lawson.

––––––

FITZ FOUND Barclay in his dim confines, illumination coming only from a desk lamp, a floor lamp in a far corner, and ambient light from the outside. Classical music hung in the air.

Barclay had moved some more furniture into the room by this point, and he was sitting in one of four burgundy tufted leather wingback chairs surrounding a glass coffee table. Fitz took a chair opposite him and said that Lawson was right behind him and he would wait on the detective before beginning.

Lawson entered the room and commented on the lack of luminescence, to which Barclay replied, "With all these windows, when my lights are on, and it's dark outside, it's like being in a fishbowl. Besides, I find this relaxes me after a long day." He gestured to a roughhewn wooden tray in the middle of the coffee table and said, "Drink?"

Fitz and Lawson both said yes, and Barclay poured a measure of Col E.H. Taylor rye whiskey in three rocks glasses and handed two to his guests. Lawson and Barclay helped themselves to ice in a silver bucket on the tray.

"The Colonel makes a fine whiskey...and not easy to find," said Fitz after lifting the glass to his nose. "How'd you come by this?"

"Luke Jackson brought it by this afternoon. A congratulations gift."

"Very nice."

They took a moment to enjoy their good fortune before Barclay, staring into his glass, said, "So what did Mrs. Burrows have to say?"

Fitz leaned forward, elbows on knees, and said, "She said that Kathryn had gotten to know a guy from her job at the hamburger place—a cop would come in almost nightly for dinner. She said that as far as she knew, this had been going on for at least two months, and he had been getting more friendly with her."

Barclay knew that sex, revenge, or money was at the root of every murder in some form or fashion, so he raised an eyebrow as he leaned back in his chair and draped a leg over a knee. Throw in the fact this mystery man was a police officer, and Fitz had his attention.

He continued, "At first, they were just chatty with one another. She was being nice to a restaurant regular—that's how Kathryn put it to Sylvia way back then. Then things started getting flirty between them. This guy starts in, and she flirts back. That type of thing." Fitz took a drink, and the other two followed suit. "One day, this fella asks her out."

"How old was this guy?" Barclay asked.

"I asked that, and Sylvia didn't know. She got the impression he was older but not overly so. He tried to get Kathryn to take a ride with him when she got off work. Even offered to drive her home, but she told him she would have to ask her parents, and he didn't care for that—at all."

"How long was this before the shooting?"

"Sylvia couldn't say for sure. A few weeks was her best guess."

"Did this guy keep coming to see her?"

"Oh yeah. Kept coming around, being all friendly. Sylvia said Kathryn liked the attention but wasn't so sure about going out with the guy. She didn't think her father would approve, so she didn't bother asking her parents. After a while, he finally wore her down and got her to ask her father, who told her absolutely not. Sylvia made it sound like it did not go well with her admirer. Said Kathryn cried about it. She enjoyed this man's company and didn't want him to stop coming around."

"And she told all of this to Sylvia?"

"Yep. Thick as thieves, those two; talked about everything with one another. Sylvia told her to go for it. They were seniors and almost eighteen. She didn't see any harm in it, but Kathryn was a rule follower. No way would she go against her father's wishes."

Lawson finished her drink, and the ice cube tinked dully in the empty glass. Barclay made a motion with his head that said, "Help yourself," and the detective tipped a bit into her glass. Lawson then stood and walked over to the window, taking in the view.

Barclay wanted Fitz to bottom line it, but he let the investigator unravel it in his own time. There was nothing superfluous about Winston Fitzsimmons, and Barclay knew this was all pertinent information, even if it didn't seem so right now.

Fitz said, "Eventually, Kathryn tells this guy that it ain't gonna happen. She enjoys his company and looks forward to him coming around the restaurant, but her father won't allow her to go out with him."

"Sylvia say how the guy took it?"

"According to Kathryn, he wasn't happy about it and tried to get her to go out anyway. She said Kathryn was crying because she really did like the guy."

Barclay nodded, taking it in, turning it over in his mind. "Does Sylvia have any better idea when *this* event occurred?"

"Just a few days before the shooting," said Fitz. Then, in answer to what he knew Barclay was about to ask, he said, "She remembers because it was Kathryn's last night of work before the restaurant closed for a week. The owner always closed the restaurant the week of Thanksgiving."

"Huh," said Barclay, who stood up, glass in hand, and joined Lawson at the window. He finished off his drink before turning around and saying, "Did Mrs. Burrows give you any idea who the cop was? First name? Description?"

Lawson said, "I asked her that, and she couldn't give us anything. She said either Kathryn didn't tell her or she couldn't remember."

Barclay turned his back to the window, sat on the ledge, set his glass down, and crossed his arms. He said, "Where do we go from here?"

Lawson said, "First, we need to stop looking at this as a cold case and approach it as a murder investigation. We're outthinking ourselves here; we need to do what we know. I'm going to start by putting a witness list together. Write down every witness we know about just as if we were investigating a recent homicide, then go through and determine who gave a statement, who wrote a report, et cetera." To Fitz, she said, "I know you've done this already, but I need to do it myself. This will get my mind focused." Fitz nodded, taking no offense. "Then I will work on tracking down who is still alive that we can speak with. I will also see what I can find out about officers with the department in sixty-three, try and narrow down who this mystery cop could be." She moved to her chair, setting her glass on the table. "We have to start running down leads as we get them, no matter how tenuous, and it's either going to be enough, or it's not."

"I agree," said Barclay.

Lawson: "We have to face the fact that this is an old ass case and accept that solving it will be a long shot. And, even if we do solve it, even if we do figure out who killed the Chathams, will we be able to prosecute the case with most everyone involved in the investigation almost certainly unavailable? For all we know, the killer is dead, too. So let's put our heads down, get after it, and see where it takes us. We've done more in a week than anyone has done on this case in the last fifty years. Let's build on that and see where it takes us."

Barclay picked up his glass and sat back in his chair. He set his glass on the table and leaned back, allowing the elegant harmony of a familiar but unidentifiable classical melody to flow through his brain, slowing his thoughts down.

He rubbed his stubbly chin with his left hand and said, "I think we need to get AJ Murphy down here for a meeting. Get him up to speed with what we've learned, let him see the evidence, and get his thoughts on moving forward."

"I agree," said Lawson. Then, seeing Barclay raise an eyebrow at her response, the detective said, "Like I said, time to get after it."

FOURTEEN

December 9

Towne Creek Estates was an upscale gated retirement community on the southern edge of the city. That was where DA investigator Winston Fitzsimmons agreed to meet retired Towne police officer Mike Garrett. After being buzzed through the iron and stone entrance, Fitz wound his way through the curvy streets pursuant to the eighteen miles-per-hour posted speed limit to the neighborhood clubhouse. He was immediately impressed with what the developer's sign at the entrance billed as "Luxury lifestyle for the active resident age 55+."

He passed a set of tennis courts, pickleball courts, and a small lake with a spray of water at its center. He admired the clean landscapes and manicured lawns among the abundant live oaks creating a shaded canopy along the streets and sidewalks, the preamble of fall not quite in full throat. His investigator's eye noticed that all the homes were single-story and none required stairs to gain entry, which answered his initial question of *what's different about a retirement community.*

The residents were out en masse on this chamber of commerce November afternoon, and his blacked-out Tahoe rolling down the street stood in stark contrast to the preferred mode of transportation in Towne Creek Estates: the residential golf cart. As such, he was getting plenty of attention from the octogenarian inhabitants of this *Stepford Wives/Cocoon* mashup. *This neighborhood may be for the fifty-five and older crowd,* he thought, *but it definitely trended toward the* older *variety.*

He stopped at a wide speed hump to allow two golf carts to cross the narrow street when he noticed the "Golf Cart X-ing" signs to his left and right. The occupants stared as they passed, clearly intrigued by this interloper. His left hand rested atop the steering wheel, and he lifted a couple of fingers in a wave to the curious passersby. They gave a reticent wave in return.

Fitz eased up and over the hump and followed the road's slight curve left then right before straightening out and dumping him into the clubhouse parking lot. He eased the SUV toward the portico when he saw a pink-headed bald man in a navy blue pullover, khaki pants, and white leather tennis shoes sitting in a golf cart smoking a cigarette—one leg hiked up, foot resting on the dash. The golf cart had a thin blue line flag affixed to the rear driver's side roof support post. Fitz exited the vehicle and approached the man who was holding the molded plastic roof handle with his left hand as he gazed out over the nine-hole par three golf course.

"Mike Garrett?" he asked as he neared.

Garrett turned slowly toward the sound of the voice, removed his cigarette, and said, "Investigator Fitzsimmons." Smoke poured from his mouth and nose as he spoke.

Fitz stuck his hand out, Garrett jammed the cigarette between his teeth, and the two shook hands.

"Jump in, and we'll ride."

Fitz walked around the rear of the golf cart, removing his light gray suit coat and laying it across the rear seat. He then stepped into the footwell and sat, the cart listing under the ex-tight end's weight.

"Cigarette?" offered Garrett, who Fitz noted smelled like laundry detergent.

"No, sir, but if you're going to smoke, I don't suppose you'd mind..." Fitz lifted a rolled-up pouch of Red Man from his back pocket and held it up.

"Shit, no," said Garrett as he flipped the burning cigarette stub into the parking lot. He popped another up from the soft pack of American Spirits with a flick of his wrist. He reached in through the v-neck of his pullover and put the crumpled pack back in his shirt pocket and grabbed an ancient copper-colored Zippo from one of the cupholders, flipped the lid, lit his cigarette, clicked the lid shut with a finger, and tossed the battered lighter back into the cupholder. He inhaled deeply, grabbed a well-used Atlanta Braves stadium cup from the other cupholder, and drank from it as he exhaled smoke. He set the cup back into the cupholder, and, everything seemingly in order, pressed the accelerator, popped the break, and the electric cart took off.

"You sounded a little coy on the phone, Mr. Fitzsimmons. You going to tell me what this is all about?"

"Yeah, sorry about that. The DA has us looking into the Chatham homicide, and we're trying to keep it quiet as long as possible."

Garrett brought the golf cart to an abrupt stop on the paved cart path and looked at Fitz, the crystal blue eyes set back beneath wild blond eyebrows. Fitz watched the man's watery eyeballs twitch back and forth, studying him. Finally, the old man blinked twice and said, "Thank you" in a rasp. He faced forward, took a deep drag off his cigarette, and accelerated.

Fitz was taken aback by this reaction, unsure what to say.

Finally, he opted for a direct approach. "This means a lot to you." It was said as a statement.

Garrett nodded as he took another drag, and Fitz waited for the retired badge to continue. He was about to speak when Garrett, staring straight ahead, said, "The first murder case I was ever involved in. I was just a rookie patrol officer when I got the call and responded, and, holy hell, that crime scene." He shook his head and flicked his cigarette into the lush green grass. "My biggest case, which also became my biggest disappointment as a cop." He reached inside his pullover once more, reaching for the cigarette pack, then pulled his hand back. "We all have those cases, Mr. Fitzsimmons, you know that. The ones that stick with us." Fitz nodded, but Garrett didn't see it. He laughed a quick, humorless laugh and said, "Can you imagine, as a rookie, being a part of a case that haunts you for the next six decades?" He shook his liver-spotted head.

Fitz said, "I've read the case file and saw you were the first on the scene. What can you tell me about that night?"

The golf course was busy, and they weaved their way around golf carts with bags on the back; Garrett gave the occasional wave to the men and women in golf attire. The air was punctuated with the occasional sound of a ball being driven off the tee or thudding onto the green.

"I remember everything from that night...vividly. I remember every homicide case I investigated as a detective, but this case, this one, I remember like I remember what I had for breakfast this morning." He took a drink, and water rolled off the outside of the cup, dripping into his lap. He set the cup down and said, "I got a call on the radio about shots being fired at a residence, so I hauled ass to the scene. When I get there, the neighbor is standing outside in his pajamas with a rifle." He laughs genuinely at this image. "I remember thinking this was just some guy shooting at possums or armadillos in his yard, and a neighbor had called the cops on him.

The development was fairly new, and there weren't many houses built yet, so I didn't see the big deal with him shooting outside. But then he tells me about hearing gunshots next door, and then *I* hear it. A shotgun. Very distinct."

Fitz nodded, occasionally spitting onto the cart path. He held the roof handle above his head, his biceps straining at the white dress shirt. Garrett went on to fill him in on what he did and what he saw. By the time he finished, the scene's impact on the retired cop was palpable.

Garrett finished as they began their second loop around the pint-sized golf course. He said, "Hope you don't mind if we keep driving. Helps me think."

"Fine by me. It's a beautiful day."

They rode in silence for a bit, save for the occasional *hello* and *back so soon?* quips from his fellow neighbors and duffers.

Fitz said, "The case file is awfully thin, and there isn't anything in there about suspects. Were there any persons of interest developed?"

Garrett smiled. "First of all, there wasn't any such thing as a person of interest back then. You were either a suspect, or you weren't, you know. As for suspects, we never had any."

Fitz spit and said, "Maybe no one was officially named as a suspect, but surely there were ideas. Names kicked around?"

"I can't speak much about early on in the investigation because I was a patrol guy; the detectives didn't exactly share the progress of their investigation with us. Especially not an investigation that wasn't going anywhere. They wanted to be viewed on a pedestal by us patrol guys so they wouldn't dare admit they were stuck."

"So you don't recall any chatter on the case? It was a small department..."

Garrett shook his head. "Nope. Nothing." Fitz exhaled, a little frustration riding on the air. "Find you a guy from detectives back then; they'll be able to tell you a lot better than I can." He fished the pack from inside his pullover and shook it. When a cigarette didn't immediately appear, he hooked his finger around inside and pulled one out. He squinted into the packet before crumbling it in his hand and tossing it on the dash. He lit the cigarette with the Zippo, the smell of lighter fluid and freshly lit tobacco mixing in the air.

Fitz said, "You said this case stuck with you. Did you ever take a look at it? When you became a detective?"

"Sure, I pulled it out on occasion. Sometimes just to stare at it as if it were going to talk to me. Like somehow it would magically tell me who to arrest, you know." Fitz nodded. "The guys in the department would give me a hard time about it. They gave me the nickname 'Birddog Garrett' because of this case."

"Birddog?"

"Yeah. They said once I got on a trail, I didn't give up." He shrugged. "I think they meant it as a dig, but I took it with a bit of pride. That was our job, Mr. Fitzsimmons. We're not supposed to let up until the case is solved and the bad guy is in jail. Some guys just never get it."

When he got nothing further, Fitz said, "Did *you* ever develop any suspects or theories?"

"No suspects, no. Early on, I figured it was a drifter, someone passing through. Maybe a member of a construction crew working in the neighborhood. It never made any sense that one neighbor could do that to another." He drew on his cigarette, exhaled, and said, "But as time passed and I became a detective, I got a better idea of the depravity of human beings. Even back in the seventies, in this small town of ours, my eyes were opened. Suddenly, my stranger theory didn't seem so certain. Mr. Fitzsimmons, once you realize what people are truly capable of, your suspect pool for any homicide grows exponentially. You learn not to arbitrarily discount anyone. It becomes evidence over emotion. Instinct and reason become guiding factors."

Though this seemed to be a dead end regarding the Chatham case, Fitz was enjoying this conversation. The retired Mike Garrett must have been a hell of a cop, he thought.

"So, now?" Fitz asked. "Any theories now as to who or why?"

Back at the parking lot, Garrett steered the golf cart toward Fitz's car, stopping behind it. He said, "I truly believe it was someone they knew. The problem is we don't know who the target was. Was the intent to wipe out the entire family, or was the shooter after one person? We, or rather I, could never answer that question."

"What can you tell me about the investigation? Not the initial investigation, but later on when it stagnated."

"This case was bad, Mr. Fitzsimmons. It's hard to put into words just how bad and the effect it had on our quiet little community. It nearly broke Joe Wilson. When it happened, he was lieutenant over detectives, and he took it personally that someone would come into *his* community and do such evil. When he became chief, he put an initial push into the case, but nothing came of it. The outrage was gone by that point except for me and him. I have to tell you, though, I truly thought we would solve it before he retired."

He looked to Fitz and said, "The good guys are supposed to win, right? Sure, bad things happen to good people, but our job is to see to it that bad things happen to bad people. We didn't solve every case, but we damn sure solved the big ones. This is the only unsolved homicide case during my thirty-four years with the PD."

A golf cart rode by, and two men about Garrett's age yelled something at him in passing, laughing.

Garrett continued, "He and I bonded over that case. I think he saw it as an opportunity to 'make a cop outta me,' as he'd tell young police." He then did a Joe Wilson impression: "I'll make a cop outta you yet, boy." Not having known the former police chief, Fitz had no idea whether it was a good impression or not.

Garrett shrugged and said, "He saw something in me. He once told me later on, when he was chief, that he was impressed with me that God-awful night. He mentioned the composure, detail, and precision I exhibited from the time I arrived on the scene through the walkthrough we conducted. The biggest honor of my career was when he went to bat for me to replace him as police chief when he retired." He paused here, shaking his head. "Sure, I was young for a chief's position, but I was ready."

"What happened?"

"The new mayor. He wanted his imprint on the PD, so he went after someone from outside the department. He had this great idea to hire an admin from a big city department. So he went to Atlanta and hired an assistant chief who was originally from Baltimore."

"Oh, boy," said Fitz.

"Yeah, *oh boy*, is right. It was the very embodiment of a square peg in a round hole. He and the mayor lasted one term, but in those four years, the new chief screwed me good. He knew I was the choice of the outgoing chief and my fellow officers, so he chained me to a desk in charge of evidence storage and internal affairs. After four years of that crap, I was set too far back. Absolutely derailed my career."

"That's bullshit," said Fitz, and he meant it.

"Of course it was, but what could I do? I tried to get the new chief to look into the Chatham case or at least authorize resources to re-open it, but he wouldn't do it. Instead, he spouted a bunch of new-age bullshit about *moving forward and not looking back.*"

He picked up the crumpled pack of cigarettes and looked in it as if maybe he missed one, but it was still empty, and he tossed it back on the dash. Fitz offered him his chew, and Garrett grabbed a healthy pinch and put it in his mouth.

He wiped his hands on his pants and said, "I respected the guy as my chief. You know, respect the position. But after that, after he shut me down on the Chatham case, I was done with him. I decided to look into it myself; I had plenty of time on my hands."

This got Fitz's attention. "I didn't see anything in the file that looked like it was anything other than from the original investigation. You make any progress?"

Garrett made a noise. "None." Then, "Mr. Fitzsimmons, I tried. I started at the beginning, but like you said, the file is so thin. There just isn't anything there."

Fitz hooked the chew from his mouth and slung it to the blacktop.

"There's some water in the cooler on the floor behind you."

Fitz reached behind his seat, opened a small plastic red and white six-pack cooler, and removed a bottle of water. The ice had melted, but the water was still cold. He opened the bottle, swished some water in his mouth, and spit. Then he took a long drink.

After a minute, Fitz said, "Tell me about finding Kathryn Chatham."

"She was pretty shaken up, as you can imagine. She said she heard the gunshots, and when she looked out her door, she saw the gunman in the hallway." Then, seeing Fitz's expression, he shook his head and said, "She couldn't ID him. Said it was too dark. Isn't all of that in the case file?"

Fitz nodded and said, "It is, but sometimes nuance is lost when reducing something to writing." Garrett agreed. "I hoped that by talking to you, something may shake loose."

"Mr. Fitzsimmons, I'm happy to speak with you as long as you want and as often as you want, but I've been over it in my mind more times than there are stars in the sky, and I just can't make it work."

"Hmm," Fitz said, thinking. "What can you tell me about the family?"

"They were as boring as it gets. Mr. Chatham owned the local hardware store, and his wife worked at the high school as an administrator. Not exactly the type to garner a lot of enemies."

"There weren't any statements in the file other than yours and Jeff Morris'. Was Kathryn interviewed?"

"Joe tried to interview her at the scene after he finally coaxed her off the roof. But she was shaking like I'd never seen a person shake before. She didn't seem to hear a word Joe was saying, and he had her transported to the hospital, where she spent the night. I was back on patrol the next night, and my direct involvement in the case was effectively over when the scene was released around lunchtime, so if anyone ever talked to her, I don't know about it."

He spit and said, "Joe and I would chat about the case briefly when I would come in to begin my shift, and he told me he wanted to speak with her, but the brass wouldn't let him. Said she needed to heal or some such crap." He was growing angry as he recounted this. "It was poor police work not talking to her as soon as she was able to be interviewed. And since there's no statement in the file, I can only suppose that either no one got around to interviewing her or no one memorialized it in writing."

Fitz scratched his chin and said, "We got some information that a police officer was getting friendly with Kathryn before all of this happened."

The old cop whipped a look at Fitz, saying, "She was seventeen years old."

"That's just what we were told," Fitz said, spreading his arms out in a palms-up gesture. Garrett shook his head and looked back out over the golf course. "We were told it was a young guy who would eat dinner at Gilly's every night he was on duty. Said he wore a uniform and always drove up in his patrol car."

Garrett closed his eyes and raised his head skyward. "Well, it wasn't me, and I sure don't think it was Jeff Morris, especially not if it were every night. He and I would usually meet up for our dinner break, which was rarely at a restaurant since our take-home was just over a hundred bucks a month."

Fitz let out a laugh and said, "Seriously?"

"Oh, yeah. Now, Larry Butler was a rookie, same as me and Morris, and he was typically partnered on shift with Todd Sutter. Todd was a little older than us, but I could see him still being described as a young guy."

"Anyone else?"

Garrett made a noise with his mouth, thinking, then said, "If she said this officer worked at night, then it has to be one of the four of us. We were it as far as overnight patrol was concerned, and detectives didn't work nights unless they were working a specific case, and even that was somewhat rare."

Fitz tossed that around in his mind. "Tell me about that night from a police perspective. There weren't many names listed in the file, but with a case like this, there had to have been more than the half-dozen or so folks I read about."

"It was an all-hands-on-deck night. It seemed like every officer, detective, and admin was on the scene in some capacity."

"Do you recall seeing Larry Butler or..." Fitz was searching for the name.

"Todd Sutter," said Garrett.

"Yes, Sutter. You see him that night?"

Garrett considered it and said, "I don't remember seeing Sutter, but keep in mind there were uniforms all over the place. I know I didn't speak with him or interact with him that night. But Larry, yeah, he was posted at the hospital outside Kathryn's room."

That got a visible reaction out of Fitz. "Really."

"Yes," Garrett nodded, "I remember that specifically because I accompanied Joe to the hospital to try and interview her, and Larry was walking out of her room and sat down in a chair outside her door."

"Do you know why he was the one posted outside her door?"

"No idea. I assume Al Cooper made the call—he was patrol lieutenant—but I don't know."

Fitz nodded, making a mental note of the name, and thought about what additional questions to ask the retired officer. Unable to think of anything else to ask, he said, "Any advice for us on moving forward?"

Garrett considered the question and said, "Investigate who had ties to the family. This wasn't a random act. Too damn personal what that person did."

Fitz pondered that, nodded once, and stepped out of the golf cart. He grabbed his jacket from the back and laid it across his forearm.

He said, "Mr. Garrett, it's been a pleasure."

"Indeed it has, Mr. Fitzsimmons. I've thoroughly enjoyed our talk, and I pray to God you find who did this. Even if the sono-fabitch is dead, this case needs to be solved." Fitz returned a solemn nod and turned toward his vehicle.

"Oh, yeah," said Fitz, turning back, remembering a question he needed to ask. "We went through all of the physical evidence in the case, and there was a cigarette butt that was collected; looked hand-rolled. Any idea who collected it? There's no name associated with it."

"Yeah. I did."

FIFTEEN

December 10

Winston Fitzsimmons pulled to the curb in front of the police department, where Beck Lawson was talking with a defense lawyer on the sidewalk. It did not take his investigator's intuition to realize she was talking *at* the haggard attorney. When he realized who the lawyer was, he smirked.

After a couple of minutes, the conversation abated, and when the detective turned toward the Tahoe, Fitz could see the frustration imprinted on her face. She glanced back to see the lawyer slinking off, hunched over, wearing a faded black trench coat and carrying a threadbare briefcase.

The SUV's door swung open, and the detective got in, looking at Fitz, causing the investigator to chuckle.

"Damn you, Fitz."

"What?"

"You know what." Lawson gave a frustrated sigh. "That fuckin' Morrison. Jesus Christ, how did he pass the bar?"

A heartier laugh this time.

Lawson: "Which one of the brothers was that anyway? I can't keep either of those two dipshits straight."

Fitz looked over his shoulder and saw the beleaguered lawyer standing on the corner, waiting for the light to turn. "I believe that was Carl."

"Yeah, well, *Carl* is a dumbass."

Fitz put the truck into gear and, as he was pulling away from the curb, said, "He's a damn genius compared to his brother Clifford."

"God bless their poor mother."

"Rumor is that only one of them passed the bar exam, and they share a license."

Lawson shot Fitz a look and said, "You serious?"

Laughing, he said, "No, but it is funny to think about."

Lawson shook her head, not laughing. "You want to know what that idiot wanted? He's representing a guy who possessed over two hundred thousand child porn images, and he wants me to hand over a hard drive with all the images 'so he can study them for trial prep.'"

"Jesus."

"Yeah, sick bastard wants to pad his spank bank."

"Come on, man," said Fitz in disgust.

"What do you expect from someone whose car tag says *LAWYER*?"

"That old-ass briefcase he's always carrying? Barclay saw inside it once. He said it contained a hairbrush and a banana."

"Damn."

There was a beat, then they both broke into laughter.

Fitz: "Lawyers, man."

———

THEY PULLED into the parking lot of The Magnolia Pig at 2:50 in the afternoon, ten minutes before closing time.

The two investigators walked in and stood at the entrance, looking around. The place was devoid of customers save for a retired couple at a table in the back, he reading a newspaper and she reading a paperback. Three young ladies were busy in the dining area wiping down tables or otherwise getting the place ready for when they opened in the morning.

Larry Butler was heard before he was seen yelling about making sure there was enough wood in the pit to make it through the night. Fitz and Lawson had talked strategy on the way over, and it was decided that Lawson would do the questioning, the thought being that since Butler was former TPD, he may be more open to answering questions from the detective.

The youngest-looking of the three girls noticed the two of them and made her way through the dining area, and walked behind the counter. She was wearing a red t-shirt that said *The Magnolia Pig* in white writing on the front left chest and had a white artist's rendering of the restaurant on the back. Her cheeks were flushed, she was a little out of breath, and she brushed her blond bangs out of her face, wiped her hands on her jeans, and said, "Good afternoon. What would you like to order?"

"Actually, we're here to see Larry," said Lawson.

"Oh," she said, then leaned back, looked to her right, and yelled, "Larry. There's someone here to see you."

"I'm busy," came a voice from the back.

She looked at them and shrugged as if to say *sorry*.

Lawson showed her badge and said, "Tell him it's important."

Her eyes went wide, and she disappeared stage right. Conversation between the two could be heard, though no actual words could be made out, and after just over a minute, the girl reappeared.

"He said to tell you that he will be out shortly." She spoke a bit timidly and eyed them with suspicion. "Uh, y'all want anything to drink while you wait."

Fitz said, "No, thank you." Lawson ignored the question and went to find a table.

Several minutes passed, which brought more than a couple of looks in their direction by the girls closing down the dining area. The older couple was finally leaving and nodded in their direction.

They were sitting on the same side of a four-person table, and Lawson said, "I feel stupid sitting on the same side of the table as you."

"We can't sit opposite one another; otherwise, where will Larry sit? It'd be awkward questioning him sitting right beside you."

"Still. They keep looking at us."

Fitz let out a loud breath. "You afraid they'll think we're on a date or something?"

Lawson, who was looking over the dining area, gave Fitz a look. "Of course not. It's just...awkward, that's all." A pause, then: "Besides, if we *were* on a date, you can rest assured we wouldn't sit on the same side of the table together because...well, I just don't do that."

"Noted," said an exasperated Fitz. "You and your *rules*. You're as bad as Barclay, you know that?"

She was about to speak when Fitz said, "Here he comes," as he stood up to greet the restaurant owner in his familiar uniform, complete with the soggy stogie.

Fitz extended a hand and said, "I'm Winston Fitzsimmons, chief investigator with the DA's office."

"I know who you are. Both of you," said Butler, not rudely but not quite cordially either. He shook Fitz's hand, then Lawson's. He pulled a chair from the table and sat with some effort. After Fitz and Lawson sat, he removed the cigar from between his wet, tobacco-stained lips and said, "Now, what can I do for you, fellas?"

Lawson raised her eyebrows.

Butler said, "Relax, sweetheart. 'Fellas' is just a generic term I use. I don't mean nothing by it."

Lawson cleared her throat and said, "We'd like to talk to you about your time as a police officer."

This drew a look from Butler. He jammed the cigar into the corner of his mouth and said, "What for?" He was looking between the two investigators.

"We're looking into the Chatham homicide and..."

Butler's gaze shifted and, pointing the chewed end of the cigar at Fitz, said, "Your boss brought this shit up last week. He said to my face that he wasn't looking into that case. I asked him point blank, and he said no." A pause as he bounced between the two people sitting across from him before saying, "I don't like liars."

"Well, Mr. Butler," Lawson said, "investigations are fluid. I'd say that he was telling you the truth at the time." The old man was about to speak when Lawson raised a hand and said, "Even now, I wouldn't say this is an official investigation. We're just seeing what we've got."

"Bullshit," Butler said in his familiar wet rattle, causing Fitz to involuntarily and unnecessarily clear his throat, drawing a look from the man.

"This is an important case to this community," said Lawson. "You know that as well as anyone. And as you can imagine, we aren't going to jump into a case this old without first determining solvability, which means figuring out what we have to work with. The first step in that process is the witnesses. Who's still alive, who still remembers what they did in the case—"

"Anyone on the job back then remembers what they did," Butler interrupted. "If they say they don't, they're lying to you." He leaned back, seeming to relax a bit.

Lawson nodded and said, "From what I know about the case, that doesn't surprise me. Unfortunately, it looks as if most of the people involved in the actual investigation have died, so if we are going to solve this case, it may rest on some of the younger guys at the time, which poses its own problems because young officers aren't typically allowed in."

Butler coughed, pulled a handkerchief from his back pocket, and appeared to spit in it. The rattle remained as he said, "So, what have you determined about the, what did you call it? Solvability?"

"We're still working on that. But, as I said, our first step is speaking with anyone who had anything to do with the case."

Larry Butler scrutinized them and then seemed to make a decision. He sat back and said, "What do you want to know?"

"Were you working the night of the murders?" Lawson asked.

"I already told the DA I wasn't, but I got called in." He flashed a look at Fitz, then back to Lawson, and said, "Don't you people talk?"

"Did you report to the scene?"

"I did."

Lawson waited for more, but seeing there wasn't anything forthcoming, she said, "What did you see when you got there?"

Butler shifted the cigar from one corner of his mouth to the other and said, "When I got there, I was immediately put on the perimeter keeping the neighbors out of the yard, so that's what I did. Rookie grunt work."

"Did you see anyone who didn't belong?"

Butler shrugged and said, "How was I to know who didn't belong? I really wasn't paying attention to who was there. As long as no one tried to come on the property, I didn't pay anyone no attention."

"Anyone try to come on the property?" Fitz asked.

These were the first words Fitz spoke since the introduction, and Butler stared at him for a beat. "No," he said. "Everyone was well-behaved. They came out of their houses and watched what was going on. Nothing like today, of course. Someone gets killed nowadays, and it's all camera telephones and social media and all that mess." He made a derisive noise at Fitz before looking back at Lawson.

Lawson said, "Did you see anything that night? Anything at all that could be helpful?"

"No."

Again, Lawson waited for something that wasn't forthcoming. She plowed on. "Did you do anything aside from keeping the scene secure?"

Butler narrowed his eyes and looked back and forth between the investigator and the detective. There was a long silence before he said, "The chief ordered me to the hospital where Kathryn Chatham was taken. He wanted an officer stationed outside her room in case the shooter wanted to finish what he'd started. So, I went and stood guard."

"Why were you in her room?"

"Beg your pardon."

"We were told you were seen coming out of her hospital room. Why were you in her room if you were sent to stand guard?"

Butler was beginning to simmer—color creeping up his fleshy neck. "Lady, it was a long time ago. How the hell am I supposed to remember?"

"Did you know Ms. Chatham? Kathryn?" Fitz asked, which seemed to annoy Butler.

"It's a small town, Investigator."

"So that's a yes?" Lawson asked.

Butler was done with the ping-pong questioning. "Anything else? I have to go tend to the smoker."

"Just a few more questions," said Lawson. "Did you eat at Gilly's often?"

A shrug then, "Sure. Weren't a whole lot of options back then."

"How often did you eat there as a police officer?"

"I don't remember. It was a long time ago."

"Kathryn Chatham worked there. You ever talk to her when you went there?"

"I'm sure I did, Detective. Look, I've been extremely patient with your questions. Like I already told you, I didn't see anything at the scene. I wasn't involved in the investigation, and I stood outside her hospital room on orders of the chief. And, yes, I ate dinner at Gilly's from time to time, and I'm sure I spoke to Kathryn while I was there. Now, anything else?"

Lawson said, "Tell us about Todd Sutter."

"What about him?"

"Generally, what can you tell us?"

"Not for me to say. You should ask him."

"We will. Any idea how we can get in touch with him?"

"None."

"You two haven't kept in touch?"

"No. Why would we?"

"You worked the same shift, just the two of you. You backed each other up. That tends to make friends out of most cops."

"Yeah, well, I wasn't *most cops*. When I got out, I didn't look back. I've always tended to keep to myself, so I never had any real interest in keeping in touch with anyone."

"Why'd you quit the police department?" Fitz asked. You didn't need to be Sherlock Holmes to know Butler did not care to be questioned by Winston Fitzsimmons, so Fitz decided to see if he could get a rise out of the old man.

He stared at Fitz, then looked at Lawson and said, "I got bored with it. Bored with riding around a small town all night where nothing ever happened. I didn't see an opportunity for advancement anytime soon. Not with super cops Garrett and Morris on the job." He looked back at Fitz, almost daring him to ask another question. Finally, he said, "I have work to do if you'll excuse me." And he placed a hand on the table and began to stand.

"Your resignation coincided with Kathryn Chatham moving away. Was that just a coincidence?" Fitz asked as he stared, unblinking, at Larry Butler, who stopped halfway to standing.

Butler straightened and said, "You can see yourselves out." And he disappeared behind the counter.

———

"So, what did you think about that conversation?" asked Lawson as they sat in the restaurant parking lot in Fitz's Tahoe.

Fitz turned off the radio as he considered the question. Then, he turned to Lawson and said, "He didn't seem to want to discuss the case, did he?"

"No. He sure didn't." Then, "Why do you think that is?"

Fitz slowly shook his head and said, "He told us at the beginning of the interview that he remembered everything about the night of the murders but then didn't seem real keen on answering our questions in any detail."

"He sure didn't like when you asked him why he quit, and he downright hated your ass for bringing up the timing of his resigning and Kathryn Chatham leaving."

"Yeah, that was weird." Fitz was squinting through the windshield, looking at nothing, when he made a noise with his mouth and said, "He damn sure didn't want to talk about it, did he?"

"Let's head on over and see if we can speak to Al Cooper. I'd like to get there before they serve dinner, and those old folks eat awfully early."

Fitz put the SUV in gear and exited the near-empty parking lot.

SIXTEEN

Waverly Manor was a large retirement apartment community built in a Georgian style meant to appear classic and timeless. It rose three stories and was a mass of brick with black shutters and white dormers spanning the width of the edifice. A large white portico supported by doric columns marked the entrance just beyond a weathered iron fountain.

There was a lawn crew on-site when Fitz guided his vehicle into the parking lot. He saw a guy riding a red Toro stand-on lawnmower, a guy edging the grass with a string trimmer, and at least two people bent over working in the shrubs. He parked in the visitor-designated parking spot farthest from the lawn activity. He and Lawson crossed the smooth blacktop amid the sounds of the lawn equipment and the smell of fresh-cut grass; they entered the wood and glass double entry doors.

They entered a two-story foyer and stopped, looking for where to go. Inside, the walls were off-white, with blond wood floors, stair railings, and crown molding. Tasteful prints and ornate mirrors adorned the walls. There were artificial green plants by the dozens in pots on the floor, urns on the walls, and planter boxes mounted to the second-floor railings. The air was sweet and clean, like a hospital. It was almost sterile, but you could smell floor wax and lavender potpourri. Fitz spotted what he thought may be a reception desk to the right and walked over to it, looking for a way to let someone know they were there.

A telephone rang in an office behind the empty desk, and they heard a woman answer through the partially opened door. They listened to the woman terminate the phone call, and Fitz knocked on the desktop.

They heard a chair squeak in the office, and the door opened. A thin middle-aged woman with shoulder-length brown hair and translucent pink cats-eye glasses wearing a buttoned-up sky blue cardigan with the Waverly Manor logo embroidered on the left chest.

"May I help you?" she asked with a smile as she approached. She was short, maybe five foot, maybe not, and had to look up considerably when she reached the desk.

"Yes, ma'am," said Fitz. "We are here to see Al Cooper."

"Ah, yes. Mr. Cooper," she said as she brought her hands together in a silent clap. "He's one of our more...spirited residents."

Both Fitz and Lawson smiled politely. Lawson said, "We have his apartment number, but we weren't sure if we could go on back or if there were some sign-in protocol."

"Well, Mr. Cooper is in the residential wing, so you can go back the same as if you were visiting any other apartment complex." They both nodded and were about to walk away when she said, "Now, if he was on our assisted living side," she indicated a hallway to her immediate right, "then yes, you would need to check in first, but since he is on the residential side, well, you are welcome to go directly to his room."

They nodded again simultaneously and turned to go simultaneously when the lady spoke up. She said, "Mr. Cooper isn't in his room right now."

A look flashed between the investigators, and Fitz said, "He's not?" She shook her head. They waited for her to say where Mr. Cooper could be located, but she just looked at them with a smile on her face.

Finally, Lawson said, "Aaaand where can we find him?"

She looked down at the desk and crossed her arms while placing a finger to her pursed lips. "You can check the billiard room, then...if he's not there...he'll be outside, maybe at the shuffleboard court."

Another double nod, and they turned to leave when she said, "He might be walking the grounds. It is a nice day for it, you know."

This time, only Fitz nodded, and neither turned to leave. They stared at her for maybe five seconds when she said, "Definitely check the billiard room first." She leaned in conspiratorially and said, "You walk right by it on your way outside." She winked.

They neither nodded this time nor did they turn to leave. After nearly ten seconds, they chanced an exit before stopping and turning back. The lady was smiling at them and pointed. "Take the middle hallway. It will take you where you need to go."

They waited a beat before turning and hastily made their exit.

When they left the foyer's hardwood for the purple and gold carpet of the hallway, Lawson said, "She made my head hurt."

They heard the billiard room before they saw the billiard room. They stuck their head in seeing two elderly couples standing around holding pool cues and staring at the television mounted in the top corner of the room. They were watching a White House press briefing on what appeared to be Fox News based on the chyron. Al Cooper wasn't in the room, so they made their way down the hall and through the glass double-door exit.

They stepped onto a concrete walking path that curved

around a large green Sport Court in the middle of the space with several shuffleboard layouts stenciled on the artificial surface. There were two in use, and Al Cooper did not appear to be among the eight or so people out there.

Faced with two directions to walk, Fitz approached the middle of the area, which got the attention of the residents. He smiled and said, "We were told Al Cooper might be out here. I don't suppose you've seen him or know where he is?"

"You cops?" asked a sturdy retiree with a smile and a thick New York accent wearing a plaid driver's cap and a tan Members Only windbreaker.

Fitz gave a light laugh and said, "It just so happens we are."

"Heh," the man said, "I knew it! You look like a cop." He looked at his group as if they should be impressed. A petite, gray-haired lady in a purple windsuit smiled and squeezed his arm. He pointed an arthritic finger at Lawson and said, "You're too pretty to be a cop. But I knew you were a cop, still." He tapped the side of his nose with the same gnarled finger.

Purple Wind Suit slapped his arm. "Behave yourself."

"You here to arrest him?" asked a resident with a helmet of gray-pink hair, and the whole group laughed as they slowly made their way to where Fitz and Lawson were standing.

"No, nothing like that," Fitz said with a smile. "We just want to talk to him about his time as a police officer. You know, trade war stories, that type of thing."

"Oh, he's got plenty of those," the pink-haired woman said with an eye-roll.

The New Yorker said, "He was out here for a while and walked off that way," he pointed left, "maybe ten minutes ago."

"Any idea where he was going?" asked Fitz.

"There's a nice fountain, a real bubbly thing, with some benches. He likes to go there and..." He seemed to be searching for the right word and said, "Eh, relax." And everyone in the group sniggered.

As they followed the path in the direction the New Yorker directed them, Lawson commented that it looked like a fun place to retire to, and Fitz told her that's what they want you to think and that this place gave him the creeps.

Around a bend and in a copse of trees, a single man sat on a bench by a fountain. As they approached, the man cocked his head to his right and spotted them; he watched them with his dull brown red-rimmed eyes, the whites tinged yellow. He was a frail-looking man with a Hemingway quality about him, the back of his neck etched by the sun and time. He wore a deep tan with messy sun-bleached hair and white facial hair that was more than stubble but not quite a beard; his jowly face incongruous with his slight frame. He wore a red and blue flannel shirt buttoned up to the throat but loose in the collar, light blue jeans with gold thread, and white leather New Balance tennis shoes. Under his nose was a nasal cannula attached to a transparent tube, which snaked behind each ear and disappeared off to his left.

His left elbow was on the arm of the bench, and his left hand was poised in the air with a burning cigarette between his fingers, the ash being carried off on the breeze.

Lawson spoke first. She said, "You think that's a good idea—smoking around oxygen?"

The man blinked once, slowly, and said, "Who the fuck are you?" His voice was light with a hollowness to it. Fitz introduced himself and Lawson, and the man said, "Well, hell, you should've just said so."

He made to stand by putting the cigarette between his lips and using his left hand to push himself up off the bench. He bent over at the waist and seemed to lock up about halfway out of his seat. Fitz quickly stepped to him and assisted Cooper to full standing.

The man removed the cigarette with his right hand and said, "Thanks, son."

With a groan, the man then bent and reached beside the bench with his left hand and picked up an oxygen concentrator. He held it up and said, "Smoking is bad for your health." Then, as if on cue, he began coughing—not violently, but with force—and spit a yellow glob onto the sidewalk. "What can I do for you?"

Fitz threw Lawson a look. She nodded and said, "Mr. Cooper, we wanted to pick your brain about the Chatham case from back in—"

"November 23, 1963," said Cooper flatly. "What about it?"

"So you remember it," said Lawson—not a question.

Al Cooper took one last drag on the cigarette, flicked it into the fountain, and said, "There's two kinds of people who worked that case, Detective, the ones who remember it like it was yesterday and the ones who are lying." He shook his head as he looked past Lawson and Fitz. "Nobody who had anything to do with that case walked away unaffected. Nobody."

Lawson was considering where to begin when Cooper said, "Let's walk. This is a non-smoking campus, and when I'm gone too long, the Nazis here send someone looking for me to try and catch me smoking...sonsabitches." He slung the oxygen concentrator's nylon strap over his shoulder as he turned and began shuffling down the path away from the building so he didn't see the look exchanged between Lawson and Fitz before they fell in step behind him.

"You finally gonna catch the sonofabitch who did that?" Cooper asked without looking back.

Lawson caught up to him in three strides and walked alongside. She said, "We're looking into it. Obviously, there are challenges with a case this old, but—"

"Ah, horseshit. You're cops. Just solve the damn thing." He walked with a slight stoop and a shuffle but did not appear at all frail.

"As I said, Mr. Cooper, that's why we're here."

"How can I help?" he asked in a conciliatory tone.

"I'm not exactly sure just yet. We are reaching out to anyone who is still around from back then and seeing what it is they know, and then we will be able to determine what is and isn't helpful to solving the case."

Cooper nodded as he reached into his shirt pocket and pulled out a Marlboro red hardpack. He pulled a cigarette out and offered the pack to Lawson without looking at her. Lawson said, "No, thank you," and Cooper returned the box to his shirt pocket. He lit the cigarette with a cheap gas station lighter.

They walked for almost a minute, with the only sounds being the shuffling of Al Cooper's shoes along the sidewalk and the occasional burst of laughter in the distance.

Finally, Lawson said, "You were the lieutenant in charge of the patrol division?"

Cooper nodded and said, "That's right."

"So, being admin, I assume you were eight to five?" Cooper nodded *yes*. "And from folks we've already spoken to, everyone was called out to the scene, is that correct?" Another nod. "What time did you get there?"

"I don't know that because I didn't note it at the time. I got a phone call from dispatch that told me to report to the address she gave me, so when I left the house to head that way, I had no idea what had happened or what I was getting ready to see. The time of my arrival wasn't an important detail at the time, you see."

It was Lawson's turn to nod. "That makes sense." As they continued to walk, the path took them through a dogwood-lined area with benches set every so often, and Lawson considered how big this campus actually was—it felt as if they were miles outside the city.

"Tell me about the patrol guys you supervised," said Lawson.

"That's a broad question, Detective. What specifically do you want to know?"

"Were there any...problem guys?"

That stopped Cooper. He turned and looked at the detective. "What the hell kind of question is that? What does...wait, do you think one of my guys did this?"

"We're looking at everything right now—"

"Oh, don't give me that crap," Cooper said with a dismissive swat of his hand.

"Can we have a seat and talk through this?"

Cooper seemed to consider the request. He nodded once, dropped the cigarette on the ground, and stepped on it; they walked in silence until the next set of benches. He took the one on the left, and Lawson and Fitz took the one on the right side of the walkway directly across from Cooper.

Lawson leaned forward, elbows on knees, and said, "What we have is thin right now, so we are looking into absolutely anything that could be a thread to pull."

"Pull on enough threads or pull the right thread..."

"The mystery unravels," said Lawson nodding.

"So, how do my guys fit in?"

"We have information that a young officer was spending a lot of time where Kathryn Chatham worked."

"That burger place, Gilly's?"

"Right. We don't have a name or description other than 'young police officer who ate at Gilly's practically every night,' but the impression I got was that he was on shift, which leaves us with four possibilities as best as I can figure."

Al Cooper's dull eyes were now sharp and focused as he discussed the old case—a kind of old lawman's fountain of youth.

He licked his lips and said, "Garrett, Morris, Butler, and Sutter."

"Impressive," said Fitz, picking his spot to enter the questioning.

"I could still do your job, Investigator," said Copper with a laugh that erupted into a cough. He spit another glob and said, "Growing old is a bitch."

"My father always said, 'Life's a bitch, and then you live.'"

"Your father was on to something," Cooper said.

"So," Lawson said, "any thoughts?"

"Yeah, Butler."

"Just like that?"

"Just like that," said Cooper with a single nod.

"Why Butler?" Fitz asked.

"Because Mutt and Jeff were always up each other's ass, so if it was a lone cop, it wasn't either of them."

Lawson said, "Mutt and Jeff?"

"Sorry, Garrett and Morris. Anyway, Sutter was too much of a pussy to chat up a girl like that. So, yeah, Butler."

"Tell us about him."

Cooper fired up another smoke and thought about it. Then, finally, he sniffed and said, "Solid officer, but I don't know; there was always something about him. Nothing bad, mind you. Nothing that was a cause for alarm. It was just...something."

"Can you help us understand that?" asked Fitz.

Cooper considered the question. "The first thing I noticed about him was his maturity." Seeing the look on the faces of both Fitz and Lawson, he said, "Yeah, yeah, I know, I know. It's just that we get these kids young and usually all goofy-eyed, but not him. Even Mike Garrett, who was exactly what you look for in a recruit and mature for his age, was nothing compared to Larry Butler." He paused to think, taking a drag to fill his lungs. "It was as if Larry had lived a lifetime before he got here. Guys like Garrett are eager and fast learners, but there are still things they don't know, and they don't know that they don't know. Larry was a guy that just seemed to know it. Or at least made you think he did.

"Garrett was a great student and squared away, but he still made rookie mistakes—usually a result of being overeager. Butler, on the other hand, was a decent student, not particularly squared away, but he's the guy you wanted by your side if a situation went bad. I never saw the guy get flustered."

"Did he play well with others?"

"No. Not at all," said Cooper with a quick laugh that ended in a cough and a spit. Then he thought about his statement and said, "Let me clarify. He just wasn't interested in the camaraderie of the job. He preferred to come to work, do his job, and go home." He rubbed his hand across his face before continuing. "There used to be a bar downtown called Cowboys, where we all went to drink." He shook his head. "I don't ever recall seeing him there. Other than that," he said with a shrug, "I never received a single complaint about how he did his job, not from inside the department or from the public."

"So," Fitz said, "good cop, but not exactly Officer Friendly."

Cooper pointed at Fitz with the two fingers holding the burning cigarette and said, "That's it."

Lawson said, "That night, Butler ended up at the hospital standing watch outside Kathryn's room. Any idea why the chief chose *him* to go the hospital?"

Cooper was mid-inhale when the question was asked. He shot Lawson a look and said, "The chief didn't send him there; he asked to go."

Fitz sharpened his gaze and said, "You're sure about that."

"One hundred percent."

Lawson gave some thought as to how to ask the follow-up question. She said, "We were told it was the chief's call."

"Who the hell told you that? They're wrong."

"How can you be certain the chief didn't send him?"

Cooper shook his head as he dropped his butt on the ground. He did not bother stepping on it, so it sat smoldering in the grass. He said, "First of all, the chief did not get involved in those decisions, especially not in the middle of that investigation. He had his hands more than full and was not making any personnel assignments outside of the detective bureau. Secondly, I remember Butler bringing it up. Initially, he was assigned to keep people out of the scene who shouldn't be there. At some point, after the ambulance left to take Kathryn Chatham to the hospital, he mentioned it would be a good idea to send an officer in case she was the target.

"The shooter was still at large, so, honestly, it was a good idea. I told him to give me a minute because I was organizing a grid search of the area when he said he would handle it. By the time I looked back to tell him to hold on, he was gone. I saw him walking off at a pretty good clip, so I went back to coordinating the search."

"I'll go ahead and ask, Mr. Cooper, do you believe Larry Butler would be capable of this?" asked Lawson.

Cooper contemplated the question for near on a minute. Then, he fixed Lawson with his cop eyes and said, "Detective, I've seen just about everything from all kinds, and I believe any person is capable of killing given the right circumstances. But this?" He began shaking his head and said, "I'm sitting here asking myself just how well I knew Larry—how well any of us knew him—and I realize that none of us really knew anything at all about him. Not his hometown, not his family...in fact, I'd say we didn't know anything about the man prior to him becoming a police officer."

"Is that unusual?" asked Fitz.

"It is, yes. It's the nature of the profession—you tend to know about the folks watching your back."

"How about when he left the police department?" Lawson asked. "Do you remember anything about that?"

"I remember him telling me he was leaving. He said he wanted a change."

"Did that decision seem odd to you at all?"

"This job isn't for everyone. You know that. I recall being a little disappointed because, like I said, he was a good cop."

"Anything else you remember about him leaving?" Cooper thought about it and shook his head *no*.

Cooper looked upon each investigator and readied for the next question, but when it didn't come, he said, "Anything else?"

Lawson looked at Fitz, who shook his head.

"I think that'll do it for now. We sure do appreciate your time."

Cooper began to stand and, following his lead, so did Lawson and Fitz, with Fitz easing toward the old man with a hand partially extended in an offer of assistance that he ultimately didn't need.

Cooper picked up his oxygen concentrator and took a couple of shuffle steps before getting his feet under him and gaining his stride. He said, "I've enjoyed our talk...and God bless you for trying to solve this case and find this monster. I only hope I live to see you put the cuffs on someone for this."

He began to cough.

SEVENTEEN

December 11

Barclay Griffith entered the conference room where Fitz and AJ Murphy were making small talk and drinking coffee. The citrus smell from the plug-in deodorizer was competing with the smell of the coffee and losing. The two men were seated at the far end of the table, with Fitz taking the end seat with Murphy immediately to his left. Someone said something funny because both men laughed.

Barclay said, "Where's Lawson?"

Fitz said, "She got assigned a big case this morning, so she won't be here."

"Something I should know about?" asked Barclay.

"Oh no, nothing like that. It's a dognapping."

This got a reaction from both Murphy and Barclay as they both said, "What?" at almost the same time.

Fitz nodded and said, "You heard me. Apparently, some local big shot called the police chief this morning about their missing beagle Rambo. The owner threw the mayor's name around and talked about how he was a donor. You know the drill. Well, Lawson got up to leave for our meeting this morning, and that was enough to catch the chief's eye, so she got the case."

"Poor bastard," said Murphy. Then the three of them cracked up.

Murphy stood and grabbed the coffee pot, refilling his and Fitz's cup. He offered it to Barclay, who was holding a coffee cup. He held up a hand and said, "No thanks. It'll mess up my ratios."

"What?" said Murphy as he pulled the pot back.

"Don't ask," Fitz deadpanned.

"I have something to show you. Come with me."

The investigators followed Barclay out of the conference room and through the maze of cubicles and hallways. They passed through the grand jury room, down a short hallway, and stepped through a door Barclay held open.

"What do you think?" Barclay asked proudly.

Murphy and Fitz took in the room with large whiteboards on three walls, two long tables pushed together, and a dozen or so chairs. A large flatscreen television was mounted on the fourth wall, with file cabinets on the floor beneath it. There was a large bowl of candy in the middle of the tables.

Murphy said, "Uh, well, it's nice...what is it?"

"It's our new cold case war room. The door locks, and we will be the only ones with a key. The file cabinets also lock so we can keep all of our work in here. We can put up photographs, write out timelines, whatever. We have the space to dive in and get to work."

"And candy," Murphy said, almost childlike.

"And candy," said Barclay.

"In all my time here, I've never been in this room. Has it always looked like this?" Fitz asked.

"No. It was originally used as a waiting room for grand jury witnesses but hasn't been used in years. Instead, it's been a depository for old office furniture. I cleaned it out, then came in last night and hung the whiteboards and television myself. Not too bad, huh?"

"This is fantastic," said Murphy. "A dedicated room to work these cases is just what we need."

Barclay motioned for them to have a seat. "I'm glad you approve. This case will be critical to establishing a cold case unit in this office moving forward. If we screw this up in any way, I'm not sure other agencies will trust us to work their cases."

Murphy nodded his agreement. "The PD may not realize it right now, but this could be a very big deal. Like I told you before, there's no point in beginning an investigation if the DA isn't all in, so creating a unit yourself speaks volumes about your commitment. It'll mean a lot to law enforcement, I assure you."

To Murphy, Barclay said, "Well, I know you have places to be, and I'm eager for an update, so why don't we jump right in? Since Lawson isn't here, I assume Fitz can fill us in on anything she would have told us?" Barclay gave Fitz a questioning look that was returned with a nod.

Fitz gave a quick run-through of what they found in the evidence room, and they bandied back and forth about what each piece of evidence meant and its significance.

The veteran investigator didn't touch his pen or open his notebook. He knew the value of listening and taking notes risked missing something of potential importance—that nugget of information that could mean the difference in solving a case or letting the bad guy get away. He'd developed a keen memory over the years and would put pen to paper when the meeting was over.

The evidence discussion didn't take long, and the narrative turned to witnesses.

Fitz recapped his meeting with Sylvia Burrows, and when he had finished, Murphy said, "So Kathryn Chatham has an argument with a guy, maybe a cop, and shortly after that, her family is wiped out."

"Pretty much," said Fitz.

AJ chewed on that for a minute before saying, "Mind if I write this out up there?" He motioned to one of the whiteboards.

"Go for it. That's why they're here," said Barclay.

The investigator walked to the board, wrote *Sylvia Burrows* with a blue dry-erase marker, and underlined her name. Below that, he wrote: *Best friends with Kathryn Chatham, Regular male customer (Cop?), KC rejected customer's advances, argument, shooting within a few days of argument.*

"That about sum up what she has to offer at this point?" Murphy asked Fitz.

Fitz nodded and said, "That's about it."

"Ok. We'll do this for all of our witnesses, which will allow us to view everything collectively, see how any of it fits, and figure out what we need to ask or what we need to look for to start linking everything together." Murphy snapped the cap back onto the marker, pointed toward the table, and said, "That's how we're going to solve this case."

Barclay tilted his chair back and asked Fitz, "Who else have you talked to?"

"Lawson and I paid Larry Butler a visit."

"How'd that go?" Barclay asked.

"He kicked us out."

Murphy's eyebrows went up, and he approached the white-board. As with Sylvia Burrows, he wrote Butler's name and under-lined it. Underneath the name, he made notes about the meeting at the restaurant.

Barclay said, "Let's go ahead and get everything else out before we discuss what all of this means."

Fitz said, "I met with Mike Garrett. He retired as assistant police chief but was a rookie on patrol the night of the murders; he was first on the scene. He took me through that night." Then, after filling them in on the details, he said, "And he's the one who collected the cigarette butt."

Barclay rocked forward in his chair and said, "No shit."

"No shit," said Fitz with his thousand-watt smile.

"Did he say why he collected it?" asked Murphy. "Seems like an odd thing to collect for 1963."

"He said the fact that it was right outside the rear patio doors where they believe the shooter made entry into the house caught his attention, and when he picked it up, the fact that it was hand-rolled seemed significant."

Murphy stepped to the candy bowl and popped a mini Mr. Goodbar into his mouth, then said, "Why did he believe that was significant?"

"He said his grandfather was the only person he knew who still rolled his own smokes, so he felt that maybe it was unusual enough to be identifying should they develop a suspect."

"Smart guy," said Murphy, who then wrote *Mike Garrett* on the board and underlined it in the same blue marker. Underneath his name, he wrote: *Patrolman, first on scene, first through the house, collected cigarette butt.*

"Anything else?" Murphy asked, looking back to the table.

Barclay said, "Put up there *paints picture*. If this thing goes to trial, we will need someone to set the scene and put the jury right in the middle of that house. Sounds like Garrett is just the guy to do that."

Murphy added that to the board and asked again if there was anything else to add. He reiterated this was just preliminary and that they would almost definitely add more as more information came out.

He capped the marker, sat back at the table, and said, "Who else have you spoken to?"

Fitz said, "Lawson and I spoke with Al Cooper. He was the

lieutenant over patrol back in sixty-three and has the memory of an elephant."

"Anything good from him?" Barclay asked.

"He's convinced Butler is the Gilly's frequent eater." Fitz then explained why.

"Did he have any thoughts on Butler as a cop?"

"He sure did. Said Butler was good police but kept to himself. Didn't seem to have any friends within the department. Just came to work, did his job, and went home."

Murphy: "Did Cooper give you anything as a fact witness?"

Fitz shook his head and said, "No. He led the grid search of the area that turned up the duffel bag containing the rope, but that was it. Other than that, he said it was pretty chaotic out there." Fitz pointed at Barclay and said, "He did make a point to tell me that if anyone tells us they don't remember much about that night, they're full of shit. Said everyone had memory burn from that night. Everyone."

"That's good to know going forward," said Barclay. "He have any thoughts on Butler being the shooter?"

"Only that anything is possible and that no one really knew Butler on a personal level."

"What were his thoughts on him quitting the force?"

"He said that all Butler told him was that he needed a change, nothing more than that. Cooper said he just chalked it up to not everyone being cut out for the job."

Murphy stood and walked to the whiteboard, and, like the last three witnesses, he wrote the witness's name and underlined it. Underneath the name, he wrote: *Lt. over patrol, likes Butler as restaurant customer, Butler was a loner on the job, Butler was a good LEO.*

Murphy looked back and asked if there was anything else to add, and Fitz snapped his fingers. "Butler told us he stood guard outside Kathryn's room that night because the chief sent him, but

Al Cooper said Butler volunteered—he was very clear about it. Said no way the chief would have made that call."

Murphy made a face that said this was something and turned to the board and wrote under Butler's name: *Lied about why HE stood guard at hospital.*

Barclay was about to speak when Fitz's phone rang. He looked at the caller ID and said, "Lawson." Then, into the phone, "You found Rambo yet?"

Neither Barclay nor Murphy could hear the detective's words, but what they could hear didn't sound as if she shared their good humor about the situation.

Fitz went from laughing to raised eyebrows. He said, "Really? What time?" Then, "I'm on the way." He ended the call and said, "Sylvia Burrows showed up at the PD asking for Lawson. She said she remembered something she thought we should know. Lawson's holding off on the interview until I get there. I hate to break this up, but..."

"Go," said Barclay.

Fitz nodded once and was out the door.

EIGHTEEN

E ight minutes after hanging up the phone with Lawson, Fitz was pulling into the parking lot of the PD. He crossed the parking lot and used his key fob to access the employee entrance to the Gillespie building. He took the rear stairs—his stride swallowing up two steps at a time—to the detective bay on the second floor, where he entered through the rear entrance.

Though the room had recently been renovated to remove asbestos, moldy floor and ceiling tiles, and old, battered desks and furniture, it was still very much a no-frills room. The room smelled of old paper and burned microwave popcorn. Twelve metal desks lined the walls, and all were empty save for two. On a bank of filing cabinets sat an old clock radio providing background music. The faux wooden rectangle flashed 12:00 in green digital numbers and was rumored to have been put in place circa 1992 when it was tuned to the local classic rock station; it had not been changed or turned off since. Currently, the tinny sound leaking from the speaker was The Allman Brothers riffing and singing about a black-hearted woman being cheap trouble.

In addition to the music, other sounds in the room included an oscillating fan and the arrhythmic sound of a detective hunting and pecking—pounding, really—with his sausage fingers on a plastic computer keyboard. The only other person in the room was another detective on the telephone—presumably on hold because he neither spoke nor appeared to be listening to anything important. He acknowledged Fitz with a lazy two-fingered salute.

"Where is everyone?" Fitz asked the room.

The detective on the computer stopped typing and eyed the investigator over his computer monitor. He said, "Hey, Fitz. Lawson wants you to meet her in the old conference room."

"Thanks, Billy." Fitz walked through the room between the rows of metal desks toward the front of the room. As he passed the radio perched on a beige metal filing cabinet, he cranked the volume up and was out the door. He heard someone yell, "Asshole," from inside. He smiled to himself and wound his way through the corridors until he found the conference room.

Fitz peered into the room through the narrow glass insert and saw Lawson seated at the head of the table with Sylvia Burrows sitting to her right; he knocked on the door as he opened it. This room was a well-appointed miniature version of the main conference room. It was used for victims or witnesses the police did not want to subject to the bleak confines of the utilitarian concrete interview rooms whose dreary atmosphere of depravity and malevolence hung as heavy as an anvil.

Detective Beck Lawson looked to her left at the intrusion, and the familiar cotton candy hair of Mrs. Burrows also swung in Fitz's direction.

"Mrs. Burrows, you remember Investigator Fitzsimmons from the other day."

"Why certainly I do," she said in her perfect Southern diction. "How do you do, Investigator?" The word *investigator* came out as investigatuh.

"I do quite well, Mrs. Burrows," said Fitz with a slight tilt of his head.

"Alright, Mrs. Burrows," Lawson said, "now that Investigator Fitzsimmons is here, why don't you tell us why you stopped by."

"Well, Detective—," said it as deetective, "—I've been thinking about our chat the other day. You know, when you two came to my house?" Both nodded. "Well, I don't know if it's anything important, but..." She glanced around the room as if to make sure no one was eavesdropping. "Did you know Kathryn was seeing Arnie Gillespie when she moved away?"

Silence. Sylvia leaned back with a *How about that?* look. Fitz and Lawson exchanged glances.

Finally, it was Fitz who spoke. He said, "You mean Senator Arnold Gillespie?"

"One and the same. And"—she leaned in conspiratorially— "he was married."

It was Lawson's turn to speak. "Wait, what?"

Fitz looked to Lawson, then to Sylvia, and said, "Why didn't you tell us this when we spoke to you the first time?"

"Because all you asked me about was the time around the murders."

"Well, that's true, I guess," said Lawson.

Fitz said, "How do you know this?"

"We were friends, Mr. Fitzsimmons."

"Of course," Lawson deadpanned before leaning her chair back on two legs.

After thinking about it, Fitz said, "Let's talk about when Kathryn left Towne."

"Alright," said Sylvia.

"Was that expected or unexpected?"

"It was definitely out of the blue. I had no idea she was planning on leaving."

"So her moving away was never discussed? Getting a job, anything like that?"

She shook her head. "Never."

"Had you graduated from college at that point?"

"Oh yes. We both graduated from Auburn in the spring of sixty-eight and moved back to Towne. I moved in with her. Into her family's house. She couldn't bear the thought of staying in that place by herself."

Lawson rocked forward and said, "Why didn't she sell it?"

"Officer, would *you* want to buy the infamous Chatham murder house?"

"Good point," she said and rocked back.

"So you and she would have graduated in May of sixty-eight, and she left in October, five months later," said Fitz more to say it aloud and roll it around than to get an actual answer. Then: "And the subject of her moving away never came up?"

"It did not."

"Tell us about the weekend she left."

"Well," she said, thinking. She nodded as a memory clicked into place and said, "My friends and I went to the Auburn-Clemson football game in South Carolina. We left Friday morning and got home Sunday after lunch some time. When I got home, I noticed something seemed a little off. It was far too quiet."

"And that was unusual?" said Fitz.

"It wasn't unusual that it was quiet while she was home by herself, but it was more than that. Like I immediately knew the house was empty, which *was* unusual."

"How so?"

"She had taken a job as an accountant with a real estate company. She worked in the property management section, and they had properties all over the southeast; she was all the time working. Even on the weekends." She thought some more and said, "I always thought it was because it kept her mind off what

happened to her family. I practically begged her to go to the ballgame with us that weekend. Even had her a free ticket, but she
wouldn't go."

"Did she say why?"

"She said she was tired and had work to do, which didn't make
much sense to me, but that was her after moving back from
school, poor girl."

Lawson said, "Anything stand out in your mind about the
weekend?"

A big smile crossed her face, and she said, "Auburn won
twenty-one to ten."

The detective's face went flat, and she said, "Anything else?"

Her smile grew, and she said, "After the game, we packed that
ol' Esso Club full of Auburn folks and ran those fake Tigers right
out of there. We closed that sucker down that night." She let out a
cackle of laughter.

Fitz said, "How about anything involving Ms. Chatham?"

"No. As I said, I left on Friday, and she was home. I came back
on Sunday, and she was gone."

"What did you do when she didn't come home that night?"

"Most of her clothes were gone, along with her suitcase and
makeup, so I figured she had decided to take a trip somewhere. I
was happy for her. She needed to get away."

"At what point did you begin to realize she wasn't coming
back?"

"I don't know. It wasn't anything sudden-like. A week passed,
then two, then all of a sudden, it'd been a month, and I guess I just
figured...you know."

"What?"

A shrug. "That she'd gone. Left. Moved on."

Lawson rocked back forward and said, "That didn't alarm you
at all?"

"Not really. I mean, she had been through so much. I just

figured she was trying for a fresh start somewhere far from Towne and the memories of her family." Seeing the look on their faces, she said, "You have to understand, it was a different time. There were no cell phones, no way of keeping up with anyone who didn't want to be kept up with. It was easy to leave and never be found. Just leave everything behind and start a new life. She was always going to be 'Poor Kathryn Chatham' around here. I didn't blame her for leaving."

Fitz said, "But to leave her house? Why didn't she at least try to sell it? She could have gotten something."

"How should I know? Her father had life insurance, so she wasn't hurting for money. The house was paid for. Maybe she just wanted to go and never look back."

"Let's say a month passes, and you believe she's gone for good. What did you do? Did you stay in the house?"

She put a hand to her chest and said, "Heavens, no. I eventually moved back in with my parents next door. Not long after, I met my husband—y'all met Tommy—and we got married and got a house together."

Fitz stood and walked to the window, peering out. He finally said, "What more can you tell us about the senator and Ms. Chatham?"

"She worked at his daddy's restaurant all through high school and during summers home from college, so I guess that's how they met. I don't think they dated or anything until after she graduated and moved back home from school. I don't know why she got involved with him."

"Why do you say that?"

"Well, she wasn't the same fun-loving girl she was before her family was killed, and she always seemed distracted. As for him, well, he was a jerk—all because of who his family was. Like because his daddy sold hamburgers and got elected to some position, it made Arnie something special. Not to mention he was *married*. I never did like the guy, and, to be honest, I was a little disappointed in her for seeing him—I warned her it wasn't going to end well. He had his career mapped out and the wife to match. No way were he and Kathryn going to wind up together."

"Did you ever speak with him about her?"

"Not directly, no. But this one time, they had a big fight, and I made him leave the house. He was something else, let me tell you."

"What was the fight about?" Fitz asked.

"She didn't say. He had taken her to Atlanta for a nice dinner, and they fought the entire way home. And it was all yelling and doors slamming when they got to the house. She was crying in her room with the door closed, and he was yelling at her to open the door." Sylvia was getting visibly angry at the retelling of this story. "I finally went upstairs and told him to leave. I told him that she had been through enough misery in this house, and he wasn't going to yell at her and bang on her door in her own home. I told him that he and his burger flippin' family could go to hell before I'd let him upset my friend, and if he didn't want his wife to get a phone call, he ought to leave."

Lawson crashed the chair down on all fours. "You said that to him?"

"Damn right."

"Oh, man," said Fitz.

"Yeah. He hates me, by the way," she said with a tug of a grin.

"That's awesome," said Lawson.

Sylvia gave her a wink.

Fitz sat back in his chair and said, "When was this big blow-up?"

She thought about it and went visibly pale, so much so that even her heavy blush seemed to lighten a shade. "The weekend before."

Fitz narrowed his gaze and said, "How can you be certain of that?"

"Because It was the last time I saw him at the house. I was supposed to be in Lexington for the Auburn, Kentucky game that weekend, but I got sick and gave my ticket away. I remember being angry because I woke up that Saturday morning feeling fine as frog hair and wishing I'd have just sucked it up and gone to the game. We won twenty-six to seven, which made me even madder that I didn't go. Mix in a few Kentucky bourbons to celebrate, and I was in just the right mood to tell that sonofabitch what I thought of him."

Fitz laughed, saying, "Sounds like you mark time with Auburn football."

"Wasn't much to do in these parts back then except cheer for Auburn and hate Alabama."

"Alright, so they showed up from dinner, you kicked him out, and he left. He say anything to you?"

"I don't recall anything specific other than that he left, and I never saw him with her again."

"Do you know if she saw him?"

"I don't." She took on a look of concentration, so Fitz waited her out. She finally said, "I don't recall her going out at all the following week, which wasn't unusual—she rarely went out on a weeknight. I left Friday morning for South Carolina, so I don't know about anything that happened between the time I left and when I got home."

"Did you ever hear anything from her after that weekend? A phone call, a letter, a postcard?"

"No. Nothing," she said as if considering that for the first time.

After a long moment, Lawson said easily, "I don't mean to jump around, but how did your father buy her family's house if she moved away and couldn't authorize the sale? Who got the proceeds?"

"It's a small town, Detective. No one had seen hide nor hair of her for a few years, so the assumption was she was never coming back. My father talked to a lawyer friend, and they spoke with a judge friend and got it done. He bought the house and put the money into a trust in Kathryn's name. It's probably still there."

"Anything else you can think of to tell us, Mrs. Burrows?" said Fitz.

She considered the question and said, "No, I think that's about it. Does this help at all?" There was a note of pleading in her voice.

"I honestly don't know. Detective Lawson and I will discuss what you've told us and see what we can make of it. Maybe something fits, maybe not. Right now, we're looking for any nugget of information that could lead to something else. We're very grateful for you coming in today, and please let us know if you think of anything else."

Lawson stood and said, "Here, I'll walk you out."

Sylvia stood as well as Fitz, and they said their goodbyes. As Lawson and Sylvia made their way down the hall to the elevators, Sylvia eyed the department composites on the wall.

"Is every year commemorated on your walls, Detective?"

"Every two years, I believe," said Lawson. "To be honest, I've never paid too much attention."

The most recent composite was the one on the wall nearest the conference room they had been in, and they counted down on both sides of the hallway as they made their way to the elevators.

Sylvia commented on how much the size of the department had grown as the numbers noticeably shrank the further back in time they went. She also commented jokingly on the different hairstyles and other visual cues of the changing times.

"Oh look, 1968," she said as she stopped and ran her gaze across the framed group of officer photos. "I think I told you I dated a police officer in the summer of sixty-seven. Let me see here...ah yes, there he is. Jack Trace. Isn't he so handsome?" She gave Lawson a playful look.

"Yes, he's delightful," Lawson gave back.

"That was quite a fun summer," she said wistfully. Lawson felt her face warm.

Sylvia was turning away when she stopped. She said, "Now I saw Kathryn talking to this man one night at Gilly's. It was during our senior year of high school, I think. I had gone to pick her up when her shift ended, and I sat in the car and waited for what had to be almost half an hour as she spoke to a police officer. I was worried at first, you know, her speaking to a policeman, but then I saw her laugh, and they looked quite friendly if you know what I mean." She threw that mischievous grin back at Lawson, who did not return it because she didn't see it.

She was busy staring at the officer Sylvia Burrows was pointing to. According to the name underneath the thumb-sized photo, she had just identified Larry Butler.

NINETEEN

Lawson walked back into the conference room and saw Fitz standing at the window, phone pressed to his ear.

Fitz saw Lawson in his periphery and turned to see her full-on. He said into the phone, "Hey, I have to go. Yeah, I'll call you later." He slid the phone into his jacket pocket and said, "Why do you have that look on your face?"

"Because I love Mrs. Burrows."

"Alright, now you're starting to scare me. How long has it been since you've been out on a date?"

"I have no idea, but that's not what I mean. I was walking her out, and as we walked down the hallway to the elevator, she noticed the department composites. Then, just as we get to the elevator, she stops at the 1968 group of photos to look for the cop she dated one summer—guy named Jack Trace."

Fitz squinted in thought before shaking his head.

"I don't know him, either," said Lawson. "But that's not the point. She also noticed an officer she had seen Kathryn hanging out with at Gilly's—the one she was friendly with."

Fitz's eyebrows went up, and then he smiled. "Let me guess. Our friend Larry Butler."

———

FITZ WAS DRIVING, and Lawson was in the passenger seat. Lawson told Fitz about the circumstances under which Sylvia said she saw Butler and Kathryn together. She was the first person to put Butler with Kathryn, and it jibed with anecdotal evidence given to them by Mike Garrett and Al Cooper.

They both agreed that the identification in and of itself wasn't dispositive of anything; however, it was something. It was momentum, and they would use it.

The new and potentially more significant item in play now was the revelation that Kathryn had been seeing Senator Arnold Gillespie around the time she moved away and was even seen in a fight with him the week prior. Unfortunately, neither investigator could figure out how, if at all, this piece of information fit into the case.

"On one hand, it was almost five years after the murder," said Lawson.

"Yeah, but on the other hand, it was within a week of her never being seen in Towne again."

It was when Fitz made that last statement that it clicked for both of them. No one, at least not them, had ever thought of it that way until now. It was always discussed as her "moving away" as if that were established as fact when it was not. It had been accepted in Towne that she moved away, but there had been zero evidence, at least none that the current investigation had found, that proved she moved anywhere.

Lawson said, "I've been going over everything that Sylvia Burrows has told us, particularly about when Kathryn left, and it doesn't make any sense." She turned to Fitz, who was watching the road, and said, "Does it to you?"

Fitz shook his head. "Not at all. I agree that you could easily get lost back then, but why would you want to? Why would *she* want to? I understand her wanting to move away, but cut off your best friend? I don't see it."

———

AT FITZ'S SUGGESTION, they were en route to speak with Walter Jackson to see what he could offer now that they had a tighter timeline on when Kathryn was last seen in Towne.

Fitz called Barclay and gave him a brief overview of the meeting with Sylvia Burrows. He told the DA about Kathryn's relationship with the former senator as well as the ID of Larry Butler as having been seen with Kathryn at Gilly's. He told Barclay they wanted to speak with Walter Jackson again, but he didn't have a number for him. Barclay agreed to contact Walter's son, Luke, to get a phone number.

Barclay texted the number to Fitz, who then called the Chatham's former neighbor, who happened to be at the house on Woods Way.

When Fitz and Lawson arrived at the house, a landscaping truck was parked on the street with bales of pine straw stacked on the flatbed. They marked this as the same crew seen working outside of Waverly Manor the day before. Several men were hard at work tossing pine straw into flower beds. One guy was working a gas-powered backpack leaf blower, returning stray dirt and straw from the grass to the flower beds.

The smell of gasoline and topsoil infused the air.

They mounted the stairs, and the door opened as Fitz was about to knock. Walter Jackson invited them in, and the high-pitched whine of the small gasoline engine was dulled behind the closed door.

"Can I get you two anything to drink? The place is still a bit barren, but I have water and beer in the cooler."

"Water would be nice, actually," said Fitz, and Walter got them each a bottle. The paint smell had scarcely faded since Fitz's first visit two weeks prior, but the smell of polyurethane on the hardwood floors was new.

"I'm just here to check on the landscape work, so it was fortuitous that you caught me out of the bank." Their voices bounced off the empty, hard interior surfaces.

"Completely understand, Mr. Jackson, and we won't be long." Fitz drank from the bottle. He introduced Beck Lawson, then said, "We're working together on this case."

"Detective," Walter said, offering a hand.

"Nice to meet you, sir."

"If I remember right," said Fitz, "you and your son were still deciding what to do with this place."

"Oh yes. Still not a hundred percent sure, but Luke is leaning toward moving in." He looked around. "It is a nice space, isn't it? Turned out better than we conceived."

Lawson took in the space and said, "It's very nice."

"Now, you two officers didn't come here to indulge me in real estate, so what can I do for you?"

Fitz said, "We wanted to talk more about the Chatham case."

"However I can help."

"More to the point, we want to discuss October of 1968, specifically the weekend of October twelfth."

Walter's eyes grew big. "As I said, Investigator—it is investigator, correct?" Fitz nodded. "As I said, I am happy to help however I can, but wow. Nineteen sixty-eight? I would've been, oh, thirteen in October of that year, so I'm not sure what I will remember."

"We understand, but we need to follow up on it. If you can't remember, then that's just what we've got."

Walter Jackson nodded with a sincere expression.

"If it helps, it was the weekend of the Auburn-Clemson game."

Walter laughed and said, "I guess you've been talking to Sylvia." That made the two investigators smile. "I assure you I, too, love my alma mater, but my memory isn't quite as tied to those ballgames like my sister's. She's something else."

"Yes, she is," Lawson said.

Fitz said, "Sylvia told us she went to the ballgame in South Carolina that weekend. She said Kathryn was at the house when she left on Friday, but when she returned from the trip, Kathryn was gone. That's the last sighting we have of Kathryn in Towne. As far as we know, that's the last sighting of her anywhere."

"Hmmm. Let me think." Walter crossed his arms and stroked his chin with his left hand. Then, he walked into the den, eyes on the floor. While he was pacing, Fitz and Lawson looked at one another; an unspoken hope passed between them.

After maybe two minutes, Walter looked up and turned to find the detective and the investigator. "I do believe I remember that weekend. Not because of the football game, mind you, but I remember Sylvia coming here and telling my parents about Kathryn not being home. It was dark outside, so that would have to have been Sunday, I guess." His speech was such that he seemed to be piecing things together as he spoke.

"Did your parents seem worried at all?" Fitz asked.

"Not at all." His voice was gaining confidence. "I remember my dad telling Sylvia that Kathryn was a grown woman. That type of thing."

"Did Sylvia seem worried?" Lawson asked.

Walter thought about it and said, "I don't think so. I mean, I guess she was worried enough to tell my parents about it, but I don't recall her sounding alarmed. Nothing like that."

"I know you were thirteen," said Fitz, "but do you remember anything about that weekend? Anything at all? No matter how insignificant."

Walter resumed his thoughtful pose: arms crossed, chin in hand, and gaze on the floor. Time seemed to stand still as he stood there, his head bowed. He eventually raised his gaze towards the windows that occupied the entire wall of the room and looked out at the lush green lawn and line of trees beyond. He moved toward the windows and looked off to the left—he reached for the door handle without looking. He slid the door open slowly, walked out onto the expansive wood deck, and approached the railing.

Fitz and Lawson fell in behind Walter, keeping their distance and stopping at the open door.

After another minute or maybe five—time seemingly paused —Walter said, "I saw her with a man."

———

FITZ STEPPED out onto the deck, followed by Lawson. "What man?" he asked easily. "Where?"

Walter had placed both hands on the wood railing and turned to look at Fitz while maintaining his grip on the rail. He then moved his gaze out across the yard to where the backyard of the Chatham property would have been and said, "Out there. It was during halftime of the Auburn-Clemson game." He released his grasp on the railing and turned, facing both investigators. He leaned back against the rail and, smilingly, said, "I know, I know, but this is different. I don't specifically remember that it was the Clemson game, but I remember it being the weekend my sister told my parents Kathryn had gone.

"We had season tickets to Auburn football, but when they

were on the road, we'd sit in the den and listen to Gary Sanders on the radio. Then, at halftime, my father and I would always go outside and throw the football in the backyard. Every game, without fail. It got to be where I anticipated halftime more than the game because I'd go out and run the plays that Auburn scored on in the first half, plus a few more passing touchdowns for good measure." He paused wistfully and said, "My dad bought a Canon eight-millimeter camera somewhere along that time, and my mother would film me with it. Talk about feeling big time." He was smiling at the memory. "I would hold on to my football the entire first half, and as soon as halftime hit, I was out the door.

"My dad, though, always had to go to the bathroom. He didn't dare move during the game, so he would go to the bathroom, get him a fresh beer, whatever. Well, I remember that day at halftime, while waiting for my dad, I saw Kathryn walking with a guy in her backyard. I remember wondering if they were also going out to throw the ball at halftime." He laughed, a little embarrassed. "I was thirteen, and it was 1968. What did I know about the birds and bees at that point?" He shrugged and said, "They walked into the woods, which I thought was about the worst place to throw the football, and then my dad came outside, and I didn't give Kathryn another thought."

"And you're sure about the day?" Fitz asked.

He considered the question and began to nod his head. "Pretty darn sure, yeah. I have a distinct memory of it being that weekend because I thought to mention what I saw. No one seemed overly concerned, so I didn't bother saying anything. Honestly, I never gave it another thought. So, if that's the day as you said, then yes, I believe that was that Saturday."

Lawson asked, "Do you remember anything about either Kathryn or the guy she was with? You remember what he looked like?"

"No idea. He was just a guy. I remember Kathryn being about

the prettiest girl I had ever seen, so I suspect I paid more attention to her than I did to him."

"Sounds like you knew more about the birds and the bees than you thought," said Lawson.

Walter smiled and said, "You're probably right, Detective."

Fitz said, "I want you to think back. Close your eyes if you need to, but think real hard and tell me if you remember anything about those two. Anything at all that stands out."

Walter turned and faced where he would have seen Kathryn and the mystery man. He closed his eyes and angled his face toward the sky.

He finally brought his head down and looked at them. He smiled sheepishly and said, "I think she was wearing a white halter top with lots of little designs on it...and tight blue jeans."

Lawson elbowed Fitz, winked, and said, "Thank God for the birds and the bees."

TWENTY

Fitz and Lawson were back in the Tahoe and sat in silence without cranking the SUV. They both stared straight ahead, taking in what they had learned throughout the day, and each of them thinking, but not saying, what they were both coming to believe.

Lawson was the first to speak. She took a deep breath, exhaled, and said, "It's her, isn't it."

Fitz nodded slowly.

"Goddamnit!"

Fitz looked out the car window at the grass and woods beyond, trying to envision Kathryn and the mystery man walking toward the tree line and into the woods. Finally, he pushed the *start* button, and the Tahoe roared to life. He sat for a beat, still staring, before pulling down the column-mounted gear selector into reverse and backing out of the driveway. Once in the street, he kept backing up until he had a clear view of what used to be the Chatham's backyard.

The investigator's phone buzzed. It was Barclay.

"Hey there, Boss," Fitz said, eyes still on the property. "We're

leaving his house now and about to head on in. We need to talk."
Barclay gave a short reply, and Fitz said, "Give us about twenty
minutes."

Fitz placed the phone on the console. Neither Fitz nor Lawson
said a word as the SUV was put into *drive,* and they made their
way to the DA's office.

———

NOT QUITE TWENTY silent minutes later, Fitz parked the SUV,
and they made their way to Barclay's office. The courthouse was
closed, and Barclay's was the only other vehicle in the darkened
parking lot.

They walked in and saw Barclay's face illuminated by the
laptop screen. Seeing them enter, he hit a couple of keys, a *whoosh*
sound of an email being sent emitted from the computer's speakers, and he closed the laptop.

He eyed the two investigators ambling in and sensed a problem. They both dropped into the visitor chairs in front of the desk
and sat slightly slumped.

"Well, this doesn't look good," he said across the desk.

Lawson said, "I think the remains we found in the well are
going to be those of Kathryn Chatham."

Barclay, who was leaned back in his desk chair, raised his
eyebrows and looked at Fitz, who met him with a stern gaze and
nodded once.

He took a few seconds to roll this around in his head. "You've
got to back up. Start at the beginning and tell me how you got
there."

Lawson recounted their meeting with Sylvia and then with her
brother Walter, which didn't take long. He knit the two meetings
together, showing how the dates fit and why they were confident
in the timing of everything.

"Fitz and I agreed that Kathryn dropping everything and effectively disappearing without a single word to anyone, never to be heard from again, doesn't make any sense at all. Then Walter Jackson sees her walking into the woods with a guy that same weekend..." She let the last statement hang there, feeling the point was made in the statement itself.

Barclay ran a hand through his sandy-blonde hair and leaned back in his chair. "What have we gotten into?" he said more to himself than the other two. The silence stretched on before Barclay said, "We've got her mother's blood on the nightgown in evidence, and we've got her father's clothes." Barclay was speaking a stream of thought and not directly addressing Fitz or Lawson.

After a few more seconds, he looked across his desk and said, "Let's use the mom's nightgown to get a biological sample for mitochondrial DNA. Forensics can generate a profile from the blood and test it against the DNA profile from the recovered bones. That'll tell us definitively if the remains are those of Kathryn Chatham or not." Fitz and Lawson nodded.

"Now," Barclay said, "with what you've learned about the senator and Larry Butler, do you think we've moved the needle at all on this case?"

Lawson spoke in a measured tone, saying, "I think learning about Butler's and Senator Gillespie's involvement is significant, but how significant is difficult to say. On the one hand, Butler seemingly gets awfully friendly with Kathryn Chatham before her family is killed. Then we have the senator getting in a heated argument days before she's discovered missing." She looked first to Fitz, then back to Barclay and said, "Coincidences in this business...well, we usually call that a clue."

"Yeah, but to believe it's more than a coincidence means that we have to consider that one or maybe even both of them murdered five people in a most brutal fashion and possibly murdered a sixth. Perhaps finishing what they started. And,"

Barclay raised a finger for emphasis, "managed to not only get away with it for going on sixty years but also had everyone, and I do mean everyone, believing that Kathryn simply moved away for a fresh start." Then, after a beat, he said, "That about right?"

"That's about it," Lawson said, her tone somewhere between frustration and exasperation.

The trio sat silently in the dim office, each lost in their own thoughts.

Barclay reclined in his desk chair, the squeak breaking the silence. He put his sock-feet on the corner of his desk and said, "Ain't this some shit. Just like that, we may have gone from one cold case to two."

"Technically, if that is Kathryn in the well, it's not a cold case since it hasn't been classified as a crime yet. So it'll just be a regular ol' murder."

"Yeah, not helping, Fitz."

"Oh, come on, Boss," Fitz said, a smile tinting his voice. "You're so good at your job you're solving murders no one even knew existed."

"You're funny." Then, "First of all, if it does turn out to be her, this investigation of ours is going to absolutely blow up, and everyone and their grandmother will know about it. Secondly, we haven't solved a damn thing yet. In fact, as far as I can tell, all we've really accomplished is what amounts to locating a hornets' nest, and now we're preparing to jab at it with a toothpick."

"So what's next?"

"Well, Fitz, we're still waiting on the genealogy lab to do their thing, and now we have the remains to identify, which will take a little time. So where do we stand on interviewing law enforcement officers from back then?"

"As for anyone else to speak to," said Lawson, "I'm not sure who would be left of any significance." She looked at Fitz. "I guess we could try and track down every officer on the job back in sixty-three, but that doesn't seem very efficient."

"I agree," said Barclay. "What about Butler's partner back then? Sutter, was it?"

"That's him. We definitely need to talk to him, but based on what we've learned, I don't expect he will have anything of value for us."

Barclay said, "I like where we are right now. We've gotten farther in a shorter amount of time than I would have thought, given the circumstances. I don't know that we're any closer to solving this case, but we continue to move forward, which is good. I worry that we won't get momentum back if we hit a lull or stall out at some point, but we also have to pace ourselves. Now get out of here and get some rest while you can."

The investigators stood to leave while Barclay laid back in the chair and looked toward the ceiling, thinking.

They were headed toward the door when Lawson turned back to Barclay and said, "You know, we could always get a DNA sample from Butler and the senator. Compare it to the cigarette butt. No need to wait on the genealogy lab."

To the ceiling, Barclay said, "You have lost your damn mind if you think I am going to run the senator's DNA with what we have." Then, facing Lawson, "He may be retired, but he carries heat, and I'll be damned if I'm going to do something that stupid. You get me something I can hang my hat on, and I won't hesitate, but we aren't there yet." Then, looking back up, he put his hands behind his head and said, "I've never had my nuts slammed in a drawer, but I may prefer that to what the senator would do to me if I get his DNA and I'm wrong. Now, Detective, if you're through thinking of ways to end my career before it begins, you're free to leave my office." He shrugged and said, "Or stay. I don't care."

TWENTY-ONE

December 15

At a back booth inside the Downtowner on the square across the street from the courthouse, Barclay sat with his good friend and fellow jurist Luke Jackson for one of their semi-regular breakfast confabs to discuss life, law, and the gossip du jour.

The Downtowner was the oldest restaurant in the city and possessed an irresistible charm. This venerable establishment had stood as the community's culinary cornerstone for generations, the nostalgic feel embracing all who walked through its entrance transporting customers to a bygone era of simpler times. Inside, it smelled exactly how you might imagine a diner would smell, with an interior that looked like something out of a television show if the show were set in a diner. It had black and white checkerboard tile floors, shiny red booths, aqua-colored chairs around aluminum tables, and alternating red and aqua bar stools lining a Formica-topped counter running two-thirds of the length of the inside. A rectangle was cut out of the aluminum wall behind the counter for passing order tickets and picking up plates of bacon and eggs, pancakes, biscuits, hashbrowns, burgers, and whatever other lard-laden nosh was on the menu. The food was simple and unpretentious, and that's what made it so good.

Both men had ordered coffee and were little more than half finished with it when the waitress came up and first topped off Luke's cup, then made for Barclay's, only stopping when Barclay said, "Now, Ms. Naomi. You know better."

Naomi Tyner, a waitress at the Downtowner for as long as Barclay could remember, smiled and pulled back the coffee urn as she popped her gum. "Oh, Barclay, you and your half-cup refill nonsense."

"It's the ratios, Ms. Naomi. We've discussed this."

She playfully rolled her eyes, said, "Your food's up next, boys," and moved on to the other occupied tables in the restaurant.

Luke said, "You and your damned coffee. Just let her fill up your cup. It brings her so much joy."

"I refuse to have this discussion again."

Luke drank from his cup and winced. He drank again and winced again before adding more sugar. He drank and pulled another face.

"What's the matter?" asked Barclay. "Not as good as your first cup, is it?" He shook his head and said, "It never is. Not unless you get a fresh full cup to add your cream and sugar. You see—"

"You just said that you refuse to have this discussion."

"Yeah, well, we're having it. As I was saying, your first cup is the best cup because you know how much cream or sugar you like, and you fix it that way. Then along comes the waitress and starts giving you refills before your cup is empty. Now what do you do? Add half the sugar? A third? I'm telling you, just say no to the half-cup refill."

"See, that's the difference between you and me. I'm willing to suffer through an imperfect cup of coffee so a grandmotherly waitress can take pride and joy in making sure I have a bottomless cup of coffee, you heartless bastard."

"That's a little harsh."

Luke was about to give a rejoinder when Naomi arrived with their food, placing the heavy white plates and bowls on the table with a thud. Naomi made a show of peering into Barclay's cup and made a noise before walking away.

They moved the plates around and unrolled their silverware from their napkins. Barclay reached into his pants pocket and pulled something out.

"Are you for real," said Luke.

Barclay looked up from his short stack and said, "What?"

"You brought syrup? Really?"

Barclay looked at the mini bottle of real maple syrup in his hand and said, "I prefer maple syrup to the fake, colored corn syrup this place serves. I've asked Jo-Jo to get the real thing in here, and he won't, so I have to bring my own."

Luke shook his head. "You're such a diva."

He pointed the bottle at Luke and said, "You know if you and others would refuse to pour that fake stuff on your pancakes and biscuits, Jo-Jo might change his mind and switch whatever it is he's serving to the real deal. So, really, you're partly to blame for this."

"Eat your food." And on that went for the next few minutes. Barclay and Luke's friendship went way back, and they often sounded like an old married couple.

Luke finished a bite of biscuits and sausage gravy, drank some coffee, wiped his mouth, and said, "I talked to Dad yesterday. He said you came by the house. You asked him about the old Chatham property?"

Barclay's mouth was full, so he nodded. He swallowed and said, "That's right. Maggie asked me to look into the case." He drank down some coffee and said, "I'd never heard of the case. Had your father ever mentioned it?"

"It sounds familiar, but I couldn't give you any details."

"Your dad gave us some good info, and your aunt was extremely helpful. It sounds as if she were a bit wild in her youth."

"That's my Aunt Sylvia. Poor Uncle Tommy could hardly keep up. Even now." They shared a laugh at that. "Christmases at her house, man alive. She'd be in the bag by the time lunch hit the table. My mother was forever mortified and tried to keep us kids from seeing it, but we knew."

"Well, if your Uncle Tommy ever dies, you might inherit an Uncle Fitz."

That comment caught Luke with a mouthful, and he started coughing. "Say what?"

"She's taken a shine to the big man."

"Sounds just like her." Another drink of coffee. "You making any progress on the case?"

Barclay shrugged. "Hard to say. We've gotten some info about possible leads, but who knows? It remains to be seen if we've got anything at all."

"DNA?"

"Yes, but we've yet to establish if it's of any value to us."

"Suspects?"

"We have a couple of names, but nothing much more than that."

Luke ran the last bite of his smoked sausage link around the plate, gathering up the remaining gravy, and, with his fork poised near his mouth, he said, "You think you're gonna get there?" He popped the bite into his mouth.

"I don't know," said Barclay. Then, after a moment, he went for the last bite of pancake when his phone rang. He picked it up off the table and eyed the caller ID before answering. "Hey, AJ."

"Hello, Barclay. Are you available this morning? I have something to bring to you."

"Ah, yeah, sure. What time?"

"You tell me."

"I should be in my office in about twenty minutes."

"Sounds good. See you in twenty."

He placed the phone back on the table and said, "Cold case guy. Former SBI. Helping us out on this."

"Good news?" Luke asked.

Barclay shrugged. "Just said he wanted to bring me something." Barclay finished off his coffee and scanned the diner. He found Naomi behind the counter reading a magazine and caught her attention. He held up the cup. She *harrumphed* and went back to her magazine.

"You've got to be kidding me," Barclay said, still looking at her.

"Should've taken the refill."

After an effusive apology that could, in some circles, be characterized as groveling, Naomi Tyner gave Barclay a to-go coffee in a tall Styrofoam cup.

"You're lucky I don't report this abusive behavior to Jo-Jo," he told her after he had his coffee securely in hand.

"Honey, you need to leave while I still love you," she responded with a wink.

"Bye, dear," Barclay said as he backed out the door.

———

AJ MURPHY WALKED into Barclay's spacious office and stood at the door looking for the DA. He heard a toilet flush followed by running water. A door inside the office opened, and Barclay emerged.

"Need a moment?" AJ asked with a smirk.

"Not anymore. My coffee had me floating, but now I feel much better, thank you."

Barclay was drying his hands with brown paper towels as he walked toward his desk. He dropped them in the wastebasket and sat in his desk chair. He motioned to the chairs in front of his desk, and AJ sat.

"Now," Barclay began, "what is so important this morning?"

AJ held up a thin stack of paper and said, "Genome 23 emailed me their report this morning."

Barclay sat up in his seat. "And?"

"With a high degree of confidence, they believe the DNA profile from the sample we sent them belongs to a male grandchild of a Charles and Inez Peterson."

"Who?"

AJ Murphy shrugged. "That's what it says. Is there anyone in the case file with the last name of Peterson?"

Barclay shook his head. He cursed under his breath and said, "I guess getting the name of someone we were already familiar with was too much to ask for."

"Unfortunately, that's just how it goes sometimes. I'm sorry."

Barclay waived off the apology. "At least we have something we didn't have five minutes ago."

"True."

Barclay did a quick flip through the papers before saying, "I'm going to need you to explain all of this. How they got there, their process, how certain they are of their conclusion, that type of thing."

AJ nodded. "I spoke with Katrina Anderton this morning. She's the analyst on this case and the person who did all the work. She's available for a call if you want to go through the report with her."

Barclay thought about this and said, "May as well. I need to know exactly what all this means so we'll know how to proceed."

AJ scrolled through his cell phone address book and located the direct line for the DNA analyst, which he read off to Barclay, who then dialed the number on his desk phone. When it began to ring, Barclay hit the speaker button and placed the phone in the cradle.

After three rings, an appealing voice said, "Katrina Anderton."

Barclay introduced himself and told her she was on speaker phone with AJ Murphy.

"Hey, AJ," she said through the phone's speaker. He responded, and they exchanged pleasantries.

"Alright, Ms. Anderton—"

"Please call me Katrina."

"Ok, Katrina," Barclay said, "I don't know what AJ has told you, but this is my first foray into genetic genealogy, so I know next to nothing about it. I have a general idea of its purpose, and AJ gave me a very brief overview of it, but not much beyond that. As for this case in particular—wait, are we confidential here?"

"Absolutely. We at Genome 23 realize we are handling sensitive information so you can speak freely. Anything we discuss about this case and any information contained in my report is between us. We don't even discuss cases amongst ourselves here."

"Good. If our killer is still alive, I don't want him to catch wind of what's going on."

"There's no real danger of that from our end. Besides, we don't have a name to give anyone at this point."

"Good point," Barclay said. "I need you to walk me through this report page by page and explain how you arrived at your conclusions."

"Everything about my process is in the report I emailed AJ, and I will be happy to talk you through it. I know it can be a little overwhelming." Typing could be heard through the telephone's speaker, followed by a series of double mouse clicks. "I assume you have a copy of the report in front of you?"

"We both do, yes."

"Okay, good. To start, the report is nineteen pages long, which is in the typical range for these types of reports. The report could be a couple of pages shorter or longer depending on how much information we compiled to resolve the question of identity."

Barclay flipped to the last page to verify the number of pages and nodded at the phone despite the analyst being unable to see him.

"I'm just going to start at the top of page one and walk through the entire report." Barclay again nodded to no one. "There is a lot of minutia in here that I'm not going to necessarily get into. If, at the end, you feel you need more information, I will go through any part you'd like. For our purposes right now, though, I'll just hit the high points if that's okay."

"That's fine."

"Ok. You see that it states that the person of interest's DNA was located at the crime scene, a profile was generated through reliable and scientifically accepted methods, and then uploaded to the website *GEDmatch*. Once uploaded—"

"Wait," interrupted Barclay, "what's *GEDmatch*?"

"*GEDmatch.com* is a free public website where people voluntarily upload their DNA profile in an effort to track down relatives by looking for matching DNA that has been uploaded by other citizen users. Basically, it's a voluntary DNA dumping ground, and the *GEDmatch* computers are constantly working to match people who are potentially related based on their DNA."

"Well, isn't that helpful?"

"Unfortunately, it's not quite as helpful as it once was."

"How do you mean?" said Barclay as he leaned in closer to the phone.

"When that website first started, and we began to see the law enforcement uses of it, and after we solved some cold cases, word got out that DNA that was voluntarily uploaded was being used for law enforcement purposes. As you can imagine, that didn't sit well with some people. Then, based on a tweak to the website's privacy statement, all uploaded profiles are public for anyone to see and access unless the user chooses to opt out of their DNA being accessible to law enforcement. So we went from access to over a million users to around two hundred thousand."

"Wow."

"Yeah, wow. It's still a very useful tool, but it's definitely been made more challenging. In this case, I found four promising matches, each with over one hundred centimorgans in common with the suspect DNA profile."

"What's a centimorgan?" Barclay asked.

"Alright, Mr. Griffith, this is where it's going to get a little sciency." Barclay said, "Oh, boy," and Katrina plowed on. "A centimorgan describes the length of a piece of DNA. For our purposes right now, you only need to know that I am looking for how many centimorgans individuals have in common to determine if a familial link exists."

"Is a hundred centimorgans in common good?"

"That is very good."

Barclay flashed a raised eyebrow look to AJ Murphy.

"Once I identify the matches from *GEDmatch*, I have to determine who the matches belong to. Unfortunately, it's not as simple as having a name attached to the user. In fact, in your case, only one of the profiles had a first and last name associated with it. One of the matches had a username that appeared to be a last name with a first initial plus two numbers. The other two matches were three-letter initials only. That said, I successfully identified by name all four parties of the uploaded profiles."

"How did you do that?"

"I have my ways," she said with a smile in her voice. "From there, I begin recreating the family tree upwards to the point there would seem to dictate a common ancestor; then I begin climbing down the tree to see where these profiles intersect."

"And you were able to do that in this case."

"I was. That particular aspect of my research makes up the bulk of my report. I explain my work and provide charts showing the family tree I recreated, complete with names, dates of birth, and marriages where applicable. This is the road map that led me to my final conclusion. I wasn't able to get as far down as I would have liked, but I did the best I could."

"I had no idea the amount of work that goes into what you do."

"No one ever does."

There was silence as Barclay considered what to ask next. "Wait a minute," he began, "if you have the grandparents, can't you just look up birth records, marriage certificates, that type of thing, and fill in the rest of the family tree?"

"That's an excellent question, Mr. Griffith." Barclay winked at AJ, who rolled his eyes. She continued, "My job is to take it as far as possible and give you what I have a high degree of confidence with. I charge by the hour, so I don't do any more work on a case unless I believe it will get me closer to an identity. In this case, I got as close as I could. I can do more work and get you more names, but I won't be able to narrow the possibilities down any more than I already have. I am certain it is a white male grandchild of Charles and Inez Peterson, but that's the best I can do."

Barclay sat back and scratched his chin. AJ got up and took a lap around the office, listening.

"So the next step is what?" Barclay asked.

"Identify the possible suspects based on the parameters I have laid out and get their DNA. Then, have your forensics lab run it and compare it to the blood on the sheath that we analyzed—we can send your forensics department our DNA profile."

"It would seem to me that you would be the best person to

complete the family tree and get us the names of these grandchildren. I have no idea who would do that for us, and I want to make sure the list is exhaustive. The last thing I need is to miss a potential suspect."

"I can certainly do that for you if you want."

Barclay looked to AJ, who nodded back. "Why don't you go ahead and do that? Shoot me the list when it's completed; we'll take it from there."

"That's an easy request. It'll take me a few days with everything I have going on, but you'll have it within a week or so. That work?"

"Katrina," said Barclay, "this case is sixty years cold. Waiting another week or two for a name is nothing."

The phone call ended, and AJ sat on the windowsill.

Barclay asked, "What are you thinking?"

"I'm thinking I don't want to be in a holding pattern for two more weeks or however long it's going to take Katrina to get back to us."

"What are you saying?"

"Remember what I told you at our very first meeting? 'Once you start, don't stop.'"

Barclay nodded.

"Well, we aren't stopping, and I have an idea."

TWENTY-TWO

December 17

Barclay was the first to arrive at The 8-9-8 Room, eschewing a booth for one of the seating arrangements in the middle of the room. A round, low-slung coffee table sat in the middle of four overstuffed leather chairs; Barclay was seated with a beer he purchased at the bar before entering the smoking lounge. He took a long drink of something extremely hoppy and sat the pint glass on a cork coaster resting on the high-gloss table. He leaned his head back, closed his eyes, and enjoyed the sounds of the live piano filling the dark space. At the close of the song, he leaned forward and grabbed his beer. He heard a familiar voice as he was about to take another drink.

"Am I late?"

Barclay set the glass down, stood, and turned in the direction of the voice.

"No, Senator, I was early." He waved his hand to the adjacent chair and said, "I finished up at the office sooner than expected, so

I figured I'd come on over. I've only been here fifteen minutes or so."

The retired senator tugged up the pant legs of his gray trousers as he lowered himself into the plush chair. Seated, he looked at the expectant waiter and said, "Jonny Walker Black, three cubes of ice." The obedient waiter nodded once and was off.

"A blend, Senator? Really?"

A shrug and a slight smile. "It's what I grew up with." He eyed the glass on the table and said, "Beer with a cigar?"

It was Barclay's turn to shrug and give a wan smile. "Just feels like a beer night." He glanced around the room and leaned in conspiratorially. "You don't think they'll revoke my membership over this, do you?"

The senator tossed his head back in laughter. "I believe you're safe. If that cad Milford Jones can swill his Long Island iced teas within these hallowed walls, surely your beer is protected."

"Milford drinks Long Island iced tea?"

"Like you and I drink water. Dreadful stuff. I happen to know the bar manager despises having his barmen make them." He shook his head. "Money can't buy class, I'm afraid."

The men made small talk for the next few minutes: *How is the job coming? Are you keeping busy in retirement?*

The waiter arrived with his Scotch on a silver tray. "Are we smoking tonight, gentlemen?"

"Does a bear have hair?" said the senator. "Dealer's choice, Tommy."

The waiter nodded and eyed Barclay. "My Fuente, Tommy."

"As always, Mr. Griffith," he said with a smile before turning and leaving.

Barclay reached for his beer, and the two drank at the same time. Then the senator said, "Don't you get tired of smoking the same thing all the time?"

Barclay sucked the beer from his top lip and said, "You know, when it comes to beer, if I see one I've never had, I will almost always try it. Sometimes, I get one I don't particularly care for, but for the most part, it works out...and if not, I know there's always another right around the corner. With cigars, on the other hand, I've been burned too many times—no pun intended—with bad draws, uneven burns, you name it. So now I tend to stay with what I know. I don't smoke often enough to tire of them."

"You'd think you would go with something more...premium."

"Says the man drinking blended Scotch?"

The senator considered this, smiled insincerely, and took another drink of his Johnny Walker. The two men sat in companionable silence for a few moments—Barclay enjoyed the current musical selection while the senator scanned the room, seeing who was there and, more to the point, seeing who would see *him* there.

Their cigars arrived, and a clean, heavy crystal ashtray was sat on the table between them, as were lighters. Cigars delivered, the waiter faded into the background.

Each man worked to light his cigar. Barclay eyed the lit end and ensured the burn was consistent...it was. Then, he said, "What did he bring you? Is that an R and J?" He was referring to a Romeo y Julieta.

The senator nodded as he continued puffing on the cigar as he applied the flame. He, too, pulled the cigar from his mouth to examine the foot. Seemingly satisfied it was burning appropriately, he took two more puffs.

He considered the cigar and said, "This would probably be my go-to if I had to choose just one."

"It's a fantastic stick for sure," said Barclay. "A law school classmate of mine gave me a Cuban R and J for a wedding gift. One of the best cigars I have ever smoked."

"Simple pleasures, Barclay. Enjoy them. Places like this are even more important now that you're in the public eye. A private club can be your haven from the pressures of the outside world.

No one here to judge you, no one here to take a picture of you with those blasted cell phones and post them on social media."

Barclay said, "On the one hand, it will be nice to have a place like this as a getaway, so to speak, but on the other, having a membership here can be twisted to make me appear elitist and out of touch."

The senator's face torqued into a look that said he'd swallowed a bug. "You can't worry about that stuff. Not if you want to maintain your sanity. Just do your job the best you know how, do it with passion, and the people won't care about that stuff. Your enemies will; don't be naive about that. But there's nothing you can do about them regardless." He took another drink, then said, "So fuck 'em."

He smiled and held his glass out. Barclay grabbed his beer and touched the senator's glass with his own. They both drank.

"So," the senator began, "Why did you call me here?"

Barclay didn't detect anger or frustration in the question, but he watched him intently, looking for a tell when he said, "It's about the Chatham case." Former Senator Arnold Gillespie, Jr. didn't flinch. As far as Barclay could see, he gave no indication that he was bothered at all by the revelation.

"I see. What about the case?" The senator spoke carefully, measured.

Barclay sat back, appearing to relax. "Since we last spoke, we've made some progress digging into the case."

"Oh really?" The senator sat forward.

"Well, progress may be a poor word choice." The senator seemed to scowl at that. "What I mean to say is that we have talked to a number of people about it, but, honestly, we're still at square one. No suspects, no motive, nothing."

The senator settled back in his chair. "Well, that's terrible. I was hoping you'd have more to show for what sounds like a lot of work."

"So would I, Senator, but a lot of time has passed. Memories fade, people die, they move on."

They puffed thoughtfully on their cigars, and the waiter appeared with a fresh drink for each of them. They nodded their thanks.

"What about DNA?" asked the senator. "Surely, with the advances made, there is something there."

Barclay shook his head slowly, clearly frustrated and upset. "I'm afraid not. I mean, you're not wrong about the progress that's been made in that area, but DNA wasn't a thought back then, so potential evidence was viewed differently. Now, we collect anything and everything at a scene with DNA potential, but back then? They looked for the murder weapon and fingerprints as far as physical evidence went. We have the clothes the victims were wearing because those were removed and collected at the autopsy, but other than that, nothing of any great value."

The senator seemed to be considering this as he enjoyed his cigar and sipped his Scotch. Then, finally, he said, "Pardon the question, but if you're stuck, why did you want to meet with me?"

"You offered a reward, and, looking back, I wasn't as appreciative as perhaps I should have been. I'm here to ask if that is still on the table."

"Well, Barclay, I don't want to overstep." Barclay thought he detected a hint of...what? Arrogance? It was gone as quickly as it appeared.

"Senator, please, it would be very appreciated, and with where we are, it may be our last best hope?"

"It's that important, is it?"

"Hard to say, but it could be." He drank some beer and wiped his mouth. "With a paucity of physical evidence, I'm not sure we can break this case unless someone comes forward with information. Someone who saw something or heard something."

The senator thoughtfully nodded and puffed. Barclay would wait him out.

"I spoke to the police chief about my offer after you turned me down."

Barclay knew all about that meeting, but he chose to play ignorant. "Really? I hadn't heard that."

"Oh, yes," he said deliberately. "He wasn't at all happy that you turned me down."

Barclay knew this, too. He said, "Well, I will smooth things over with him. I'm sure he wants what we all want, and that is to solve this case."

"Of course." The senator appeared very concerned now. "So, you don't have *any* evidence to tie to a suspect?"

Barclay looked quite grave. "Unfortunately, no. To be honest, Senator, had I known that, I probably wouldn't have even begun looking into the case at all."

"It's only natural to want to rush into something like this when you're new. Trying to make your mark and all. Probably a good learning experience for you."

Prick, thought Barclay.

"I've learned quite a lot through this process. Believe me," Barclay said.

For the next several moments, they sat, not speaking, smoking their cigars and drinking their beverages. Barclay finished his first beer and moved into his second.

The senator leaned forward, coughed into his hand, and said, "Let me give this reward some thought. I have the same reservations I expressed previously about the wisdom of dragging this horrible ordeal back up, and now that I hear about the lack of evidence." He stuck the cigar in his mouth and shook his head. He puffed, removed it from his mouth, and said, "I just don't know now. If I throw twenty grand out there, it will be blood in the water for all manner of kooks and crazies. And for what?"

Barclay wasn't sure if the question was rhetorical, but he chose not to answer either way.

More head shaking from the senator, "I'm sorry, Barclay. I know you say this could go a long way to solving this case, but I'm not sure I agree."

If the room had not been so dark, the senator would have seen Barclay's ears flush with anger at the condescending way he was being spoken to. Barclay was beginning to get good and pissed off but was maintaining his composure. Lashing out at this blowhard would do nothing positive for what he was trying to accomplish.

"Be that as it may, Senator, please know that your assistance would mean a lot should you choose to provide it."

"I hope you believe me when I say that I want nothing more than for you to solve this gruesome crime and lay to rest what has long been a blight on our fine community."

"I certainly do believe that, Senator." But Barclay did not believe him, not for a second.

The senator twisted in his chair, first left, then right. Then, spotting the waiter, he threw up a hand, signaling for the check.

"I've got this, Senator."

"You sure?"

"Of course. It was my meeting. I invited you."

"I wish I'd have known. I'd have ordered better Scotch." They laughed, but Barclay knew the senator's penchant for allowing others to pick up the check.

The senator downed his remaining Scotch and took a couple of last pulls on the cigar before dropping it into the crystal ashtray.

Both men stood, and Barclay shifted his cigar from his right to his left hand before the two shook hands.

"Thank you. The next round is on me."

"Macallan twenty-five it is," said Barclay as he pumped the senator's hand.

The senator laughed a laugh that said he wasn't sure if Barclay was serious. "Yes, well, until next time."

Senator Gillespie exited the lounge, and the waiter approached —Barclay handed over his Amex. When the waiter left to run his card, two figures from the darker recesses of the room approached and sat down.

"Did you get it?"

"Sure did, Boss. In perfect high definition." Fitz unplugged a cord attached to a small black box from an iPhone and handed the iPhone to Barclay, who viewed a few seconds of his meeting with the senator.

He said, "Perfect," and returned the phone to his chief investigator. He undid a single button on his dress shirt beneath his tie, removed the wireless microphone he wore, and handed it to Fitz. "Now photograph his glass and cigar before you collect it, and we've established the provenance of the evidence." To Detective Lawson, he said, "The audio come through?"

She pulled the AirPods from her ears and said, "Loud and clear. That guy's a real asshole."

Fitz snapped several photos with his iPhone before placing it back inside his coat. He then reached into his right outer coat pocket and retrieved a black latex glove, which he slid onto his right hand. He then pulled a clear plastic back from his left coat pocket, snapped the bag so the mouth opened, and dropped the glass inside. Next, he peeled back a piece of paper, exposing an adhesive strip, then folded the strip over and sealed the bag. He handed the sealed bag to Lawson, then extracted another bag from his left coat pocket and repeated the process with the half-smoked cigar after making sure the fire was out.

When the cigar bag was sealed, he said, "I'll get this down to forensics in the morning."

"Remember to hand it directly to Pevey, okay? No one else."

"Got it, Boss."

"I will call him when I leave here—he'll be expecting you."

The waiter arrived with a leather bi-fold holding Barclay's credit card and receipt. Barclay took the bi-fold and slipped a folded hundred dollar bill into the waiter's hand. "Appreciate you letting my friends take up a table."

The waiter accepted the money with the furtiveness and dexterity of one used to receiving such handshakes. He gave a half-bow and said, "Certainly, sir."

TWENTY-THREE

December 21

It was mid-morning, and Barclay was writing a letter to the Alabama parole board objecting to the early release of a man who had only served five years of a twenty-year sentence for assault. During a meth-induced fight with his girlfriend, he bounced her eight-month-old baby boy off a bed and into a wall. After he did that, he held the girlfriend at knifepoint so she couldn't call an ambulance for her critically injured child. She eventually got away from him and called the police from the neighbor's house. Barclay wanted to make certain the parole board knew every sickening detail of the incident, including the fact that the assault resulted in permanent brain damage for the baby. He would do everything in his power to see this evil human serving every day of his sentence.

He was proofreading the two-page letter for the third time when his desk phone rang. His assistant, Peggy, told him that FBI agent Cody Rich was on the line.

"Hey, Barclay," Cody said. "I have an agent from the San Francisco field office on her way in from Atlanta who wants to meet with you today if you're available."

Barclay, who still had half of his attention on the parole letter, said, "Wait a minute. What's the San Francisco FBI want with me?"

"You know what I know at this point. My SAC popped his head in my office about three minutes ago and told me a couple of agents landed in Atlanta and are heading our way and wanted a meeting with you."

"Hmm. That's all he said?"

"That's it."

Barclay thumbed open his iPhone, opened the calendar app, and said, "I've got a couple of things set this afternoon, but nothing I can't reschedule. Shoot me a text when you're on the way."

———

BARCLAY'S PHONE dinged at 1:32 PM, signaling an incoming text message. It was from FBI agent Cody Rich, and the message read: *Be there in 10.* Eight minutes later, his assistant let him know three FBI agents were at the front desk, and he asked her to send them back to his office. Cody walked in first, followed by a black woman and a younger, shorter white guy.

Cody Rich was assigned to the Montgomery field office but lived in Towne, so he handled a lot of the Fed's business in East Alabama. He was six feet tall with closed-cropped salt and pepper hair and a matching three-day beard—always a three-day beard. He wore an untucked plaid flannel shirt, khaki cargo pants, and sand-colored boots. He shook Barclay's hand and made the introductions.

The female was Daisy Adams, the Assistant Special Agent in Charge for the FBI's San Francisco field office. She was light-skinned, had stunning green eyes, and wore her hair pulled back in a bun. Her charcoal Brooks Brothers skirt suit was paired with a white dress shirt, black heels, and small gold ball earrings. She had a warm smile and smelled of citrus with a suggestion of...something. Cardamom?

When she extended her hand for a handshake, her coat sleeve rode up, exposing an Apple watch with a Day-Glo orange strap. Anything but the dull, stodgy G-man stereotype, Barclay thought. However, the man with her, Special Agent Mason Simpson, was precisely that.

Agent Simpson was short, maybe five-seven. He wore his black hair with a severe part and plenty of pomade. He wore a black suit that was a size too large, a white dress shirt with a purple and white striped tie, and sensible black shoes. The moment Barclay saw him, he thought, *Military*.

Barclay introduced Fitz to the out-of-town agents, explaining that he was his chief investigator and right hand. The visiting FBI agents, Barclay, and Fitz, took the four seats around the coffee table while Rich sat outside the group; he was merely the intermediary and only stayed out of curiosity.

Barclay asked if anyone needed anything—water, coffee—and they all declined.

Rich said, "They wanted barbecue for lunch, so I took them to The Pig."

"Ah, what did you think?" Barclay asked the two agents.

Simpson looked at Adams, which Barclay thought was odd, and she smiled and said, "Excellent. Unfortunately, the barbecue scene in northern California is pretty much non-existent, so this Texas girl tries to find it where she can."

"Texas, huh," said Barclay. "I do like our barbecue in Alabama, but nothing beats Texas brisket."

"I agree with that," she said, smile widening.

"Well, The Magnolia Pig is the most popular smokehouse in

Towne, so Rich didn't steer you wrong there." Daisy nodded with a smile, her glossy lips reflecting the ample light in the room. Simpson, on the other hand, sat there, his mouth set in a line.

"So, what did you want to discuss?"

Daisy Adams cleared her throat and crossed a leg over her knee. "If you'll indulge me, I'd like to start at the beginning so you'll have some context for why we're here." A nod from Barclay, then: "Are you familiar with the 1962 escape attempt from Alcatraz prison?"

That was definitely not how Barclay expected this to begin, and it showed on his face. He said, "If that's the one the Clint Eastwood movie was about, then yes, I'm familiar with it, and by familiar, I mean I've seen the movie."

Daisy smiled and said, "Yes, *that* escape attempt. As you might imagine, that movie was based in reality, but it didn't tell the entire story."

"Imagine that."

"According to all the reports, official or otherwise, three men attempted an escape on June eleventh of sixty-two and, although no bodies were ever recovered, the escape attempt has been officially classified as just that: an attempt. Meaning no one ever made it to the mainland."

The prosecutor in Barclay already had questions he wanted to ask, but he stayed quiet and let her tell her story.

"The three men everyone talks about are Frank Lee Morris and brothers John and Clarence Anglin." Barclay recognized the names once he heard them. "Well, and this brings me to why we're here..." She paused, then said, "There was a fourth prisoner."

Barclay considered this with a creased brow. Daisy was silent, and sensing she wanted him to say something, he said, "Yeah, seems like I remember that from the movie. There was a guy that was supposed to go with them, but he couldn't get out of his cell or something like that."

Daisy was nodding before he finished his sentence, going exactly where she expected him to. "You're thinking of Allen West, and you're right. Unfortunately for him, he didn't make his hole large enough to squeeze out of his cell, and he got left behind. But that isn't who or what I'm talking about. What I'm telling you is that there was a fourth person who made the attempt with Morris and the Anglins. Unlike those other three, however, it appears he made it."

If she wanted a reaction from Barclay, she got it.

"Hold on," Barclay said after maybe five seconds. "You mean someone actually made it to San Francisco? Made it to freedom?"

"Well, yes and no. We believe the prisoner made it to shore but not San Francisco." Seeing the look on Barclay's face, she said, "Let me explain. Of course, we don't know what their plan was other than to leave the island, but common sense says San Francisco would have been the most likely destination because it was the closest shoreline, and its dense urban setting would be conducive to blending in and getting lost. That said, it's hard to fathom four men on a homemade raft of glued-together raincoats and makeshift oars would be substantial enough to overcome the whims of the resolute tidal currents of the Bay.

"In the days after the escape, there was very little evidence as to where they went or what happened, but over the ensuing week or so, debris believed to belong to the escapees was recovered in the water, but nothing of any value as to their whereabouts. Fast forward about a month, and a call comes into the warden's office from a citizen claiming to have seen a man soaked to the bone and wearing denim-blue clothing head to toe wandering through the streets of Sausalito within hours of the escape." She exhaled and said, "Alright, I have given you a lot up to this point. Any questions as to what I've said so far?"

He considered the question and said, "That's a lot to process, but the first question I have is what this has to do with us?"

"Right to it, I see. We're jumping a little ahead, but the long and short is that we got a CODIS hit, which led us here."

"Ok. Now you really have my attention." A moment, then, "Just so I'm not misunderstanding, DNA from your escape tracks back to a profile belonging to a person here?"

"Not a person—a case. There is no name attached to your profile. However, the DNA *we* have is from a guy named Eddie Howard."

"Based on the names you mentioned earlier, am I to assume this Eddie Howard is the fourth escapee?"

"That is our man number four."

"Wow. Ok. Let's talk through this. Where is your DNA from, and how do you know it belongs to Howard?"

Daisy inclined her head toward Barclay. "Let me pick up where I left off. The man seen in Sausalito was too tall to be Morris, who was around five-seven. He was about the right height but too thick to be John Anglin, who was about five-ten, one-forty. And Charles Anglin was of similar stature to the man spotted in Sausalito, but he was fair-haired while our mystery man was dark-headed...as was Eddie Howard."

"That's a compelling identification."

"It is. As for the DNA, when the FBI found out about the sighting in Sausalito, they descended on the southeast coast of the Marin Headlands and concentrated their search northward to Horseshoe Bay. The northernmost end of the Golden Gate Bridge makes landfall at the Marin Headlands coastline, and there is a large concrete piling there. That's where they located a handmade life vest similar to what we found floating in the Bay. The vest had blood on it, and that's the source of the DNA."

Barclay opened his mouth to speak, closed it, thought, then said, "I'm curious, why has no one ever heard of this Howard guy? I imagine this has been written about and reported on for decades. So why does no one know about this fourth person?"

"Enormous resources were poured into this case from day one but faded over time. The warden, in particular, was pushing for a quick resolution and was adamant that the inmates didn't make it. He wanted the investigation shut down and the matter put to bed so no other inmates would get even the barest of notions that the Rock was vulnerable to escape."

"Makes sense," Barclay interjected.

"And to be fair, the evidence weighed heavily in favor of that hypothesis. The Bay is a cold, nasty body of water. The idea that four inmates in the dead of night with questionable floatation devices could have successfully navigated the choppy waters was not given much credence at all. So, after a few weeks, the search was called off, and the investigation was quietly shut down.

"Fast forward some fifty-odd years to early 2019, and Agent Simpson here"—she motioned to him with her head—"came to me asking to look through the files of some unsolved cases. I told him to stick his nose in the Alcatraz file."

"Wait," Barclay said, "how is the Alcatraz escape considered unsolved? I thought you knew what happened?"

ASAC Adams shook her head. "There's a public consensus that the case is closed, and the warden back in sixty-two was certainly of the opinion that the case was closed, but, officially, the FBI has it classified as unsolved." A pause as she made sure Barclay's attention was on her. "That's why we're here; hoping you can provide that missing piece because this DNA hit is our first real lead since the Howard sighting was reported a month after the escape."

Barclay seemed to accept that, then nodded to Agent Simpson and said, "That was a pretty fortuitous decision, giving the case to him."

She shrugged. "Dumb luck."

"I don't believe that for a second."

"Yes, well, Agent Simpson has done yeoman's work on this

case. He found the supplement documenting the Sausalito sighting and ran with it. He tracked down an old prison guard." To Simpson: "What was his name?"

"Jerry Dascenzo," said Simpson without hesitation.

"That's him," said Daisy. "Guy was like ninety years old. Anyway, Simpson asks him about this fourth person whose description clearly did not match Morris or the Anglins, and he got one mother of a story." To Simpson: "Why don't you tell him."

A short nod, then, "I was trying to learn what I could about the case, so for the first few weeks, I watched as many documentaries about Alcatraz that I could find, hoping I would see something that may help. I would work on the file during the day and watch videos and read articles at night. I came across this sighting and immediately knew the description didn't track with the other three. I searched all manner of records of inmates coming and going, hoping to narrow down the possibilities of a fourth person."

"Wait, you knew there was a fourth person from the beginning?" asked Barclay.

"Oh, no. It took a few weeks before I came across the witness in Sausalito, and even then, I was so ingrained in looking for three people that it didn't quite click. I knew the description didn't fit any of our guys and attributed that to witness error. The more I considered it, though, the more I wondered if we were missing something. That's when I started exploring the idea of this other person.

"One night, I'm watching something on the History Channel or PBS, something like that, when I see Jerry Dascenzo speaking about his time as a guard. The show was a few years old, and he was listed as the oldest living Alcatraz guard. He had this halting, raspy voice, and I hoped upon hope that he was still alive; after a quick search, I found him."

Barclay said, "Very impressive."

Simpson allowed himself a slight smile. "I appreciate that. Well, I call him, and during the conversation, I take a flyer and ask him about this fourth prisoner, and he goes silent. Like for more than a few seconds. I wondered if we'd lost our connection and hoped he hadn't just dropped dead. When he finally speaks, he says, 'Eddie Fuckin' Howard.'"

Barclay's eyebrows shot up.

Simpson nodded. "Yessir. He knew all about it. He said the warden was a real piece of work. Ran the prison like a dictator—his own little fiefdom. When the breakout happened, every prisoner went on lockdown, and no one was allowed to leave the island—including the guards. The FBI showed up, and it was them, and the warden all closed up in his office. When the initial meeting broke up, the warden made it clear the guards were to stay out of the way and keep their mouths shut. The warden even shut off the phone lines so no one could call out.

"The escape alert sirens alone were enough for San Franciscans to know something happened, so the journalists began poking around almost immediately. However, with no phone access to the island and no way to get there—all transport to the island was ceased at the warden's command—information was impossible to come by. Finally, after a few days, the warden knew he couldn't sit on this forever, so he crafted his narrative: three people escaped—Morris and the Anglin brothers—and they died in the water during the attempt."

"But why keep Howard out of it?" Barclay asked.

"I asked Dascenzo the same thing. He said it was because Howard was a bad, bad guy. Killed six people during a bank robbery in Oakland. We looked into that, and Dascenzo was exactly right. Howard goes in and points a pistol at a teller, and throws a pillowcase at her. She fills the sack, and after she hands it over to him, he shoots her. He then shoots five more people on his way out as they lay face down on the ground. Puts the gun to the back of their head and pulls the trigger one by one until the gun goes click. A bank executive hiding under his desk saw it all happen."

"Whoa."

"Yeah, so Howard gets caught and convicted, and the warden specifically requests Howard be sent to Alcatraz. He had the Bureau of Prisons scared to death that Howard was an escape risk because he busted out of a small county jail down in Salinas some years before. The way Dascenzo figures it, the warden was worried about his station in life should it get out that Howard escaped, so he threw a bone to the local media by giving them the names he did. Those cons were small time. Bank robbery, escape, nothing too dangerous.

"Then, according to Dascenzo, things get back to some semblance of normalcy after the warden makes his statement to the media. Fast forward, and the report of the sighting comes in from Sausalito, and all hell breaks loose. He said he'd never seen the warden so out of sorts. Here the warden has kept it quiet about this six-time murderer getting off the island and convinced himself he died with the other three when all of a sudden, he gets a call that one of his prisoners made it to dry land, and he knows from the description precisely who it is.

"He can't exactly put out an alert that Howard is on the loose because, at best, he's incompetent, not knowing his prisoner was gone, and at worst, he's a liar who has put an entire community at risk with an escaped multiple murderer on the loose."

"Oh, boy," said Barclay. "Politics." He thought, then said, "But still, to keep it secret all these years?"

"I wondered that as well, but Dascenzo made a good point. He told me the inmates didn't know what was happening outside their little home on the Rock. As far as they knew, Howard's absence was reported along with Morris and the Anglins. The prison guards weren't going to talk, what with the warden and all. And by the time the prisoners were released or transferred off the island, it wasn't a story anymore. The press had moved on from three dead convicts who died in the Bay during a prison escape." He paused, then said, "Eddie Howard just fell through the cracks."

Barclay: "The warden sold a story, the press bought it, and the public can no longer be convinced otherwise." Sounds of agreement. "I do have a question about identity. How do you know the blood on the life vest was Howard's and not one of the other three?"

Daisy took over the conversation: "Because we had DNA standards from Morris and the Anglins. The FBI relied on the warden to tell them who the escapees were. When the FBI investigated the cells of each of the escapees, you'll recall the men created dummy heads to make it appear they were asleep in their bunks throughout the night." Barclay nodded. He remembered that from the movie. "Well, Howard had no such fake head or any other indication of wrongdoing in his cell, so it was wholly ignored, whereas the entire content of the cells of Morris and the Anglins were seized, so we had toothbrushes and shaving razors to access their DNA."

"Ok, you've got me convinced about Eddie Howard. Now, which case of ours is associated with your CODIS hit."

Daisy Adams said, "It's a murder case. Last name Chatham."

———

THE CHATHAM REVELATION hit him like a sledgehammer to the solar plexus. After Barclay worked through the implication of the FBI's revelation, ASAC Adams agreed he could get Detective Lawson on speaker phone. Barclay reasoned things were about to get complicated, and he wanted the detective to hear everything firsthand so nothing would be lost in translation.

He got her on the phone and quickly caught her up to speed before continuing the meeting and drilling down for more detail. He learned that the CODIS hit was based on a DNA profile generated through the cigarette butt found at the Chatham crime scene. If that was true, and he had no reason to believe it was not, he wondered why the cigarette butt profile did not generate a hit after it was uploaded to CODIS?

Every forensic biology analysis report from ADFS included the statement: *Any appropriate DNA profiles developed in this case have been entered into the Combined DNA Index System (CODIS) and will be searched on a routine basis. If any investigative leads are generated, you will be notified in a separate memorandum.*

Based on his experience, he knew the profile would have been run and a report generated, so why had he not seen anything from this submission? Special Agent Mason Simpson told him that their DNA profile had been uploaded a few months before the profile from the cigarette butt, so it should have kicked out a match when ADFS uploaded it. Why had it not? That was a question for Ken Pevey, and he made a mental note to call him after the meeting.

Cody Rich got a call and left Barclay's office to take it. The four people remaining in the room, Adams, Simpson, Fitz, and Barclay, probed the ramifications of the DNA discovery.

Assistant Special Agent in Charge Daisy Adams said, "We noted the submission of the source of the matching DNA occurred recently, which would put our guy committing a homicide or at least being at the scene of a homicide, at eighty-one years old. That's a bit long in the tooth to commit a murder. On the other hand, we don't know anything about the case, so I guess the first question is, does this look like a murder an old man could have committed."

Barclay, who had stayed standing while they were on the call with Lawson, had picked up the baseball he kept on his desk and was absently spinning it into the air and catching it, thinking. In response to Adams' comment, he stopped and looked back at the ASAC and stared for a beat. His gaze clicked to Simpson, then back to Adams. He said, "You mean you don't know about the murders?"

Simpson spoke unprompted for the first time. "Murders? As in multiple victims?"

"Five victims. And slaughtered would be a more appropriate term." Seeing the look on the agents' faces, he continued, "Probably the worst crime scene I've ever seen." He returned to his chair and sat on the edge of his seat. "And you need to know these murders happened in 1963."

"Oh," was all Daisy could muster.

"Yeah. This is an unsolved homicide that we began looking into a month ago. We examined all the physical evidence, took a flyer on a couple of pieces for possible DNA, and I guess we were successful."

Daisy Adams suddenly looked like she was sucking on a sour candy. "So, our hit dates back to a homicide committed sixty years ago."

Simpson: "So Howard could be dead or, if he's still alive, long gone from here."

Barclay shrugged. "Or he could still be here. Or he could not have had anything at all to do with the murders. He could have left that cigarette there at any time."

Daisy: "I'd be lying if I said I wasn't more than a little discouraged at this revelation. I thought we were onto something—perhaps the biggest break in this case in sixty years."

"You might be," said Barclay. "If nothing else, it proves Eddie Howard escaped Alcatraz...and survived."

TWENTY-FOUR

December 29

Diana Krall was crooning Christmas tunes in the Griffith family kitchen, and the air was suffused with the pleasant scent of wassail simmering on the cooktop, and the hint of a fir-scented candle lingered in the background. Barclay was still in his work clothes—gray suit pants and light blue dress shirt—as he stood drinking a beer and talking through the day's happenings with his wife, Brittany. Lasagna was in the oven, still several minutes from being done.

He wanted to go wake his daughter, who was still asleep from her afternoon nap, but Brittany threatened him. "She's been cranky all day, and I finally got her down. You go wake her up, and I will beat your tail."

He held his hands up in mock surrender before bolting from the kitchen.

"Barclay!" she whisper yelled.

He returned and said, "I just had to look at her...I needed that."

"Mm-hm."

He dropped onto one of the barstools and took a long pull on his beer.

"You look worn out," she said.

"I am."

"Anything particular?" she asked as she worked a waiter's corkscrew around the mouth of a bottle of wine, removing the foil.

Barclay took another drink and said, "No. Just the job. When Maggie told me I had been appointed to take over for her, she warned me that it was like the dog chasing the car, only now the dog finally caught it and was like, now what?" He paused as he thought. "They don't exactly give you a 'how-to' manual when you take office. I know how to be a prosecutor, how to try cases and all of that, but the rest?" He shook his head. "It's a lot, and I'm just trying to figure it all out."

The foil on the bottle was removed, and as she was twisting the corkscrew into the cork, she said, "No one said you had to figure everything out overnight, Barclay. I can't imagine you're any different from anyone else in your position. There's a learning curve, and it will take time; you need to pace yourself. You gave your office some time off for the holidays, yet you haven't slowed down yourself."

"I know. It's just...look, the positive is that Maggie had things running well, so I'm not in a position of having to do a complete rebuild, but there are things I want to do—ideas I want to implement."

"I get that, but you don't have to get it all done overnight."

"I know, but I want it done. I've been waiting for this opportunity, and now that I've got it, I want to go, go, go."

Brittany pulled the cork with a *pop* and said, "I know you very well, Mr. Griffith, and that's why I'm telling you: *slow down*." She poured a glass of cabernet and slid it to him. He downed the rest of the beer, took the glass of wine, and, holding it at the base, swirled the dark maroon liquid around in the glass.

Krall's version of *Christmas Time is Here* began, and Barclay said, "I have to tell you, I'm beginning to wonder about jumping off into this cold case right off the bat."

She dismissed that with a noise and a wave of her hand. "Please, Barclay. *That* is why you are going to be a great DA. You don't shy away from the tough cases. You're willing to take on any challenge, and you do it because you want justice for the victims regardless of how long ago the crime occurred. That's what made you so good at your job as an ADA, and it's why Maggie trusted you with the appointment." She poured herself a glass, swirled it in her hand, took a sip, and made a face that said, *Not bad.* "You're like a pig in slop with this case. Anything else you say about it is a lie." Then, after another, bigger sip, she said, "Guess what? No one will blame you if this case isn't solved. It's cold for a reason, right?"

Barclay was sitting on a barstool, resting his elbows on the island, staring into the wineglass. "I wish I could turn it off. I wish it didn't affect me so damn much."

"Liar."

He cut his eyes to her. Smirked. She did know him.

———

DINNER WAS FINISHED as the two of them sat sipping wine, dinner plates pushed toward the middle of the black granite-topped island, music still playing. Barclay reached for one more piece of buttery garlic bread, and Brittany topped off their wine when his phone rang.

The phone sat face down to his left, so he picked it up, looked at the caller ID, and answered. "What's up, Ken."

"Hey, Barclay, I have the results of the DNA analysis on the cigar."

"It doesn't match the cigarette," Barclay interjected. He dipped his head, silently cursing himself, considering for the first time that he should have told the lab director what he had learned, mainly because he had asked for the favor of a rushed analysis.

A long pause, then, "Wait, you knew?" Frustration edging in.

"Ken, I'm sorry." He went on to tell his friend about the visit from the FBI eight days before and the revelation that the cigarette butt's DNA tracked back to the Alcatraz prison escape attempt of 1962. "So," he said at the conclusion of his story, "unless Arnold Gillespie, Jr. is a prison escapee, then he's not our guy."

Ken Pevey had risen to his position as much for his temperament and ability to handle people as his acumen in all things forensics. He took a moment to gather himself and said, "How does that jibe with what your genealogy lab told you? Is there anyone else who fits that description?"

"You know, I haven't given it any thought. I was so stunned to hear from the FBI..."

"How about this? Let me have a look at your evidence. Maybe there's an opportunity for additional testing. Maybe I'll be able to identify a piece of evidence that we can get something from that you may have missed or didn't realize had any forensic value. Our testing and instrumentation are constantly evolving, giving us some pretty incredible evidentiary opportunities."

"Brother, I would welcome your help any way you can give it." He thought for a moment, then said, "Fitz has photographs of all the evidence. How about I get him to email them to you, and if you see something you'd like a closer look at, we can get the evidence to you."

Pevey weighed this and said, "That'll work."

Barclay rang off and dialed up Fitz. When Fitz answered, Barclay could hear music in the background. Pop music. When he commented about Fitz and pop music, his investigator said something about being well-rounded in the arts.

Barclay told Fitz about his phone call with Pevey, and Fitz said he would email the evidence photos when he got off the phone.

———

THE FOLLOWING MORNING, Fitz was downstairs at the courthouse entrance chatting up court security over coffee and Chick-fil-A chicken biscuits. He was catching up on the latest gossip: who's getting promoted, who failed to qualify at the gun range, who the judge yelled at in misdemeanor court.

When Fitz's phone rang, one of the court security officers was in the middle of a story about a deputy threatening to punch a defense attorney in court. Seeing the caller ID, he stepped away but not before telling the officer to hold the rest of the story until after the phone call.

The caller was Ken Pevey. He had reviewed the photographs and requested two pieces of evidence be brought to him for further examination. Fitz told him they would be in his hands before lunch and rung off.

When he hung up, a chorus of laughter erupted. *Dammit, he finished the story.*

TWENTY-FIVE

January 4

Barclay sat at the heavy oak desk in his home office, proofreading all four hundred-plus case summaries for the upcoming Grand Jury set for the following week. It was after 9:30 in the evening, and he was little more than halfway through.

He was reading this particular summary for the third time, trying to decipher if a crime had even occurred, when the sound of the pocket doors opening interrupted his task.

"Hey there," Barclay said, seeing Brittany, her copper-colored hair and smattering of freckles a welcome diversion. He was a little bleary-eyed from staring at the computer the last few hours. Then, "Well, hey there," he said, eyesight focusing on the man behind her. In his left hand, the man carried a paper bag with a pronounced lump at the bottom, and under his right armpit was tucked a long cardboard container. He held a red folder in his right hand.

Barclay rolled his soft leather oxblood executive desk chair back away from the desk, stood, and walked around to greet Ken Pevey and take the box from under his arm. He could tell from the markings on the box what it was, which confused him even more. He laid the box across the arms of one of the visitor chairs in front of his desk, and Ken sat the heavy sack down at his feet.

They caught up for a minute, Barclay introducing his wife to Ken, who said he thought they'd already met, and Brittany agreed. They went back and forth trying to figure out where they had met and, after no one remembered for certain, agreed they had met once before and left it at that. Brittany announced she was going to bed to get caught up on her reading, and Barclay offered Ken a seat across the room in a forest-green leather wingback chair.

Barclay joined him in a matching chair and said, "Not to sound rude, Ken and I'm glad to see you, but...this is a surprise."

Ken Pevey had begun smiling before Barclay finished speaking. "Well, I thought you'd want to know what I learned. Laura left with the kids a couple of days ago to visit her parents outside of Atlanta. I stayed behind to finish a few things at work, and now I'm headed up there; since your place is on the way, I figured I'd drop in."

"You've lost me."

Ken motioned his head toward where the packages were left. "Your evidence."

Barclay turned in his chair toward the box and bag, then back to Pevey.

Ken said, "Fitz didn't tell you? After Fitz sent me the evidence log and photos, I asked him for the machete and flashlight. Those two items looked the most promising and—"

"Promising? As in having some evidentiary value?"

"That's right. In the photo of the machete, I noted that it appeared to have a cloth-like wrap around the handle, which is an ideal conduit for DNA such as sweat and skin cells." He produced the file folder and handed over a stapled two-page document.

Barclay recognized it immediately as an *Examination of Biology* report from the Alabama Department of Forensic Sciences. The form listed the suspects as Eddie Howard and Arnold Gillespie, Jr., and the "subject" line listed the slaying victims. In addition, the lab case number and other tracking information were listed.

It stated the date the evidence was received and that the evidence was received from Winston Fitzsimmons, Chief Investigator, Towne County District Attorney's Office. Then it listed the items submitted: *1. One (1) brown paper bag containing a silver Winchester flashlight identified to be from the living room of the crime scene. 2. One (1) cardboard box containing the following evidence: 2A One (1) machete approximately twenty-four (24) inches in length.*

Under the "Results" section, the report stated: *The following items were examined and/or analyzed for the presence of blood; however, none was detected. Item 2.*

Barclay held up the paper and said, "No blood detected? The blade—"

Ken saw where he was going and began nodding before he got there. He said, "We just focused on the handle. I didn't figure there was any dispute that the blood on the blade belonged to the victims. But we can test it."

Barclay nodded and went back to reading.

The "Results" further stated: *The following items were processed for the recovery of trace evidence: Item 2.*

The genetic traits detected from the swabbing (Item 2) are a mixture of at least two (2) individuals, both of which must be male. Eddie Howard is included as a potential contributor of the mixture of genetic traits detected from the major component of the DNA detected from the swabbing (Item 2).

The probability of including a random, unrelated individual as a potential contributor to the major component of this mixture is

approximately 1 of 121 quintillion (1 of 1.21E+20) African Amer-
ican individuals and 1 of 33.3 quintillion (1 of 3.33E+19)
Caucasian individuals.

Arnold Gillespie, Jr. is included as a potential contributor to the
mixture of genetic traits detected from the machete handle (Item 2).
The probability of including a random, unrelated individual as a
potential contributor to this mixture is approximately 1 of 16
African-American individuals and 1 of 25 Caucasian individuals.

Barclay scanned the document one more time, flipping to
page two, which contained only the signature of the reporting
forensic scientist. Finally, he said, "I'm guessing this is good, but
you're going to have to explain it to me."

Ken's eyes sparkled. He slid up onto the edge of the chair and
said, "This was Eddie Howard's machete...but we also have
Arnold Gillespie, Jr., Mr. Senator himself, handling it."

Ken could tell that Barclay was still not seeing it. "Ok, first
things first, on the machete handle, we have what we call a 'complex DNA mixture,' which means we have two sets of genetic
material: a major contributor and a minor contributor. This
means that the biological sample originated from more than one
donor, which is not at all uncommon and is usually easily
explained.

"Let's say two or more people handled this machete, sweated
into the cloth handle. In all likelihood, each person would leave
his or her DNA behind, but consider that maybe one person left
more or less DNA behind. Maybe person one handling the
machete had extremely sweaty hands, while person two's hands
were relatively dry. Person two left their DNA behind, but it was a
fairly low contribution. In this scenario, person one would be the
major contributor, while person two would be the minor contributor. It could also be that the major contributor handled the item
after the contributor of the minor sample, thus wiping out a
majority of biological evidence."

Barclay was beginning to understand the science but was still unsure of the ramifications.

Pevey continued: "Here's what we can definitively say: We can place one of the murder weapons unequivocally in the hands of Eddie Howard. You follow me there?"

Barclay nodded. "Yes, it's a solid DNA match to Howard. Put that together with the cigarette butt, and he's our guy—no doubt." He paused, looking over the page once more, feeling stupid for not seeing what Ken wanted him to see. He finally said, "I see where the senator is listed as a minor contributor, but at only...one in twenty-five. That's hardly overwhelming, Ken.

"Let's assume that the population of Towne in 1963 was, say, thirty-five thousand people." Barclay got up and walked to his desk, and grabbed his iPhone. He unlocked it, worked his fingers across the screen, and said, "At a population of thirty-five thousand people, that leaves fourteen hundred potential contributors of the DNA at one in twenty-five."

Ken was shaking his head, "In the first place, the one in twenty-five number is for white people, not the entire populace."

"Come on, Ken. Towne, Alabama, in 1963, wasn't exactly Detroit. I have to believe it was pretty damn white back then, and that doesn't even factor in a potential stranger from out of town."

Ken put both palms up in a *calm-down* gesture. "And in the second place, you have to look at who was connected to the Chatham family. Out of those fourteen hundred possible contributors—it's less than that, but I will use your example—how many of those folks knew the Chathams?" Barclay could see where he was going but was still unconvinced.

Ken smiled, and Barclay said, "What have you got? What are you not telling me?"

Ken slid back in his chair and said, "How many of your fourteen hundred potential contributors also left their fingerprints at the scene of the most gruesome homicide the city has ever seen?"

Barclay, who was leaning against the front of his desk, was up and took a step toward the forensics man. "Fingerprints. What fingerprints?"

"The flashlight," Ken said.

Barclay flopped down in his chair, "Look, man, it's getting late, and I still have a few hours of work left to do."

Ken continued, "I noticed in the photograph of the flashlight that it was covered in what I assumed was fingerprint dust. Back then, smaller police agencies sent their prints to us for processing. On a hunch, I went through our archives and found where the prints were cataloged. I ran them through IAFIS and got a hit. The senator provided his fingerprints for a background check to obtain a security clearance while serving in D.C. Solid match, too. Whoever took the prints in sixty-three did a damn fine job. That chrome was also an optimum surface to retain prints. So...yes, Barclay, he, or at least his flashlight, was there that night."

TWENTY-SIX

January 5

By lunchtime, Barclay had the two reports he was waiting on. The first arrived via email from Katrina Anderton, whose name Barclay didn't immediately recognize when he first saw the message. However, when he clicked to open the email, recognition bloomed, and he remembered her as the analyst from Genome 23.

The body of her email stated that a report was attached regarding the completed family tree to include all the grandchildren of Charles and Inez Peterson. Barclay opened the attachment and scrolled through the PDF report until he got to the part he was looking for. According to Katrina Anderton, the Petersons have five grandchildren, and only one of them is a male: Arnold Gillespie, Jr.

Barclay read the report twice, sure he was missing something. He stared at the results, trying to make sense of what he was reading. He began mentally ticking off what he knew: the first time they spoke, Katrina assured him that the DNA on the cigarette belonged to a male grandchild of the Petersons; the only male grandchild, Barclay now knew, was Arnold Gillespie, Jr. Not only did the DNA on the cigarette not match the senator, but it matched a man named Eddie Howard who was an escapee from Alcatraz in 1962.

Barclay rolled that information around in his head for a few minutes as he leaned back in his chair and gazed out the window at nothing particular. A chorus of laughter from somewhere in the office interrupted his train of thought, which frustrated him. He reached out to his laptop and slammed the lid shut. He stood and walked to his office door, and slammed it shut. Had he given Katrina Anderton too much credit? He knew nothing about genealogy DNA and had given her effusive praise when they spoke the first time, but had he been wrong? She was well aware of his lack of knowledge and understanding in the field of genealogy DNA, so had she taken advantage of that ignorance and made herself seem much smarter than she was? Was her initial report bullshit? Was the whole idea of solving a crime with genealogy DNA bullshit?

No, he thought. AJ Murphy had vouched for her, and she had even helped him solve a cold case; she'd personally assisted in solving dozens of cold cases around the country. Moreover, he was a seasoned, savvy prosecutor who was not easily taken.

What am I missing? He walked to his office window, shoved his hands into his pockets, and looked out upon the cold gray sky. He absently pulled out his Kershaw pocketknife and thumbed the blade open, then closed, open, then closed, like that repeatedly as he ran through everything. He couldn't make it work and, after several minutes, allowed himself that he didn't know squat about genealogy DNA and needed to trust Katrina. There must be an explanation if he didn't get the expected outcome. He chastised himself for questioning her ability. He was the one who was off into a world he knew nothing about, not her.

He resolved to call Katrina Anderton. In that moment, he had a strong, unexplainable belief that she was the key to solving this case.

———

"Katrina Anderton," said the familiar voice on the other end of the line.

"Hey, Katrina. This is Barclay Griffith in Alabama."

"Oh hey there, Barclay Griffith in Alabama," she said with mild surprise. "I just sent you an email, probably not thirty minutes ago."

"Yeah, that's what I'm calling about." He paused, searching for how to ask the question he needed answered. "I need some help here."

"Sure. What's your issue?"

He ran through the problem: her report identifying the senator as the only male grandchild and the DNA from the cigarette matching someone else—a man from twenty-five hundred miles away, no less.

"Well," she began, "my report was based on a profile we developed from blood on the machete sheath. I never tested a cigarette butt."

Silence on the line.

After several seconds, Katrina said, "Barclay? You there?"

An exhale. "Yes, I'm here." Silence, then, "I'm an idiot."

A laugh on the other end of the line. "Sorry, I don't mean to laugh."

"No, no. It's fine. Ah, jeez." Then he explained. "This whole time, I've had it in my head that the killer left the cigarette behind. We got a name and a match on it, so when I got your completed family tree and didn't see the name I expected, I got a little frustrated. I felt like we were getting so close, and your report seemed like a complete reset of the investigation."

"I take it this Arnold Gillespie, Jr. is not the DNA match to your cigarette?"

"He's not."

"I don't want to insult your intelligence, but maybe he's the match to the blood on the sheath. Like I said, that's what I based my research on."

Barclay was nodding, eyes closed, and said, "Yep. I realized my mistake when you just mentioned it."

"Mr. Murphy and I discussed the cigarette butt when he first reached out. He wanted to send me the profile forensics generated, but I told him we needed a fresh DNA source because we develop our profile differently from the state people. That's when he sent me the cardboard sheath."

"I can't believe I could be so stupid. I got so damned focused on that cigarette..."

"Don't beat yourself up. Often times, when law enforcement first dips their toe into genetic genealogy to try and solve a case, they think it's a silver bullet when it is anything but. While we believe a great deal in what we're doing, and I've seen it solve numerous homicides, it's not quite the magic pill police think it is. The successes get the headlines, but there are a lot of cases we work on that don't end with an arrest or conviction."

"That makes sense," said Barclay, deflated.

"If it helps, we rarely use the entire extract to develop a profile, so we can send what we have left to your state lab. Maybe that will match Mr. Gillespie."

"Well, Katrina, if your research is correct, then it has to match. He has to be our guy."

———

AFTER HANGING up with Katrina Anderton, Barclay picked up the phone and dialed Ken Pevey. He left a voicemail, hung up, then dialed the lab director's cell phone. The phone didn't even ring in Barclay's ear before it was answered.

"Damn, Ken, you staring at your phone? It didn't even ring."

"Actually, I was dialing your number when you called."

"I've already had one major disappointment this morning, so I hope you have something good for me."

"I'm standing in the DNA lab, and we just got an identification on the remains from the well. It's definitely Kathryn Chatham."

"Ah, man."

"That a good thing or a bad thing?"

Barclay's shrug was lost through the phone. "Neither, I guess. It just is."

"Were you calling for anything particular?"

Barclay shook his head, clearing it, then said, "We sent a piece of evidence to a private lab for analysis." Ken made a noise of faux derision. "Look, until you start doing genealogy DNA, I don't have many options, and you're not one of them."

"Yeah, yeah, yeah."

"Anyway," Barclay said, moving the conversation along, "the lab was able to narrow down our list of suspects in this Chatham case. Only the DNA profile from the cigarette butt didn't match any of the suspects they gave us."

"A private lab?"

"Yes, a private lab. But that's not the point. The point is they developed the suspect pool through other biological evidence, and now I need you to check the senator's DNA against this other evidence. Katrina Anderton is the scientist we've been working with. She will send you the remaining extraction to develop a profile to test against the profile you developed for Arnold Gillespie, Jr."

The silence that followed conveyed Pevey's annoyance better than anything he could have said.

"What?" Barclay finally asked.

"We don't typically work from an extraction taken by another lab."

"Well, this isn't a typical case."

"Is there any biological evidence left on the item they tested? Maybe we could get the original piece of evidence and test it ourselves."

"No, sorry. It wasn't a large sample, to begin with, and there isn't any left to test. I'm afraid the extraction is your only option."

Barclay could hear Pevey scratching the hair on his chin. "I suppose if that's all we have, it will have to do. What did you say her name was?"

Barclay gave Ken the scientist's name and contact information and asked him, unnecessarily, to let him know the moment the lab made the comparison.

They were about to end the call when Ken said, "Oh, wait. You still there?"

"I'm still here."

"The ME's report is back on the autopsy of the bones, and no cause of death could be determined. The defect in the skull, by itself, didn't give the ME enough to make an official finding. The manner of death was ruled as undetermined because although she was found in the well, it's possible she just fell in. Keep in mind that this doesn't rule anything *out*; it's just what protocol dictates in these instances."

"That makes sense. I wasn't optimistic about that, but I'm glad we went ahead with the examination. Appreciate you indulging me with the private lab."

"Yeah, yeah, yeah."

TWENTY-SEVEN

January 27

The preliminary hearing docket was rolling into its third hour, and most of the cases still remained. He was in the middle of a case involving an individual who attempted to cash a forged check at a bank. The defendant was arrested on the scene and confessed to forging the check and attempting to cash it. Defense counsel was cross-examining the case agent, and Barclay wondered why they were even bothering with a prelim in such an open and shut case when his cell phone buzzed on the tabletop.

He saw it was Ken Pevey, so he dashed off a text stating he was in court and asked if it were urgent. Ken responded that it was not urgent but involved DNA in the Chatham case.

That made it urgent to Barclay, so he texted an ADA in his office asking them to come down and handle the rest of the prelim docket.

While he waited to be relieved, the forged check case was bound over to the grand jury. He began another prelim involving a traffic stop, an odor of marijuana, a probable cause search of the vehicle, and the subsequent discovery of a backpack that held the defendant's wallet, ID, a prescription pill bottle with the label scraped off and a couple of dozen assorted pills ranging from Alprazolam to Oxycontin to Adderall. A quantity of Meth was also found in the backpack, along with marijuana, a small glass smoking pipe, a digital scale, an assortment of small baggies, and a stolen handgun. The defendant told police he didn't know anything about the backpack or its contents despite the fact it contained his personal effects.

The ADA sat beside Barclay at the counsel table as he tendered the witness for cross-examination. After nearly ten minutes of fruitless and repetitive questioning by defense counsel, the case was bound over to the grand jury, and the judge called the next case. Barclay handed off the docket to the ADA and went back to his office, where he called Ken Pevey.

———

"Tell me you have something."

"Oh, I've got something, alright," said Ken. "Only I don't suspect it's what you want to hear."

Barclay was perched on the corner of his desk with his phone to his ear. Then, hearing Ken, he dropped his head, hissed, "Shit," and said, "Tell me."

"No match."

"Are you fucking kidding me, Ken?"

"Nope. The DNA from the machete sheath does not match Arnold Gillespie, Jr."

"I just don't get it," Barclay said more to himself. "Alright, Ken. I appreciate you getting back to me on that."

"Sure thing, but I did find something interesting if you'd like to hear it."

"Ken, I'm not really in the mood right now. If you've got something, just tell me."

Ken got right to it. "On a hunch, I compared the DNA profile from the cigarette to the machete sheath. They matched."

This got Barclay's attention. "You're shittin' me."

"Nope."

Barclay began to pace. "Well, okay. That's definitely...something."

"And another thing," said Ken, "we have to do some more research, but it looks like the person whose DNA is on the cigarette and the sheath is related to Mr. Gillespie."

Barclay almost dropped his phone. "Say that again."

"The DNA profile from the cigarette and the sheath have a number of consistencies with the DNA profile of Arnold Gillespie, Jr. I don't know how they're related, but my analyst assures me they are."

Barclay did not quite know what to do with the information he was just given. Ken had nothing else for him, so he ended the call.

Barclay rolled this revelation around in his head and took off for Fitz's office, where he found his chief investigator on the telephone. They made eye contact, and Fitz waved him in. The smell of a sandalwood candle filled the space, slightly relaxing a now amped-up Barclay Griffith.

He walked behind the investigator, who was up and resting his elbows on the desk, and peered out the window. They shared a similar view of the square, although the investigator's office had only a single window to the outside. Within a minute, the phone call was over, and, hearing the call coming to a close, Barclay went to stand in front of Fitz's desk.

Phone back in the cradle, Fitz said, "What's up, Boss?"

Barclay leaned on Fitz's desk with both hands and asked him

to get Beck Lawson on the line. Once that was done, he told them what he had just learned from Ken.

It was Lawson who spoke first. "How does that fit with the information we got from Genome 23?"

"Good question," said Barclay as he dropped into a chair in front of Fitz's desk. "Dr. Anderton told us the DNA belonged to a male grandchild of the Petersons, and then she further confirmed the Peterson's only male grandchild was Arnold Gillespie, Jr. Only now we know Gillespie isn't a match." He said this more as an expression of thought than conversational as he put two fingers to his lips, looking past Fitz out the window. "Do either of you have any thoughts? Because I'm lost."

Fitz shrugged.

Lawson said, "Let's walk through it logically. If the DNA tracks back to a male grandchild of the Peterson family and that person is not Gillespie, then he's clearly not the only male Peterson grandchild, right? It would seem to me that there has to be another male grandchild out there that Anderton hasn't identified."

———

BARCLAY AND FITZ convened in the war room, soon joined by Lawson, who came over from the PD. The first thing they did was call AJ Murphy to fill him in on the developments, and then they called Katrina Anderton. They got a recorded message stating the offices were closed for lunch, which they hadn't considered. The lab was located in Tempe, Arizona, which was on Mountain Standard Time and one hour behind them in Towne.

"Who ate all the candy?" Fitz asked, pointing to the near-empty candy bowl in the middle of the table.

Lawson peered into the candy bowl and said, "What're you talking about? There's candy in there."

Fitz gave a withering look. "Almond Joy ain't no candy."

Lawson and Fitz debated the merits of Almond Joy, and while Fitz begrudgingly agreed it was candy, in the technical sense, Lawson agreed with *him* that as far as candy rated, it was at or near the bottom.

The great Almond Joy debate settled, they moved on to reviewing and updating the whiteboard with what they knew. Under the senator's name, Fitz added that his DNA was not a match for either the cigarette butt or the blood on the machete sheath. Fitz wrote *Possibly Related?* next to the latest additions to the list. He then included the low-percentage DNA match to the machete handle and the fact that his fingerprints were found on the flashlight at the scene.

Fitz added a line under the name Eddie Howard: *DNA located at Chatham crime scene (inside and outside) November 1963. Related to Senator Gillespie?*

When Fitz finished writing, he said, "Boss, did the FBI mention whether or not this Eddie Howard was still alive? Anything at all about his whereabouts after escaping from Alcatraz?"

Barclay considered the question and said, "I don't believe they ever did. Surely he would not have lived under the name Eddie Howard after his escape."

"Probably not, but someone needs to run it down, tie it off," said Lawson

"You're right. Fitz, why don't you reach out to that FBI Agent, Simpson, and see what they have."

Fitz nodded as he capped the dry-erase marker and laid it in the tray beneath the whiteboard. They both stood back, studying the board—nothing sliding into place.

"What are you thinking?" Barclay asked.

Fitz slowly shook his head, not taking his eyes off the board. "I just don't know, Boss."

Silence as they studied the board further. Then Lawson said, "Let's talk about what we know...or at least what we strongly believe. Eddie Howard is the likely killer, or at the very least, he was there and involved."

"Ok," said Barclay. Fitz nodded.

"If he is our guy, then, on its face, it would appear to be a random stranger home invasion murder, right?"

"True, except for the fact that the senator's fingerprints were there and possibly his DNA on one of the murder weapons," said Barclay

Fitz weighed that statement with a waggle of his head from one shoulder to the next. "Playing devil's advocate here...the senator knew the Chatham's, right? Or let me say we know he knew Kathryn Chatham. I suppose we would need to find out if he knew the Chatham family beyond Kathryn, but I say that to say maybe the flashlight and the machete were his and Mr. Chatham, the father, borrowed them, and the killer, Howard, grabbed them before going in. Maybe they were in the garage, and he took them inside the house with him."

Lawson: "The killer shows up ostensibly with a shotgun but goes into the garage searching for a flashlight and machete before going in? I don't see it."

Fitz: "What if the killer forgot his flashlight and needed one? He goes into the garage to find one, does, and while he's in there, he sees the machete and decides to take it and use it. It's quieter than a shotgun."

"Hmmm...plausible," Barclay said with a slow nod.

Lawson: "But the elephant in the room is the senator's possible relationship with Eddie Howard. How does that square with any of this?"

Fitz: "Well, this is either a stranger home invasion or it's not. If it is, then Eddie Howard's a lone actor. He's a dangerous escaped prisoner and somehow makes it from San Francisco to little ol'

Towne and wipes out a family for some damn reason. *Or* it's someone the Chathams knew which could still make Eddie Howard our guy. I mean, maybe he was doing odd jobs for them around the house, or maybe he worked for Mr. Chatham at his hardware store or any number of other possible connections. But if it is someone the Chathams knew, this entire board becomes a suspect list."

Lawson: "But let's not lose sight of the evidence, Fitz. The physical evidence points to two people: Howard and the senator. That's it."

Fitz: "True."

Barclay: "My head hurts."

———

FIGURING they had given the folks at Genome 23 enough time to return from lunch, Lawson, Fitz, and Barclay stared at the telephone in the middle of the table in the war room—Fitz seated and Barclay standing but leaning on the table the same as Lawson. On the third ring, an automated voice answered, and through a series of prompts, including typing the first three letters of Katrina Anderton's last name, they connected directly to her desk.

When she answered, Barclay introduced himself and told her she was on speakerphone. She told them she had a conference call at the top of the hour and would call them back if that didn't leave enough time. Barclay said he didn't think it would take long and jumped right in.

"Alright, Katrina, you did fantastic work narrowing down our suspect field. And after we last spoke, you sent the DNA extract to our lab, and they tested against the known standard of a possible suspect based on your research."

"Ok," she said in a way that told Barclay she was listening and following closely.

"Well, that DNA did not match our suspect."

"Ok."

"The problem is, based on your research, he should be the guy —Arnold Gillespie, Jr. He's the Peterson's only grandson."

"Hmmmm." The sound of tapping on a computer keyboard came through the phone's speaker.

Barclay continued, "Our lab says that while the DNA profiles from the cigarette and the sheath and the known standard from Gillespie don't match, they are related to some degree."

"Oh...I wasn't expecting that," said Anderton.

"Yeah, neither were we. Can you give us some insight into what could explain this? And if I sent you the suspect's DNA profile, could you then tell me if or how they are related?"

"Yeah, I should be able to do that, no problem. But are you sure about this?"

"Truthfully? I'm not sure about any of this stuff. You gave us a name that fits from the standpoint of time and place, but that's about it. Nothing else about this particular person's involvement makes any sense at all. Then a second person's DNA shows up in the middle of this case; only he turns out to have escaped from Alcatraz a little more than a year prior to these murders."

"My goodness," she said reflexively.

"On top of all of that, I'm being told the two people may be related." Barclay plopped down in a chair as if exhausted from laying it all out there.

"My goodness," she said again. "What have you all gotten yourselves into?"

"I'm afraid to even find out."

"I've got to go. Send me what you've got, and I will get back to you."

TWENTY-EIGHT

February 3

Barclay, Fitz, Lawson, and AJ Murphy were back in the war room. They had a call scheduled with Katrina Anderton in less than an hour, and they were using that time to review the updates to the whiteboard in the hope that it may shake something loose.

The group went back and forth, agreeing and disagreeing, debating and discussing, pounding mini-Reese's cups—gold foil wrappers littering the tabletop—and mini-Mr. Goodbars—their familiar yellow labels littering the surface as well.

They ran through the list of names on the whiteboard and were left with only three as far as suspects were concerned: Eddie Howard, Senator Arnold Gillespie, Jr., and Larry Butler. Every other name that had come up had an iron-clad alibi for the time of the murders.

Eddie was at the top because of the DNA, while Larry Butler was relegated to merely a tangential concern at best. They had come to believe Butler was associated with Kathryn Chatham on a more than friendly basis around the time of the murders, and coupled with the fact that he quit the force shortly after what they now know to be the time of her death, kept him on the shortlist as a person of interest. Throw in the fact that he lied about why and how he ended up standing guard outside her room at the hospital, and he could not be completely ignored. His general demeanor and response to being questioned about the case was discussed, but it was agreed that it wasn't enough to move him from where he now sat in their collective minds.

Senator Gillespie was the wildcard, and there was no consensus about what to do with him. They all agreed that he could not be discarded, but try as they may, they couldn't make it work. Murder was one thing. Everyone in the room had been around long enough not to be surprised by any particular person committing any particular crime; however, this case was especially heinous. It was worse than anything any of them had ever been a part of, and that was what was especially confounding trying to determine the senator's involvement.

"Even figuring Eddie Howard for it...why?" asked Murphy. "It wasn't a robbery. Why go in and systematically annihilate an entire family like that?"

A few moments passed when Barclay said, "Do you just chalk it up to evil in the world?"

"No. This is beyond evil. That man had a reason. I'd bet my pension on it."

———

THE PHONE RANG, and Fitz pushed the speaker button to answer it—Katrina Anderton's voice filled the room. Fitz asked for a minute before they began because Barclay had stepped out.

Time passed with AJ and Katrina making small talk. When Barclay finally walked into the room, she was telling AJ about being interviewed for the CBS crime show 48 Hours regarding her role in helping solve a twenty-one-year-old cold case.

She finished her story, and Barclay said, "Please tell me you have something to make all our dreams come true."

"Well, I don't claim to know your wildest dreams, but I can tell you that Arnold Gillespie and Eddie Howard are related. Half-brothers would be my guess."

"So, another male grandchild of Charles and Inez Peterson?" Lawson said, flashing a satisfied look at Barclay and Fitz.

"That's exactly right, Detective," Anderton said.

Barclay, Fitz, and Lawson were still locked in a stare-down. She mouthed, "Told you."

"You still there?"

"We're here," said Lawson. "My coworkers are just letting this little nugget soak in."

Fitz smiled; Barclay did not. The DA looked down at the phone and said, "I guess my first question is, why did this Eddie Howard not make it into your family tree?"

"How did I know that would be your first question?" Her voice was light and absent any animus.

"That is not a criticism. I'm just trying to understand."

"Uh-huh," she said. Again her tone was light. "My reports and their conclusions are only as good as the information and records I can access. If there is, say, an illegitimate birth, and the folks involved want it kept quiet, then..."

"Got it."

"Now, before any of you go and get too excited, I need to tell you that I was only able to determine relation via DNA commonality. I could not find anything connecting Eddie Howard to the Gillespies, which is where this connection most likely originated. In other words, based on everything I know about familial DNA and genealogy, I'm guessing they share a common father and that

Mr. Gillespie, Sr. dipped his pen in the wrong inkwell somewhere along the way."

That last statement straightened everyone up at the table.

Barclay said, "Now, I know you have more to give us."

"I see you are finally coming around to my abilities."

"Oh, you're a certified badass, which is why I'm certain you have more."

He could hear her grinning through the phone line. Finally, she cleared her throat and said, "I dug around and could not find a birth certificate for an Eddie Howard, born in 1939. Based on that, I expanded my search to include adoptions, which, incidentally, is how I got started in the field of genetic genealogy, so I am especially proficient in that area. Those can be tricky, with privacy laws and a scarcity of public information, but, as luck would have it, California is one of only a handful of states that allows public access to adoption records. Since he served time in Alcatraz, it was the first place I looked." She paused, and Barclay was about to speak when she continued, "Eddie Howard was adopted by Mr. and Mrs. Anthony Howard of Sacramento, California, in 1941. Eddie Howard, it turns out, came into this world as Eddie Jones, born to a Rebecca Jones of Macon, Georgia, April 30, 1939."

THE PHONE CALL WAS COMPLETED, and with the rush of new information, they sat in silence as each of them weighed what they had just been told.

"AJ?" Barclay said.

AJ took a deep breath, slid his chair away from the table, walked over to the whiteboard, and grabbed a marker. He stood before the board, staring at it, tapping the marker in the palm of his left hand. After more than a minute, below *Eddie Howard,* he wrote: *Born Eddie Jones April 30, 1939. Birth Mother-Rebecca*

Jones (Macon, GA). Adopted 1941 by Mr. and Mrs. Anthony Howard (Sacramento, CA).

He capped the marker and returned it to the tray. He turned to face the table and made a sucking noise through his teeth.

"Here's what I think we need to do," AJ began. "We need to focus our efforts on Eddie Howard slash Jones, Arnold Gillespie, Jr., and Larry Butler."

"You sure we've reached that point?" Barclay asked.

AJ nodded. "The thing about cold cases—particularly those that are this old—is that people, evidence, and information will all be sparse. Barclay, the mountain that was this case six weeks ago when we first met, cannot be understated, yet here we are." He gestured with his hand to the whiteboard. "How much more do you think you can get? Is there anyone left to talk to?"

Barclay was about to speak when AJ held a hand up and said, "Now, don't get me wrong. We still have a lot to do, but at some point, we have to choose a path and take it."

Lawson said, "I agree. Shit, or get off the pot."

"That was eloquent," said Barclay.

"She's right," said Fitz.

"You have three damned good suspects on this board, in my opinion. Hell, you've got DNA at the scene for two of them." AJ's voice was rising now, not out of disrespect but out of passion. "Sure, you can keep digging and continue looking into this or that and trying to speak to this person or that person, but, realistically, would that truly get you closer to an answer than we are now? And keep in mind, with each new name you throw in the mix, that's one more thread that needs to be explored and tied off."

He made his way to his seat at the table and said, "Let's put our energy into Howard, Gillespie, and, to a lesser extent, Butler. Who knows, maybe Howard's our guy, and we find out he's dead and exceptionally clear it through a grand jury." He shrugged. "Maybe we clear all three suspects and reassess. But, honestly, I believe the killer or killers are listed on that board." He pointed a beefy left index finger across his body to the board. "It's time to build our case...or clear them."

He glanced at Lawson, which prompted Barclay to do the same.

"You know what I think," she said.

"They're right, Boss," said Fitz.

Barclay eyed AJ and said, "How do we move forward?"

"The first thing we need to do is see what we can find out about Eddie Howard after the escape. I would have thought he'd head straight for Mexico or some other such place, and maybe he did. But we know for certain he was in Towne, Alabama, on November 23, 1963. Whatever he did after his escape, it's hard to imagine him not living under an alias, so I don't expect to find much, if anything, after June 1962, but we gotta look. Do a deep dive into the name, DOB, and social to mark it off the list as done. We need to do the same with Arnold Gillespie, Jr. and Larry Butler." AJ rocked back, putting his chair on its rear legs. He said, "There was a motive here; just have to find it."

TWENTY-NINE

February 5

AJ Murphy sat on his twenty-eight-foot Bennington QX Tritoon in the middle of a quiet Lake Martin. It was approaching 1:00 in the morning, and the cloudless sky allowed the full light of the three-quarter moon to be reflected on the glass-like water. Custom blue LED lights ringed the boat's deck on both the exterior and interior, giving it a glow reminiscent of police lights. The lights had a functional purpose, serving as a visibility and safety feature, but it was also cosmetic—Murphy thought they looked cool.

The retired and sometimes part-time investigator routinely operated on only a few hours of sleep per night, rarely getting to bed before midnight, the result of living a 1980s undercover narc life. When he was active on a case, he would wait for his wife to go to bed, then pack a cooler of beer or tote a bottle of bourbon, depending on weather and mood. He would pilot his boat to one of his favorite spots and dig into his case file as he drifted with the current.

The night was mild—temperature around forty degrees. With no wind to speak of, the combination of layers, and the warm orange glow from his small propane-powered Mr. Heater knocking down the chill in his immediate area, he was quite comfortable. He never felt as productive as he did sitting on his boat under a clear sky, free from the city's light pollution, with a canopy of so many stars. Jupiter held its usual spot as the brightest object in the night sky; a reddish-orange glow was also present. Murphy had spent enough nights out here to know Mars when he saw it.

He was reclined in the leather chaise, his back against the cockpit, and he was reading through the black three-ring binder for the umpteenth time. It contained everything he had compiled regarding the background of the three players they had agreed to focus on: Howard, Gillespie, and Butler. He was developing an idea, a theory, and he knew he needed to be absolutely certain about it before bringing it to the district attorney. If what he believed to be true was true, then oh boy.

He closed the binder, switched off the reading lamp clipped to the top, and laid the binder on the deck. He blindly groped for the bottle of Old Forester as he stared off into the distance. Finding it, he refilled the rocks glass and raised it to his lips—the warm feeling spreading through his chest. He took another drink as he thought through what he believed he had figured out.

He was working through how to present it to Barclay when a gust of wind kicked up, gone as quickly as it appeared. He finished off his glass and set it on the deck, then zipped his orange Arcteryx down jacket the rest of the way up, covering his neck and throat. He sniffed as he lay his head back and closed his eyes, running through it one more time.

His body shuttered awake—he'd dozed off for a few minutes. He checked his watch: 2:38 AM. He took a moment to get his bearings before swinging his legs to the side and standing up. When he stood, he kicked over the quarter-full bottle of bourbon.

He leaned down with a grunt as he bent to retrieve it and placed it in a cup holder. He sat behind the wheel and reached for the key when he noticed running lights a mile or so to the northwest. He cranked the boat, and the rumble of the dual outboards vibrated the deck just a little.

He pushed the throttle forward, slowly at first, as he oriented himself and shook the sleep from his eyes, then pointed the boat home and opened up the engines. It didn't take long for the brace of frigid wind to start his eyes watering as he squinted into the chill. He was thinking about his discovery as he glided over the moonlit water, not overly optimistic he'd get any sleep now that he knew there was a killer in their midst.

———

BARCLAY WAS FINISHING up the first passes of his straight razor on the right side of his lathered face when his cell phone rang. He looked down at the phone lying face up on his bathroom counter, and the caller ID read simply *Fitz*. Barclay paused an episode of *The Andy Griffith Show* playing on his iPad and answered the call.

He activated the speakerphone and said, "Hey, Fitz, what's up?"

"Morning, Boss. You have a minute?" His radio baritone bounced around the hard surfaces of the bathroom.

"I've got as much time as you need," said Barclay, looking in the mirror as he continued to shave.

"Remember Walter Jackson telling me and Lawson about seeing Kathryn Chatham walking with a man in the woods when he was out throwing the football?"

"Yeah." Barclay was working on the left side of his face now.

"I woke up about 3:00 this morning to go to the bathroom, and as I laid back down, I had a thought. Something Walter told us during that interview. He mentioned his family had a video camera; said his mom would use it to film him playing football with his dad."

"Mm-hmm," Barclay said, concentrating on shaving and trying not to slit his throat with the finely-honed blade.

Fitz said, "You need to call me back?"

"Hmm? Oh, no. Sorry, just finishing up. I'm listening. You mentioned a video camera."

"Right, well, I got to thinking. What if Kathryn and this mystery man were caught on video?"

That drew Barclay's full attention. He looked at the phone. "What do you mean caught on video?"

"He told us that his mother would film him playing catch, running routes, that sort of thing. What if, while filming him, she caught something in the background? Like maybe Kathryn Chatham being walked into the woods. I mean, he did say he saw Kathryn and this mystery man while he was outside at halftime of the ballgame."

"Huh." After several seconds of silence, Barclay said, "That seems like the longest of long shots."

"I hear you, Boss, and I don't disagree, but, man, what if?"

Barclay made a noise that told Fitz he was thinking.

Fitz said, "I thought I'd reach out to Mr. Jackson today and see what I could find out. See if he has those home movies somewhere." After no immediate response, he said, "What else are we going to do? Better than just sitting around, right?"

"No, I'm with you, Fitz. Just running it through...You know what? Go for it. Damn sure don't want to look back and think we left any stone unturned. See if Lawson will go with you."

"Already spoke to her and told her what I wanted to do."

"And what did she say?"

"What do you think?"

"She loved the idea," Barclay deadpanned.

Fitz barked a laugh. "Hardly."

"I bet she didn't hesitate to help you, though."

"I didn't even have to ask."

———

ON HIS WAY TO WORK, Barclay pulled into the parking lot of his favorite coffee shop, The Knockbox. He was reading an email on his phone as he opened the door and stepped inside, almost colliding with a customer leaving.

"Whoa," said the customer. Then, "Ahhh."

Barclay looked up, embarrassed, and began to apologize when he saw who it was.

AJ Murphy transferred the cup from his right hand to his left and started shaking spilled coffee off his now-empty hand. Barclay shook his head, still holding the door open, and said, "Ah man, I'm sorry."

"It's fine. Just a few drops, so no damage done." He wiped the back of his hand on his blue jeans. "I was actually headed to your office to meet with you."

"Well, you just want to grab a table here?" He inclined his head toward the store's interior.

"We can do that." AJ backed into the coffee shop and claimed the rear-most table. The shop had a steampunk vibe and smelled strongly of brewed coffee, freshly ground beans, and the earthy tang of incense. The business was busy, but with customers primarily grabbing coffees and pastries to-go, only four of the dozen tables were occupied.

The large, commercial espresso machine hissed and gurgled as it worked on a shot of espresso. The sound masked the chatter of people in the cafe and mixed with the whirr of the coffee grinder and the pings of steam warming the milk for cappuccinos and lattes to serve as a kind of coffee shop orchestra. Combined with the soft EDM music that spilled from ceiling-mounted speakers, an ambient soundtrack was produced, creating a sonic tapestry that provided them with just enough privacy.

Barclay was following Murphy to the table when he caught the attention of Kelly, one of the baristas. He ordered, and the barista, a brunette with a loop nose ring and a neck tattoo of the guy from Shel Silverstein's poem *My Beard*, gave him a head bob as she poured steamed milk for a cappuccino.

The chairs for the customers were blonde wood with rebar legs, making them heavy to move. Barclay pulled a chair out and sat at the table. "Is this your first time here?"

AJ had the lid off his coffee, steam rising. "I've been here once before. I'm more of a Maxwell House guy, but I needed something strong because I'm running on about two hours of sleep."

"You, too? Fitz called me this morning. He had an epiphany about the case during the night and didn't get much sleep either."

Barclay heard his name called, and he saw Kelly placing his dark roast pour over on the counter. He got up and walked to the counter, pulled some cash out of his pants pocket, peeled off a five and two ones, and laid the money on the counter. Then, he moved down the counter, added cream and sugar, stirred with a wooden stick, and sat back at the table.

AJ took another drink of coffee and said, "What did Fitz come up with?"

"Just a hunch. A long shot, really, but what the hell, you know."

"What the hell, indeed," AJ said before sipping more coffee.

A minute passed as they sat, enjoying their coffee and watching the hustle of the crowd.

"You mentioned not sleeping last night. This case keeping you up, too?"

"Actually, yes..."

Barclay took a sip and stared at the investigator over the rim of his cup. Finally, he said, "You going to tell me what you found out?"

Murphy leaned in and said, "I believe Larry Butler is Eddie Howard."

Barclay let out a noise that sounded like a laugh but wasn't. He shook his head and said, "What?"

"You heard me. And I'm about ninety percent sure."

Barclay, rarely at a loss for words, was speechless. He opened his mouth and attempted more than once to say something, but he had nothing.

"Let me explain," said Murphy. "I first started digging around on Eddie Howard. I reached out to contacts at ACJIC and ROCIC, and as I figured, there was nothing from him after the prison escape. Nothing at all using his name, date of birth, or social security number. Nothing from anyone named Eddie Howard even remotely matching his description. Which is what you'd expect, right?"

Barclay nodded and sipped.

"So then I moved on to Larry Butler. Not because I suspected anything—he was just next on the list. Well, I couldn't find anything on him prior to 1963. Nothing. Zilch. In fact, the first record of any kind I have for him is his employment with the Towne PD."

"But AJ, come on, that doesn't mean anything—"

"Age is right. His build is right."

"Yeah, but...I mean, come on. How trustworthy are records or the lack thereof from sixty years ago." AJ began to speak, and Barclay said, "And how does he get hired on at the PD with no records check, fingerprints, background, anything?" His voice rose as he spoke before catching himself and looking around the coffee shop. No one was paying them any attention.

AJ said, "You're applying present-day standards to sixty years ago; it was a different time then. I don't know what the hiring process was like for police departments, but I doubt it was a very intensive check. They run the guy's record, and nothing shows up —then what? They couldn't exactly Google the guy or check his Facebook page. And as far as reliability of records...look, it's entirely possible I'm totally wrong here...but I don't believe I am."

"What am I supposed to do with this information? That's not enough to go to a judge with, let alone a grand jury."

"But DNA would, right?"

"What do you mean?"

"You've got Eddie Howard's DNA. You found a way to get the senator's DNA." A shrug, "So do the same with Butler."

An audible, tired exhale from Barclay. "Alright. We can work on that." Then, "Ah shit."

"What?"

"If Butler is Howard, then he and the senator are brothers; half-brothers, according to Katrina Anderton."

"Gee, this case keeps getting better."

THIRTY

L arry Butler arrived at his barbecue restaurant at exactly
4:00 in the morning, the same as he did every day except
for Sunday when The Magnolia Pig was closed. As he
always did, he pulled his early model red Ford F-150 around to the
rear of the building and parked. He slid out of the cab of his truck
wearing a buffalo plaid shirt-jacket over his usual coveralls and
went to the rear wall of the building and unlatched and swung
open a metal door set in the brick that was about two feet high
from the ground. He half walked, half limped to the stack of split
hickory logs, swung back the blue plastic tarp covering the wood-
pile, and made three trips tossing wood into the firebox.

After loading the firebox, he went inside, started a pot of
coffee brewing, and began making the biscuits that were most
responsible for packing his restaurant for breakfast. Biscuits now
in the oven, he poured coffee into a tall Styrofoam cup, sprinkled
in sugar from a cylindrical container, followed by non-dairy
creamer from a similar canister. When he was done with his coffee,

he would pour one more, and when he finished that second cup, he would use the cup to spit in as he chewed tobacco.

Once his coffee was poured, he set about checking on the pork shoulders he put on at closing the day prior. He pulled off what was ready, which was usually everything, and replaced it with new meat—he would repeat that process at closing time to be prepared for the following day's customers. He also served smoked chicken and turkey, but he wouldn't put those on for another couple of hours since they didn't take as long to cook.

Pulling meat from the smoker and replacing it typically led right up until the first customers began showing up at 6:00 AM, and today was no different. Employees—kitchen and wait staff— got to work at 5:30, preparing to meet the day's demands.

It may be in the upper thirties outside, but it was pushing ninety degrees inside the pit room. And Larry Butler began to sweat. He had the exterior door to the pit room opened just a crack for the cold February air, which didn't do much good, but it was something. Opening the door too wide would affect the airflow in the carefully constructed room, adversely affecting the meat, so he opted to sweat. He was constantly asked why he drank coffee as he sweltered in the pit room, and his response was always the same: *Because I want to.*

After half an hour or so and maybe a hundred pounds of meat out of the pit, he took his first haul to the kitchen. He then returned to his office, where he tore open a clear plastic bag containing a dozen freshly laundered white terrycloth hand towels from Cintas and wiped his face, neck, and forearms. He slung the towel over his shoulder, fixed his second cup of coffee, and went back to work pulling meat off the pit—he hung the towel on the handle of the raised pit cover.

After about twenty minutes, the remaining meat was pulled and loaded onto a metal pushcart. He reached up and pulled the towel from the handle of the counter-weighted pit cover and wiped his sweat-laden face. He hung the towel back up, took a long sip of coffee, and pushed the cart to the kitchen.

He unloaded the cart and wiped it down, cleaning all the grease and other meat juices from its surfaces. As he loaded it with new meat to add to the smoker, he made small talk with Jackie, Larry's right hand for the last fifty years. Jackie, an older black man about the same age as Larry, was lean and sinewy. He wore the same coveralls as Larry but no hat on his shiny bald head. He had two primary responsibilities: season the meat pre-smoke and chop, pull, and slice the meat as customers ordered it. It had been decades since he needed a scale to know how much meat to serve. He was busy rubbing down the meats with their secret rub when Larry was chatting him up. They talked about this and that—mainly sports and politics, depending on the time of year. As of late, it seemed sports and politics were becoming increasingly intertwined, which neither man liked.

Jackie told him what was ready to go into the pit, and Larry piled it up on the cart and then returned to the pit room. After the cart was empty and the meat was loaded onto the smokers, he scanned the pit area, making sure everything was in its place. He reached up absently and grabbed for the towel hooked through the handle attached to the pit cover and grasped only air. He continued to grope for the towel before finally looking up. The towel was gone.

He looked down to his right and saw his coffee cup, half-full, in the same spot he'd left it. He looked around the space, hazy with smoke. He was more suspicious than confused. He was eighty-four years old, but his mind was still sharp. He was not forgetful and knew where he'd left his towel—the same place he always left it when working in the pit room. The added leverage from the towel helped him lower the heavy lid.

And that was when he noticed it. The exterior door was open wider than he left it. Not by much, but it was. Perhaps not noticeable to anyone else, but he noticed it and knew Jackie would also. He slowly made his way across the dirt floor to the door. He looked out the expanded opening for several seconds before sliding it open further, the blast of chilled air feeling even colder on his sweat-covered face, cooling him almost instantly. He took a careful step outside and looked left and then right. Nothing.

The rear of the property backed up to a wooded lot, and he stared into those woods, not seeing or hearing anything.

"Larry."

Larry Butler was still scanning the area behind his building when he said, "What is it, Jackie?"

"Just checking on you, friend. We got lots more meat to put on them pits, and when you didn't come back...Well, I was just checking on you."

"Thank you, Jackie," Larry said, not taking his eyes off the exterior landscape. "I'm fine. Go on back into the kitchen. I'll be there in a minute."

THIRTY-ONE

February 15

W hat do you think about the wine?"
Barclay finished chewing and said, "It's fine, I
guess. You know all wine tastes about the same
to me."

Brittany gave him a look. "I realize you're no wine aficionado,
but all wine tastes the same? Come on."

"What can I say? I have a very unrefined palate."

She let out a sound of derision and jest, heavy on the jest. A
pizza box lay open on the kitchen island between them. It
contained two slices of pepperoni, feta, and banana pepper pizza.
Barclay had worked late and decided that it would be pizza night
for dinner, so he ran by their favorite pizza place and picked up
their preferred pie.

"Well, for your information, this particular pinot was
suggested to me by Molly, so do *not* tell her you didn't like it."
Molly Pheiffer was the widow of Barclay's best friend, Duncan
Pheiffer, who was murdered some eighteen months ago.

"First of all, I never said I didn't like it. Secondly, why in the world would I mention the wine to her? Even if I thought it was the best wine on the planet, I doubt I'd say anything to her about it."

"Mr. Griffith, you're telling me that if someone suggested something to you that turned out to be the best thing on the planet, you wouldn't let them know that and thank them for it?"

"Ok, yes. If someone gave me the best thing on the planet, I would tell them thank you."

"What if it were the second-best thing on the planet?"

Barclay shook his head and said, "Nope. Only the best thing."

"What? Someone gives you the second-best thing on the planet, and you wouldn't acknowledge it?"

"I would not. My cutoff is the best thing on the planet; otherwise, where do you draw the line? If you do it for the second best thing on the planet, then do you do it for the third best thing?"

"Yes, you do."

"You see, now you're in trouble because you can keep extrapolating it until you're thanking someone for something that's like the world's hundredth best thing. That's why I have a standard, and the standard is the best thing on the planet. Period."

"Don't be silly. It wouldn't get that far."

"Then what's your standard? Where do you draw the line?"

"I don't know. I guess I don't have one. If I like it, then I acknowledge it."

"And if you don't like something someone suggests, you lie and say you liked it."

She cut her eyes at him and made a playfully angry face. "I hate being married to a prosecutor."

Barclay crumpled the paper towel he had used as his plate and walked around the front of the island to throw it in the trash. He was finishing his glass of wine where he stood when his phone rang.

He fished it from his pants pocket and said, "Hey, Fitz." Fitz began to speak, and Barclay interrupted, "Say, Fitz, are you a wine guy?"

This got Brittany's attention. She was rinsing out her wine glass and turned off the water to listen.

Barclay lowered the phone and told her, "He says he's a wine guy." Then, he put the phone on speaker and said, "I've got a pinot noir from Australia. Is it supposed to be good?"

Fitz: "Now, how am I supposed to know that based on that limited amount of info?"

"You said you were a wine guy."

"What year is it?"

"What year is it?" Barclay circled the island and grabbed the bottle. "I have no idea. How do you find that out?"

"Forget it. I'd need to taste it anyway."

"Hmm. That's fair, I guess."

"You and Brit arguing about wine?"

He eyed Brittany, who was watching him. He said, "Brittany and I were *not* arguing about wine." This caused her to laugh out loud.

She jabbed a finger at Barclay and whispered, "That's why he's such a great investigator." She dried her wine glass, put it back in the cabinet, and left the kitchen.

"So, do you need anything in particular, or are you just calling to chat?"

"I finally got up with Walter Jackson this morning about those home movies."

"Dang, Fitz, I'd forgotten about that."

"Yeah, well, he's been traveling and just got back into town yesterday, and he allowed me and Lawson to come by and search through his attic."

"Ok," said Barclay in a tone asking why Fitz was telling him this.

"I'm still here."

"What?" Barclay looked at his watch. It was 7:30. "When did you get there?"

"Just after eight this morning."

"Holy cow. I hope you found something." Barclay drained the last of the wine and set the glass on the counter next to the sink.

"That's why I'm calling. I suppose the best answer is yes and no. We believe we've found the video we were looking for, and it shows a man and woman walking behind the Chatham house. Problem is, I'm not sure the quality is such that we can identify anyone."

"Well...," Barclay said, thinking.

"Any chance you can come over tonight and take a look? It's on eight-millimeter film that requires an old projector. We have everything set up here, and it would be a pain in the ass to move it. Rather not if we don't have to."

"Yeah, I can come by. Give me about twenty minutes."

Barclay ended the call, told Brittany what had come up, and left.

———

WALTER JACKSON LET Barclay in the house and took him upstairs to the room above the garage. The entire house still smelled of new construction and contained almost no furniture. He was led upstairs to the room where everything was set up. It was long and narrow with light brown carpet, and the walls and ceiling were painted a yellow-orange. It wasn't a color Barclay would have chosen, but he thought it worked. In the middle of the room, on a square card table, sat a reel-to-reel projector with film threaded through the machine.

Fitz said, "Okay, so I told Mr. Jackson what I was looking for. It took us a while, but we located several boxes of film in the attic along with this old projector. The film was not organized, and only a few reels were even labeled, so we just started watching rolls of film until we finally found what we were looking for. It took us a few dozen home movies, but I believe we found it."

Fitz nodded to Walter, who walked over and turned out the lights.

"What you're going to see," Fitz said, "is young Walter here running a pass route, his dad making a bad pass, and in an attempt to catch the ball, he loses his balance and falls into the fence. I'm guessing that makes a noise because the guy with whom we presume to be Kathryn Chatham whips his head around in the direction of the fence. It appears as if the couple slows down when he sees this before getting his head back around and walking her toward the woods."

Barclay nodded as he stared at the frozen image on the screen. Lights off, Fitz turned a knob on the side of the projector, and a warped sound came from the projector's speaker, followed by the fast clicking of the reel turning and the film moving through. The image on the screen began to move.

On the screen, a young boy—Walter Jackson—was wearing a blue three-quarter sleeve shirt with two orange stripes around the biceps and an orange interlocking AU on the front. He was holding a football under his right arm, smiling at the camera, and waving his left hand. There was no sound.

The boy tosses the ball to an older man with a cigarette in his mouth and a can of beer in his left hand—his father—and takes a wide receiver stance to his dad's right. His father says something, bobbing his head hard, and the boy takes off right to left on the screen. The boy runs straight before angling inside, and the pass comes in a bit out front. The boy reaches for the ball and loses his balance, falling headfirst into a chain link fence. He curved his body at the last minute, so his back took the brunt of the impact.

At the sound of the boy hitting the fence, the man with the

woman in the background looks over his right shoulder, appearing surprised, before gathering himself and continuing off camera, headed toward the woods. Fitz stops the film.

"Can you play that again?" Barclay asked.

Fitz rewound the film and played it back through.

"Ok, now play it back and stop it when the man looks back."

And that's what he did. The man and woman were now frozen on the screen. The image, though not great, was better than Barclay expected. Blown up on the wall, the image was plenty large enough for an identification...if the image were clearer.

Barclay walked closer to the image and stared at it, unable to make out much detail. He turned first to Fitz, then Walter, and said, "Thoughts?"

Walter said, "I didn't know the man then, and he doesn't look familiar now. Any idea who he is?"

Barclay looked back at the image and said, "We have an idea who it *could* be, but that's about it. We were hoping to get some manner of confirmation with this. Unfortunately, I'm not sure we got it. Can you at least confirm the girl in the film is Kathryn?"

"I think it's her...Yeah, I believe it is her."

To Fitz, Barclay said, "What did Lawson think about this?"

Fitz said, "Maybe. Maybe not. No way to tell."

"That's a good summation." Then, to Walter Jackson, he said, "Can we borrow this? I'd like to take it to Cameragraphics and have them make a digital file from it. Something we can watch on the computer."

"Of course. Absolutely."

"Appreciate you working with us, Mr. Jackson."

"I do hope you can solve this."

"We're getting damn close."

THIRTY-TWO

February 18

Murphy and Fitz were in the war room staring at a whiteboard when Barclay walked in with Detective Lawson. AJ glanced at Barclay before focusing back on the board. He opened his mouth to speak when Barclay said, "Before you say anything..." Barclay paused, looking between the two investigators before settling his gaze on Fitz. "I've already told Lawson, but I got an email from Ken Pevey during court. That towel you grabbed from the Pig's pit room? It's a match."

Fitz's eyes went wide. He said, "To the cigarette butt?"

"To the cigarette butt, the blood on the sheath, the handle of the machete, all of it. Butler is Howard—no question."

"And he's our murderer," said Fitz.

"You're damn right he is," Lawson interjected.

Fitz did a hard fist pump. They were getting close.

On the whiteboard, held in place by round magnets at each corner, were two photographs side-by-side. On the left was Arnold Gillespie, Jr.'s senior portrait from his college yearbook, and to the right was a still shot from the video. The still shot was a frame showing most of the man's face. Barclay noticed the television was also on and paused on the same image.

"Tell me something great, AJ. Keep the good news flowing," said Barclay with renewed energy.

He glanced again at Barclay, who'd walked up and stood beside him to his right. AJ said, "It's him. He's our guy. No doubt in my mind."

Barclay groaned, not trying to hide his disappointment; he walked away from the board. He raised his arms out to the side and said, "This is what you have? Come on, man. How can you tell that?" He let his arms fall limply to his side.

"I've been a cop for forty-two years. I've watched thousands of hours of surveillance footage; I know what to look for. First of all, we got lucky in that the angle of the face in the video and the angle in the yearbook are very close. That makes comparing the two easier."

Using his pinky finger, AJ first pointed at the yearbook photo, specifically the eyes. He said, "Look at how he has a slight squint. Now"—he moved his pinky to point at the frame from the video —"look here. Same thing. It's the way he holds his eyes. And here" —he moved back to the yearbook photo—"look at his hairline, particularly on the side of his head. See how it curves back a little, then just above his eyebrows, it juts forward before slightly curving back? That's distinctive."

Barclay was not convinced, but he could see what AJ was saying. *Was he just seeing what he wanted to see?* He looked to Lawson. He knew she was the hardest to convince of the group.

"Fitz sent me these last night. I've studied them six ways to Sunday, and I believe he's right."

"Do this," AJ said. "Walk to the back of the room and face the wall. When I tell you, I want you to turn around and look at these

photos. I don't want you to think about it—just react to it."
Seeing the look on Barclay's face, he said, "Humor me."

Barclay did as he was asked and stood facing the wall opposite
the photographs. AJ told him to turn around. He did.

———

AGREEING that the video likely showed the senator walking
Kathryn Chatham into the woods, they moved to discussing what
the video did and did not reveal. Their discussion spilled over into
The Downtowner, where they currently sat for a late lunch. They
were waiting for their food as they talked.

Fitz was missing from the group because he was helping an
ADA rundown a witness, so he told them to update him if
anything was decided.

"But you have to admit," said AJ, "when you immediately see
those two pictures side-by-side, it's him. Not definitively, of
course, more of an impression, but you saw it, and if *you* saw it,
then a jury will."

"I don't know," said Barclay. He was going to be the one to try
the case, and it was his ass in the jackpot if he charged but didn't
convict a man like Senator Gillespie of murder. "I mean, I get it,
and I agree with you, but that is a long way from an ID the jury
will need to convict a person of murder." He took a drink of his
sweet tea and continued, "Besides, and I hate to sound like a
broken record, but what does the video show other than a young
couple going for a walk in the woods?"

"I said the same thing," said Lawson.

"A good defense lawyer could probably raise doubt that the
girl in the video is even Kathryn Chatham. Of course, that's a
tougher sell because it's her house, and it does look an awful lot
like her, but still..."

"I understand and realize it's not the nail in Gillespie's coffin, but I believe we can work with it," said AJ.

"Run through it one more time," said Barclay.

AJ sucked Dr. Pepper through a straw, wiped his mouth with his hand, and said, "One thing I've learned in all my years as a cop is that you should never underestimate the fact that the bad guy knows what he did. Evidence that you think means something big, they may see it as not significant at all because they know what they did and what the evidence shows. Conversely, evidence we may see as insignificant, they may view as being the smoking gun because, again, they know what they've done and what that particular piece of evidence means. You follow me? I once had a case—"

AJ stopped talking as the waitress, Naomi, delivered their food. She set three heavy white plates brimming with mashed potatoes, vegetables, meatloaf, hamburger steak, and fried pork chops on the table.

She gave Barclay a sideways glare and said, "No coffee today?"

"Not this time," he said. She winked at him, and he smiled back.

AJ watched her walk out of earshot and then, ignoring his meatloaf, said, "I had a case involving an undercover drug buy with a CI, and we used a camera embedded in a pair of glasses. The CI goes in, and, stupid us, we gave him sunglasses for an indoor buy, so the dealer starts getting all suspicious. He's up in this guy's face—and consequently up in the camera—asking our confidential informant why he won't take his sunglasses off inside. The CI is scared shitless and won't even look at the dealer. He's trying to avoid eye contact, just wanting to make the deal and get his ass out of there.

"So they make the transaction, and we've got it all on video... except the video is garbage. We didn't have a clean look at the dealer. Didn't even see the transaction. Total bust. Fast forward a few months, and the guy wants to plead guilty. We are about to

walk into the courtroom, and his lawyer asks to watch the video. I
thought we were screwed. You know, because he's going to see
how lousy the video is."

Barclay and Lawson had begun eating, but they were listening.

AJ continues, "The ADA pops the tape in the VCR—yes, I'm
that old—and the video plays. I swear it was worse than I
remembered."

"So what happened?" asked Lawson before eating a forkful of
green beans.

"The defendant watches about ten seconds of it and says, 'Ah,
they got me.'"

"Really?" said Barclay.

AJ wagged a finger at Barclay and said, "The guy knew he sold
our CI some dope, so when he saw it, he saw himself making the
deal. He knew what the tape was supposed to show, so he saw it as
if it were playing in HD."

Lawson laughed and said, "Dumb ass."

"Right? The lesson is never to underestimate the guilty mind.
They know what they've done, and they know when they've been
caught." AJ then attacked his plate of food like he hadn't eaten in
days.

"So, what, we show him this video, and he confesses?" Barclay
asked.

AJ shook his head, eyes down on his plate, moving food
around with his fork. Finally, he looked up, finished chewing,
drank some Dr. Pepper, and said, "Of course not. But we have to
create movement. We show him what we've got and see what
happens. Personally, I don't believe he'll simply ignore it. He'll
know what he's looking at, which will prompt some action. I have
no idea what that will be, but he'll do something."

Barclay sat his fork down and surveyed the empty restaurant.
He leaned into the group and said, "If we do this, I don't think we
approach it from an adversarial point of view." He paused, think-

ing, and said, "Maybe we approach it as 'We recovered her remains from the well.' Let him in on that."

AJ said, "That's good. He'll like that; make him feel like an insider."

Barclay continued, "Then I show him the video and say something like, 'This was the last day she was seen alive. We found this video, and someone mentioned that it's you and Kathryn. Did you see anything that day, or can you give us any information that could help us figure out who killed her?' Something like that."

Murphy and Lawson weighed it out, looked at each other, and AJ said, "Let's talk it out, but I think you're on the right track. We come at him hard, accuse him of killing her, he may call our bluff because, let's be honest, clarity of the video aside, it doesn't really prove anything, and he's not stupid." More Dr. Pepper. He cleared his throat and said, "Slow play it. Show him the video and allow *him* to make the connection. The only way this works is if he figures it out for himself and feels like he is still in control of the situation." He grabbed a piece of meatloaf with his fork and pointed it at Barclay. "Then we hope that prompts him to make a move."

Barclay rubbed his hands on his thighs and began shaking his head. "I see where you're coming from, AJ, I do, but like you already said, the video is weak, and he's not stupid. I get that *he'll* know, and *he'll* understand the significance, but if he believes that's all we have...I just don't know that the video will be enough of a nudge."

Lawson said, "Larry Butler."

The two men looked at her.

"How do you mean?" Barclay asked.

"Both his and Butler's DNA is at the scene—on a murder weapon, no less. If we're traveling under the theory that they're both involved, maybe *confiding* in the senator about the DNA evidence putting Butler there will be enough of a push." Lawson made air quotes when she said *confiding*.

AJ said, "We need to be real careful here. Butler is potentially the only person who can implicate the senator. If we let him know what we have on Butler...well, who knows what this man will do."

"But didn't you say you wanted movement?" Barclay asked.

"Yeah, but...I just don't know. That's putting an awfully big target on Butler."

Silence, as they all considered it, and Lawson was the first to speak. She looked at Barclay and said, "Whatever we decide, I think that whenever this meeting is held, we need to be prepared to have eyes on him from the time the meeting ends and stay on him until he either does something or we're convinced that he's not going to do anything. Twenty-four-hour surveillance."

"She's right," said AJ.

Barclay said, "Can the two of you and Fitz cover surveillance? That will keep us from having to involve anyone else."

AJ said, "I think the three of us should be able to handle it, but I would feel better if we had one more person. Fitz and I are good for it, but Detective, if you get pulled away by your people..."

Barclay thought about it. "Let's keep to just three for now. I'll reach out to Sally Ramos at the sheriff's office if we need a fourth. It'd put her in a tough spot, but I think she'll do it if we need her."

———

BARCLAY PILOTED his Tahoe deep into the county, far from the traffic and well-lit streets of the city. He needed to think, and going for a quiet night drive away from everything sometimes helped. He was mentally running through his upcoming meeting with the senator—everything had to be right.

There were no neighborhoods out here, and due to no zoning standards, he drove past a mobile home, a single-family home set well off the road on an adjacent property, and an array of storage units directly across the street. On his drive, he noticed a pick-up truck parked outside an open storage unit, which struck him as odd—more like suspicious—given the time of night.

This area's lack of population density was great for those who prized their privacy, but it was also conducive to burglaries. Drugs were a constant issue in the county—specifically meth-amphetamine—which accounted, in large part, for the prolifera-tion of property crimes in the area. The DA made a mental note of the storage unit with the late-night visitor figuring it as a likely cache of stolen property or possibly even a meth lab or maybe both. He would ask the sheriff's office to check it out.

Barclay approached a pulpwood plant and took the first right past the considerable metal building. After a quarter mile or so, he rumbled over a railroad track and slowed, creeping along, looking for the turnoff. His headlights illuminated a rolled aluminum utility gate secured with a thick chain and padlock. He got out, unlocked the gate, and drove through. Once through the gate, he got out and pushed it closed, wrapping the chain around the post but not engaging the lock.

He slowly wound through the narrow dirt road that was little more than a rutted path and emerged onto an open green space occupied by a hunting cabin. The cabin belonged to his friend Luke Jackson, but he had access to it whenever he wanted; it was not unusual for him to stay here on the weekend before a big trial to prepare.

The cabin wasn't large, but it was well-appointed and sturdy —built with white pine timbers. The inside smelled distinctly of the cedar trim present throughout, from the cabinets to the fire-place mantel to the exposed ceiling joists. It was a homey smell, a welcoming smell that tamped down the slight scent of a cabin that hadn't seen recent use.

Barclay made his way up to the loft area, where there was a gas fireplace and comfortable chairs. He turned the fireplace on with the flip of a switch and poured himself a rye whiskey. Next, he paired his phone with a Bluetooth speaker, turned on classical music—the soft background sound helped him think—and began organizing everything they knew about the case up to that point.

He was on his second glass when his phone rang. Since the phone was joined to the speaker, the phone rang through it, which caused him to jump. He saw it was Detective Lawson and scrambled to disconnect the Bluetooth.

"What's up, Detective?"

"Ever since our meeting, I've been reviewing the case file... just...I don't know...seeing if there is *anything* we've missed. Anything you can use with the senator."

Barclay let the silence hang. Beck Lawson was not one to merely call for a chat.

"Well, something's been bothering me about it."

"Only one thing, Detective?" Barclay said with a bit of a laugh.

"Yeah, right. It's just that as I was reading the ME's report identifying the remains from the well as Kathryn Chatham, I got to thinking about everything we knew or thought we knew up to that point. Correct me if I'm wrong, but the thought was that she moved away, right?"

"Right. Sylvia Burrows believed she moved away for a fresh start."

"And no one questioned it. I mean, nobody believed she had come to any harm. But after discovering she was in the well—most likely this entire time—one thought kept niggling at the back of my mind...what happened to her car?"

"Her car?"

"Yeah. Her car."

"What do you mean?"

"Unless I'm wrong, her car was never found, right?"

"I guess. Never really thought about it," he said, not understanding the point she was trying to make.

"The thing is, if she left voluntarily, as everyone thought at the time, then she takes her car with her, right?"

A slow, tentative nod from Barclay. "Yeah."

"But, if, as we now know, she didn't leave Towne and instead was killed and dumped in the well, then where did her car go?"

Barclay set his glass down and stood up. He began doing laps around the small loft area. "But I don't—" And then he got it. His mouth formed as he said a silent "Oh." After a beat: "Ok. I'm with you, but how does that help us?"

"It may help us if the car is still around, right?" There was something in her voice. Something light and...mischievous?

"Hold on," said Barclay. He sat back down, put the phone on speaker, and set it on the coffee table. Barclay began scrolling through reports on his iPad. He found Fitz's summary of Sylvia Burrows' interview. "Sylvia said Kathryn's car was gone when she got home."

"Well, sure. Whoever killed her needed to make it look like she up and left on her own. In her statement, Mrs. Burrows mentioned Kathryn's suitcase, clothes, and makeup were also gone, adding credibility to the notion that she left of her own volition. But the killer would have to do something with her car; otherwise, no one would believe she left on her own accord. She's not getting very far without her car, and why would she leave it behind?"

Barclay considered this. "This is a small place, even smaller back then. No way the killer dumps her car anywhere around here without it being noticed. I suppose he could have driven it out of the county and abandoned it. But he would have needed help to do that, and I don't see that happening."

Lawson said, "Even so, someone would have eventually located it. Some police department somewhere would have run the tag, discovered who it belonged to, and tried to contact them. Perhaps they would have eventually contacted Towne PD about a car abandoned in their jurisdiction. But that never happened."

Barclay didn't know what to say. He could only stare dumbly at his phone, trying to comprehend.

Lawson: "What if there were a place, close by even, that someone could dump a car and no one would ever bat an eye."

He was ready to argue. "But where—" He froze. "Holy shit."

———

BARCLAY HAD SHUT everything down in the cabin, locked the gate behind him, and was speeding back towards town. The ringing phone echoed through the Tahoe's interior—Fitz answered on the fourth ring.

"Hang on, Fitz. I'm going to try and conference in Lawson and Murphy."

Barclay fiddled with his iPhone, trying to ring a second, then a third number without hanging up on Fitz. He had never attempted this before, so he watched a quick YouTube video before leaving the cabin. It worked, and now Murphy and Lawson were a part of the conversation.

Barclay told them who was on the line, and then he got to the point of the phone call. "Detective Lawson just gave us what could be a hell of a lead. She has a good idea about where we can find Kathryn Chatham's car."

Fitz said, "What?" and Murphy said, "Car?" at almost the same time.

"You heard me."

"Wait, wait, wait," said Fitz. "Her car? What are you going on about, Boss?"

"I wish I could take credit for this, but it's all Lawson. She saw something none of us even considered. She realized Kathryn

Chatham's car was never found, and she believes she knows where it may be, and I agree with her."

It was Murphy's turn to sound incredulous. "I'm going to need you to back up and explain all of this."

Barclay turned the call over to Lawson, and she explained her thoughts on the car. She ran through everything the same as she had for Barclay, but more to the point.

"Well, damn," said Murphy when she was finished. "That never even dawned on me."

Fitz said, "So where is this car supposed to be? You said she knows, right?"

"It's just a hunch," said Lawson.

"It's a lot more than a hunch, and I think she's dead on," said Barclay.

"Well," said Fitz. "You gonna tell us?"

She said, "At the well."

Silence for a few beats, then realization hit Fitz, who said, "All those cars."

"Yep," said Barclay. "Hiding in plain sight."

"What are y'all on about?" Murphy asked. "What cars?"

"I'll explain later," said Barclay. "First, we need to either get permission from the landowners or get a search warrant to go on the property looking for the vehicle."

"Can't we just go have a look-see?" Fitz asked.

"I don't know, Fitz. Any other time, I may chance it. But this case? We need everything done by the book. Everything. Contact the landowner, but go ahead with the search warrant regardless. Make sure it allows us inside the car if we do find it."

"Understood."

"Work your magic, Fitz. We need those people found."

"I got you, Boss. As for the warrant, I need the color, year, and make and model of the car we're searching for." Then, "What's our probable cause?"

"What do you mean?"

"We need probable cause for a search warrant, and, no offense, Lawson, but your theory, no matter how well thought out, doesn't get us there."

"No," said Barclay. "It doesn't." He thought about it and said, "We need to find some nexus between that piece of property and the senator."

Lawson said, "What do you mean?"

"We have to show a judge that we're likely to find evidence of a crime on that property. Ostensibly, we're saying her killer left evidence there, and we have to explain why we believe the killer would have left the car there. Why we believe evidence would have been left there. At a minimum, we need to show that Gillespie had access to the property or at least had knowledge of the property. I don't believe a judge will give us the warrant absent showing some connection. Why it's reasonable to believe there is evidence of a crime—this crime—there."

Lawson said, "Are you done? I know what probable cause is. I just don't understand why it's an issue here."

"What don't you understand?" Barclay's tone was harsher than it should have been, and he caught himself. "I'm sorry, Beck. That wasn't right. This case is just so damned frustrating."

"I'm guessing you don't know."

"Know what?"

"The current landowners bought the property from Arnold Gillespie, Sr."

THIRTY-THREE

February 19

When Fitz arrived at work that morning, he dug even deeper into his skip tracing tool bag to locate anyone connected to the Lockhart family who owned the property they wanted to search. He was able to locate someone who turned out to be a cousin of Stan Lockhart's granddaughter. Through the cousin, Fitz contacted the granddaughter, who lived in south Florida, and explained who he was and what he needed.

The granddaughter informed him that her mother—Lockhart's daughter—still owned the property and she would have her mother call the investigator. Fitz gave her his cell number and told her it was important they speak as soon as possible. The granddaughter said she would call her mother as soon as she got off the phone.

Forty minutes later, Fitz's phone rang, and the caller ID said it was a number from Jackson, Tennessee. He answered the call, and it was Erma Waites, Stan Lockhart's daughter. She told Fitz she was unsure about talking to him, what with all the telephone scams nowadays, so he proposed she call the office's main switchboard and ask for him. She agreed that would assuage her worries.

After hanging up with Ms. Waites, he called the front desk, told the receptionist he was expecting a call, and had her send the call back to the war room. Two minutes later, the phone rang.

Fitz answered with the speakerphone so everyone in the room could hear. "Hello, Ms. Waites. Thank you for calling." He explained the purpose of his phone call, including the discovery of the human remains found in the well, without going into detail.

"Oh, my dear fathers," she gasped. "Who would do such a thing?"

"That's what we're trying to find out, ma'am, and that involves conducting a search of your property."

She made several tsking sounds before saying, "Oh, my dear fathers," again. Fitz let her come to him in her own time. Finally, she said, "I haven't been on that property in probably twenty years. Have you been out there, Mr. Fitzsimmons?"

"Yes, ma'am. When we extracted the remains from the well."

"So, you've seen all the cars."

"Oh, yes," Fitz said lightly. "If you don't mind me asking, what's the story there?"

"My crazy father," she said playfully. "He was a mechanic and wanted something to keep him busy in retirement. So he had this idea that he would buy some land and make a car museum of sorts. He purchased the property from Mr. Gillespie in maybe nineteen sixty or sixty-one, somewhere in there. He then started looking for old cars. Junkers that people abandoned at the shop, cars he saw for sale that he could get a good deal on, and even going through the junkyards. He didn't care about how well it ran or if it even ran at all because he could fix near about anything. As long as the body was in decent shape—he didn't do body work— he'd take it.

"He planned to build a shop out there and work on the cars.

His intention was to wait until after he retired to build the shop, but he wanted a steady supply of cars to work on when he got everything ready, so he amassed quite a collection over the next few years. Sadly, he had a heart attack the day after he retired, and everything out there is just as he left it. My mother didn't have any interest in the property, and, quite frankly, I think it hurt her to visit the place because of what it meant to my father."

"Well, Ms. Waites, I can tell you that several people commented on your father's car collection—it's very impressive. A lot of fine automobiles out there."

"That is nice to hear, Mr. Fitzsimmons. After Mother died, I inherited the property as an only child. I looked into selling it once and got a few offers, but I couldn't make myself do it. The property isn't that valuable, and, fortunately, I don't need the money, so I decided to hang on to it."

"Ms. Waites, do we have your permission to go on the property for the purpose of a search? We are getting a search warrant, but we wanted to let you know what was happening, and we are hoping for your approval."

"Of course, Mr. Fitzsimmons. Anything I can do to help. Can you tell me what you're looking for?"

"Unfortunately, I can't. I may not be able to tell you what we find if we find anything, but I will let you know something."

"Oh, that would be so nice of you, Mr. Fitzsimmons. I will be praying for you and the family of that poor person you found in the well."

———

JUDGE ARNETT'S discretion was unassailable. He never played the political game, preferring, instead, to let his job speak for itself. As for gossip, he neither engaged in it nor did he indulge it in those around him. This approach to the job has resulted in the county's first—and, to date, only—black judge and the longest-tenured judge in the county's history.

He and Barclay had a bond far beyond the courtroom, so he called and told him that Fitz and a detective with the PD would be coming to him for a search warrant. "We need this fairly quickly."

"You send 'em up, and *I* will decide whether they get their warrant, emergency or not."

———

ARNETT SAT at his open third-floor office window, puffing on one of his *Mexican ceegars* as he listened intently to what Fitz was laying out.

After he had finished laying out the probable cause, the judge considered everything he was told and spit between his teeth out the window.

"Damn, son," he finally said to Fitz in a voice that was all low notes and silk. Then he held out his hand to Fitz, who handed over the search warrant request. He laid the cigar on the windowsill.

The judge finished reading the two-page document and flipped back to page one. Then back to page two.

"A little light on the facts, no?" Judge Arnett said, eyeing Fitz and sliding the half-moon readers up to his forehead.

Lawson said, "We didn't want to put a lot of what we know in there should we be wrong and that document leaks somehow."

The judge had not looked at Lawson and instead had kept his gaze on Fitz. His watery brown eyes bore down on the investigator, who finally said, "We found skeletal remains in a well on the property. Those remains have since been identified and tied back to a cold case murder from 1963. We believe evidence of a crime exists on said property in the way of an automobile. We have a suspect. We've established the suspect's knowledge of the property by way of his family having owned it until they sold it a few years prior to the individual found in the well going missing. We also have a witness and video evidence of the suspect walking the victim into the woods on the weekend she was last seen." The last bit of information was not included in the search warrant. Still, the judge was allowed to consider additional information outside of the four corners of the document, such as officer testimony. This allowed the judge to have the information without putting it in writing.

"And you're certain this is the car you're looking for?" the judge asked.

"Yessir," said Fitz.

"Tell me how."

"We were able to find vehicle registration records for Frank Chatham, the father of Kathryn Chatham—"

"The Chathams," Judge Arnett said. "That's what this is about?"

"Yes, Judge," said Fitz, "and as I was saying—"

"Wait. Just wait one damn minute." The judge's gaze bore in on Fitz, then Lawson. Finally, he spit—in the trashcan this time—and said, "What's it been...gotta be what..." He mentally did the math. "Sixty years ago now?" Fitz nodded. "You've solved that family's murder?"

"Not exactly," said Fitz. Arnett narrowed his eyes, and Fitz said, "Sir, we located Kathryn Chatham's remains in a well on the property that's the subject of the search warrant before you."

The judge looked uncharacteristically stunned.

Detective Lawson said, "Judge, this investigation was initially begun to look into the five homicides back in 1963, but as the investigation has unfolded, we are now focusing on the possible murder of Kathryn, which, as I'm sure you know, no one even knew was dead. And certainly not dead at the bottom of a well mere yards from her property."

"And you think her death could be connected to her family's murders?"

Lawson said, "We don't know anything for certain. What I can tell you is that this portion of the investigation has unfolded fairly quickly."

The judge nodded. "Barclay indicated as much." Then, the professional that he was, he quickly shifted back to judge mode. "Tell me more about what you're looking for...specifically."

Fitz said, "Specifically, we're looking for a car. Kathryn's car. Or rather her father's car. The vehicle registered to him at the time of his murder was a 1962 Chevrolet Impala, blue with a white top. We confirmed through a friend and roommate of Ms. Chatham's that she drove a blue car with a white top."

"She couldn't confirm the car this woman drove was her father's car?"

Judge Arnett could be difficult, and he was putting Fitz through it right now. Fitz and Lawson knew probable cause had been established, and they knew that the judge knew it. But, in spite of it all, Arnett was playing one of his games, and Fitz was the recipient of the judge's charm this time.

Lawson chimed in. "No, Judge. Her roommate was not a car person and did not bother learning the year, make, model, and VIN number of her friend's car."

The look on the judge's face said *Touché*, and that seemed to wind him down.

"It's not lost on me that there is no name in this search warrant, nor have you mentioned a suspect here in my office." He waited, and seeing no response forthcoming, he asked, "Do I want to know?"

Fitz gave him a look, and the judge said, "Forget I asked."

Arnett spit into the trashcan again, thinking. He ambled back to the windowsill, picked up his cigar, and reviewed the document once more before flashing a look at Fitz. He gave a slight nod toward his desk, and the investigator walked over and grabbed a sleek black ink pen from a pen stand. He walked the pen over to the judge, who flipped to the second page, whipped out his signature in the appropriate place, and held out the completed search warrant to Fitz, who took it.

The judge tossed the pen onto the windowsill, jammed the cigar in his mouth, and said, "Now go catch this motherfucker."

————

The Tahoe hopped the curb and rolled over the grassy field, coming to rest at the wood line. The four individuals in the SUV piled out, and as if on cue, they all zipped up their jackets a little higher, closed their respective doors, shoved their hands into their pockets, and made their way to the front of the vehicle. The clouds were a harbinger of rain; the moisture in the air combined with the lack of sun created a hard chill, the evidence of which could be seen with every breath.

"Alright," said Barclay, "not far past the tree line, there is a barbed wire fence, so watch your step. That is where our target property begins. Fitz?"

Fitz said, "Let's spread out to cover the width of the property. AJ and I will be the bookends—set the edge of the search area. Based on the make, model, and year of the car, along with the description from Sylvia Burrows, I texted each of you a picture of what we believe the car looked like. I also texted you the tag number based on the last registration by Kathryn Chatham." He eyed AJ Murphy and Beck Lawson. "Any questions?"

Silent shakes of the head.

A nod. "Let's go."

They set off into the woods and gradually spread out as they approached the target property line, with AJ setting the left edge and Fitz setting the right. Over the course of nearly three months since Fitz and Barclay ventured into these woods, the chilling grasp of winter had descended upon the land. The skeletal fingers of hardwood branches now dangled ominously, casting an eerie atmosphere reminiscent of the haunted woods from Sleepy Hollow, making for a fitting backdrop for their foreboding mission.

The lack of foliage allowed visibility from one edge of the property to the other, and the snap of dead branches being crunched underfoot cracked loudly as the sound bounced among the hardwoods.

Less than a minute after crossing the barbed wire fence, AJ Murphy said, "Wow!" The other three stopped and turned expectantly.

"This place is amazing!" AJ yelled.

The collective groan of the other three registered their displeasure. They tromped on.

———

THEY FOUND THE CAR.

It took nearly three-quarters of an hour to make it through the veritable graveyard of antique cars; it was tucked into some of the more dense scrub. The light blue color was faded and mottled with rust, and the once-white top was a dingy speckled gray from decades of weather and tree sap. The vehicle wasn't easily identifiable due to the only visible portion being the rear end. Fitz, however, recognized the six distinctive round taillights from the photo he'd downloaded from the internet. But it wasn't until he brushed the coating of dirt off the license plate that he knew for certain he had found the car they'd been looking for.

All four individuals were now gathered at the rear of the vehicle.

"This is the car," said Barclay, looking at the car's tag. "We need to get inside. Did you bring your Slim Jim?" He directed the question to Fitz.

"It's in the truck. Let me go grab it."

While he was gone, Murphy and Barclay worked their way into the scrub, trying to clear a path to the doors and create space to get the doors open. Lawson was peering in through the rear passenger glass, first on the right side, then the left. Unfortunately, the windows were cloudy with filth, so her efforts were for naught.

Fitz was back with the door access tool. He squeezed into the narrow opening, crunching over and through branches and scrub brush, and slid the tool down into the door panel. After fishing around for a few seconds, a satisfying *clunk* was heard. He worked the tool free and pulled it from the door panel. He handed the tool off to Barclay, and the door squeaked open after some effort.

After breaking the seal, he stepped to the side to open the door further. With so many brambles and a small gauge pine in the way, Fitz had to wedge himself into the narrow opening between the door and the car. He pushed the door open with both hands, crushing the brush in its path.

The blue vinyl seats were ripped and puckered along the seams, with pieces of yellow foam squeezing through the tears. Fitz took a moment to look around to see if anything stood out. Nothing did. He eased into the front bench seat, trying not to snag the seat of his pants on an exposed spring. The door swung back slowly, forced by the rebelling limbs, and came to rest against his left leg, which was outside the vehicle with a foot on the ground.

"We've got a key in the ignition," he announced. He produced black latex gloves from his coat pocket and slid them on. He removed the key by the attached keyring, not wanting to handle the key itself any more than necessary. He held the keyring as he scanned the car's interior, seeing nothing of interest. He then extricated himself from the vehicle with a groan matching that of the door.

He moved to the trunk, worked the key into the lock, and wrestled the lid open.

Someone let out an audible gasp.

"Welp," said Lawson. "We've found Kathryn's suitcase."

THIRTY-FOUR

N estled on Samford Drive, Senator Arnold Gillespie, Jr.'s residence commanded attention among the exclusive enclave of just ten homes that graced this tranquil, tree-lined dead-end street. The senator's abode, a striking testament to the enduring charm of the antebellum South, bore the unmistakable marks of time, its classic facade a centerpiece within the cul-de-sac, flanked by other residences similarly steeped in the historical architectural tradition.

The lawn was dormant and brown, creating a subdued backdrop to the elegant home. The flower beds, devoid of blooms yet meticulously groomed, added a sense of order and grace to the landscape. Illuminated by a multitude of warm, welcoming lights, Senator Gillespie's residence shone as the beacon of the neighborhood, an emblem of Southern hospitality amidst the quietude of this charming enclave.

Barclay parked in the driveway and, as he made his way to the front door, opened the voice recording app on his iPhone, started it recording, and placed the phone microphone up in the outer breast pocket of his wool navy blue sport coat behind his red and white microcheck pocket square. The idea to record the conversation was not to use it against the senator but to have a record of the meeting for the others to analyze afterward. They all agreed that a recording was better than Barclay trying to recount the details of what was said. They'd tested the phone's placement in the coat's breast pocket both for concealment and recording quality. That particular location proved adequate for both.

The doorbell was a resounding gong that repeated itself three times. The senator answered the door in gray wool dress slacks, cordovan penny loafers—a penny in each shoe—and a light yellow cardigan over a blue-striped dress shirt.

"Hello, Barclay. Come in, please. I don't believe you've been here before, have you?"

"First time," he said, shaking the man's hand.

"I've hosted events here and was unsure." The senator held up a rocks glass containing a small amount of brown liquid and said, "Get you a drink?"

"Sure. Whatever you're drinking." That seemed to please the host.

As Barclay cleared the door, the senator closed it—the sound of the door shutting reverberated, emphasizing the weight of the moment—and glided past his visitor, leading him to the senator's inner sanctum on a spicy oak scent trail of bourbon. The senator's hard-soled shoes clomping on the heart pine floor.

The house had a distinct motif about it, from the scarred hardwood floors to the chipped plaster moldings to the underlying smell of age, a subtle reminder of the home's history. Barclay cast a glance through an archway to his right and saw a formal living room that looked fixed in time, complete with a grandfather clock, the pendulum arrested, and the time halted at 2:40. Barclay heard a member of the Rat Pack crooning from somewhere in the house before entering the well-appointed study.

If the exterior and other parts of the interior showed their age, the senator's study did the same, but in a handsome, learned way. The room seemed to embrace its age with a refined grace. An antique desk messy with papers sat in the middle of the room, and beyond it, a full bookcase built into the wall stained dark brown. The rest of the walls were painted a deep tan and bereft of any decoration, though the base of each wall was lined with framed awards and certificates of a life in public service waiting to be hung but likely never would be.

Whereas a hint of must and dampness rode on the air when Barclay entered the aged home, this room smelled distinctly of leather, wood polish, and old paper.

The senator went directly to a bar cart and poured a generous amount of bourbon—Blanton's by the look of the bottle.

"Ice?" the senator asked with a look over his left shoulder.

"Please."

Several cubes were placed in the glass from a silver ice bucket, the crack of the ice caused by the warm liquid audible in the otherwise silent room. The senator refilled his own glass and motioned for Barclay to join him where two leather wing-back chairs sat facing the wood-burning fireplace warming the room.

They sat and enjoyed their drinks for about half a minute when the senator said, "So, what is it you wanted to discuss?"

Barclay cleared his throat. "It's about the Chatham case." After discussing at length how to approach this conversation, it was agreed that Barclay needed to come off as tentative, as if he were uncomfortable even bringing it up. The thought was that this would give the senator a sense of power and authority. AJ felt that the longer the senator felt in control, the more likely he would be to try and handle it...whatever *it* was.

Seeing that Barclay wasn't going to say anything else, the senator slid back into his chair and said coolly, "What about the case?"

"Well, as you know, Senator..." *Use his title*, AJ had said.

Create that sense of power and authority and respect. "As you know," he repeated, "we, well, I...my office has been looking into this case." He took a drink.

"Yes? And you've found something?"

Barclay was sitting on the edge of his seat, leaning forward, elbows on knees, looking down. Finally, he raised his head and said, "Your name has come up in the investigation."

"Really? My name? In what way?" Another drink from Barclay. "It's ok, son. Whatever you have to say, just say it."

"It appears your fingerprints were at the scene of the murders." Barclay was paying close attention when he made this statement and thought he saw something. It was only a flash, but it was there.

"Fingerprints, you say? *My* fingerprints?"

A grim nod. "On a flashlight."

The senator took a drink. *Was there a slight tremor in his hand?* Barclay wondered.

"There must be some kind of mistake. I..."

"Of course, of course," said Barclay. "That is exactly what I told my investigator when he gave me the news." Then he began shaking his head. "Fingerprints are tricky things. There is no standard for what qualifies as a match—"

"That crime was, what, almost sixty years ago. How in the world could fingerprints even stay around that long?"

"That's what I said," exclaimed Barclay as he stood up. He began to pace now. "I...I'm not sure what to do."

The senator slid to the edge of his seat, facade fading even if only a little. He pointed at Barclay with the hand holding his glass. "You said it yourself. Fingerprint evidence isn't reliable."

That isn't what Barclay said, but that *is* the leap they'd hoped he'd make.

"Only there's something else." Barclay finished off the bourbon. The dull clink of the ice hitting the bottom of an empty tumbler.

"Something else?"

"You know those remains we found in the well?" A nod from the senator. "They turned out to be the remains of Kathryn Chatham."

The senator's eyes flicked to the right, and his face drained of color.

"How sad." It was the senator's turn to stand up. His gaze fell to the floor, and he shook his head. "Poor, poor girl."

"Here's the thing, Senator, we have a witness saying they believe they saw you and Kathryn walking into the woods behind her house on the last weekend that anyone recalls seeing her alive?"

"What? That's preposterous. Other than when she worked for my father, I had nothing to do with her." The senator was clearly more comfortable being angry. That emotion allowed him to focus, and Barclay was seeing the man so feared and respected on the floor of the United States Senate. "Who is saying such inflammatory things?"

"I'm not at liberty to say at this point." Then, seeing the senator about to explode, he held up a hand and said, "It's not what we would call a solid identification. In fact, the witness threw out a couple of possible names. Yours was just one of them."

The senator walked to the other side of the room, shaking his head. He reached the wall, turned on Barclay, and hissed, "This is my reputation we're talking about."

"I know. That's exactly why we are keeping this very quiet."

He narrowed his eyes and fixed Barclay with a hard stare. "Who all knows about this?"

"Just me and my chief investigator."

"Can I count on his discretion?"

"Absolutely. He understands the dynamics. Trust me."

More head shaking. "It is quite scary what a rogue, unfounded statement can do."

Barclay walked to the bar cart and poured more bourbon, covering the ice. He capped the bottle and said, "There's a video."

"A vid...what the hell are you talking about? A video of what?"

Barclay made his way to the fireplace mantle where the senator was standing. "An old home movie. I can only say there is an old eight-millimeter film with Kathryn in the background. She is with a man as they walk into the woods. We believe it was filmed the weekend she went missing."

"She didn't go missing. She moved away!" the old man spat.

"The remains in the well, Senator."

The senator shook his head as if that didn't change anything.

Barclay pulled out a piece of paper folded lengthwise down the middle. He passed it to the senator.

"What's that?" he asked, looking at the paper but not taking it.

"It's a printout of a frame from the video. It shows the face of the person with Kathryn that day.

He snatched the paper from Barclay's hand and opened the paper. He extended his arm, trying to see it better. He walked over to his desk, opened the wide middle drawer, and pulled out a pair of readers. He put them on and looked at the picture once more. He stared at it. His eyes flicked to Barclay, then back down at the paper.

"That could be anybody," he said without conviction and tossed the paper and his glasses onto the desk. He wandered back to the bar cart and downed the remaining bourbon in his glass, which was a lot, and splashed more into the empty crystal tumbler.

The senator gave Barclay a sidelong glance and said in a low voice, "How do we control this?"

Barclay thought about how he was going to answer. They had

all agreed on a loose script. AJ said to give him just enough—only give him a nudge. Give him too much, and there was no telling what a man of such considerable power would do. Barclay took a drink of bourbon, buying time.

He turned toward the fireplace, showing his back to the senator. He slid the phone out of his jacket pocket, thumbed the screen open, and ended the recording.

"Barclay?"

He slipped the phone back into his pocket and turned around.

"We may have a problem, Senator." He took a few steps to where Gillespie stood at the bar cart. "As I said earlier, the only people who know your name's been mentioned are myself and my investigator. To be honest with you, neither of us put much stock into what we've been able to turn up in our investigation. Just not much new information floating around so many years later, you know."

"Then what's the goddamned problem? You're the DA. Just quash the damn thing. It is your investigation, after all." Then more to himself, "That bitch Maggie Gamble couldn't let sleeping dogs lie."

It angered Barclay, hearing him speak of Maggie like that; however, he tempered his anger, knowing this conversation was having the desired effect...maybe too well. This was not like the senator. His composure under pressure was legendary, but then again, being investigated for murder has a way of shaking up even the most even keel person.

"Senator, I don't know how, but the attorney general has gotten wind that the investigation is back open on this case. And he has this new cold case unit he's been itching to show off—"

"And he wants this case?"

Barclay gave the senator an uncertain look. "He doesn't know anything. That I am certain of. But if he wants to commandeer the case, he has the authority to do so."

Barclay waited for a response, and when he didn't get one, he said, "I hear he is gearing up for a gubernatorial run. You know the old saying, you only become the AG if you want to become the governor."

"That motherfucker! That goddamn *weasel*! If he thinks he's going to step on my neck on his way to the capital...no. Fuck that!" He was fuming now. "I helped get him elected." He turned on Barclay. "You know that?" Barclay wasn't about to interrupt him. "It never fails. A guy gets a taste of power and suddenly becomes an asshole."

"There's nothing more dangerous than a politician with an agenda."

If looks could kill, Barclay would have been struck dead where he stood. Barclay weighed out what to say next. He wondered if he'd pushed the senator as far as he needed. If he were honest with himself, he'd admit that he had gotten him more fired up than he ever thought possible. But he'd come this far.

Barclay said, "Senator, there's more. Now, I don't know how any of this plays, but, well, you know Larry Butler, right?" A nod from the old man. Seeing his face right now almost made Barclay feel sorry for him—almost. "Well...and I would ask that you not tell anyone about this. I'm serious. It could jeopardize everything."

"What? What?" The senator greedily sought information like a parched land sought water.

"We have Butler's DNA at the crime scene—on the murder weapon, to be exact. We also have it elsewhere at the Chatham house." Barclay watched the man's Adam's apple bob up and down. He even thought he *heard* it bob up and down. "He killed Kathryn Chatham's family, Senator."

The man's eyes narrowed. "I take it you haven't arrested him?" Barclay shook his head somberly. "Why not? If you have DNA and all."

"We have to make absolutely certain we have everything lined up because we'll probably only get one shot at him."

"One shot? What do you mean 'one shot?'"

Here we go. "Because we believe he had help."

The senator set his crystal tumbler down on the bar cart. Hard. "Help?"

"Yes. And that's why we haven't pulled him in yet. If we are going to ask him to give up his accomplice, we have to make certain we are ready because if we're not, he'll know, and he won't feel like he has to give us anything."

"But...how can you be sure he had help?"

"We have a second, as yet unidentified DNA profile at the scene."

Barclay thought the senator's legs were about to give way, and he actually moved to catch him, but the senator stayed upright.

"How close are you to being ready? To 'pull him in' as you say?" He was like a child sucked into a crafty bedtime story.

"Close."

———

St. Barnabas' Episcopal Church was all stone and wood and stained glass; the building was small, but the congregation was dedicated. It was located about a quarter mile from Samford Drive, which was why it was chosen as the meet-up spot following Barclay's meeting with the senator. Two cars were waiting for him.

Barclay pulled around to the rear of the church and killed the headlights. He exited his Tahoe and slid into the backseat of Fitz's SUV next to Lawson—Murphy sat in the front passenger seat.

"How'd it go, Boss?" Fitz said.

Barclay had spent the short drive contemplating how much to say. His trust in Fitz was sacrosanct, and he knew the investigator would have his back no matter what. He also knew Lawson would make no judgment whatsoever. She just wanted the bad guy. He had to be more careful around Murphy, though. The retired cold case man was no dummy. He knew he pushed the senator much harder than Murphy thought wise, so he figured the best course of action was to limit how much information he gave them. He also wanted Fitz and Lawson to have deniability if this whole gambit blew up.

"He didn't give away much. A couple of times, I detected something from him when I mentioned his prints being at the scene and when I showed him the still shot of the video. I'm not sure how moved he was by either revelation, but"—he nodded at Murphy—"he got the significance just as you predicted. He's definitely worried, but more so regarding his name being attached to it than actually being implicated in the act. At least that's how I read it."

AJ: "You got everything recorded?"

"Well, most of it. Unfortunately, I got a call during the meeting, which terminated the recording. I actually had it happen to me once before, and I kicked myself for not setting it to airplane mode before going in. After the call, I would have had to open the app and start a new recording, which was too big a risk to try. The senator isn't stupid."

"Damn," said Fitz. Barclay hated lying to him, but he didn't feel he had much choice with AJ sitting there.

"Yeah. The phone needs to be in airplane mode to avoid interruption. I'm sorry I forgot about that."

A look passed between AJ and Barclay. AJ's was skepticism, and Barclay's a challenge to pursue it.

He texted all three the recording that was made, and they agreed to listen to it and discuss it further in the morning. AJ volunteered for the first watch—he was already out, and home was forty-five minutes away—and they discussed the best place to set up. The location of the senator's house made surveillance tricky;

the neighbors would undoubtedly notice an unfamiliar vehicle parked on the street. It was agreed that the senator was not a risk of undertaking anything too covert. They didn't expect a man his age to go hopping over fences and running through backyards to avoid detection. If he left his house, he would most likely turn left off his street toward the church, so AJ opted to stay in the church parking lot. He would pull around to the front and sit in a spot that afforded him a view of the street's entrance while providing him enough cover so he wouldn't stand out.

None of them expected anything to happen that night—too much information to process, and the senator was known for being methodical. That said, Barclay didn't expect the sun to rise more than twice before the senator did what so many politicians do best: cover his own ass.

THIRTY-FIVE

February 26

Twenty-two hours after the previous night's meeting at the senator's home, Fitz was parked in front of the Episcopal church in the same spot AJ had taken the evening before. Detective Beck Lawson had taken the day shift, relieving Murphy at 7:30 in the morning with a large coffee and two Krispy Kreme doughnuts.

The senator had not left his home all night but moved around the following day. Lawson stayed in contact with Fitz, who was in charge of the surveillance detail. The only action of note was the senator's meeting with the sheriff early that afternoon. Ordinarily, a father meeting with his son was nothing to note; however, the two men met behind an old, rusted-out warehouse deep in the county.

Lawson had nothing of detail to report because she didn't feel she could observe the meeting without her cover being blown. So all she could tell Fitz was that she followed the senator until he turned off the road toward the warehouse at 2:18 PM. She kept driving past the entrance because there was no way to explain another vehicle going down that road. She kept the entrance in her rearview until she found a place to turn around. She sat for another six minutes when, at 2:24, Sheriff Gillespie turned down that same dirt road.

At 2:36, the sheriff exited and drove back the way he'd arrived, followed by the senator at 2:39. The senator made a couple of other stops—Wal-Mart and the hardware store—before she saw him turn onto his street at 3:42 and that is where he had been since.

"At least that's the last time I saw his car. I guess he could have snuck out without me seeing him," she told Fitz as they made the swap.

"I'm sure he's still at home," Fitz said.

————

AT 12:36 AM, Barclay's phone rang. He'd been too geared up for sleep, so he was lying in bed reading *The Barbarians at the Gate* when Fitz called.

"He's on the move, Boss."

Barclay pulled the phone from his ear to look at the time. "I don't know the man's habits, but I'm guessing this is not normal for him. Let me know if he stops anywhere out of the ordinary. I don't want to raise the alarm if he is merely out for a drive."

The call was disconnected, and Barclay left the bedroom for his study, where he went back to reading. He re-read the same page probably six times when he acknowledged he couldn't concentrate.

He opened his phone and composed a text to Fitz asking for an update. He was about to press send when he considered it, told himself that Fitz would let him know as soon as he had something to report, then deleted the unsent message.

Twenty-six minutes later, Fitz called back, and the phone was answered at the echo of the first ring.

"Where is he?" asked Barclay by way of greeting.

"That's the thing. He's stopped...nowhere."

"What do you mean 'nowhere?'"

"Well, he pulled into the Publix parking lot, circled the building, and stopped on the side furthest from the road."

"Publix? But they're closed."

"Yessir. And he took a pretty circuitous route to get here."

"Hmmm. Where are you now?"

"Across the street. I'm down far enough that I can see his car."

"What could he be doing there?"

"You got me, Boss."

"Alright, I guess just call—"

"He's getting out." Barclay stayed silent, waiting on updates he knew would be coming. "He's walking toward the shopping center perpendicular to the grocery store...He just walked behind the building."

"Where could he be going?" Barclay said more to himself. "Any way you can get eyes on without him seeing you?"

"Let me see." Barclay heard the car begin to move. "I'm going to move to the gas station across the street. That should provide me some cover."

"Don't get caught." As soon as he spoke, Barclay felt stupid for saying it.

"Alright, he's out from behind the row of shops and just took a right on Wrights Creek."

"On foot?"

"Yes. What do you want me to do? I don't see how I can follow him. A car creeping along behind him will definitely look suspicious."

Barclay had activated the speakerphone and asked Fitz to hold on, telling him he was looking something up.

Bingo.

"He's headed to Larry Butler's house."

"What?"

"I've got *Maps* open, and if you take a right out of that parking lot, Butler's neighborhood is, oh, maybe a quarter mile or so from there. Maybe more."

"Text me Butler's address."

"Sending now. Keep me updated." And Barclay hung up.

———

FITZ'S PHONE dinged with Barclay's text message. He pulled up Butler's address in his phone's maps app and switched it to satellite view. What he saw was a typical neighborhood. The houses looked to be set apart more than current neighborhoods, and there appeared to be plenty of trees.

He took his foot off the brake and slowly rolled through the darkened gas station, and exited. He caught sight of the senator a hundred yards or so up ahead, and he extinguished his headlights as he crept down the quiet street. He consulted the app once more and saw that the entrance to Butler's neighborhood was on the left, so the senator would have to cross the street if that was where he was headed. A few minutes later, he saw the senator quick-walk across the roadway without bothering to look back.

Fitz sped up nominally and rang Barclay. "That's exactly where he's going." Fitz turned into the neighborhood but could not see the senator. He stopped at the entrance and scanned the area, rolling his windows down—the dark tint making visibility difficult at night—saw nothing and relayed that to Barclay. Barclay cursed.

Fitz crawled along the route laid out by the app, keeping an eye out for the senator. The cold air was bracing and would have served to energize him had his adrenaline not already kicked in.

He was coming up on Butler's street—the app indicating he was supposed to turn right—when he noticed what appeared to be a creek bed that ran off to the right. It was difficult to make out, but the full moon reflected off what could only be water. The creek ran behind the houses on either side of it. He consulted the map and saw that Butler's house was almost at the end of his street and past a curve to the left.

He sped up a little and made the right onto Butler's street. He stopped in front of the first house and strained to see if he saw any signs of movement. He leaned forward over his steering wheel and saw nothing.

"Anything?" Barclay asked.

"No." Barclay could tell from his voice that Fitz was concentrating and focused.

Fitz sped up only slightly and was approaching the curve in the road, so he slowed down. He didn't want to risk driving up on the senator and spooking him. He put the car in park and got out, opting to take the rest of the way on foot. He grabbed his phone off the console and told Barclay he was walking the rest of the way. He kept the call connected.

He was too exposed on the sidewalks with the streetlights, so he ran, half-crouched, for the shadowy cover of the houses lining the street. He estimated the target house was two hundred fifty to three hundred yards ahead on the right.

He had direct line of sight with Butler's house now. Nothing appeared out of the ordinary, so he made his way forward at a steady pace in the anonymity afforded by the shadows.

He was less than a hundred yards away now and could better make out the details of the house. From what he could see, the front part of the house was dark, while lights were on in the rear portion. He didn't see any movement inside.

"I've got eyes on the house," he said into the phone in not quite a whisper. "Still no sign of the senator." He dropped his phone hand back by his side and was now a dozen houses away. He stopped to assess the situation. He made the decision to move quickly from house to house at this point, so that's what he did. He sprinted across the yard of one house, stopping at the corner of the next. Watch, listen, repeat.

He was now nine houses away when he heard a single pop... then another...both sounds accompanied by flashes of bright light illuminating the darkened portions of the single-story home.

Fitz bolted.

————

SENATOR ARNOLD GILLESPIE, Jr. hadn't achieved what he had in his life by sitting on his ass. He was a man of action, and his plan wasn't perfect, but he didn't have the luxury of time and committees. He had to move...now. He would not allow that dumb shit, Larry Butler, to send him to prison for what remained of his life. There was only one option, really.

He spent a couple of hours earlier that afternoon getting ready. He had gone by Walmart and purchased dark clothing: sweatpants, a sweatshirt with a hood, a black watch cap, shoes, and gloves. His plan was to do the shooting and then dispose of the clothes, gloves, cap, and shoes.

He then stopped at the hardware store and bought pepper spray. He wasn't sure why, but he'd never killed anyone before, and it seemed like something he might need.

Then he went home and waited.

He knew from Google Maps that a creek bed ran past the rear of the property, so that is where he would make his approach. He also knew, because everyone in Towne knew, that Butler went to bed early on account of getting up at 3:30 every morning. So he waited until he felt the man would be good and asleep before knocking on the door.

Despite the cover the late hour would provide him, he did not want to chance some nosey neighbor seeing his car and telling police about the strange vehicle arriving after midnight and leaving a short time later, so he decided to park at the Publix shopping center and go in on foot. He was, after all, a runner and the fittest eighty-three-year-old he knew.

Before getting out of the car, he reached over to the passenger seat, grabbed the Hi-Point .40 caliber, and held it in his hand. He wasn't a gun guy, so he wanted to feel the weight of the gun and make sure he knew where the safety was. He racked the slide as he'd seen done on television, ejecting the round already in the chamber, which scared him. Comfortable that it was loaded, he got out of the car and put it into his sweatshirt pocket.

He made his way through the darkness behind the row of stores adjacent to the grocery store and onto the road leading to Butler's neighborhood. He stayed off the roadway and in the brush line in case a car happened by. When he was adjacent to the entrance of the neighborhood, he threw a look left, then right, then darted across the road.

The night was cold, which kept his energy level up. He wasn't sure he could have done this in July or August—not in Alabama. He made his way to the creek bed, and on his first step, his foot sank a few inches into the cold mud. "Shit." His foot made a sucking noise as he removed it, and he stepped to the side where it was more grass than mud and made his way to Butler's property. Like most of the houses he passed, Larry's did not have a fence, nor was the rear of the property illuminated. He gathered himself, reached into the pocket of his sweatshirt, and wrapped his hand around the pistol's grip. He slid his right index finger through the trigger guard and rested it on the curved trigger. He took a breath and made for the back door.

He knocked on the door lightly at first, not wanting to wake the neighbors. Seeing it wasn't loud enough to wake the person he was there to shoot, he knocked again, louder, and on the glass this time. He was about to knock a third time when he registered a light turn on at the far right side of the small house.

A few seconds later, the kitchen light came to life, and a silhouette filled the curtain-covered window in the door. Butler snatched the door open, ready to light into whoever had awoken him when he caught himself. The remnant odor of fried spam escaped the house.

"You," Butler said. "What the fuck do you want?" He looked the senator up and down, taking in the senator's dress. Realization set in. He backed up, leaving the door open.

The senator stepped up the single concrete step and crossed the threshold into the small kitchen. Larry Butler's expression was a mixture of fear and confusion with an undertone of rage.

After maybe two seconds, and his mind saying, *shoot the motherfucker*, the senator pulled the pistol, pointed it at the barrel-chested oaf in front of him, and pulled the trigger. Larry Butler instinctively put his hands in front of his face as if that were enough to stop a bullet.

The senator missed.

"Shit," he hissed and pulled the trigger again. Nothing. He brought the gun to his face and stared at it. "Shit, shit, shit." Then, unsure what else to do, he racked the slide, ejecting a round, pointed the gun at the now charging Larry Butler, pulled the trigger...and ran.

As he moved through the yard, retracing his route back to his car, he replayed the last event over and over. He couldn't get the image out of his mind.

The bullet had hit Butler. He didn't know where, but he knew he shot him because the last image he had was of the fat man sprawling backward onto the floor, bringing a yellow kitchen chair with him.

———

BARCLAY HEARD the unmistakable pops through the phone and began yelling for Fitz, asking if he was okay. He screamed "Fitz!" into the phone three, four times.

Finally, a breathless Winston Fitzsimmons came on the line. "Two shots fired inside the Butler residence." He was whispering. "I'm at the neighbor's house now. The porch light and floodlights are on, making an approach dangerous. I don't want to walk right up on it, or I'm a sitting duck."

"Keep yourself safe, Fitz. I'm going to hang up and call the PD. Then I'm on the way."

"Boss," Fitz began, then stopped. "I'm going to clear the house. I doubt the shooter will hang around, but if he did...."

"Wait on the police."

Fitz shook his head. "If he's not inside, he's headed back to his car. He doesn't know we're on him, so no lights, no sirens. Don't want to alert him. Tell the PD to send a couple of units to sit on his car—out of sight. He will walk right to them."

"You're going in there? Alone?"

"Got to. I'll be fine. Just tell them what I said. Gotta go."

"What if Butler was the shooter?" Barclay yelled into the phone. But Fitz was already gone.

He looked at Brittany, who was now standing in the doorway of the study, looking as scared as he had ever seen her. He said, "There's been a shooting." His mind was awash in thoughts at that moment. He reflected back on his conversation with the senator. If his actions got Fitz shot, he'd never forgive himself.

THIRTY-SIX

February 27

Seventeen minutes later, Barclay followed Lawson, whom he had called on the way to the scene, into the kitchen and approached the body. They joined Fitz and a patrol officer he didn't know standing over a dead Larry Butler—a perfect black circle under his left eye. Lawson ordered the young patrolman to establish a perimeter and not to allow unauthorized persons to pass.

"And write down every person who so much as dips a toe into this crime scene," she said. A nod from the wide-eyed rookie, and he was gone.

"Dammnit," Fitz said as he paced, hands on hips, shaking his head. "Dammnit, I could've done something."

"Nothing you could have done, man. Nothing at all." Barclay knew the best thing for Fitz was to get him into investigation mode, so he asked, "How does this play?"

The investigator seemed taken aback by the question. He stared at Barclay for a beat, then began to speak. He waved a hand at the back door that opened directly into the cramped kitchen. "No forced entry. I doubt it was unlocked this time of night, so I'm guessing he opened right up for him."

"Hit him at the perfect time," said Lawson, hands in the pockets of her jeans, eyes on the man who lay on the dark red clay tile of the kitchen floor. He was wearing only a pair of thin white boxer shorts that were tugged down but not quite far enough to expose anything. "He was in bed and probably asleep, so I doubt he was clear-headed enough to do much of anything in the way of defending himself."

The kitchen was open to a small den, which Fitz reached in four strides, stepping over the body in the process. He walked to the opposite wall and pointed to a hole in the wood paneling. "There were two shots. Not sure if this was the first or the second, but it was one of them." He looked back to the door, making a visual measurement of trajectory, and Barclay followed his gaze. It made sense. "There's also an unspent round on the counter by the door." Barclay looked and eventually spotted the copper-colored bullet.

"How do you explain that?" Barclay asked.

"Gun probably jammed, and he had to clear it." Fitz let his eyes play over the scene a bit more before saying, "I bet he fires the first shot and misses because this isn't television, and he's never tried to shoot a person before, then pulls the trigger again, and nothing happens. He gets the jam cleared, then bam. Right under the eye. Lucky ass shot, Boss."

"You believe he had time for all that? Surely Butler didn't just stand there waiting to get shot."

Fitz shook his head. "I didn't register much time passing between the shots when I heard them." A pause, then: "Consider this: The first shot scares the shit out of Butler; probably thinks he got shot from that distance. Then he and the shooter realize he wasn't shot, the gun jams, Butler's mind processes what he's

seeing, jam is cleared"—he points at the bullet on the counter—
"then he goes after the shooter before he gets it in the face.
Would've been over in a matter of seconds."

"Huh," was all Barclay could think to say.

About that time, an additional detective arrived, announcing
himself as he entered through the front door and then a second. A
few minutes after that, a third detective arrived, and eventually,
there were six roaming the property inside the house and out.

––––––

It was just before 6:00 AM when Barclay made it to the
Towne police department. After leaving the crime scene, he went
to his office to prepare for his upcoming conversation with
Senator Arnold Gillespie, Jr. The senator had already invoked his
right to a lawyer, which only prohibited the authorities from
asking him questions. It did not prevent anyone from speaking *to*
the suspect. The collective decision was made for Barclay to talk to
him. It was felt that a man such as the former senator would be
offended being spoken to by a regular old cop. Barclay was elected
to his position, and the senator would see some dignity in that.

Barclay knew that once an attorney got involved, he would
never get the chance to speak with the senator alone, so he wasn't
going to pass up this opportunity. He gathered everything he
thought he'd need and headed to the PD.

The precinct was buzzing. Everyone knew this case would be
big because of who the shooter was; however, only a handful of
people knew just how big this case was about to get. The first
person Barclay saw when he was walking through the parking lot
to the rear entrance of the police department was AJ Murphy. He
was in a gray SBI quarter-zip fleece, jeans, and cowboy boots. He
was wearing a baseball cap with the name of a marina on it. He
pulled up alongside Barclay as they approached the door.

He began to speak, and Barclay said, "Not now, AJ."

———

INTERVIEW ROOM two at the Towne police department was the same as interview room one. Small—approximately seven feet by five feet—with a metal table shoved into a corner, two folding metal chairs, and a camera over the door. The senator sat in one of the metal chairs unshackled, his white hair a mess. The once great senator was reduced to a murder suspect, a once titan of Towne now looking small and frail in a cheap metal chair. He sat beside the table while Barclay sat in front of the table, separated only by a couple of feet. A grocery-sized paper evidence bag sat open at his feet.

"I already asked for a lawyer." His eyes flicked more than twice to the bag at Barclay's feet.

"I know. I won't ask you any questions, and I don't want you to say anything. I'm going to talk, and you're going to listen. First things first, you're cooked on the murder of Larry Butler; my investigator followed you last night. He followed you from your house to the Publix and then to Butler's neighborhood. That's how we knew where to pick you up." Barclay saw the senator's face slip hearing this.

"You gave my investigator the slip, unintentionally as it was, and he lost you in the neighborhood; you took the creek while he stayed on the road. He heard the shots and ran to the house, but it took him a few minutes to gain entry because he was worried the shooter—that's you—might still be inside, and he was by himself. Looking back, that allowed you to affect your escape from the scene the same way you came in." With a clunk that echoed in the barren room, Barclay set a clear evidence bag on the metal tabletop.

"This is your gun from tonight. It's hard to see what with all the mud smeared around the inside, but this is the shitty little Hi-Point you used to kill Larry Butler. We found it in the creek bed where you tossed it. It was partially submerged in the muck, so it took a while, but we got it. The bullets in the magazine match the two shell casings in the house and the unspent bullet we found there." Barclay paused before saying, "Those Hi-Points are notorious for jamming." The look on the senator's face was priceless. He had to wonder if Barclay was some type of wizard for knowing that. "I'm not that smart, of course," Barclay said as if reading the senator's mind. "Just top-notch work by very experienced detectives. Whoever gave you that gun did you a disservice. That's a cheap gang-banger piece. It's gotten more people killed than it has killed people because the damn things jam or don't shoot straight, and the shooter is left holding their dick in their hand. I bet you got pretty nervous when you missed your first shot, and the second didn't happen, am I right?" A pause, then, "Again, not me. I'm not smart enough to have put it all together.

"Oh, we also found the unspent round in your car that matches the rounds in the magazine. I'm guessing you racked the slide, not knowing one was already in the chamber?" Another look of recognition. "Now that one *was* me." Barclay leaned in conspiratorially: "I've done that before."

Barclay had seen enough recorded interviews from this very room to know the limits of the microphone. A soft-spoken suspect—typically a female—can be difficult to hear.

He scooted his chair toward the senator, leaned in close, and, in slightly more than a whisper, said, "I didn't bullshit you about having evidence proving Butler murdered the Chatham family. I know that you know he did it because you were there." The senator leaned back, but Barclay followed him. "We know you were there because of your fingerprints. I told you that already. But we also found your DNA at the scene."

Seeing the senator's micro-expression, he said, "Yep. On the machete handle. It's the damnedest thing finding DNA from that long ago. But found it we did. You held that machete. Probably swung it, too, didn't you?" Senator Gillespie was backed up as far as he could get, back straight against the wall, peering down his patrician nose at Barclay, who was leaning into him.

"And I know you killed Kathryn Chatham, too." Barclay was nodding slowly. "Want to know how I know? The first thing is that video. I didn't see it at first, but knowing it's you, I can't unsee it. And I saw the look on your face when you saw the still printed from the video. You knew it was you. That was you leading her to her death."

Barclay moved the gun to the edge farthest from the senator before going back into the paper bag. He came up with another clear evidence bag. "We found her car." The senator's eyes went wide before he caught himself. "That's right. Credit where it's due, Arnold. That was a genius idea, hiding it in plain sight like that. Anyway, we dusted the interior for fingerprints, and wouldn't you know, we didn't find any. None. Strange, isn't it? I mean, you'd expect to find Kathryn's, right? It's her car. But nope."

He tossed the bag on the desk with a *tink*. "I actually misspoke when I said we didn't find any prints. We did. Yours." Barclay tapped the bag with his finger. "A nice thumbprint, your thumbprint, on the key that was in the ignition." He reached back into the paper bag and came up with another clear plastic evidence bag, which he placed next to the key. "It's the rearview mirror. Your thumb and forefinger." He held the rearview mirror up and to the side, demonstrating adjusting the mirror to show how his prints got there. "You forgot to wipe the mirror down. Probably didn't even think about it when you adjusted it. Habit."

He stared at the senator for a moment. "Anyway, you missed those items, and we're glad for it. I must say that packing her suitcase to sell the story of her moving away was brilliant. For sixty years, no one batted an eye at that story. We only found her by dumb luck, really. You almost"—Barclay held his thumb and forefinger close together but not touching—"*almost* got away with it."

A crowd had gathered in the detective bureau, watching the interview on different computer monitors with access to the camera feed. They were all frustrated because they could not make out what was being said. The camera, though, was sharp enough to see the expressions on the senator's face. Whatever Barclay was saying to him was hitting its mark.

The senator swallowed hard, a varnish of sweat making his face shine. His lips parted, he licked them and cut his eyes up and to the right, settling them above the door before bringing his gaze back to Barclay. Confused for a beat, Barclay looked to where the senator's eyes had gone and saw what garnered his attention. He looked back at the senator, nodded, and sent a text from his phone.

He looked back above the door and stared at the camera until the red light blinked out. A collective groan from the crowd on the other side of the hollow wood door could be heard in the interrogation room.

"Ok," said Barclay. "No one's listening, no one's recording." He narrowed his eyes, sizing up the situation. "You already know anything you say is inadmissible absent a signed rights waiver, so... no witness, no recording, no proof. We can both speak freely."

The senator cleared his throat and seemed to regain some of his composure. "What can you do for me?" Ever the horse trader.

Barclay stared at the senator as he pondered the question. The truth is, he didn't want to do anything for this man, but he did want answers. Answers that only the senator could provide.

"Tell you what, Arnold. We've got Butler dead to rights on the Chatham murders. I also know you were there and handled the machete, but I don't see any reason to drag you into that case. You tell me about that night, why it was done, what your involvement was, and Butler carries all of it. No one ever knows you were even a thought in that crime. Otherwise, your legacy will no longer be that of a revered public servant. Instead, it will be Arnold Gillespie, Jr., murderer of five people in the most heinous crime in the history of your hometown."

"I did not murder five people," he spat through gritted teeth as he pounded a fist on the hollow metal desk. The sound reverberated in the room. "I didn't murder anyone."

Barclay didn't say anything. He allowed the senator to work it out in his mind; he didn't need to prod him. The senator heard what he said, and it was now his decision. One more glance at the camera above the door, making sure the red light had stayed dark.

He plunged ahead with his story.

―――――

November 21, 1963
1:42 PM

LARRY BUTLER LIVED in a rented room above a hobby shop. The room was bare bones with a bed, a dresser, a bedside table, and a toilet; it didn't even contain a shower. For that, he used the locker room at the police department. He had a hot plate and a single pot in case he ever wanted to cook a hot meal, which he never did. It wasn't much. In fact, it wasn't a significant departure from the prison cell from which he escaped, but it was what he could afford on a rookie cop's salary. More than once, he wondered if this really was better than prison.

He was lying on his bed reading an old paperback western when there was a knock at his door. He laid the open book face down on the bed to keep his place—he was almost at the midpoint of the story. He opened the door, and Arnold Gillespie, Jr. barged in all khakis, cardigan, tasseled loafers, and entitlement.

The place smelled of stale cigarettes and beer farts. Arnold made a face when he walked in. He said, "Ever consider opening a window?"

"Come on in," Butler said to the little shit who was already by the window peering down at the street below.

He was still looking out the window when he said, "I need you to do this. Tonight."

Butler closed the door and said coolly, "I'm working tonight." He grabbed a loose, hand-rolled cigarette from a bowl on top of the dresser and lit it with a silver Zippo he snapped shut with a flick of the wrist.

Arnold spun on him. "I need this to happen."

Butler exhaled a plume of smoke at Gillespie. "You keep throwing around the word 'need.' This isn't exactly a situation where murdering someone qualifies as a 'need,' Arnie."

"I've told you not to call me that."

Butler walked over and flopped down on the bed, bouncing his book up, closing it, and losing his place. He made a face. "You know, Arnie, you sure are quick to demand someone else commit murder for you."

"Quit saying that word."

A laugh. "What word, Arnie? Murder? That is what you're asking me to do, right?" He flicked his ash into an ashtray that ran out of room a week ago.

Arnold paced at the foot of the bed, crossing the small space in three and a half strides before hitting the door, then turning around and retracing his steps. He was shaking his head. "She embarrassed me, and it's all her father's fault."

Another laugh. "For not going out with you?"

"Look, *Eddie*, it's not for you to question why, okay?" He stressed the name "Eddie" to make a point, and it struck its mark.

The expression on the face of Larry Butler, nee Eddie Howard, hardened. He had done time, hard time, with men who would toss this little prick out the window without a second thought, and he was threatening to turn him in if he didn't carry out his request.

Since making his way to Towne after his narrow escape from Alcatraz, he'd gotten clean papers and a new identity thanks to his father, Arnold Gillespie, Sr. The look on the elder Gillespie's face was priceless when he showed up on his doorstep. Eddie Howard saw recognition in the man's eyes the instant the man opened the door. Fortunately for Howard, the senior Gillespie now had everything to lose, so the small favor of a new identity was nothing to be granted. He'd considered larger cities—Atlanta, Miami—but settled on the quiet, small-town life with an unsophisticated police force. It had all gone well until now. Until this peckerwood asked him to kill someone for him.

The act of killing wasn't what bothered him—he'd done it before. He knew he was a real sonofabitch. But he'd always had a reason; at least, he told himself that. He did not like being treated like the hired help available on the whim of a spoiled rich kid.

But he would do it. When he decided to help his little brother —he hated thinking of him that way—he had made it abundantly clear that this was the last time he would do anything for him, and if he ran his mouth to anyone, he would snap his neck. He knew he made his point with little Arnie Gillespie, so he wasn't nervous about getting caught.

This *job,* as it were, was better than the alternative of leaving and having to start over. He couldn't trust Arnie wouldn't give him up to the police if he up and left without doing what was asked.

"I can do it tomorrow night," Butler said lazily, exhaling a stream of smoke.

Arnold punched a fist into his palm and said, "Ok. Good. I'll leave the stuff by the well on the property behind the house. You know where that is, right?"

He just looked at Arnold. Then, after a beat: "And Arnie, I do this, and you get your father to set me up in something other than being a cop. You'll do that for me?"

"What else do you want to do?"

"I'll let you know."

———

November 23, 1963
2:52 AM

ARNOLD GILLESPIE, Jr. sat on a fallen tree in the woods at the rear edge of the Chatham property. He'd dropped the supplies off at the well at midnight as instructed. Instead of going home, though, he chose to stay. To watch what was going to happen. It wasn't that he didn't believe his half-brother wouldn't carry it out; no, he was certain he would. He just wanted to watch. He'd been in this spot for almost three hours, and his confidence in the man who would carry out his wishes began to wane, if only slightly, when he heard the crack of a tree branch and the rustle of ground cover.

He saw Eddie Howard stride confidently from the wood line to the rear entrance of the house. He watched him take one last long drag on a cigarette and drop it on the patio. He then watched him slide open the glass door and draw his hand back as if he had gotten shocked. He then saw him enter the house.

He waited, not hearing anything...until the explosion and flash of a gunshot. He waited a moment more and heard a second gunshot followed by a third. He then ran-walked to the backdoor and peered inside, shining his flashlight around the room. He saw Mr. Chatham lying on the couch shiny with blood and dropped the flashlight in shock. Then, he heard another gunshot—loud, deafening, inside the house...*upstairs.*

He went to the couch and saw the machete sticking out of the man where his neck and shoulder met. The flashlight was on the carpet just inside the entry, indirectly illuminating the dead man. Another gunshot. He looked up as if he could see through the floor what was happening above him. He then licked his lips and grabbed the machete. It didn't move.

He tried rocking it back and forth, but nothing. Another gunshot. He looked up again. He then put his left foot on the edge of the couch, grabbed the machete with two hands, and pulled as he pushed his foot against the couch for leverage. He began to rock the blade until it eventually slid out with a sucking sound.

He held it up and tested the weight of it. Another gunshot. Another look upstairs. He weighed the machete in his hands once more before bringing the blade down hard on the man's neck with a two-handed chop near where he had just pulled it from.

He attempted to remove it once more, but once again, it was stuck. He was scared. Scared he would get caught and scared because he didn't hate what he had just done. He tried once more to remove the blade, but when it didn't budge, he ran.

————

BARCLAY STARED at the man sitting in front of him, trying, but failing, to rationalize the person he thought he knew with the story he had just heard. The senator had told this story as dispassionately as if he were reading from the phone book. Barclay thought he had it figured out, at least to some degree, but this? Arnold Gillespie, Jr. is a sociopath.

"Why did you want the Chatham family murdered?"

The senator looked appalled. "I only wanted her father dealt with."

Dealt with, Barclay thought. That was a euphemism if he ever heard one. He said, "If he was only supposed to do the father, then why the rest of the family?"

The senator looked at Barclay with some mix of horror and disgust. "When I found out what he'd done, I confronted him at his little apartment. I told him he wasn't supposed to wipe out her entire goddamn family. He said it was to show me what he was capable of should I decide to fuck with him or rat him out as Eddie Howard." A pause, then, "He's a goddamn monster, that man."

"The barbecue restaurant. That what he asked you for in return?"

A single nod. "The arrogant bastard tried to take my father's restaurant. Can you believe that? It took me a while to get him off that notion and convince him that wasn't happening. My father had no idea about any of it, of course. I went to him and convinced him to set Larry up with the barbecue place. Convinced him that it would make Larry self-sufficient and get him off the family tit."

Barclay stared at the senator, trying to understand everything he had heard up to that point, but he couldn't make himself do it. He couldn't rationalize any of it.

There was one last reveal for Barclay to make, and after almost a minute, he reached into the paper sack and produced one last evidence bag. "We served a search warrant on your place and found this." It was Kathryn Chatham's journal. "Interesting reading, but you know all about that, don't you? She makes it abundantly clear she chose your brother over you. That had to have really pissed you off."

Seeing the look on the senator's face, he continued, "Oh yeah. She writes about how you asked her out on multiple occasions when she was in high school and working for your father. When she told you her father would not allow it, you became outraged. She feared you would hit her because you were so angry. She also confides that she liked the police officer who frequented the restaurant...a lot. That would have been your brother, Larry, right? But, once again, same as you, he was too old for her, and her father forbade it."

More silence, then: "Choosing a murdering escapee from prison over you? I bet it took everything you had not to tell her the truth about Larry." Barclay paused and studied the senator. "Was that why you enlisted Larry to handle your business? Did that provide you some perverse satisfaction having the man she essentially chose over you to be the one to murder her father?"

Barclay was getting angry now. The more he talked, the angrier he became, but he was keeping it contained...barely.

"You're a coward, Arnold. The guy always getting someone else to do his dirty work."

The senator didn't react.

"I understand you don't want to discuss it, Arnold, but do you know that wasn't even the best part of her diary? What am I saying? Of course you do. How often did you read it?" He watched the senator, who eyed him wearily, dreading what was coming next.

"Kathryn was pregnant with your baby when she died, wasn't she? She goes into great detail about it and lays out how you tried to make her go to Georgia for an abortion, but she wouldn't go— she wanted the baby. Only you were married, and that wouldn't have boded well for your burgeoning political career, would it? A young family man like yourself fathering a child with a woman who wasn't your wife?" A pause, then: "Is that what you two argued about on the drive back from Atlanta the week before you killed her?" Seeing the senator's expression, he said, "Yeah, Sylvia Burrows told us all about that."

He let that hang in the air before saying, "Your father made the same mistake, didn't he? Except his mistress had the baby." A flicker of recognition. "Larry Butler, or should I say, Eddie

Howard, was the result of your father's illicit tryst. I guess adultery runs in the family, same as murder, huh, Arnold?"

He finally leaned back but kept his voice low. "Did you know you were going to kill her when you took her into the woods that Saturday in October 1968, or were you still trying to talk some sense into her? I imagine she kept refusing you, so, what, you hit her over the head and dumped her in the well?"

The senator looked away.

Barclay said, "Not going to say anything about Kathryn? About how you killed her?"

There was a stretch of silence that seemed to absorb every possible emotion.

After what felt like minutes, the senator cleared his throat and, with all the authority he could muster—which wasn't much at all —asked, "You'll help me, now?"

You motherfucker, thought Barclay as he slowly shook his head. "I made you a deal, and I'll stick to it. Your name will be kept out of the Chatham murder case. Instead, we'll announce it solved and closed by the death of the man responsible for the murders, Larry Butler, formerly Eddie Howard."

"And no mention of his relationship with my family?"

Barclay laughed a mirthless laugh. "Sure, why not."

The senator seemed to relax. "Ok, so how do we handle this?" he asked, looking around the room.

"What do you mean?"

"I mean, what do we say about me being released?"

"Released? Arnold, you murdered a man tonight and killed Kathryn Chatham." He searched the eyes of the person across from him, seeing if any of that was sinking in. "You're going to die in prison."

Gillespie stood abruptly, "But you can't. I can't."

"Can't what?"

Then there was something in his eyes. Recognition of some

kind as if something had just clicked into place. He looked down at Barclay, who was leaning back in his chair.

"The attorney general was never going to look into this case, was he?" the senator croaked.

A smile played at Barclay's lips. "No. I'm afraid not." He raised a finger and said, "I didn't lie, though. I was prepared to, of course, but you made the leap all by yourself."

The senator's eyes went a little wild, roaming around the room as if looking for a way out. Finally, they came to rest on Barclay. "You wanted me to kill Butler, didn't you? That's why you told me all of those things."

Barclay seemed to consider this. He knew he pushed the senator to take action, and he certainly knew Butler's death was a possible outcome. What did he expect to happen when he essentially told the senator that the only thing between living the remainder of his life a free man or dying in prison was the testimony of a scumbag like Larry Butler?

Had Barclay crossed a line in the name of justice? Did that rationalization make it easier to manipulate the situation? What he knew for certain was that neither Butler nor Senator Gillespie were victims in this circumstance. Not even by the smallest measure. He also knew that he didn't feel any guilt whatsoever. None.

He motioned for the senator to sit back down, which he did. Barclay said, "You're going down for both of those murders because we prosecute people like you. It's what we do."

Barclay saw real fear in the senator's face for the first time.

"It's a shame, really," said Barclay.

"What?"

"This is going to play out very publicly. If this goes to trial, it *will* come out about Eddie Howard, you killing Kathryn Chatham and Larry Butler." He shook his head as if he was disappointed by this. "Hard to see how it doesn't. Even if you plead guilty, the warrants will be public record, your guilty plea will be open to the public, and I'm sure the media will be there for all of it, Arnold." He leaned back and crossed his right leg over his left. "Yep. You walking out in that dirty orange jumpsuit, handcuffed and chained at the waist. Leg chains, too. They probably won't let you shower before court, so your hair will be greasy and messy. It's going to be awful. That's a lot for a man like you to go through. That's a lot for a man to put his family through."

Senator Arnold Gillespie, Jr. tried to muster his dignity. Tried to put on a strong face, but he couldn't pull it off. Not very well, anyway.

He said, "I'd like to make my one phone call."

"You watch too much television, Arnold. They'll let you make as many calls as you like. Who would you like to call?"

"My son. The sheriff."

THIRTY-SEVEN

T he only thing left was transporting Arnold Gillespie, Jr. to the Towne County Jail, about a twenty-minute drive from the police department. Barclay stepped out of the interview room and arranged for a phone to be brought in for the senator. He even agreed to give him privacy to make the call.

Barclay and the police chief huddled in the chief's office to discuss the next steps. Barclay gave him a brief rundown of the investigation. Even the CliffsNotes version took fifteen minutes to explain. He went over the evidence showing Larry Butler as the killer in the Chatham murder case: he discussed the DNA that was found on the machete handle, the machete sheath, and the cigarette butt. He explained about the towel Fitz had taken from the smokehouse almost three weeks prior to secure a DNA standard for comparison. In answer to a question, Barclay admitted he hadn't considered the admissibility of the evidence from the towel. In truth, it likely wouldn't be admissible, "But," Barclay said, "Butler's dead, so who's going to complain?"

He also explained that Larry Butler was an alias and the half-brother of Arnold Gillespie, Jr. He touched on the genealogy

DNA evidence but didn't mention Alcatraz because he didn't feel like stepping off into that right now.

As for charges against the senator, they agreed they had enough for a murder warrant for shooting Butler but decided to hold off on charging him in Kathryn Chatham's death. There were still some loose ends that needed tying off, and since he would already be charged with murder, there was no need to rush. The chief pulled Detective Lawson into the room along with the lieutenant over detectives, and they talked through the Butler murder case once more in detail as they got ready to prepare the arrest warrant.

They were finalizing the probable cause language for the warrant when Fitz walked in. "Boss, you're not going to believe this. The gun Gillespie used to shoot Butler? It was used in a murder back in twenty-ten."

After a moment to process the news, Barclay said, "How do you know that already? We haven't sent anything to ballistics."

"We ran the serial number, and it came back to a murder. An arrest was made, and the guy pleaded guilty in twenty-twelve—case never went to trial."

No one seemed to understand the significance of what he was saying. Then it hit Barclay. "That gun was evidence in a murder case?"

"Yes." Fitz nodded, seeing his boss beginning to understand.

"Let me guess. It was the county's case."

"Yep," said Fitz.

"That motherfucker!"

"What?" asked the chief.

Barclay rubbed his face with both hands. "The gun Gillespie used to shoot Butler was evidence in a murder case that never went to trial, so the gun should still be in the evidence room of the sheriff's department...but it won't be." Barclay nodded toward Lawson and said, "We know he met with the sheriff yesterday afternoon in a secluded location for a few minutes." He let that hang in the air for about five seconds. Then: "Sheriff Gillespie gave his father the gun used to kill Butler."

"Whoa," was all Chief Greenhaw could think to say.

A long pause, then Barclay said, "That makes the sheriff guilty of murder."

"Whoa, now. Whoa, now. Whoa—"

"Relax, Chief. We're not there yet. He could always say his father asked for a gun for protection, that he didn't know he was going to kill somebody with it. It'd be bullshit, but we have to consider that. We have time to work it all out." He could see the chief's relief at this decision. "Besides," Barclay said with a smile, "by law, the coroner is the only person who can arrest the sheriff, so you're off the hook if the time comes."

The chief was not amused.

The meeting broke up, and Barclay walked back into the detective bay as Senator Gillespie was being brought out of the interview room. He was handcuffed, hands in front, and told he was being taken to the jail where he would be formally arrested and booked for murder. A detective was handing him off to a patrolman for transport.

Barclay followed them outside, and as he passed by the officer with the senator in tow, he leaned in and whispered, "I know who gave you the gun."

The senator stiffened but did not comment or so much as glance at Barclay.

———

BARCLAY PULLED out his phone and sent a text that read: He's on the way. ETA about 20 mins.

He did not receive a response. He hadn't expected one.

Barclay arrived at the jail a minute or two before the car transporting the senator. As he was walking into the jail, he heard his name. He turned and saw Wendy Wade looking more casual than usual—hair in a ponytail, toothpick jeans, white Treetorn sneakers, and a red quilted Barbour jacket. This time, her iPhone was on a tripod, and he walked over to her.

Wendy: "I am live at the Towne County Jail, and Towne County DA Barclay Griffith has just arrived. Barclay, what can you tell our viewers on Facebook Live about the events that occurred overnight?"

Barclay: "I can tell you there was a homicide, a shooting death to be more specific, but it's an ongoing investigation, so there isn't a whole lot I can say at this point."

"Has an arrest been made?"

"No arrest has been made yet, but a warrant is being drawn up and sworn to as we speak."

"Who do you have in custody? Who is the warrant for?"

"I can't comment on that at this time. When a warrant has been served, I will discuss it then."

"Thank you, DA Griffith."

This interaction went exactly as they had discussed when Barclay called her from the police station to alert her about what was going down. At the end of the brief phone call, he agreed to text her when the senator was en route to the jail.

The interview over, Barclay stepped out of camera range and pointed back to the parking lot as the patrol car pulled up to the gate that was the entrance to the sally port.

Her eyes got wide, and she mouthed, "That him?" to which Barclay nodded. Then, she deftly removed the phone from the tripod and walked right up to the rear driver-side window, and said, "Folks, inside the back of this police car is former Alabama and United States Senator Arnold Gillespie, Jr." He did what he could to shield his face, but it was obvious who he was.

She said, "As you can see, he is handcuffed. Senator, why are

you in the back of a police car? Why are you in the back of a—"
Before she could finish her question, the car drove into the sally
port, and the gate rolled closed behind it. She went up to the gate
and filmed between the slats; she got the senator being removed
from the car in perfect high definition. As the event unfolded
and word spread across social media, the number of people
watching the live broadcast increased exponentially by the
minute.

Barclay understood what many in law enforcement did not.
The media isn't the bad guy—at least not around here. Be good to
them, and they will be good to you. Everyone knew Wendy Wade's
influence on public opinion...especially a man in the public eye
like Senator Gillespie.

And that's what Barclay was counting on.

The stench of vomit permeated the booking area of the jail
and hit Barclay the moment he stepped through the steel door. He
quickly located the source, which was a wreck of a man swaying in
front of the height chart getting his booking photo taken. He had
vomit in his ample gray beard and down the front of his faded
black Iron Maiden t-shirt.

Barclay was talking with a jailer inside the desert-colored
booking area when the senator was brought inside and sat on a
metal bench. Detective Lawson walked in about three minutes
later, approached the senator, and helped him stand. She told him
he was being arrested for the murder of Larry Butler, and then a
female jailer began the booking process.

The sheriff had been standing back while all of this was going
on. When the booking process was completed, the sheriff stepped
up, took his father by the arm, and guided him to a cell. Barclay
watched as they exchanged words no one could hear. He removed
his father's cuffs and walked him into the cell, where he lingered
for a moment before exiting and closing the heavy steel door with
a thud and a click.

The sheriff turned to look at Barclay and said, "What the fuck are you doing here?"

Barclay was about to give a smart-ass answer when a muffled *pop* was heard. Someone screamed, and everyone instinctively ducked their heads and began to look around. The patrolman from TPD was crouched with his gun out, as was Lawson. The jailers didn't carry guns, and they looked confused.

A sheriff's deputy was there because he had recently booked in a DUI—the man covered in vomit—and had been hitting on a jailer. He had his gun out and yelled, "Is everyone ok? Anyone hurt?"

Barclay noticed in all the confusion that the sheriff hadn't moved, hadn't so much as flinched. Having gone to a knee, Barclay slowly stood up. He eased toward the sheriff and peered around the wide man into the cell the senator was just placed in by the sheriff himself. He saw the blood spatter high on the wall before he saw the body. The gore rose up from below the viewing window, heavy at first, but grew light as the blood's velocity slowed the higher it climbed. He directed his gaze at the man before him.

"Was that gun also from your evidence room, Sheriff?"

The sheriff absorbed what Barclay said. He wheezed a heavy breath. And charged like a bull.

———

THE STEEL DOOR to the jail under the sally port burst open and slammed into the brick wall with a loud bang, which got the attention of Wendy Wade, who was in the process of packing up and leaving to file her story. The gate to the sally port was rolling up across its track with a hum and a rattle.

Barclay was being half pushed and half carried through the entrance and into the parking lot by the deputy and Detective

Lawson. There was a lot of shouting, but no specific words could be discerned. Wendy made a move toward the scrum but thought better of it.

Once they had cleared the sally port by twenty or thirty feet, they let Barclay go, and he turned and adjusted his coat as he stomped off, away from the jail. Like Barclay, the deputy and Lawson were breathing hard. They stood watching Barclay, making sure he wouldn't make a run back into the jail.

After stepping off a few more feet, Barclay turned back to the jail, getting his breathing under control. He noticed Wendy Wade running toward him.

She was bringing up her phone, and Barclay held up his hand and said, "Not now, Wendy. Please."

She stopped and lowered her phone. "What just happened back there?"

Barclay sat on the curb, reached up, grabbed her wrist, and pulled her down beside him. He glanced back over his shoulder at the jail, then back forward. He looked down at the ground between his feet, gathering himself.

"Off the record," he said.

"Yes, of course."

He pulled his head up. Then, without looking at her, he said, "Senator Gillespie just shot himself."

"What?" She looked back at the jail and made to stand, but Barclay put a hand on her narrow shoulder, keeping her seated. "My God, Barclay. What...what's going on?"

He recapped the events of the last three months and, for the first time Barclay could remember, Wendy Wade was at a loss for words, and he told her so, which lightened the mood if only a bit.

"Can you give me an interview about all of this?"

"Not right now, Wendy. I will talk to you about it. All of it— the cold case, everything—just not right now, okay?"

They heard a noise and looked back toward the jail. Barclay said, "I do have something you can ask the *sheriff* about."

———

THE SHERIFF WAS STANDING at the open sally port entrance, staring at Barclay through a haze of vape smoke.

Wendy looked at Barclay, who nodded at her, then toward the sheriff. She smirked, stood, and began doing something with her phone. She walked confidently up to the sheriff, her phone out front, and said, "Sheriff Gillespie, I'm broadcasting live on Facebook. Would you care to tell us how a gun from your evidence room was used by your father to shoot and kill a man early this morning?"

A stunned sheriff worked his mouth, jowls shaking. "Goddamn you, Griffith!"

Wendy Wade went wide-eyed. "Sheriff, we're live on Facebook!"

"Oh shut up, bitch!" He spiked his vape pen on the pavement, sending glass and plastic flying, and stalked off back to the jail

Barclay watched as a mortified Wendy Wade stuttered through an apology to her viewers about what just happened.

Barclay retrieved his phone and dialed. After four rings, the call was answered.

"I retired in part so I'd quit getting these early morning phone calls, Mr. DA." Barclay smiled wearily at Maggie Gamble's greeting.

He was about to respond when a familiar SUV turned into the parking lot practically on two wheels. It braked hard in front of Barclay.

"Sorry, Maggie, I have to call you back. I promise it's worth being woken up." He ended the call as Fitz and AJ got out of the SUV.

Barclay extended a hand to his chief investigator, who reached down and pulled Barclay to standing. Barclay explained what happened in the jail and asked Fitz to go see what was going on. "I don't need to go back in there. Not right now."

Fitz nodded and walked off toward the jail.

Barclay could feel AJ watching him. He considered what to do or say before deciding the best option was not to say anything.

In a low voice, AJ said, "Just what did you say to that man?" Barclay ignored the question. Murphy glanced toward the jail, then back at Barclay. "Your little conversation with the senator at his house and then at the PD. What did you tell him? I know there was no phone call at his house—you stopped that recording on purpose. And then having the camera turned off in the interview room? Come on, Barclay. It's as if you planned all of this." AJ was looking around, trying to make sense of it all. "Is this really the outcome you wanted?"

Barclay couldn't discern if AJ was angry, disappointed, or genuinely curious. He weighed the question for a long moment. Not because he didn't know the answer, but because he didn't know how honest he should be with this man. AJ Murphy was a zero-sum cop, but would he approve of Barclay's...methods? He didn't believe so.

Against the advice of Murphy, he pushed the senator—hard. He did so because he wanted a resolution. Not years from now and not after a long, drawn-out public trial dredging up ghosts of the past. This outcome would bring some degree of healing to this community—his community.

Sixty years had been long enough.

The guilty had been dealt with.

Was this the outcome he wanted?

"Don't ask questions you don't want the answers to, AJ."

The two men stared at one another, wheels turning, decisions being weighed.

Finally, Barclay said, "I have a phone call to make." He broke eye contact and walked away.

AJ watched his back as he walked off, saw him raise the phone to his ear, and after a beat, AJ heard him say, "Maggie...we got him."

THANK YOU FOR READING

Please take a moment to leave a review on Amazon, Goodreads, or wherever you purchased this book.

Visit BrandonHughesBooks.com and sign up for updates regarding his next novel. You can also follow Brandon on Facebook, Instagram, and Twitter. Email him at Brandon@brandonhughesbooks.com and let him know what you think about the book, or just drop him a line to say hello.

FOLLOW QR CODES TO LEAVE A REVIEW

Leave a review on Amazon

Leave a review on Goodreads

ACKNOWLEDGMENTS

The writing process is a largely solitary endeavor; however, there are always others who contribute a great deal to the finished product. I hesitate to name anyone in particular because to name everyone would be impossible. But in this case, there are some people who need mentioning.

In March 2020, as I began researching *The 4th Prisoner*, the first person I spoke to was George DeVincenzi. When we spoke, he was 94 years old and the oldest living Alcatraz prison guard. It was a wonderful conversation, and he provided me with a great deal of insight into the inner workings of the most famous prison in America. Having visited Alcatraz some years before, I had a spatial feel for the place and a sense of its foreboding eeriness, but Mr. DeVincenzi breathed life into it with his first-hand knowledge and stories.

Secondly, I'd like to mention Anthony Jones, a true friend. He has been with me on this writing path since day one and has served as an early reader for each manuscript, providing insightful commentary, critiques, and, best of all, encouragement.

Lastly, because we save the best for last, a huge thank you to my wife, Karen. She serves as a sounding board in the early stages of the process, reads early drafts, and offers her thoughts and opinions. She is extremely supportive (and patient) with my writing endeavors. She tolerates the whiteboards and the swaths of paper as I work through the process and puts up with my constant questions of, "What about this?" and "What about that?" This could not have happened without her.

There are many others, of course, including some who were even the inspiration for a character or two in *The 4th Prisoner* (you know who you are). To each of you, I say thank you.

ABOUT THE AUTHOR

Brandon Hughes brings two decades of experience in the criminal justice system to craft an authentic mystery novel and utilizes his real-world knowledge to take the reader inside the inner workings of a criminal investigation. Criminal cases he has handled have been featured on numerous television programs.

When he isn't writing, Brandon enjoys cooking, reading, and cheering on his Auburn Tigers. He and his wife Karen are empty nesters save for their chocolate lab, Murphy. They live in Auburn, Alabama.

The 4th Prisoner is his second novel.

Visit Him Online:
BrandonHughesBooks.com

facebook.com/BrandonHughesBooks

x.com/BrandonHughes74

instagram.com/the_4real_brandonhughes

amazon.com/author/brandonhughesbooks

Printed in Great Britain
by Amazon

37297823R00209